Secrets in the Babby House

Gloria McBreen

Cover design: GetCovers

Cover image: Des Connors

ISBN: 978-1-3999-4404-5 (paperback)
ASIN: B0BQSWWDRH (ebook)

For my dear dad

I'm sorry I didn't get my book finished before you departed from this life. I know you have been with me in spirit right up to the end. Thank you for all the stories, especially the one about the wee red stocking, and for answering all my questions about times gone by. Thank you for believing in me and for passing on that little stubborn gene that I have within me. You have left me with a million beautiful memories. My one regret is that you are not here to hold my book in your hands!

The best things in life are the people we love, the places we have been, and the memories we have made along the way. ~ Irish proverb.

PART ONE

1956

CHAPTER ONE

Frank Connolly used the butt of his cigarette to light another one. He inhaled the fresh smoke deep into his lungs, hoping it would give him courage. He hated the thought of breaking the bad news to his girlfriend—again. He didn't care if she cried or fell to her knees like a demented banshee, she would have to accept that they were finished.

Alice Ward inflated Frank's ego and made him feel special. She had her pick of men but she'd chosen him. Her bold green eyes conveyed fun and excitement. Her curves tantalised him—and every other man she came into contact with. The thrill had worn off for Frank. She had her pick of men for a reason, and that reason didn't fall into his list of preferred qualities in a woman. He had his eye on someone else; someone a bit more graceful and ladylike. Flossie Lynch was the only girl on his mind these days.

Frank walked at a slow pace, with no rush. He needed time to think and to be clear about the exact words he'd say to Alice so that she got the message loud and clear. After four months of being her fella—as she called him—he didn't want her anymore. She stifled him. Twice in one week she waited outside work for him to finish; the lads had a great time jeering and laughing at him. He'd told her not to come near his work again but she'd accused him of being embarrassed by her. 'Aren't you proud of me?' she'd asked.

As Frank approached Town Lake, he pulled on what remained of his cigarette. He flicked the butt into the ditch and blew thick smoke into the grey sky. He rolled his tongue around his dry mouth to accumulate spit. Alice and her friend, Joyce Rafferty, sat on the lake wall, waiting. *He might've known Joyce would be with her.*

Alice stood and kissed Frank on the cheek, the scent of her perfume catching in the back of his throat. 'You're late... as usual.'

'Sorry. Josey needed a hand on the farm.'

She rubbed his cheek where her red lips had stained him. 'Hasn't he got that young lad helping him?' she asked. 'Tell him you haven't time in the future.'

'Hiya, Frank,' said Joyce with a meek smile.

'Where ya heading, Joyce?' he asked.

'She's coming to the pictures with us, aren't ya, Joycie?'

Joyce glanced at Frank, checking for approval. He looked ahead, silent.

'Aw dunno, Alice. I might head up home,' she said.

'That'd be nice,' Frank said. He sat on the wall and lit up a cigarette. 'I don't feel like the pictures tonight anyway.' He took a small comb from the pocket of his overcoat and ran it through his chestnut waves.

'Why not?' asked Alice.

'See ya tomorrow, Alice,' Joyce said as she headed back towards town.

With hands on hips, Alice turned to Frank. 'Why aren't we going to the pictures?'

'You can go if ya like but I'm not going.' He bit on his lip. He stood up and kicked at a tuft of weeds.

'What's wrong?' she asked.

'Look, the thing is, I can't go with you anymore.'

'Don't start that again.' Alice linked her arm in his and started walking.

'Alice, stop, please.' He pulled away from her.

'But we're going steady.'

'No. We're not going steady,' he said.

'Four months is going steady.'

'Two of those months I've spent trying to break it off.'

'But you love me.'

'Did I say that?' Frank reached inside his pocket for his cigarettes. 'When did I ever say, "I love you"?'

'Well, I love you.' Alice pulled a tissue from her handbag. She sniffed and turned her back.

'There's no point wailing.' He paced back and forth.

'Well, if you must know, Frank Connolly... it's too late.'

'What's too late?'

'You can't leave me.' She grabbed his box of Players and lit one.

'I'm not leaving you. I'm breaking up with you.'

'It's the same thing. Why are you doing this?' She turned her back again and cried into a tissue.

'I'm going now,' Frank said.

'I was going to tell you this tonight, after the pictures.'

'Tell me what?'

She took a long pull on her cigarette. 'Nothing.'

'Turn round, Alice.'

She faced him. Tears trickled down her pink powdered cheeks.

'Oh, for feck sake. Dry your eyes. Go on, tell me again, how you love me more than life itself. You can't live without me. You'll die if I leave you. Well, I don't want to hear it again. We're over.'

'We are not over. This is only the beginning of our lives together.' She glared at him, her lips pursed tight. There was only one way to get through to this woman. He took a deep breath.

'How about I tell you something? You're going to find out sooner or later anyway.'

The words he wanted to say next lay heavy in his parched throat. *Would she make a scene?* Like the night outside the pictures when he hadn't enough money on him to buy her sweets. She'd shouted at him, called him a useless imbecile and slapped his face. Some people had looked on in disgust, but the lads laughed and slagged him for days after. His brother Josey heard about it and warned him to get rid of Alice.

'What am I going to find out?' Her eyes probed his.

'I have a new girlfriend.' *A lie, but not for long*. 'And I'm mad about her.' He held his breath, bracing himself for her outburst.

But it wasn't the outburst he expected. Alice's icy stare pierced him. He tugged at his coat collar as a cold shiver ran down his spine.

'Do you remember a few weeks ago, Frank? When we got carried away behind the old church?'

'What about it?'

'And do you remember the part where you said you had

things under control?' Alice took a step closer. 'Well, you didn't have things under control.'

'What do you mean?' Frank asked, fearing he knew exactly what she meant. The hairs pricked the back of his neck.

'I love you and you're going to marry me, Frank Connolly... whether you like it or not.' She placed her hand on her belly.

As he tried to process her bombshell, images of Flossie flashed through his mind. Alice took another step closer. *He had to get away from her.* His head spun as he turned to leave, but like a snared rabbit, Frank knew there was no getting away from Alice now.

CHAPTER TWO

Flossie Lynch cycled slowly up the path leading to St. Anne's Church. She checked her watch again. Quarter to eleven. Almost time. Her stomach churned as she approached the church doors, her legs weak with nerves. She hopped off her bicycle and parked it against the hedge before making her way over towards the small crowd that had congregated. The bells rang out and everyone chattered as Alice Ward emerged from the church, linking arms with her new husband, Frank Connolly. Flossie watched intently. She studied Frank's face for signs of melancholy, hoping he'd catch her eye. He stood rigid beside Alice, his troubled eyes betraying the broad smile he wore for the clicking camera. He took a sidelong glance at his brother, Josey, who stood close by talking to Joyce, the bridesmaid. Then his eyes met with Flossie's. He frowned, then looked away.

The well-wishers cheered as they threw confetti over the newlyweds. The children who gathered with their mammies ran to catch the fragments of colour to throw them in the air. Their laughter filled the church grounds. People being happy about something they knew nothing about. *They think this is a happy couple? Are they blind? All they see is romance, beauty, a nice dress.* Flossie focused on Alice's face. She could see why men were attracted to her.

The bells stopped. The Widow Johnson—who showed up at all the weddings in town—turned to Flossie. 'Don't they make a lovely couple?'

'I only came to light a candle for Daddy,' Flossie said. 'I'm not here to see the wedding.'

The widow's warm smile faded. She folded her arms and glared at Flossie. 'What's wrong with you, Miss Lynch?'

'I'm sorry, Mrs Johnson. I don't feel very well, that's all.' Flossie walked away. She edged her way through the crowd, her eyes fixed on the ground. Once inside the church, she closed the solid wooden doors behind her, dulling the sound of chatter and laughter. She pressed her back against the door and, with a heavy sigh, closed her eyes. Mental images of Frank's smiling face compelled her to open them again. She wanted him to be happy, but she wished she was the bride, not Alice.

Her footsteps echoed through the empty church as she walked briskly towards the votive candle stand. She lit a candle for her late father and prayed for his soul. Her hands trembled. She lit a second candle for Frank, but she didn't say a prayer.

'Marry in the month of May; you will surely rue the day,' she whispered.

CHAPTER THREE

'Hurry up, Flossie, or we'll be late,' Goretti called from the bottom of the stairs. Flossie didn't care that they might be late for yet another monotonous evening at O'Malleys', listening to her mother's boasting and exaggerating her children's talents and achievements—all to impress her friend Ruth.

Her mother often baked cakes for the O'Malleys, pretending Flossie had made them. She once crocheted a white chignon cap and presented it to Mrs O'Malley at a Legion of Mary prayer meeting—the same meeting she brought Flossie along to. She took pride in her crocheting but had paid extra attention to this piece, decorating the brim with tiny pearls. The circle of women believed that Flossie was the creative one with the crochet hook. She sat among them while they praised her, her insides curling with embarrassment.

'Great lassie you have there, Goretti,' Mrs O'Malley said as she passed the finely stitched cap around.

Molly Fagin gently circled her bony freckled fingers over

the soft cotton fibres. 'Oh, Goretti! You're blessed with your Flossie!'

'Sure I know! She'll make a lucky man a great wife someday, so she will.' Goretti's heart skipped several beats when Ruth said, 'Well now, I'd be shocking happy if my John were to end up with a girl like Flossie.'

They spoke as if she wasn't in the room. She swore she'd never attend another one of their meetings. The following evening, after Flossie and her mother prayed The Angelus, her mother asked Jesus to bless Flossie and her future husband, John O'Malley.

'What are you talking about Mammy?' Flossie said. 'I am not marrying John O'Malley... ever.'

'Why not? You'd be perfect for him. He'll be taking over Frederick's business eventually and he's highly respected in the town. And sure, he's not a bad-looking lad at all.'

Flossie stared at her mother. 'He has funny eyes and he smells like mothballs. I don't even like him, never mind love him.'

'Oh, don't be silly. What has love got to do with anything? Get those notions out of your head, my girl, or you'll end up on the shelf. Do you really think I loved your father when I married him? I learned to love him. It happens over time.'

'John hardly speaks to me when I'm at their house.'

'He's shy, that's all. Maybe if you tried talking to him instead of sitting with a big puss on your face, it might be different. He's the catch of the parish and you won't get any better. He's very interested in you. His mother as much as said so! Don't be so fussy.'

Goretti was deaf to her daughter's protests when it came

to John, so as the months passed, Flossie learned to ignore her.

§

Sitting on the edge of her bed, Flossie lifted the small, framed picture off her locker. Three smiling faces lit up the dull brown frame—Flossie, her sister Catherine and their brother Danny. Even though the photo had been taken ten years ago, she still had clear visions of her father behind the camera making funny faces to make them laugh, like he always did when he took their picture. He used to tell them that a photograph without a smile was like a sunny day without the sun. Catherine always replied, 'Don't be silly, Daddy. If there's no sun, then it can't be a sunny day. It'd just be a horrible dull day'.

'Exactly, my leanbhín. And a photograph without a smile would just be a dull lifeless piece of paper.' Then they would all laugh at the silly faces he'd make.

Danny, aged ten at the time, had the biggest smile of them all. Smiling came easily to him and Flossie often wished she was more like him. She asked him once why was he always smiling and he replied, 'Because I'm always happy.' Everyone who met him loved his loud hearty laugh. It didn't seem like three years since he'd joined the priesthood. Flossie missed him dearly. She traced her finger around the outline of his face. His blond hair, like hers, was the colour of vanilla ice cream.

God took Catherine too, when she was fifteen, sent by their parents to a cloistered convent to live a life of solitude with the Carmelite Sisters. With a priest and a nun in the family, Flossie's mother had told her that she was to marry a good man and bless the family with grandchildren. Flossie loved children and looked forward to having her own one day, but she had always hoped that Frank Connolly would be the father.

§

John O'Malley loved when Saturdays came to an end, especially Saturdays like this one, with that Mrs Lynch and the daughter coming for tea. The conversation would be the same as every other time. The Legion of Mary, Danny the holy one, Catherine the blessed one, and of course idle talk about other people's business. It amused John how Mrs Lynch and his mother thought he didn't know what they were up to, trying to pair him with Flossie, what with all the subtle hints and the delight on their faces when the two so much as glanced at each other.

He watched Flossie with interest, especially over the last few months. She'd be an acceptable wife for him, he supposed. Not too demanding or silly like some of the girls who came into the shop. The proper height for him—about five foot four, he guessed. He would consider marrying her now that Connolly was out of the picture. The years were quickly passing by and he certainly didn't want to end up with the completely wrong woman. Flossie Lynch wouldn't exactly be the right woman, but he could do worse. She didn't love him and he didn't love her, but that was irrelevant.

§

Flossie's mother had her long cardigan buttoned up and her headscarf securely tied under her chin. Anxious to get going, she called out, 'Hurry up, Flossie, please.'

Flossie groaned as she ambled down the stairs.

'Wear your green Aran cardigan. It's more respectable than that skimpy thing, and you know yellow makes you look sick.'

Half-way down the stairs, Flossie turned to go back.

'It's hanging here beside your coat,' said her mother wearily as she lifted the cardigan off its hook. 'Liven yourself up, girl.'

They walked the short distance from their house on Anne Street—known as The Green—to O'Malley's on Main Street. Frederick O'Malley was tidying up outside his shop as he bade farewell to his last customer of the day. The familiar whiff of mothballs hovered in the air as long as his shop door stayed open.

'Good evening, Mr O'Malley.' Flossie gave her best 'Danny Smile'.

He smiled back. 'Hello there, Flossie. And Mrs Lynch.' He nodded his head politely towards Goretti.

'Hello, Frederick. You're late closing this evening.' Goretti knocked firmly on the door of the private entrance.

'I am indeed. Sure, they all come in at closing time,' he said, laughing.

John appeared in the shop doorway with a broom, pausing when he saw Flossie and her mother. He adjusted his glasses as if doing so might change the view in front of him. He put his head down and scurried across the footpath, and, with long strokes of the brush, he swept aimlessly. Flossie cringed, thinking of other things she'd rather be doing on a Saturday evening. Anything would be better than trying to make small talk with John and listening to her mother and Mrs O'Malley gossiping.

Goretti was about to knock again when the door swung open and Ruth O'Malley ushered the two women into the hallway. The distinct fragrance of furniture polish was more pleasing than Mr O'Malley's mothballs. The rich mahogany staircase gleamed, and the weary red carpet on the stairs had been revived by the stiff bristles of the Widow Johnson's brush.

To the envy of Goretti, the Widow Johnson cleaned for the O'Malleys a couple of times a week along with many other townhouses in Bailieborough. She took great pride in her work, often expressing that the only thing needed was plenty of elbow grease and no call for half of that fancy cleaning stuff at all.

Ruth led the way up the steep narrow stairs to the family's living area on the second floor. The smell of freshly baked bread reminded Flossie of how much she relished Mrs O'Malley's cooking. She sat by the window, where she had a good view of Main Street. Some shops still had their doors open, happy to serve the last-minute shoppers. She could see John, still sweeping the footpath. Pointless on such a blustery evening, she thought.

Ruth poured Goretti a small glass of sherry and Flossie her usual red lemonade. She had hunger pangs now and wished the men would hurry up so they could eat. The spread made her mouth water. Only in the O'Malley house would you find garden peas mixed through the potato salad, and rolls of fresh-smelling ham decorated with cucumber slices and tomato wedges. The platter of hard-boiled eggs, barely visible under dollops of salad cream, was specked with finely chopped parsley. Homemade soda bread was already sliced and buttered. The crust broke away from the corner of one slice. Flossie picked it up discreetly and popped it into her mouth. She swallowed it quickly as she glanced up at St. Therese watching her from an ornate gold frame on the wall above the dining table. The exact same picture hung in their own house, her eyes always watching.

St. Therese had been fifteen when she joined the Carmelites, like Catherine, but she joined of her own accord, whereas Catherine didn't. For three nights before she left, Flossie listened to her sister sobbing. The image of Catherine sitting beside a nun on the Dublin bus with puffy red eyes clouded every other memory Flossie had of her. For months after, Flossie thought she might die. She felt like her heart had moved to a different part of her body and a hard rock had taken its place. She had rubbed her chest vigorously to make the rock disappear, but it stayed for weeks.

They wrote to each other every fortnight, and over time Flossie found her heart again. Catherine had a whole new family—women, young and old—who she called her sisters. She settled into the Carmelite way of life, she said, with the help of the kindest person she ever met: Sister Anne. She took Catherine under her wing and guided her through her first difficult months in the monastery. Flossie accepted that her sister would no longer be a huge part of her life, and instead of tormenting herself with unanswerable questions, she found herself reminiscing about the good times.

Catherine didn't attend their father's funeral three years later, but Danny's presence eased Flossie's disappointment, even though she didn't get to spend much time with him. She didn't spend much time with anyone really, except her best friend, Mary Connolly, who hardly left her side for three days. She remembered the kindness of Frederick O'Malley too and the way in which he consoled her.

'You can be sure that a good man like Eddie Lynch is gone to heaven anyway. There's no doubt about that. Your daddy was very proud of you, Flossie; he was proud of yas all.' He bent down and whispered in her ear, 'You were his favourite, you know, but don't tell the others that.' She had felt as if a warm blanket had been wrapped around her when he gave her hand a soft squeeze. He had a gentle way of expressing himself that put Flossie at ease and gave her a sense of reassurance; the complete opposite to his wife's loud penetrating voice. Mr O'Malley often said, 'Her bark is worse than her bite; pay no attention to her.'

Mrs O'Malley interrupted Flossie's thoughts. 'How are you getting on helping Miss Kennedy in school?'

'I'm getting on grand, so I am. Miss Kennedy said I'm a good teacher. She said I should go to the college in Dublin to get proper training and I'll get a diploma there too.' Flossie gauged her mother's expression.

Ruth's eyes widened and her head bobbed from Flossie to her mother. 'That'd be a great thing for her to do, Goretti. You must be delighted.'

Goretti shrugged and chuckled. 'Oh, I don't know if there's any need for that. Sure, isn't Miss Kennedy doing a fine job with Flossie as it is? And she'll be looking to get married in a year or two anyway, so I don't see the point of traipsing off to Dublin looking for diplomas and the like.'

'Ah, here's the two men now. I'll wet the tea.' Ruth bustled over to the cooker and lit the gas ring under the kettle. Flossie fixed her gaze firmly on the window to avoid her mother's scowl. Frederick rubbed both his hands together as he entered with a big smile. 'These Saturdays are getting longer every week,' he said.

'It's the bread and butter, Frederick, don't complain,' Ruth said. He laughed. Everyone knew Mr O'Malley loved the shop and all his customers.

John sat directly across the table from Flossie. He greeted her with a nod and the bare minimum of a smile. She couldn't help wondering what went on inside his head. She hadn't known him in school because he was a few years older than her and he'd left when he was fifteen to work in the shop. Could she learn to love him? She imagined Ruth as her mother-in-law. Flossie didn't dislike her; she just talked so much. She could have a worse mother-in-law, she supposed. Sure, maybe going with him mightn't be the worst thing in the world. She didn't have to kiss him—not yet anyway. Then she wondered if anyone ever died from boredom.

'Did I hear you on the phone to Roy earlier?' Ruth asked as she poured Frederick's tea.

'Indeed you did. We're going for a quick round in Kells tomorrow.'

'Do you ever play golf, John?' asked Goretti.

'No, he doesn't. It's not his kind of thing. Golf isn't for everyone, you know,' Ruth answered. John glanced at Flossie while his mother continued. 'No. My John knows all about aeroplanes. He still has all his wee models that he built himself, you know. And about a hundred books all about how they work. And stars. He knows all about astromily... don't you, John?'

'It's astronomy,' he answered, taking off his glasses to

clean them with his hankie. His nose looked more in harmony with the rest of his face without his glasses on, Flossie noticed.

'I might go to the dance next Sunday,' Flossie said.

Ruth's voice vibrated the cups and saucers. 'John was thinking of going too, weren't you, John?' she said as she took her place at the table between him and Frederick.

John straightened himself. When he opened his mouth to speak, she nudged him with her elbow. 'The two of you could go together.'

'That'd be lovely... so it would,' Goretti said, thrilled with the idea.

'Tell them about Dublin. She's going to teaching college in Dublin. Aren't you, Flossie?' said Ruth.

'Well, it's not for sure yet. I wrote to Auntie Bridgey about it. She might let me stay with her. She once said I could whenever I want.'

'She's far more than a nurse, you know, she's a matron. The boss of them all up there in St. James's,' Goretti said with a sniff.

'Yes, you told us all about her a million times before,' said Ruth.

Goretti boasted about her sister-in-law at every opportunity. She'd fallen out with her for a short while after Catherine joined the nuns. Although Goretti had a tendency to dominate and speak over people, she disliked animosity and had since made her peace with Bridgey.

'John, tell her about the time you were talking about leaving us all to go to America,' Ruth said. She continued before John could answer. 'He wanted to go with those Finnegan lads. They all high-tailed it to America as soon as they left school. Except for young Pete, he had to stay to run the farm.' Ruth blessed herself. 'Thank God John has the shop here and there's no need for him to leave. The Finnegans tried to inveigle him away. Same as in school, always trying to get him into trouble!'

Goretti scrunched up her face, defending the Finnegans. 'Sure in a way, weren't they right to go? There's nothing for them here. They're not all as lucky as your John.'

'And the poor Connolly fella, the one that married the Ward lassie back in May. Did you hear what happened?' asked Ruth in a tone lower than her usual high pitch.

Goretti sat up straight, neck out, ready to hear the gossip. Ruth only spoke in hushed tones when she was spreading rumours. Flossie couldn't control her blushes. She tried to appear uninterested by fiddling with the doily on the table.

'The poor girl had a miscarriage. In the outhouse. Frank came home from work to find her in an awful state. There wasn't one around to help her. Poor lassie.'

Goretti's eyes widened, egging Ruth on. 'God help them all. That's awful. How many months was she?'

'Well now, they're only married a couple of months, but everyone says she was that way at the wedding... so you can imagine,' Ruth replied, her thin pencilled eyebrows arched higher than the church windows.

'Was it a shotgun wedding then?' Frederick asked.

'To be sure it was.'

'I'll help you tidy up, Mrs O'Malley.' Flossie sprang from her chair.

'Not at all; sure there's no rush. Sit down there and have more tea,' Ruth said.

'I'm full, thank you.'

'Sure you and John go on into the sitting room and talk about the dance.'

'Well, I'm looking forward to the golf tomorrow,' Frederick said.

'How is Roy keeping anyway?' asked Ruth.

§

Relieved to get out of the kitchen, Flossie flopped onto the couch in the sitting room. 'You're like one of those puppet things, John. You don't speak out because your mother says everything for you. Our Danny said you were very brainy in school, so I know you're not stupid. And I've seen you talking to customers in your shop.'

He laughed, shaking his head.

Flossie hadn't heard John laugh properly before. He had a gentle laugh and nice white teeth.

'Mammy can't stop herself. Me and Dad talk plenty when she's not around. She's not that bad... not really.'

'You should tell her you're not a child anymore.'

John tilted his head to study a row of books on the bookcase.

'So, what do you like doing apart from building toy aeroplanes and looking at the sky?'

He turned and looked at her over the rim of his glasses. 'Do you have any hobbies?' he asked.

'One or two.'

He went to the window, stood straight, with his back to Flossie. 'Your mother thinks you'll marry me, you know. Well, I know you don't like me much, but if you don't find yourself a husband, you can marry me if you want.'

'And what makes you think I won't be able to find a husband, Mr O'Malley? Excuse me! And who said I didn't like you? You're a bit boring, that's all.'

He turned to her. 'Don't underestimate me, Flossie. "A quiet man is a thinking man". Haven't you heard that one?'

'"Beware the quiet man". Have you not heard that one?'

He laughed again. Flossie's feelings for John O'Malley shifted slightly.

With a stolid expression, he said, 'I've watched you coming here, having tea with our mothers, listening to them gossiping and giving out. I might not say much, but I hear and I see plenty. Frank Connolly is the man you thought you'd marry and I know you're angry that he married Alice. I saw you in there at the tea, when they talked about him. I saw the look on your face. The same look every time any of the Connollys are mentioned.'

Flossie curled her toes, and her scalp tingled. *The cheek of him!*

'For your information, I have no intention of getting married. I'm away to Dublin as soon as Auntie Bridgey says she'll have me. I'll be a working woman and I might never get married—just like Bridgey. She says women don't have to get married if they don't want to.'

Flossie's heart thumped so hard she imagined he might see it if he were to look down at her chest. Her feelings shifted again.

'Funny to think that he married her because of the baby and now it's gone. God can be cruel sometimes,' said John.

'So, are ya coming to the dance with me or not?' Flossie asked.

'Sure, I suppose I will.'

§

In bed that night, Flossie pondered over her muddled thoughts. *Frank married Alice because of the baby, then God took it away. A cruel act. Why did God give him to Alice? Why couldn't she have him?* She didn't think much of God's plans. She imagined her mother praying night after night that John would become her son-in-law. Surely God only answered prayers that were meant to be. *For the good of all. Was it God's will that she should marry John? What would Catherine think? Should she ask in her next letter?*

CHAPTER FOUR

Auntie Bridgey wrote several letters to Goretti to convince her that a few years in Dublin would be the best thing for Flossie. She offered to pay for her education so there'd be no need to worry about money. Her words: *proper education, status, highly respected,* swayed Goretti into believing that it would be good for Flossie.

'Is that another letter from Auntie Bridgey?' Flossie recognised the writing.

'Indeed it is.'

'Did you decide yet? Can I go to Dublin?' She crossed her fingers behind her back. Her mother didn't know Auntie Bridgey had already enrolled her into college.

'Oh... I don't know. That Bridgey one is so pushy. I wish the woman had children of her own, then she might stop telling me what to do with mine.' She folded the letter and put it in her apron pocket.

'We're the only family she has, Mammy. She cares, that's all.'

Flossie filled the kettle. She'd made buns earlier to please her mother. 'Did I tell you John's coming to the dance with me this Sunday?'

'No, you did not tell me! Sure that's the best news I've heard in a long time.'

Goretti sat at the table and took a bun from the cooling rack. She had that look on her face that made Flossie nervous.

'John said he'd be very proud to have a girlfriend with a diploma and experience of city life.'

'He said that, did he? Well, it would be a nice thing. Not everyone is fit for college, you know, and not everyone can afford college.' Goretti sniffed and pursed her lips.

Flossie poured the tea and sat on the chair beside her mother. *It's only small lies. Not even big enough to tell in the confessional.*

'Mammy, I was thinking. If John becomes my boyfriend and I go to Dublin, sure he can visit me there because he goes to Dublin a lot anyway, for shop supplies and stuff like that. And we can write to each other as well.'

Goretti cut a bun in half, keeping her gaze on Flossie. 'Do you think he'd do that?'

'He said he'd do anything for me. Last Saturday evening when we were in their house, we had a really long talk. He likes me, you know.'

'Of course I know. You two were made for each other.'

'Will you please tell Auntie Bridgey I can go?'

'I'll see. Now get to bed.'

Flossie prayed extra hard that night, making all sorts of promises to God and all the saints in Heaven.

§

Alice Connolly lay in bed, feeling sorry for herself. Frank had gone to work even though she'd asked him to stay at home to be with her in her time of need. He had been so good for the last few days, looking after her, consoling her, trying to convince her it wasn't meant to be. *Of course it wasn't meant to be.*

Hunger pangs prodded her out of bed. She slipped on her dressing gown and made her way downstairs. The kitchen smelled of smoking coal. *At least he lit the fire before he went.* She half-filled the kettle with water from the bucket and put it on the range to boil. He had plenty of logs stacked up against the wall beside it, plenty to keep the fire going for the cooking. Not that Alice intended doing much of that today. She hated that range in the summertime. Frank had promised her a gas cooker, a proper one with an oven. Be no need then for the big fire on warm days. She opened up the damper and threw in a couple of logs and a shovelful of coal.

One of Josey's scrawny cats peered through the window, hoping for scraps. Alice let him in. 'Hello, Snowy. I think if it wasn't for me, you'd starve,' she said as she stroked the meowing tomcat. She took a tin of sardines out of the press and scooped the contents onto a saucer. 'There ya go.'

She'd had a cat once called Tabby. Her father often used him as a threat against her. *Do it again and that cat'll disappear and ya'll not see him again.* Alice wet the bed one night, as she often did. Tabby disappeared the next day and didn't return. She didn't want another cat of her own. She got enough pleasure from feeding Josey's.

The wireless crackled on low volume on the sideboard, some fella going on about the hurling. Alice didn't care what happened in the world of sport. She fiddled with the knob and moved the wireless around the kitchen until she got a clear reception from Radio Luxembourg. Jazz music trumpeted from the airwaves, and she turned up the volume.

Alice turned her ear to the kettle—not as much as a whisper from it. Flames crackled and roared up the chimney. She closed the damper and willed the water to boil. She sat at the table and lit up a cigarette. Rubbing her tummy, she thought about what it must be like in there for a baby. Warm and safe. The outside world was no place for the little mites. Some women were good at looking after babies, others not so much. Alice didn't think she'd be any good at looking after a baby. *Just as well there wasn't going to be one.*

Snowy rubbed against her legs. She picked him up and held him in her arms like a baby. He wriggled and hissed and jumped down, then he leapt onto the worktop and darted out the window.

'Stupid cat,' said Alice as she dabbed at the scratches on her chest with the sleeve of her dressing gown. As she closed the window, she caught sight of Joyce coming towards the door. Joyce let herself in and entered the kitchen through the scullery. 'Hello, Alice.'

'Morning,' Alice replied. 'Sit down. There'll be tea in a minute.' She gestured towards the range.

Joyce took a bottle of Lucozade and twenty cigarettes out of her shopping bag and put them on the table. 'Very sorry to hear what happened. Are you okay?' She sat across from Alice.

'Aw thanks, Joycie. I'm nearly out of fags.'

'How are you keeping now? I said I'd wait a day or two before coming to see you.'

'I'm grand. It's all probably for the best.'

Joyce frowned. 'Why?'

'Sure how would I know what to be doing with a baby?' Alice pulled on her cigarette and blew smoke rings towards the ceiling.

'You'd learn as you go along. No one knows in the beginning.'

'Frank is disappointed. He was looking forward to having a son.'

'A son? Did he say that?'

'Men prefer boys.'

'That's not true, Alice. Not all men are like your father. Frank would love a girl just as much as a boy.'

Alice wasn't so sure about that. Her father's words cut through her thoughts. *Bloody women, only good for one thing. Have you no more lads in there, in that belly of yours?*

Eight-year-old Alice was watching her new baby sister, Nellie, feeding from her mother's breast. Alice and her sister Carol were happy that Nellie came out alive, unlike the two sisters that went back to Heaven on the very same day that they were born. Her father stabbed a finger in Alice's direction. 'She and that other one upstairs are of no use to me. And then you give me another one.'

'You can get pregnant again,' said Joyce.

'If I ever do have a baby, would you be its Godmother?'

'Of course I would. But would you not ask one of your sisters?'

'No.'

'I wanted to ask you this at the wedding but I didn't,' Joyce said. 'Why did no one from your family go to your wedding?'

'They don't like me, that's why. I'm glad they didn't go

and I'm glad I don't have to live with them anymore. And the best thing of all is that I won't have to be riding that shite of a man's bicycle in and out of town.'

'Do they know you lost the baby?'

'I didn't tell them I was pregnant.'

'But... you do know people were gossiping anyway. Surely they'd have heard it by now.'

'So what if they did? I don't care. I'm a married woman now and I don't have to see them again if I don't want to.'

The kettle hissed. Alice made no attempt to wet the tea.

'Will I do the tea?' Joyce said.

'Aye, go on.'

Joyce went out the back door with the teapot to empty the used tea leaves. The dustbin lid balanced on top of the overflowing rubbish. Alice wasn't overly fond of keeping the house in order, but these days she had a good excuse. *Poor Alice.*

'What does Frank think about the miscarriage?' asked Joyce when she returned to the kitchen.

'Why are you asking me so many flipping questions, Joycie? Are you working for the guards all of a sudden?' Alice stubbed out her cigarette in the ashtray.

'Sorry, I'm only asking. Look, will I stay a while and help you clean this place up a bit?'

'Yeah, okay.'

CHAPTER FIVE

Flossie didn't look back as the bus took her up the Kells Road out of Bailieborough to a new life in Dublin. She felt nervous and excited at the same time. *What would it be like living with Auntie Bridgey? Would she be bossy like Flossie's mother? Probably not.* John had seemed pleased when she told him he could be her boyfriend and how he should visit her in Dublin. She dreaded her mother's reaction when she broke it all off with him. She'd wait a few months.

The long trip to Dublin allowed Flossie some time to reflect on her life. She wanted freedom, yet she needed the comforts of home, like a fledgling ready to fly her nest but not quite ready to be alone in the wide-open sky.

Security and stability, Flossie, her mother's voice niggled. *Dissidence and recklessness,* a different voice tempted.

She swallowed the lump in her throat. *What if she didn't get along with Auntie Bridgey? Was she foolish to be running away from a potentially good life with John O'Malley? Maybe her mother was right: she might do no better than him.*

Tears flooded her eyes and she dared not blink for fear

they'd fall. She'd promised herself she wouldn't cry. *She was eighteen, a big girl now, starting a new life as an adult.* She pushed her shoulders back and thought of her friend Mary and her life in Manchester, how brave she and her husband Jim had been to head off to England as soon as they got married. She envied them and now she had the same chance too. She should be happy, not sad. She tried to think of all the good things that might come her way. Thoughts of Frank pushed their way into her mind. She tried not to think about him. Life in Dublin would make her forget about him, as though he didn't exist.

Flossie took a ham sandwich out of her bag. She took one bite and chewed it slowly. She struggled to swallow it. *Maybe later*, she decided as she wrapped it up again. The man sitting right in front of her lit a new cigarette from the one he had just finished. She opened her window to let the smoke escape, but the draught whipped the back of her neck, so she closed it again. *Maybe he'd get off soon.* She folded her coat and rested her head against it. The bumpy road made it hard to doze off, but she kept her eyes closed and let her mind drift back to a time when she remembered being carefree; a time when her family lived in Primrose Cottage.

Perched neatly on a small hilltop in Bailieborough, overlooking the white gates of the wood entrance on the Cavan Road, Primrose Cottage held her favourite childhood memories. The Connollys lived two fields away, on the back lane that led to a different part of the woods.

Danny and Josey Connolly were friends, just like she was friends with Josey's sister, Mary. Catherine played along with everyone. Frank was the leader, deciding what would happen next and who should and shouldn't do what. He made fishing rods from the branches of a hazel tree and took them all fishing to Castle Lake. In the warm weather, they had picnics and paddled in the shallows. When he left school to start working in Corrie's Forge, he still found time for everyone. As Flossie grew older, her feelings for Frank deepened. Strange sensations stirred within her when they were together—a tingling up her spine and soft flutters in her tummy. When they weren't together, she daydreamed about him. Thinking about Frank made Flossie feel like she was floating on a cloud.

Mrs Connolly had a different way of going on than Flossie's mother. The children never bothered her, it seemed. She didn't shout or complain when they made noise. A lot changed when she died from a brain haemorrhage. That was a day Flossie would always remember because it was her tenth birthday. With no experience in dealing with grief, Flossie had no idea how to help Mary cope with losing her mother. She didn't know what to say or how to comfort her. Sometimes she said nothing at all; she just let her cry. She overheard her mother talking to Molly Fagin about Mary.

'Poor child, twelve years of age and entering into womanhood. A time when she needs her mammy more than ever. Who's going to look out for her? Who'll teach her about... "you-know-what"?'

'It'll not be the father or the brothers, I hope. God help them.'

Flossie didn't know what they meant.

When Catherine left, Mary then became Flossie's shoulder to cry on, taking her mind off her own pain. But when Mr Connolly died less than two years later, grief consumed Mary once again, but in a different way. She was angry with everyone. She rarely went to school, and when she did go, she spent most of her time staring out the window. Miss Kennedy—who usually had a spite to Mary—didn't chastise her. She let her be. Flossie liked Miss Kennedy for doing that.

Once again, the Connolly children became a regular topic of conversation. They were pitied, comforted, and praised at how they dealt with their unfortunate circumstances.

'Poor wee Mary, taking over the role of the mother, and then for the father to go as well. Died of a broken heart,' Molly Fagin said.

'Aw now, t'was the fags,' said Goretti. 'God bless them, is all I can say. That Josey lad's a great worker; cut out for the farming, he was. The middle lad Frank spends all his wages on the family, you know! They're a credit to the parents.'

Fun and games stopped in the Connolly household after that. Josey took over the farm, and soon after that, Mary left school to work in the shoe factory.

Thinking about her childhood days warmed Flossie's heart, but a deep sense of longing churned inside her. The smell of the woods, Mrs Connolly's scones, even thoughts of her mother making all her decisions for her gave Flossie some comfort.

CHAPTER SIX

The bus rattled and jolted as it pulled into Busaras. Flossie woke, sore and her eyelids heavy. She stretched her arms out in front of her, yawning and twisting her neck.

This was only her second time in Dublin. Once, her mother brought her and Catherine for 'a day out', she said. They came on the bus, browsed around some clothes shops and a great big chemist. The only thing her mother bought was Yardley perfumed soap.

Then they met Auntie Bridgey in a small café where they had tea and sandwiches. After that, they went for a walk along the Liffey and across the Ha'penny Bridge. Auntie Bridgey told Catherine to stop saying hello to everyone they met or she'd lose her voice.

§

Flossie thanked the bus driver and stepped out into the exhaust fumes and the smell of diesel. She stood alongside the other passengers, waiting for the man to fetch her case from the baggage compartment of the bus. Hers was possibly the biggest one there, and the heaviest. She thanked him and lifted the case, then made her way into the station where she hoped her aunt would be waiting. The air was cooler inside. She saw Auntie Bridgey straight away, standing along the wall. Flossie's jittery tummy settled down when her aunt smiled and waved in her direction. She looked a bit different, younger maybe. Her bright red cotton skirt and white blouse seemed inappropriate for a trip to the bus station. Flossie wondered what age she was. She daren't ask. She got whipped around the legs with her mother's tea towel the day she asked Molly Fagin her age.

'You look nice, Auntie Bridgey.'

'Thank you, my dear. Now we'll have less of the "auntie", please. I'm not listening to that every day for the next two years. Do you need the toilet before we get the bus?'

'No, I'm grand, thanks. Are we going on a double-decker bus?'

'We are indeed.'

'Can we sit upstairs? Please.'

'Of course we can. It's not far; fifteen minutes or so.'

§

Bridgey took several sly glances at her young niece sitting beside her on the top deck of the bus. It amused her how she took all in with wide eyes and an open mouth. She looked the other passengers up and down, recoiled in her seat as the couple across from them began arguing—the man appeared to be the main instigator of the row. Not a scene young Flossie would be accustomed to.

'Do you think I'll like it here, Auntie Bridgey?'

'Why wouldn't you? It'll take a while to get used to, but there'll not be a bother on you.'

'Mammy gave me some money and I've a few pounds in the Post Office too. Can't I withdraw money from the big Post Office here? Could we go shopping for clothes?' Flossie eyed up a stylish young girl getting off at her stop. 'And a nice handbag. I only have this awful thing.'

Bridgey couldn't help but laugh at her enthusiasm. 'Plenty of time for all that. Your bag is grand enough, so it is. You don't have to be anything special living in the city, Flossie. You'll see all sorts of everything and everyone up here, you know.'

'But I want to be something special.' Flossie opened her bag and took out her ham sandwich. 'I'm starving.'

Bridgey had seen it so many times with the student nurses down through the years. They came to the city expecting their lives to be magically transformed. Oh, they changed, yes, but not always in the way they imagined. They thought it was all glamour and excitement; they let their illusions get in the way of reality. They forgot about the hard work involved in gaining their independence. Only the well-grounded girls with reasonable expectations got through it without too many tears. Bridgey had no doubt that Flossie would make mistakes, like the others, and she'd watch her niece experience the lows as well as the highs. But she knew Flossie would be okay.

§

All thoughts of home strayed from Flossie's mind as the bus dropped them off on Kimmage Road in Harold's Cross. They had a short walk from the bus stop to the house, during which time Bridgey kept the conversation going.

She had a Saturday job organised for Flossie in a nearby grocery shop. She was expected to start the following weekend.

'It's important to have your independence. I'm paying for your education and I'm happy to do that for you, but with money from your wee job, you can give me a bit of rent. Bills don't pay themselves, you know. If you work hard, Mr Reilly might keep you on.'

§

The house was red brick—like all the others in the row—and covered with ivy. It was bigger than their house on The Green, but not as big as her mother had described it. Maybe the windows made it look bigger than it really was, the way they protruded outwards.

'You've big windows, Auntie Bridgey.'

'They're called bay windows. The first thing I liked about the house, I must say.'

A hedge surrounded the small garden. Two huge terracotta flower pots, blooming with marigolds, sat each side of the three steps leading up to the dark green door.

'Welcome to my home, Flossie Lynch.' Bridgey smiled as she turned the key.

The hall smelled a bit like O'Malleys'—the same polish. Flossie followed Bridgey into the sitting room. Freshly washed clothes hung on a clothes horse giving the room a clean linen scent.

'Will a cup of tea do you for now? The dinner will be in an hour.'

'That's grand,' Flossie replied.

Bridgey reached into the press and took out a small package wrapped in brown paper and tied with a piece of red wool. 'A little present to welcome you,' she said as she handed it to Flossie.

'Oh, thank you. But I didn't get you anything.'

Bridgey flicked her hand in the air and scoffed. 'Stop it.'

Flossie carefully untied the wool and uncovered a blue hardback notebook. She traced her fingers across the embossed floral design on the front cover. 'It's so pretty.' She fanned through monthly labelled pages. 'Oh, it's a diary.'

'Yes, but you have to fill in the dates yourself. So you can start using it straight away if you like.'

'Oh, I will,' said Flossie. 'Then, in years to come, I can read back on my time living here with you.' She wanted to hug her aunt, but she didn't think Bridgey liked hugs.

She wandered around, taking in her strange new surroundings while Bridgey made the tea. She searched inside herself for the sense of security she feared she'd be lost without. But she didn't feel lost at all.

The kitchen was small, but the spacious dining room made up for it. *Very fancy*. At home, the dining took place in the kitchen. No one she knew in Bailieborough had a separate room for eating in.

Bridgey called from the kitchen, 'Tea's ready.'

'You have a telephone,' Flossie said as she sat at the small round table in the kitchen. 'Does Mammy know you got the telephone in?'

'I didn't get round to telling her yet. It's only there a week or so.'

'When the O'Malleys got theirs in, Mrs O'Malley had the whole town told about it the very same day.'

'Oh, that one. Don't mind what she'd do,' Bridgey said.

'Do you not like her?' asked Flossie.

'She talks too much.'

'Do you know that her bark is worse than her bite?'

'Mmm, I'm sure it is,' said Bridgey, smirking. 'Your mother can call you from the phone box if she wants.'

'I'll tell her the number when I write to her,' Flossie said, hoping John wouldn't start ringing her too.

After they finished their tea, Bridgey showed Flossie to her bedroom. She carried her case upstairs for her, joking that she must have brought half the house in it.

'This can be yours while you're here. It's a bit bigger than the back bedroom and has a nicer view. I'm in the one next door and the bathroom's across the hall. You settle yourself in and I'll get on with making the dinner.'

'Thank you. It's lovely.'

The bedroom was similar to her own at home, although far tidier, with no clutter. A clunky, dark brown wardrobe stood against one wall with a matching chest of six drawers. A metal-frame single bed was pushed up against the opposite wall, so high off the ground another person could easily sleep under it.

§

Flossie sat on the small, padded stool at the dressing table in front of the window. She could see the steeple of Mount Argus Church behind the oval mirror if she tilted her head to the side. *Won't have far to go to Mass.*

She lay on the bed looking up at the cracks in the white ceiling, waiting for her mother's voice to boom up the stairs. In a way, she missed not hearing it but quickly convinced herself how lucky she was to be here, away from them all. She wondered how long it would take for her to feel that sense of freedom people talked about.

CHAPTER SEVEN

Flossie felt more like an adult with each passing day. She liked the way Bridgey asked her thoughts about certain topics being discussed on the wireless. 'Times are changing, Flossie,' she'd say. 'What do you think?'

The suffrage and women's rights were the main topics of conversation. Bridgey lectured Flossie about her rights as a woman in a male-dominated society. Most of it made little sense to Flossie. She wasn't used to such talk. 'Depend on nobody, only yourself,' Bridgey would say.

She got the notion that Bridgey didn't really like men. 'Watch that fella—he has a dodgy eye in his head,' she said about the young man who worked in the shop with Flossie. 'His eyebrows meet in the middle—that's a bad sign,' she said about the man at the door selling encyclopaedias.

Although many aspects of life in Dublin appealed to Flossie, she still yearned for home and familiar faces. Part of her relished being a stranger to everyone she met as she walked the city streets, but she also missed the comfort of familiar faces. Her heart lingered in Bailieborough, yet her head didn't want to be there. She used her studies as an excuse to stay in Dublin at the weekends.

College wasn't as hard as her mother had made it out to be. *I'm not sure you have the brains for it...'tis hard work... all those books.* Flossie liked the work. It kept her mind off Frank... sometimes.

Most students were friendly; some were rude. Flossie made friends with Sheila from Kildare. She wasn't her best friend like Mary, but Flossie liked being with her and she knew a lot about city life.

They often socialised on a Friday night with Sheila's cousin George from the Docklands. He studied history in DCU. Although too much history bored Flossie, George fascinated her. He was the most curious person she'd ever met. He wore bright-coloured patterned shirts and chequered trousers, and dickie bows. He had wavy hair blacker than boot polish, that bounced when he walked. Hair that Ruth O'Malley would die for.

John wrote seven times between September and December, each letter longer than the last one. He had tidy joined writing, easy to read. He wrote on blue Belvedere Bond writing paper, not on both sides like some people did, and he numbered the pages at the bottom. She expected his letters to be boring, but they weren't at all.

He kept her up to date on the local gossip, and he mentioned how his mother and Goretti made several remarks about their friendship becoming much more. Goretti had asked twice if he planned a trip to Harold's Cross any time soon. Getting to know each other through their letter writing had a mysterious feel to it, like reading a book when you couldn't wait to read the next chapter. Writing gave them the privacy they didn't get at home.

Flossie wrote about her new friends, Sheila and George. She wrote about her studies, the films she'd seen at the pictures and all the mad stuff Auntie Bridgey said.

John's letters were mature and interesting, as if they were written by a person she'd never met. His words absorbed her full attention. They stilled her and left her sitting in a haze of wonderment about him and the parts of him that she had yet to discover. The passionate side of him seemed to thrive in his writing. John O'Malley was like a poet! Unlike Mary, who wrote like she spoke, although her letters were fun and gossipy.

§

Flossie's mother phoned her a couple of times from the phone box on Main Street, reminding her she could go home anytime she wanted. *Did she need any money for a bus? Be careful in the city. Don't be out gallivanting at night-time with those new friends. Are you learning anything at all? Did you write to John? He's a great lad. Father Tierney was in hospital with ulcers. He's home now.* When the phone would beep to alert her mother that her money had run out, Flossie would practically kiss the telephone. Although a part of her really did miss her mother.

As Sheila and the other girls on her course made plans to go home for Christmas, Flossie offered to stay in Dublin with Bridgey, but Bridgey told her she'd do no such thing and that she had better not dare let her mother hear such nonsense.

She lent her a small suitcase and left her to Busaras on Christmas Eve.

§

As soon as the bus stopped in Bailieborough, warmth radiated through Flossie's veins. As she stepped out into an air of cheerful voices, a thousand bubbles fizzed up inside her.

Joyce Rafferty's uncle Billy, with a cigarette hanging out the corner of his mouth, was trying to get rid of his last few sprigs of berryless holly. It grew in abundance beside his house, and the few bob he made on it bought him his beer in the pub on Christmas Eve.

Neighbours greeted Flossie as she made her way across The Green to her home. She realised at that moment that she'd missed her hometown more than she thought. She missed the friendliness of the neighbours. There was a smile around every corner, people greeted her by her name, a quick chat was always available if she needed one. Colourful lights twinkled in the townhouse windows, cosy and welcoming. She imagined the children getting ready for bed hours earlier than usual, with freshly washed hair and wearing new pyjamas.

As Flossie reached her front door, it swung open. Her mother beamed. 'You're here! Happy Christmas.'

'You too, Mammy.'

Goretti Lynch reached out and hugged her daughter. Flossie held her breath and let her case drop to the ground. Until that moment, she hadn't paid much attention to the fact that her mother hadn't hugged her since Catherine went away. Wasn't it normal? When children grew up, they didn't get hugs and kisses anymore. Flossie put her arms around her mother's slim waist and gave a gentle squeeze, welcoming the familiar smell of hair lacquer and a whiff of cinnamon sweets.

'I didn't think I missed home, Mammy, but I did... a little,' said Flossie as she stepped into the hall.

'The house has been very quiet without you. I've been talking to the walls for the last four months. God, I wouldn't like to live on my own forever.' They went through to the kitchen.

Flossie felt silly for wanting to stay in Dublin for Christmas. It was enough that Danny was staying in the seminary for the holidays. Auntie Bridgey was right to send her home. She put her case inside the sitting room door and stood for a moment to look around. Christmas ambience filled the small room. The fir tree by the window smelled a hundred times nicer than Auntie Bridgey's artificial Christmas tree. Presents were stacked neatly on the coffee table, all wrapped in the same patterned paper—red and white candy canes and red bows tied on silver bells. Firewood crackled in the open hearth, sending a soft flicker of light up to the sprigs of holly that lined the mantlepiece.

She joined her mother in the kitchen. 'You've the sitting room looking lovely, Mammy.'

'Did Bridgey put up any decorations?'

'Just a few. Do you need help with anything?' Flossie noticed a ham sitting in the biggest saucepan they owned, ready for boiling. 'The ham's very big.'

'Oh, I didn't get telling you. We're going to Ruth's for dinner tomorrow. I'm bringing the ham. I'll boil it tonight and bake it in the morning.'

'Oh... lovely. Nice of them to have us.' Flossie sighed and then quickly reminded herself to be grateful. Christmas wasn't a time for complaining and moaning.

'So how many times did John write to you?' her mother asked.

'Danny wrote twice. Pity he couldn't come home for Christmas. I'd love to see him.'

'I know, I know. Did John write?'

'Yes, Mammy. He wrote and I wrote back. Now, tell me what I can do around here.'

'Oh, that's good. You can tell me all about it later then.'

Flossie covered the prepared ham with cold water and put it on the gas cooker to boil.

§

Christmas Day dinner in the O'Malley house was more enjoyable than Flossie had expected. Mrs O'Malley even offered her a sherry, which she declined. They all wanted to hear about college and her adventures in the city—none of which sounded very exciting at all.

After dinner, Flossie and John went for a walk to Town Lake. They strolled in comfortable silence. A soft white mist fell from the dull sky and hovered above the still waters, creating a sense of calm and peacefulness. The reflection of skeletal trees with their bony branches gave the illusion that the muddy lake concealed a secret mystical land. Flossie imagined the kind of people that might exist in this other land, fairylike and magical. Or maybe monstrous and devilish. John picked up a flat stone and skimmed it across the lake, rippling the smooth surface and snapping Flossie from her daydream.

'You'd like George. He knows all about history... not only Irish history. And politics. You'd like all that stuff. It's okay that you're a bit shy because George does most of the talking anyway,' Flossie said.

'Do you like him?' John asked.

'I do. He's my friend.'

'Well sure, that's marvellous.'

'You should visit me the next time you're in Dublin. Meet him and Sheila.'

'I could, I suppose. We'll have dinner somewhere.'

'Why don't you stay overnight and come out with us?' Flossie said.

'I suppose, I could. I'll stay in Foley's.'

'Bridgey has a telephone... if you want to ring me sometime,' Flossie said.

'Maybe. I'd rather write to be honest.'

'Me too. I like your letters, John. You write more than you talk.'

He smiled and skimmed another stone.

§

Flossie spent the best part of her Christmas holidays at home with her mother. She visited John a few times, but she avoided everywhere else for fear of meeting Frank or Alice. She was happy that Mary didn't come home for Christmas. Otherwise, she'd have had to visit the Connollys. She enjoyed the few days in Bailieborough, but she was glad when the time came to return to Dublin.

CHAPTER EIGHT

Mary wrote in January about her pregnancy news. She said she was afraid of her life about the whole thing but was excited at the same time. Flossie replied with words of joy and support. She almost told her about John but told her all about George instead. She wondered how her friend would react when she read that her new friend was a man. She gave her Bridgey's telephone number so that Jim could ring when the baby was born. Mary never mentioned Frank or Alice in her letters, and neither did Flossie.

§

For several months, John and Flossie met in The Brazen Head for dinner on the last Wednesday of each month. By the end of the college year, he still hadn't met her friends. He didn't ask to because he had little interest, and she didn't offer him the opportunity because she hadn't yet told them about him.

Auntie Bridgey talked Goretti into letting Flossie stay in

Dublin for the summer. She got full-time hours in the grocery shop, which meant she had extra money to spend on herself.

With her friend Sheila's help, she added some colour to her boring wardrobe of brown skirts and cream blouses. Sheila told her once that she was beautiful and had no need to hide behind *all that drab*.

That summer, George worked in The Punch Bowl pub. On his time off he delighted in taking Flossie and Sheila out in his recently purchased old Baby Austin to educate them on the city's heritage and culture. He paid ninety pounds for the 1922 car at an auction—he said it was a bargain. Sheila and Flossie knew little about cars and their worth, so they took his word for it.

'I have a boyfriend back home, you know,' Flossie said to Sheila as they sat in the car eating ice cream by the baths out at Blackrock. George was on the promenade talking to some college friends.

'Oh, really? You didn't mention him before.'

'Aw, sure I don't know what to make of him. I once sort of hated him. Well, I know now I didn't. I only hated how Mammy always tried to get us together.'

'So, she succeeded then.' Sheila grinned, focusing on licking the melting ice cream that dripped down her cone.

'It was the easiest way for me to come to Dublin. I planned on breaking the whole thing off by Christmas. Mam wasn't keen on me coming here, you see, but agreed when I let her think we were going out together.'

'So why didn't you break it off?'

'You see... that's the funny thing. He's not that bad once you get to know him properly. He's kind, he's polite, reliable, and respectable.'

'Is he handsome?'

'I looked closer at him at Christmas, and he's not all that bad looking. His eyes are handsome, dark and deep, a bit lost behind his glasses. The kind of eyes you could easily dive into if you wanted. Do you know those kind of eyes?'

'Not really.'

'He writes to me. I think he's lonely... or something.'

'He probably misses you,' Sheila said as she opened the door to let some cool sea air circulate inside the car.

'No... that's not it. We haven't even kissed yet. You'll meet him soon, and then you can tell me what you think of him.'

'You haven't kissed yet?' Sheila's jaw dropped.

'He's a gentleman.'

'Should you not be at home for the summer then? With this boyfriend?'

'Probably. Mammy wasn't too happy when she heard I wasn't going home.'

'So when will I get to meet him?'

'He's very shy about meeting my friends. He's shy about most things, in fact.'

'Maybe that's why he hasn't kissed you yet, because he's shy.'

'I'm his first girlfriend, so yes, maybe. But he really is a gentleman. Were you ever in love, Sheila?'

'Only with ice cream.' Sheila closed her eyes and took a big lick of her cone. Flossie laughed. She liked Sheila's sense of humour.

CHAPTER NINE

Work on Saturday had been busy. Flossie couldn't believe the amount of extra people around during the summer. She arrived home at five o'clock and collapsed onto the couch beside Bridgey. She closed her eyes.

'I dropped a bottle of lemonade today, and it smashed into a million pieces. The shop was full and Mr Reilly wasn't too pleased.'

'Jim Fitzpatrick phoned,' Bridgey said. 'Mary had a wee girl.'

Flossie opened her eyes wide and shot up straight. 'Oh my God, that's the best news I've heard in a long time! What did he say? Have they a name? Is she really tiny?'

'Maureen Frances, he said. She came a bit early, so she's only five and a half pounds but healthy. Mary's doing grand and will ring you soon.'

'Oh, I can't wait to talk with her. I can't wait to see the baby. She'll have to send me a picture.'

Flossie sat back and sighed. *Mary was so lucky. Jim was a*

good man and he made her happy. She closed her eyes again and imagined Frank's face.

'John O'Malley rang too,' Bridgey said.

Flossie straightened herself again.

'He said he's coming to Dublin this evening. He's booked into Foley's.'

'What?'

'That's what he said.'

'Oh, okay.' Flossie rose from the couch, her face flushed.

'I know all about you and John O'Malley. You hardly thought your mother would keep that to herself, did you?'

'Does everyone know?'

'I couldn't tell you who knows and who doesn't. Why, is it a secret?'

Flossie sensed that Bridgey expected an explanation. 'You know how Mammy didn't want me to come to Dublin? Well, I knew if she thought I was courting John, she'd back down. Knowing I'd go back home and not stay away forever.'

'And are you going back home? To John?'

'I don't know yet, Bridgey. I'm not gone a year yet. I like Dublin, but I like home too.'

'Home will always be there,' Bridgey said. 'What are the things you like about home? Your friend is in England and she's the only one you ever really got on with. If you liked it that much, you'd have gone home for the summer. I don't know what to say about you.'

'I got along with the Flemmings too.' Flossie examined her chipped nail polish.

'And where's the Flemmings now?' asked Bridgey, knowing well they went to America as soon as they turned sixteen. 'Does John O'Malley think he's your boyfriend?'

'Well, he is... sort of.'

'Christ of Almighty, Miss Lynch... cop yourself on.' Bridgey scowled.

'But he's not that bad. I like him better than I used to. He writes good letters and I've got to know him now.' Flossie glanced over at her aunt, who stared back with a furrowed brow. She went to the kitchen for a drink of water. Bridgey followed.

'I can't tell you what to do, but I know if your father was alive, he'd have none of it.'

'Daddy always did everything Mammy said. He didn't exactly want Catherine to join the nuns, but he didn't stop it, did he? So, don't be telling me he'd stop me from marrying John O'Malley if he was here.'

Bridgey's face turned red. Flossie had crossed the line. Her mother would slap her for being so cheeky. 'I'm sorry, Bridgey, I swear I am. But I know what I'm doing.'

'I'm not sure you do. Anyway, I've to get to work. I'll see you in the morning. I told young O'Malley to come here tonight, if that suits the pair of ye. There's ham and tomatoes in the fridge. Make sandwiches,' she said without taking a breath.

Flossie had learned that Bridgey spoke at ten miles an hour when her humour wasn't good. 'Okay, thanks.'

§

Flossie had made plans to meet Sheila and George that night. She didn't want to cancel. John would have to come too, whether he liked it or not. She phoned George to tell him John would be joining them.

John pulled up at Bridgey's in his father's car. Flossie watched through the net curtains in the sitting room. He didn't get out straight away. He took off his glasses and wiped them with his hanky. He ran both hands through his greased hair. When he did get out, Flossie—despite herself—thought he looked quite attractive in his lemon short-sleeved shirt. He wore a dickie bow instead of his usual tie. *Holy God! Himself and George will look like twins tonight,* she thought.

He carried himself well—something her mother said about people who walked with a straight back and their head held high—more so now than ever before.

Flossie opened the door with a spring in her step. 'It's not like you to come and see me with such short notice,' she said.

John raised his eyebrows. 'Hello,' he said.

'Hello. Sorry. Hello. Come in.' Flossie stood aside and ushered him in.

He stepped past her into the hall, his scent cool and refreshing, like peppermint floating on a sea breeze. The smell of mothballs was a million miles away.

'My father has a young lad working in the shop for the summer, so I got a half day. I felt like coming to see you. Is that okay?' said John as he followed Flossie into the sitting room.

'Of course it's okay. Sit down there... anywhere.' Flossie swept her arm around the room. He sat in the armchair beside the fireplace.

'Is your auntie here?'

'No, she's at work. There's no one here, only me. Will you have a sandwich?'

'No thanks. I'm fed.'

He sat forward in the chair with his elbows resting on his

thighs. He turned the toes of his shoes up as if admiring the high shine.

Flossie stood by the window. 'I'm going out with Sheila and George tonight, so you'll have to come. Sheila's only here for the weekend, so I want to see her.'

'Sure, isn't it time I met them?'

'That's what I was thinking. They should be here soon.'

'So you told them about me.'

'Of course I did. You're not a secret. Sure, every time I go out with my friends, I have men tripping over themselves to get a date with me, so I have to tell them I'm already spoken for.'

John sat back in the chair, pushed his glasses up his nose and sat forward again. He tapped his foot, admiring his shiny shoes again.

'They'll be here any minute,' Flossie said.

He cleared his throat. 'You look nice. You've new clothes on.'

'Thanks. You look well yourself.'

'You're wearing lipstick too.'

'John... how come you haven't kissed me yet?'

'Well, as a matter of fact, I was going to kiss you tonight.'

Flossie turned to the window, blessing herself when she saw George pulling up. 'Oh, they're here. Come on, let's go.'

John was already on his feet. Flossie ignored what he'd said and avoided eye contact with him; she scurried past him into the hallway. That was the last thing she expected him to say. She wasn't even sure if she wanted to kiss John O'Malley and she didn't even know why she'd asked him about kissing her.

George got out of his Baby Austin to introduce himself to

John. He shook his hand. 'I've heard all about you, my good man. Nice to meet you at last.'

That was a bit of a lie. She'd told him hardly anything about John. But it made her look good, so she didn't mind.

'Good to meet you too, George.'

Sheila got out of the passenger seat and walked round to introduce herself. She looked John up and down, slowly, chewing gum, a half-smile on her lips.

'Awfully nice to meet you, Johnny. Flossie told me all about you, so she did,' she said in a lilting voice, throwing a glance at Flossie.

John passed no remarks of her smart tone and kept his cool posture. Heat rushed to Flossie's face. Sheila offered John the front seat and climbed into the back with Flossie. 'You're a dark horse,' she whispered into her ear.

'His name's John, not Johnny,' she whispered back. They giggled.

George usually stayed close to his friends, keeping strangers at a distance, but he hit it off with John like they were long-lost twins. They talked fluently in the car about economics and politics, the kind of things Flossie knew they'd chat about.

§

They went to a pub, and after two drinks, George announced that The Harry Boland Band was playing in the Kingsway in Parnell Square. George and Sheila loved the big bands and enjoyed dancing.

'We should go,' Sheila said. 'Flossie, will you come this time?'

'I think it sounds like great fun. And sure, I'm wearing my new skirt, so I might as well. You'll come along too, won't you, John?' Flossie smoothed down her lilac skirt.

When they entered the balmy, smoke-filled dance hall, Flossie's heart raced with a mixture of excitement and self-doubt. The music vibrated up her legs, the floor a rainbow of swinging frocks. Women smoked carelessly, no worries about tittle-tattlers. The scent of perfume and hairspray wafted through the air. George and Sheila took straight to the dance floor.

'Are you coming out?' John asked Flossie.

'Out where?' Flossie furrowed her brow.

'On the dance floor, where do you think?'

'Can you dance, John O'Malley? Because I don't want you making an eejit of me in front of everyone.'

John took her hand and led her to the floor. 'There's not much room,' she shouted over the booming band. He ignored her and swung her into a jive.

Jesus, John O'Malley could dance. Other girls shot admiring glances in their direction.

Maybe her mother was right. *If you don't marry the one you love, love the one you marry.* Could she learn to love him? Bridgey's words found their way into her thoughts, but she mentally swiped them to one side and let the songs of the dance hall take them away.

John had an air of confidence about him that Flossie hadn't seen before. *Why does he hide behind a scrupulous altar boy mask when everyone would love him as this high-spirited man?*

At the end of the evening, he said goodnight; no kiss, no flirtation. Relieved but also disappointed, she wondered again about the puzzling John O'Malley; *who was he really*? He certainly wasn't the same John she knew from Bailieborough.

CHAPTER TEN

'Will you stay with him?' Sheila asked Flossie as they drank tea in Bewley's, one Saturday lunchtime.

'I can't seem to break it off. I don't think I want to. There's so much about him I like, but there's things I'm unsure about.'

'Like what?'

Flossie's forehead wrinkled. 'If I'd be happy with him; if he'd be happy with me.'

'Do you love him?'

'Sheila! You're the only person in this world who asks private things. You can't ask people things like that.'

'But you're my friend and I know you want to tell me,' Sheila said.

'I love him, sort of, but a bit like I love my friend Mary.'

'Does he know?'

'Of course not. But I don't think he loves me. He hasn't kissed me yet.'

'I don't think he knows what he wants. Neither of you do.'

'Sometimes I think I'll meet someone here in Dublin, someone I'll fall properly in love with. So then I can tell John I can't stay with him.'

'Do you think that's a normal thing to do?' Sheila asked.

'Of course it's not. Anyway, I'm not meeting anyone, am I? There's no man I can fall in love with.' *There's only one and he's married to Alice Ward.*

Sheila sat back in her chair, tilting her head to the side. 'If you want my opinion, I don't think John is the man for you. You say you don't really love him and you've admitted that you're hoping to fall in love with a man you haven't even met yet.' She sat forward and looked Flossie firmly in the eyes. 'You can't stay with him.'

Flossie knew deep down that Sheila was right. But would Sheila say the same thing if she knew the whole story? She swirled the tea leaves around the bottom of her cup, as if they held the answer. She didn't love John, but she liked him. She was curious about him and a part of her wanted to be with him. Her mother's voice butted into her thoughts. *You'll learn to love him.*

§

John visited more often, sometimes for a couple of hours, and at other times he stayed in Foley's for the night. He and Flossie learned more about each other during his visits.

'You're like a different person away from home... and your parents,' she told him. He laughed and said, 'Well, you're the same as ever, Miss Lynch.'

The long silences between them lessened. They talked and debated about politics, literature and the end of the world. Flossie's knowledge of politics improved by being in the company of George and Bridgey, but she was no match for John.

Sometimes religion caused arguments between them, John saying he only went to Mass to be seen and to please his parents. Shocked by his agnostic attitude, Flossie refused to discuss God with him in the future.

Their relationship developed further when John dropped her home after the pictures one evening. He'd been quieter than usual on the way, like his old self again.

'Sure I'll walk you to the door,' he said as he pulled up outside Bridgey's.

'There's no need.'

He got out of the car and walked round to her side.

'Afraid the bogeyman might get me?' she asked.

When they reached the door, John took a deep breath. 'Goodnight, Flossie.' He leaned forward and kissed her on the cheek.

'Night,' she whispered.

He dashed back to his car like an embarrassed schoolboy. Flossie stood watching as he turned the car and drove away. The first kiss from John O'Malley left a warm tingle on her skin. She liked it and it made her smile.

A few weeks of pecks on the cheek turned into quick pecks on the lips, his touching hers long enough to warrant it a kiss. No lingering, no caress. No attempt from either of them to hold the kiss for even a second longer than the one second it took to display affection. John O'Malley was a gentleman who respected his girlfriend, and she was a lady who showed manners and decorum, as she was raised to do.

CHAPTER ELEVEN

Bridgey made a pot of tea. She took a packet of Kimberley biscuits from the back of the press and put a few on a plate, alongside two slices of Madeira cake. Flossie had only a couple of months left in college and Bridgey needed to talk with her.

'Now miss, take a break from the books and have some tea with me,' she said, putting the tray on the coffee table in the sitting room.

'Oh, Kimberleys! Yes, please. Flossie said, shoving her books aside to sit forward.

Bridgey had grown very fond of her niece during the last couple of years. She reminded her of her younger self in certain ways. 'What do you want from your life, Flossie?'

'To be a schoolteacher, you know that.' Flossie bit into the gingery mallow sandwich and closed her eyes, savouring the sweetness.

'Tell me about John O'Malley.'

'I told you all about him.' Flossie's jaw slowed as she realised Auntie Bridgey was buttering her up for a lecture.

'Tell me again. His intentions, your intentions, is there love involved?'

'What's love got to do with anything?'

'So you don't love him, or he doesn't love you. Which is it?'

'We do love each other. And we respect each other.'

'What I'm really wondering is whether you intend going home to Bailieborough or staying here in Dublin after you complete your training.'

'Sheila and George asked me the same thing.'

'What did you tell them?'

'I told them I couldn't make up my mind.'

'Did John ever mention marriage?'

'He did... a long time ago.'

'What did you tell him?'

'I told him I wasn't desperate.'

Bridgey chuckled.

Flossie relaxed, realising this wasn't a lecture but concern from someone who treated her as an equal.

'I'd like to ask you something,' said Flossie.

'Go on.'

'What age are you?'

Bridgey raised her eyebrows, and her jaw dropped.

'Well, aren't you the brave one?'

Flossie held her breath, but Bridgey smiled.

'Going on fifty. So if I live to be a hundred, I'm only half-way there.'

'Well, I thought you were much younger than that.'

'I like you, Flossie Lynch.' Bridgey winked.

'Why did you never get married?'

'Nursing became everything to me, Flossie. I worked

hard, you know. I studied morning and night. Daddy drove me on, encouraged me. I wanted to make him proud.' Bridgey closed her eyes and took a deep breath before continuing. 'I almost got married ten years ago, but I gave him up for my job.'

'Ten years ago? Mammy never told me that.'

Bridgey reached forward and poked at the hot coals in the small grate. 'Your mam and dad didn't know anything about my private life. Anyway, I was on my way to becoming a matron and I couldn't jeopardise that. I didn't have a choice, Flossie. I loved him but I also loved my work. I haven't fallen in love since and maybe I never will.' There was an unfamiliar softness in her voice. She frowned slightly and clasped her hands together. 'Be careful of the choices you make, Flossie.'

'Sometimes we don't have a choice. You had no choice because if you'd chosen marriage, you might have lost your job,' said Flossie. 'Do you think now you made the wrong decision, Bridgey?'

'Neither decision was the wrong one. I could have chosen one or the other. I wish we didn't have to make those kinds of choices. It's a man's world, Flossie, and don't you forget it.'

'But aren't things changing? You said they were.'

'We've a long way to go yet, I'm afraid.'

Thoughts went spiralling around Flossie's head for the rest of the evening. She wrote them all in her diary to try and make sense of things.

§

Her mother expected her home soon. Bridgey wanted to keep her in Dublin. Flossie had no doubt she'd live happily with Bridgey but parts of home niggled away at her. Like a spider, she had weaved herself a web of mixed thoughts and feelings. No matter how hard she tried to unravel the voices in her head, she ended up back at the root of all her emotions: Frank Connolly.

§

When Flossie finished college, John invited her to a celebration dinner in The Beaufield Mews restaurant in Stillorgan.

'Have you made up your mind about what you'll do now?' he asked.

'I miss home. But I like living with Auntie Bridgey.' Flossie broke up her chocolate torte with the side of her fork.

'I'd like you to be my wife.'

'What?'

'What I mean is, will you be my wife? If you want to be. Of course, I know you could have any man that your heart desires, and you...'

She put her fork down and swallowed a mouthful of chocolate and cream. 'Yes,' she said. Her mother was right: he was a kind man with prospects and she'd be mad not to accept.

John reached into his blazer jacket and took out a small red box.

'I was hoping you'd accept. I got this last Christmas with the intentions of asking you then, but I... lost my nerve, I suppose.'

Flossie held out her hand, and as John put a pear-cut diamond ring on her finger, he said, 'I really do care about you. Always remember that.'

'Thanks, John, it's a beautiful ring. I know you'll be a good husband; I care about you too.' They both meant every word.

§

Dear Mary,

I hope you, Jim and Maureen are well. I can't believe Maureen is nearly a year old. Will you have a little party for her?

So that's it... college is over and I'm returning to Bailieborough. The city life is not for me, even though I did enjoy my time here. I'll miss Sheila and George. It's a pity you didn't get the chance to meet them.

I hope you're sitting down because the next thing I have to say might shock you a little bit. You might want to light up a cigarette too. Are you ready?

I'm engaged to John O'Malley. I got to know him really well in the last year or so and I swear to God, Mary, he's not like you think at all. He's kind and generous (you should see the ring). He has the utmost respect for me.

It was such a romantic proposal. He took me to The Beaufield Mews restaurant in Stillorgan—you wouldn't know it, Mary—it's beautiful! He got down on one knee and declared his love for me, right there in front of everyone. And presented me with the ring. It was nearly like a wedding itself.

Mammy is beside herself, as you can imagine. Will you

please be my bridesmaid? The wedding will be on the 5th of September. A Friday. I hope you can come.

Love from your best friend, Flossie. 31/05/58

CHAPTER TWELVE

When Flossie arrived back home in Bailieborough, her mother and Ruth fussed around her like she was royalty. Goretti couldn't wait to tell everyone the good news. Flossie to marry John O'Malley, at last!

Of course, her mother would have liked a July wedding, but she said September was a nice month too. She wondered what Ruth might wear to the wedding.

'No doubt she'll have to go to Dublin for a new hat. Well, she can if she wants... I'll be buying in town. I have my eye on a lovely lilac suit in Mrs Hall's window.'

Flossie needed a break from all the wedding talk—and her mother. 'Mammy, I'm going for a spin.'

'Okay, but don't be too long now. We've to visit people,' Goretti said.

The thought of being dragged around all Goretti's friends as though she was a film star or something made Flossie light-headed. It was going to be a long day.

She pulled her bicycle out of the shed, wiped down the saddle and pumped the soft tyres with her hand pump. She had missed the woods while she was in Dublin. Two years was a long time to be away from your favourite place in the world. *Everything will be okay. John is a good man. Things will fall into place.*

She welcomed the country breeze blowing in her face as she pedalled out the Cavan Road. She kept her eyes firmly fixed on the road ahead as she approached Connollys' lane. As she sped past it, a shiver ran through her veins. She imagined Frank watching her, her hair blowing in the wind and her skirt flapping behind, showing too much leg. She wondered where he was and what he might be doing.

She shook her head and tried not to think of him. She had to think about her future and forget the past. Father Tierney had called to see them the previous night. He was pleased that she was marrying John, but that wasn't the reason for his visit. He was letting her know about the teacher's job in the new national school, St. Anne's. She imagined Auntie Bridgey's voice in her head as the priest informed her the job was hers, instead of asking her first if she'd like to consider it. Flossie had already considered it since her mother wrote to her a few weeks ago about it—around the same time that John proposed.

I already told him you'd take it. Sure, why wouldn't you? Isn't that the reason you went off to Dublin in the first place, to get the proper training? she wrote.

When Flossie reached the wood gates and Primrose Cottage, she got off her bicycle and inhaled the familiar smell of pine and honeysuckle. Her favourite memories were in that house and in these woods—especially the woods.

She took her time strolling through the woody, winding trails. She missed this, slow walks in the peace and quiet. The sounds of nature were music to her soul. Yes, it was good to be back.

The sight of a man fishing at the lake reminded Flossie of her father. He'd often taken them to that part of the lake to fish and have picnics. She still missed him. He would have approved of her and John... probably. She took a deep breath of the crisp, mid-morning air. A family of swans floated towards the bank, seeking shade in the rushes.

Flossie loved nature, especially in the summer when everything captivated her senses. The sun glistened on the lake, making it look like a million stars had fallen from the sky. Shimmering speckles of sun sparkled on the leaves of the unshaded trees.

She closed her eyes and took a moment to bathe in the serenity surrounding her. She reflected on the contented family of swans, the stars on the water, and the diamonds in the trees. She looked at John's teardrop diamond on her finger. A shadow fell upon her, blocking out the warm sun.

'Well, there's a face I haven't seen in a while.'

'Jesus!' Flossie said, slamming both hands to her chest. 'You scared the life out of me.'

Frank Connolly's broad grin suppressed a laugh. 'Sorry, I didn't mean to.'

'And what's so funny?'

'You. Standing there with your eyes closed, smiling away to yourself like a nutcase.'

She sat down on the grassy bank. 'You shouldn't sneak up like that. You could give someone a heart attack.'

'Well, you shouldn't be standing there like a cod with your eyes closed.'

Despite herself, she laughed along with him.

He sat on a tree stump opposite her. His brown, muscular arms made her pasty limbs look like sticks of chalk. She tugged her dress further down her shins. The soft breeze carried his scent in her direction. Frank always smelled like the wind—fresh and invigorating. Today he also smelled like the damp rushes that nestled the swan family.

She had forgotten what it felt like to crave a person in this way, to be aroused by the presence of a man. The sixth commandment came to mind: thou shalt not commit adultery. But surely thinking about it wasn't a sin. *God forgive me.* She mentally blessed herself.

She had to keep her sinful thoughts where they belonged—buried deep inside.

'How's the city treating you?' Frank asked.

'It's grand, but I'm home for good now. I'm starting in the new school, St. Anne's, in the second week of September.'

'It's a fine school. So you're a proper teacher now,' Frank said.

'Still a smart arse, I see. Some things never change, Connolly,' she replied.

He laughed and offered her a cigarette.

'No, thank you. I don't smoke.'

He looked sideways at her and laughed again. 'You used to,'

'And what would you know about what I used to do?'

'I know you and Mary used to steal my cigarettes and smoke them in the hayshed—not as innocent as you pretend to be, Miss Lynch.'

'I never touched them. It was only Mary, if you must know.' *So he had noticed her—sort of.*

Flossie took a deep breath. 'Have you heard from Mary lately?'

'Not in ages. She doesn't really write that much. She sent Josey a photo of the baby. Does she write to you?' Frank's eyes softened.

'We write to each other a fair bit. Do you know she's coming home in September?'

'No. Maybe she wants to surprise me,' he said.

'She's coming for my wedding,' Flossie said. 'She's my bridesmaid.'

'Your wedding? Janey Mac! Are you marrying some fancy lad from Dublin?'

'Well, indeed I'm not. I'm marrying John O'Malley, if you must know.'

'John O'Malley? Mammy's boy O'Malley? Is he going to spend his confirmation money at last?' He threw his head back and laughed as if it was some kind of joke. 'It must be a big secret or I'd have heard about it.'

'Of course it's not a secret. Sure I'm wearing the ring.' She fanned her fingers at him.

'Didn't think he was your type.'

'And what exactly is my type, Mr Connolly?' Flossie said. 'Is Alice Ward your type?' Her jaw clenched. As soon as the words were out, she regretted them.

Frank picked up his fishing rod. 'Well, the best of luck. Nice to see you again. Better get on and see if I can catch something.'

'Frank. I'm sorry about what happened with the baby,' she called after him.

Without turning back, he saluted her. Flossie cursed herself for being so childish. *He was as bad. Should she follow him? No. Damn. Why did he have to be here anyway? Spoiling her peaceful walk. So much for feeling sentimental.* At least when she lived in Dublin, she never had the worry of bumping into bloody Frank Connolly. She'd make sure to avoid him in the future!

She turned John's ring round on her finger. Its teardrop diamond sparkled in the sun like a real teardrop would.

CHAPTER THIRTEEN

Mary arrived in Bailieborough the evening before the wedding. Josey met her and Maureen at the bus and took them straight to Graham's for tea. They both agreed it would be best if they stayed with him while she was home, rather than with Frank and Alice. They were exhausted after their journey and Maureen fell asleep as soon as Mary put her into the pram.

'I wish Jim had been able to come. I didn't think it would be so hard travelling with a baby,' she said.

'You can head on over to Flossie's after this if you want. I've a few messages to get anyway. Meet me back here at six,' Josey said. 'You can leave your cases here with Mrs Graham if you want.'

'I'll leave the big one, but I'll take the small one with me. It's got my bridesmaid dress in it and Flossie wants to see it.'

§

'Ah, Mary... and the baby. Come in, come in,' Goretti said when she opened her front door. 'You're a bit pasty looking. Are you alright?' she asked. She poked her head into the hood of the pram.

'I'm fine, Mrs Lynch, just tired.'

'Aw, look at her. Out like a light with not a care in the world.' Goretti put a coin underneath Maureen's blanket. 'There's a wee shilling for luck.'

'Thanks, Mrs Lynch.'

Goretti led the way into the kitchen. She grabbed the broom and banged it on the ceiling to let Flossie know her visitors had arrived.

'Your hair's lovely, Mrs Lynch.'

'Well, thank you. Nan did it for me. I hope it stays nice for tomorrow.' Goretti waved her feather duster towards the ceiling. 'I'm going upstairs to finish cleaning. I'm getting Danny's room ready—he's coming on the early bus in the morning.'

Flossie whizzed into the room and embraced her friend with a squeal. Mary laughed and put a finger to her pursed lips. 'Shh... the child's asleep.'

Flossie lowered her voice. 'Oops, sorry.' She peered into the pram. 'Oh, she's just beautiful, Mary. You're blessed. I can't wait to cuddle her. She's huge.'

'I know. Sure she has an appetite like her father. Now show me that ring.'

Flossie held out her hand.

'Jesus, that's gorgeous. Can I make a wish?'

Flossie slipped the ring off her finger and handed it to Mary.

Mary tried it on; it wouldn't go past her knuckle.

'Oh sure, my big bones letting me down again.' She turned the ring towards her heart three times as she silently made her wish.

'It's great to be home, Flossie. I'm dying for a decent cup of tea, so I am. It's like dishwater over yonder, so it is. Now, show me your dress. Here's mine. I hope the colours go well together.' Mary pulled the dress out of her small brown suitcase. 'It's a nice green, "apple green", the woman in the shop called it.' Mary held up her new dress for Flossie's approval.

'Oh, it's lovely, Mary. Green always suited you. Will you be careful not to get it all creased? Hang it up as soon as you go home,' Flossie said. 'Who are you staying with?' She beckoned for Mary to follow her upstairs.

'We're staying with Josey. You know I'm not fond of Alice, so I don't think I'd manage living with her for any length of time. Frank can visit us in Josey's.'

Mary sat on the edge of Flossie's bed and leaned back on her elbows. 'Now, show me your dress,' she said.

'I know I told you it was blue, but the more I look at it, I think now it's more of a greeny colour.' Flossie held up a turquoise dress.

'Ah, Flossie, you're colour-blind; that's not blue! That's as green as a gooseberry.' Mary's hearty laugh vibrated the thin walls.

'I wanted blue. I didn't want green.' Flossie felt panic in her voice. 'Are you sure it's green?'

'Honestly, Flossie, it's green, but it's gorgeous. We'll be like two peas in a pod.'

'But Mary, you don't understand. Marry in blue; you're sure to be true. Marry in green; ashamed to be seen.'

'Okay, it's blue,' said Mary.

'I should have picked white.'

'Marry in white; you're sure to be right?' Mary raised her eyebrows. 'Why didn't you then?'

'I don't know,' Flossie whispered as she opened the small cardboard box which sat on her bed.

'I'm wearing these flowers in my hair. Look, Molly Fagin made them into a slide for me. Aren't they lovely? She's great at doing up flowers.' She held the small arrangement of pink roses to her head.

'You'll be gorgeous. I have the wee hat I wore on my own wedding day.'

'We'll be lovely.'

'Flossie, are you sure you're okay? You seem a bit... I don't know.'

'I'm just nervous, that's all. Come on, let's get that tea you're dying for.'

In the kitchen, Flossie filled the kettle. 'How was Maureen on the boat?'

'She wasn't too bad. I'm exhausted from running around with her, so I am. She didn't want to stay in her pram at all.'

'Who'll be minding her when you're at the wedding?'

'Miss Dunne, the priest's housekeeper.'

'That's nice of her. She'll spoil her rotten.'

'She might wake up before we go and then you'll see her properly,' said Mary.

'Would you ever think about coming back home? I miss you.'

Mary's shoulders dropped.

'Frank and Joe would be delighted too,' Flossie said.

'Oh, I don't know. I like Manchester, but I miss home as

well... and you. But sure, what would we be doing coming back here?'

'Ah, maybe you will in a year or two.'

Goretti's voice boomed the lyrics of *Danny Boy* through the ceiling.

'Flossie, do you love John?'

'Of course I do. That's an awful thing to ask.' Flossie felt a lump in her throat. *Was it love?*

'It's just that... I don't know... He's a bit of an oddball.' Mary grimaced.

'No one knows him like I do, Mary. He's different when he's away from his mother. We had lovely times up in Dublin, and I know I'm doing the right thing.' Listening to herself was like listening to someone else. Flossie's temples throbbed.

'Oh, I'm sorry, Flossie. I suppose I always thought he'd be the last person you'd end up with because of the way your mammy always went on about him. And you told me once he reeked of mothballs.'

They giggled like they were teenagers again.

'Ach, that was ages ago. He smells far nicer now. I don't think his father is as fond of the mothballs as he used to be.'

'You'll be called Mrs O'Malley now.'

'I know.' Flossie screwed up her face. 'Although everyone still calls you Mary Connolly.'

'In England, I'm Mrs Fitzpatrick.' Mary tossed her hair proudly. 'So, where are you going for your honeymoon?'

'No idea. Mr and Mrs O'Malley said it's a surprise. All I know is it's two nights away.'

'You're lucky they're paying for it. Me and Jim only went to Laytown for one night.'

'Here, have a drop of sherry in that tea before Mammy

comes back in.' Flossie jumped up from the couch and grabbed the bottle from the press. 'She's busy getting the house in order for *Father* Danny.'

'There's a quare smell of lavender polish alright.' Mary laughed as she wrinkled her nose.

'There'll be twenty people coming, y'know,' Flossie said, a knot forming in her belly. *It was really happening. There was going to be a wedding and there was no turning back.*

'I'd say you're looking forward to seeing Danny?'

'Can't wait.' The thought of seeing Danny lifted her spirits. 'I wish Catherine could be here too.' Flossie put the sherry back in the press.

'She never talks about her, y'know,' Flossie said. 'She writes to her the same as I do but rarely mentions her.'

'Who made your wedding cake?'

'John's mother. It'll be the main focus of the wedding breakfast, as you can imagine. She's bringing it over this evening.'

'Right now, you two girls.' Goretti clapped her hands as she marched into the kitchen. 'I could do with a bit of help here.'

'Well, I have to be heading off now, Mrs Lynch. Josey's waiting for me at Graham's. I'll gather my stuff.'

'You have to show me your dress,' Goretti said.

'Sorry, Mrs Lynch, but I have it all packed away again. You'll see it tomorrow.'

'But what if it's not right, the colour and everything?'

'Mammy, it's a lovely dress,' Flossie said. 'Do you think Mary's going to go back to England to change it? Hardly!'

'Don't be so cheeky, madam,' her mother said.

'Sorry.' Flossie meant it. She didn't mean to be so contrary. 'Mammy, what colour do you think my dress is?'

'Blue. Why? What colour is Mary's?' Goretti frowned.

'Don't worry, hers is green.'

'I still wish you'd have shown me.'

'It's grand. You'll see it in the morning. C'mon Mary. I'll see you out,' Flossie said.

'So, I'll meet you at Nan's in the morning,' Mary said as she manoeuvred the pram out the door.

Flossie retired to bed with mixed feelings. She tossed all night, falling in and out of sleep. She was with Frank in her dreams, but Alice was there too, in the background, holding a baby. The dream turned into a nightmare when the baby's face turned into a mirror image of Alice: round cheeks and green marble eyes.

CHAPTER FOURTEEN

Goretti's knock on the bedroom door woke Flossie from her restless slumber. She shuddered and looked at the clock on her bedside table. Seven o'clock.

She got up and marked off another day on the calendar that hung on her door. Friday the fifth of September. Catherine always teased her about her superstitious beliefs, but Flossie swore by every saying and proverb she knew.

Marry in September's shine; your living will be rich and fine.

Flossie tried to fill her lungs with air, but they felt crushed. Her shallow breaths made her feel lightheaded. Rich and fine perhaps, but loving and joyful... not. Her mother was wrong. She'd never learn to love John. She loved Frank. Those feelings weren't learned, they were created. Frank made her feel in love. Being with him, seeing him, thinking of him, created those blissful sensations inside her. Frank held her heart in his hands and she had no control over it. What she felt for John wasn't love and never would be, but she was about to become his wife.

§

Flossie sat on the doorstep to wait for Danny. As soon as she saw him walking down the street, she ran to meet him, her smile almost as big as his. He grabbed her and swung her round, laughing. 'You weren't this heavy the last time I swung you round in my arms.' He huffed and puffed dramatically as he put her down.

'It's great to see you, *Father Daniel Lynch*.'

'And you, my wee leanbhín.' He gently tapped the tip of her nose with his finger, like their father used to do.

'I wish he was here now. But you are, so I'm as happy as can be.'

'Are you really?' he asked.

'I swear I am. I know Mammy was always going on about me marrying John, but when I got to know him better, I found him very nice. I know he'll be good to me, Danny. Yes, I love him and he loves me.' She hated lying to Danny, but she couldn't tell him the truth.

'That's all I need to know. God be with the pair of ye. Now, shouldn't you be getting ready?'

§

Not a soul in all of County Cavan wore as big a smile as Goretti Lynch. Her Flossie marrying John O'Malley—the catch of the parish!

Sitting in the second row of seats in the church, she glanced across at Ruth in the opposite row and smiled. She compared her lilac, midi-length dress to Ruth's, which was a similar style, but a more daring blush pink. Everyone knew

Ruth had a fine eye for well-made clothes, but Goretti satisfied herself that both dresses were equally beautiful.

They both wore a pillbox hat. Ruth's was clearly brand new and exactly the same shade as her dress. Goretti tightened her pursed lips and sniffed, annoyed that she had to make do with one of Bridgey's, which were all either cream or grey. She had chosen a grey velvet one with netting that veiled her eyes and cheekbones. But she wasn't going to let a little thing like a borrowed hat spoil her day.

As Danny handed his sister over to John O'Malley at the altar, he shook his hand and gave Flossie a reassuring wink. She smiled and looked up to the stolid face of the man she had chosen to spend the rest of her life with. John took her hand and whispered, 'You look beautiful.'

She struggled to stay focused during the ceremony. Images of last night's dreams flashed through her mind—Frank holding her hand as he looked into her face, Alice standing behind him, and the awful baby.

''Til death do us part,' John vowed.

The priest turned his full attention to Flossie. Her chest thumped so hard, she felt breathless. The congregation's eyes bored into her as they waited for her to say her vows. With God and the people as her witnesses, she promised John O'Malley that she would love and cherish him from this day forward, for better, for worse, for richer, for poorer, in sickness and in health, until they parted in death. Goretti Lynch's sniffles could be heard all over the church.

§

The wedding guests were all back at Goretti's house before mid-day. Hungry mouths tucked into the spread of cold meats and salads.

Some of the women drank sherry, while others went straight for the porter. John's best man, Tony, an old school friend, was well on it before he even began to eat (he'd likely had a few before the ceremony). He was doing a clumsy job of chatting up Molly Fagin's daughter, Mags, who sat with her legs crossed, sipping on her lemonade. She looked down her nose at Tony before twisting around on her stool to face the other way. Tony stuck out his chest and grunted at her before moving on.

Frederick entertained his golfing friend Roy, from Kells, while Ruth drank sherry and nattered to his glamorous wife, Norah. In the sitting room, Danny took out his old accordion and Bridgey sprung to her feet. 'Woohoo, Danny. Give us *The Kesh* like a good lad,' she hooted. She got the fun going and Danny had them all dancing the jig. Mary beckoned at Flossie to follow her outside.

Flossie was relieved to get out of the stuffy house and away from all the well-meaning wishes from the guests. The air outside was warm, but it refreshed her stifled lungs.

'I'm dying for a fag,' said Mary. 'I still won't smoke in front of your mother. She still scares the life out of me.'

'Well, you'd better not let her see that you're a bit drunk.'

'Well... well, indeed I'm not one bit drunk. I'm only tipsy.' Mary giggled. She sat on the low windowsill and lit up her cigarette. She inhaled deeply, and as the smoke streamed out of her nostrils, her breath sounded like the groans of a man in deep slumber.

'You got a great day for your wedding, Flossie. Pity you

didn't have a garden party, y'know, like the high society ones.' Mary stuck her nose in the air and put on a posh voice, 'Law de daw.'

Flossie giggled. 'You've had far too much sherry. And I saw you gulping down a bottle of Guinness.'

'Sure it's ages since I had a drink.' She took another long pull of her cigarette. 'So, you're a married woman now. How d'ya feel?'

'I feel I might need to start smoking again,' she replied, puffing on an imaginary cigarette.

'If Mammy could see...' Flossie began but Mary butted in.

'Oh, here's Frankie the boi.' Mary called out to her brother who was walking towards them. 'Where are you heading?'

Flossie pressed her back against the cool shaded wall and wished at that moment she was inside it.

'I was in town and thought I'd drop over to wish Flossie and John good luck.'

'Can he come in for a wee drinkie? Your Danny would love to see him.' Mary looked at Flossie as she squashed the cigarette with her foot.

'I suppose he can. But I think you've had enough.'

Mary linked Frank's arm and smiled up into his face. 'She thinks I'm drunk.'

'She could be right.' He grinned. 'I'll go in for a few minutes then... if the bride says I'm invited.'

Flossie knew if she said no, it would make her look petty and Mary might question her.

'Yas are looking lovely,' Frank said, glancing at Flossie.

She ignored him and led the way into the house. Mary dragged Frank into the sitting room to dance. Flossie stood at the doorway watching. Everyone clapped as they skipped and hopped to Danny's tunes.

John appeared by his wife's side. 'How come Frank Connolly's here?'

'He was just passing by and Mary asked him in for a few minutes. Now, how about we cut our cake? I'm sure your mother can't wait for the compliments to begin.'

'There was a wild colonial boy, Jack Duggan was his name...' Frank's singing had everyone's attention.

Mary sat crouched on a three-legged stool, elbows on her knees with her face resting in her hands. Melancholy filled the room and Flossie's gaze was fixed on Frank. His rich, mellow voice stirred up all the memories of their time together. He sang with passion, his eyes alive, and his body moved in time with the music. Flossie swallowed the tingling in her throat.

'So are we cutting this cake or not?' John asked.

'Yes, I'm coming.'

'You're gone very red in the face,' John said as they went through to the kitchen.

'Sure I'm roasting.'

'Are you?'

Mrs O'Malley took charge of organising everybody around the two-tier wedding cake on the kitchen table. A little plastic bride and groom sat on top. Danny took photos with their father's old box camera, and Frederick boasted about how his brand-new camera took eighteen photos on one film.

Cheers and whistles echoed across The Green when the knife sliced through the rich fruit cake. Ruth applauded with short little claps, relishing the compliments on her perfectly baked cake. She glowed as she sliced the bottom tier of her creation into evenly sized rectangles.

'I wonder if I'll be re-icing this one in pink or blue next year?' Ruth said. She chuckled as she put the top tier to one side. She wasn't one to crack jokes, so the laughter was stilted and all eyes looked to Flossie and John.

Danny held up his glass and called, 'To the bride and groom.'

Everyone cheered and Flossie relaxed. She and John made their way around the room, stopping to chat with the guests individually, each one telling her that John was a lucky man.

Frederick came towards them. 'Well, my son and my beautiful daughter-in-law. Soon time to head off on the old honeymoon.'

'About that, Mr O'Malley. Thank you very much. It's very kind of you and Mrs O'Malley to pay for our honey-moon,' said Flossie. 'So, where are we going?' she asked.

Frederick shuffled his feet. Flossie wasn't sure if he was excited or nervous, which worried her. She felt intrigued, but she didn't like surprises. She preferred to know what was happening, so she could be properly organised and prepared.

'Haven't you guessed yet, John?' Frederick bore a wobbly smile.

Flossie glanced at Ruth for a sign of reassurance, but her expression was blank.

'No, Dad. I have no idea. Tell me.'

'Our favourite, of course. The Grand Hotel in Malahide! Two nights.' Frederick didn't take his eyes off John and his wobbly smile was now a beaming set of crooked teeth. Ruth gave another round of gentle applause.

'Auntie Bridgey's been there. She showed me photos. It's lovely,' Flossie said. *Why the big secret?* A wonderful present indeed, but she thought he was going to announce somewhere amazing, like a golden beach in Spain, or somewhere awful like Butlins. Their favourite? How come Ruth hasn't bragged about their *favourite hotel?*

John was silent. He and Frederick stared at each other. 'So what do you think, son? It's been a while, so your mother and I thought you'd like to revisit the ole haunt.'

'Yes, it's been a while alright,' John said. 'Thanks.'

He took Flossie's hand. 'Let's get our things together. It's time we left.'

Flossie followed, certain she wasn't the only one to notice his crassness.

§

Pink satin ribbons shimmered across the black polished bonnet of Frederick's Ford Coupe Utility.

'Your carriage awaits, Mr and Mrs.' Frederick smiled, skimming his hand along the bonnet. 'I want her back the same way, mind.'

Flossie had changed into a light pink swing dress speckled with tiny white polka dots. She wore cheap, white-rimmed sunglasses, even though the hazy grey clouds already shielded her eyes from the sun. She could see her distorted reflection in the wheels, exactly how she imagined she might look if somebody were to turn her inside out: disjointed, crumpled.

'You can take the ribbons off, Dad,' John said.

Ruth bustled over. 'He'll do no such thing. They look lovely.'

Flossie was glad to be getting away from everyone and their 'just married' jokes. She was about to enter into a life that wasn't hers. Like an imposter. Taking what didn't truly belong to her. She was no better than Alice Ward—marrying a man who was meant for someone else. Did John believe they would learn to love each other? Just like her mother said they would?

Mary hugged her friend tight. 'Tonight's the night,' she whispered in her ear.

Flossie repressed a giggle and slapped Mary's arm with the back of her hand. 'Goodbye, Mary. I'll write to you next week,' she said with a grin. 'Now, where's that brother of mine? Hey, you, don't be hiding.'

Danny stood in the doorway. His eyes were misty, making them look more grey than blue. She squeezed him tight. 'Thank you so much for coming home, Danny. Write to me, please.'

'Be happy, Flossie. Enjoy that posh hotel.' Danny smiled, but it wasn't his usual big toothy grin.

Frank leaned up against the rear end of Frederick's car with a grin on his face. 'Wouldn't be much of a family car, would it, Johnny?'

'Excuse me, young Connolly. Do you mind getting off my car?' Frederick's short legs moved swiftly, like a terrier's, to protect his pride and joy. He shook out his crisp white handkerchief and buffed the spot where Frank had his arm.

'You're wasting your time, Mr O'Malley. Those skies are about to burst open,' Frank said.

My God, what is he doing? It's at home with his wife he

should be. He was always a smart arse, but now he's being an eejit. Flossie ignored him and carried on saying goodbye to the guests.

'Enjoy the honeymoon, you two. Yas make a lovely couple.' Frank kissed Flossie on the cheek and saluted a red-faced John. He sauntered down the street, whistling the melody of *Let Him Go, Let Him Tarry*.

John opened the passenger door. 'Are you ready, Flossie?'

Raindrops pinged on her bare arms, making her shiver. She swallowed hard to soften the lump in her throat. 'Thanks, everyone. See you soon.'

CHAPTER FIFTEEN

The drive to Malahide was longer than Flossie expected. The rain lashed down on the uneven, bumpy roads, but at least it provided a topic of conversation—for a while anyway. The wipers got on Flossie's nerves, swooshing across the windscreen, over and back continuously.

The stuffy air stifled her. The back of her knees stuck to the seat and she couldn't get comfortable. The rich sweet smell of the leather seats reminded her of the day Frank Connolly kissed her.

It had been her eighteenth birthday and she was spending the evening with Mary. She lay flicking through a magazine on Connolly's old two-seater leather couch while Mary was in the kitchen making tea and buttering biscuits. Flossie's legs dangled across one shabby arm, and her head rested on a puffy patchwork cushion. She loved the soft scent of the leather.

Frank came in, carrying a box of fire logs. A blast of frosty air followed him. Flossie stiffened, as she always did when he came near. She breathed in the smell of freshly cut timber, then sank further into the couch in the ridiculous hope that he wouldn't notice her.

She peered over the top of the magazine, keeping it close to her flushed face. He was on his hunkers, poking at the fire. His shirt sleeves were rolled up above his elbows. She wanted to wipe away the sawdust that stuck to the hairs of his brown arms. Even in January he was tanned. She closed her eyes and sunk deeper into the leather. *Please let him leave now; please let him leave.*

'So, I hear you're eighteen today.' His voice was right beside her.

Flossie flipped the magazine onto her chest. 'Yes.'

'Well, happy birthday.' He looked down at her.

Her heart thumped under the magazine. She swung her legs from the arm of the couch to the floor. As she struggled to pull herself up, Frank took her hand. His touch sent shivers right through her.

'Are yas going out tonight?' he asked as he helped her up.

'Why do you want to know?'

'Because I'm Mary's big brother and it's my business to know. Is Jim going with yas?'

'If he was, then I'd be a gooseberry.'

The last time she had stood this close to him was when she was ten or eleven.

His rough hands were cold and dirty, but she didn't care. 'You're still holding my hand,' she said.

'I know.'

'They're freezing. Have you no gloves?'

'I work better without them. A bit of frost won't do me any harm,' he said.

She tried not to stare into his hypnotic grey eyes, but she

couldn't stop herself. They were like magnets, pulling her in. Something inside her was desperate to burst.

'If you must know, we're not going anywhere. We might go to the pictures tomorrow night.' The smell of sweat and sawdust sat in the back of her throat. She pulled her hand away, but her bare feet stayed stuck to the floor.

'Happy birthday, Flossie.' He kissed her on the forehead like you might kiss a small child. The heat of the kiss stayed on her forehead as if he had branded her with the poker he held in his hand.

'Is that the only kind of kiss you can give a girl on her eighteenth birthday?' she said.

'I'll take you to the pictures next Friday if you'll come. Mary and Jim will be halfway across the Irish Sea. I could cheer you up.'

'What about your girlfriend? You can't take a girl out if you have a girlfriend already, it's not right.'

'I won't have a girlfriend by next Friday night.'

§

The rain stopped. Tiny pools on the bonnet glistened in the soft rays of the evening sun. John switched off the wipers, to Flossie's relief. They were both quiet, deep in their own thoughts, nothing shared between them. It was more strained than the comfortable silence that usually shrouded them when they were alone. They had gotten used to the long breaks in their conversations; it had become normal.

Things were different now. They were man and wife. *Would they have sex? Would they fall in love? Would they have children? They'd have to. Did he find her attractive?*

Flossie wasn't attracted to John even though he was handsome in his own way. He always kept a clean-shaven face and wore Brylcreem in his thick wavy hair. He wore a shirt and tie every day, like his father. She had no desire to wrap herself up in any part of him and didn't yearn for his lips to touch hers. Her bones ached for Frank's arms around her, and her lips wanted only his. She tortured herself day after day, night after night, hating him because she couldn't have him, and loving him more each time she saw him. She should have stayed living with Auntie Bridgey in Dublin. It was too late for that kind of thinking. *She'd made her bed and now she had to lie in it.*

§

Pulling into the car park of The Grand Hotel, John gripped the steering wheel with sweaty palms, wishing they were still miles away. His shirt stuck to the seat. His armpits were soaking wet. He should have organised his own honeymoon, but as bloody usual, his parents had to interfere in his life. Bloody marvellous how they always ended up making decisions for him. Telling him what to do. He had been looking forward to spending a quiet weekend with Flossie. Away from the shop, his parents and Goretti—although Goretti was bearable most of the time. At least she treated him like an adult, and he was certain that living with her and Flossie would be easier than living with own his mother. He loved his mother, but she smothered him.

His father knew damn well that this was the last place on earth he would want to go on his honeymoon. No wonder he'd kept it a secret until the last minute. After the whole shame and horror of what had happened all those years ago, why would he send him back? John's jaw tightened as he pulled the ribbons off the car and shoved them under his seat. The other problem with this place was Julie. And if this was her weekend for working, he'd have a lot of explaining to do.

The dark clouds still lurked in the sky, threatening more rain; the heat had gone from the evening sun. John carried both their bags while his new wife admired the impressive building and delighted in the smell of freshly cut grass. Every step towards the main door of the Grand Hotel was like stepping through a wall of steel.

At least Flossie seemed happy. He might even learn to love her. She had a pretty, pear-shaped face, the kind most men would find attractive. Her wistful, pale blue eyes hid behind long, fair eyelashes. He wondered if he would ever replace the sadness in her eyes with some form of happiness.

Rain spat again and the couple hurried inside.

§

Flossie took a deep breath and told herself everything would work out for the best. She'd learn to love John in the way he deserved to be loved. They would have a lovely weekend and a good life together. *Frank Connolly doesn't exist.*

John's mood hadn't brightened since they left Bailieborough. *Was it something to do with his father and this present? Was he nervous about their wedding night like she was? Or maybe it was because Frank turned up at the house.* She felt the need to reassure him.

'It's a beautiful hotel, John, isn't it?' She smiled. 'We'll have a lovely time. Let's check in and go straight to dinner. I'm starving. I didn't eat much today.'

'Okay.'

The biggest vase of freshly cut flowers Flossie had ever seen sat on the centre of a round mahogany table beside the reception desk. She inhaled deeply; their soothing scent and pastel colours relaxed her. The receptionist made them feel very welcome and important. She addressed them as Mr and Mrs O'Malley.

Their room smelled of fresh linen and the bedclothes matched the thick, full-length, curtains. Her mother would love all these floral patterns. Even the picture on the wall was a field of bright yellow sunflowers.

John unpacked his bag in silence. He hung his clothes in the wardrobe, pushing them all to the left, and left his socks and underwear in the bag. Flossie followed suit. He stood looking out the window while she sat at the dressing table, brushing her hair. She freshened up her makeup and applied more lipstick. She desperately wished she wasn't a virgin. She wished this wasn't their first time. Maybe then they could both relax.

'Are you looking forward to it?' John asked as he spun round.

'To what?'

'The dinner. You said you were hungry.'

'Oh... yes. Yes, I am. Will we go?'

§

Flossie was glad to find the dining room quiet. Mellow music played in the background and the other guests appeared relaxed and happy. One couple looked quite young, maybe her age, and she wondered if they were on their honeymoon too. They looked very much in love and excited to be there. She was certain nobody would realise she and John were on their honeymoon.

The waiter served them roast chicken with sage and onion stuffing and a complimentary bottle of white wine. The wine was the nicest Flossie had ever tasted (even though she had only ever tasted wine twice). It had a light fruity taste and it smartened her tongue. The waiter said it was from France and was a popular wine with their guests in the summertime. *Very fancy.*

The flutters in her stomach had calmed down now, and John seemed to be more relaxed too. *They had nothing to be worrying about. The consummation of their marriage was inevitable and there was nothing to fear from it at all.*

Before she married Jim, Mary had told Flossie all she needed to know about having sex. Flossie suspected she and Jim had done it before their wedding, but she kept her suspicions to herself and lit a candle for them one Saturday after confession. The two friends were the same age but Mary, at five foot six, was a few inches taller and much heftier than Flossie. 'A fine big lassie' was how Molly Fagin described her one day. She had matured at a faster rate than most teenage girls, physically and emotionally.

She educated Flossie about periods when she was only fourteen and gave her a bra when she was fifteen—one of her own that she'd grown out of. Although it drowned Flossie's apple-sized breasts, she wore it anyway, feeling like a proper woman.

She suppressed a giggle when she thought back to the day

Mary had found out how babies were made. In school one day, she whispered to Flossie that she had an important secret to tell her after school. She had to cross her heart not to tell anyone or they'd be in big trouble. The day dragged for Flossie, and when the last bell of the day rang out, she gave Mary a knowing grin on the way out the door.

The two friends ventured home the long way, as they often did, through the church grounds and into town by the Virginia Road. Hidden between the hedgerows that lined the church avenue, Mary checked there was no one around.

'You won't believe what I found out last night, Flossie.'

'I've been dying to know all day. Tell me.'

'Do you know how a baby gets into the mother's belly?'

'It just does, Mary. God puts it there. It might be from kissing because Jerry Duffy once said it was.' She faced Mary, and her mouth opened. 'It's not really from kissing, is it?'

'No. Worse than that.' Mary took a step closer to Flossie and whispered in her ear.

'What?' Flossie's eyes blinked rapidly.

'Can you imagine?'

'Jesus Christ, Mary, if anyone heard you saying such a thing. That's disgusting and the worst lie you've ever told.'

'I swear to God and hope to die, it's true, Flossie. I was in the library and there was a book all about it, drawings and everything. I took the book, put it in my bag, only for the lend, but I'm afraid to go back with it in case I get caught.'

'God forgive you, Mary. That's stealing. You'll have to show me or I won't believe you.'

Mary did show Flossie the book, and for weeks, she couldn't believe it was true. She put the whole thing to the back of her mind and tried not to think about it. She decided there and then she would never have babies, like Auntie Bridgey.

§

'Flossie, will we get more wine, or do you want tea? I feel like wine.' John interrupted her thoughts.

'Yes, okay. The wine's lovely.'

John looked uncomfortable again.

'Auntie Bridgey was here three years ago, shortly after it was all done up. I wonder what it was like before that?' Flossie was interested in the history of the hotel and John loved talking about old things.

'The last time I was here was eight years ago. It looks a bit different, alright. Feels the same though,' John said, as he raised his hand to a waiter.

'With your parents?'

'Yes, we came here for a weekend every August. This is the hotel that once belonged to my grandfather, the one my father sold to marry my mother and live in Bailieborough. This is actually where they first met.' He ordered the wine.

'Really? This is a lot different than a drapery shop in a small country town. Why didn't your mam move up here and run the hotel with your father?'

'Daddy didn't want to be in the hotel business, and she wanted to carry on her parents' shop. She didn't really like Dublin anyway. I think she felt too small in a big place, compared to feeling like someone important in a country town. You know how snobby she is.'

'I know what I'd pick,' said Flossie.

'I would've liked it if they'd chosen to live in Dublin,' he said, with a tone of regret.

A waitress stopped at their table with a tray holding two glasses of wine.

'Your wine?' The petite redhead, who was somewhere in her mid-thirties, gave Flossie a polite smile and then faced John.

'Oh... hello.' Her face went the colour of a raspberry.

John's eyes widened slightly, and he pressed his glasses against the bridge of his nose. 'Hello,' he said. His jaw clenched and he loosened his tie.

'Our wine. Yes, thank you. This is my wife,' he said with a swift nod in Flossie's direction. 'Today... we got married today.'

'Married?' Her eyes widened as she craned her neck towards John.

'This is Flossie. Flossie, this is Julie.' John licked his lips and then wiped them with his napkin; his eyes skimmed the room.

Julie's raspberry face turned a mushroom colour. She shook her head and blinked rapidly, as if snapping herself out of a daydream.

'Well, that's lovely. Congratulations.' She looked at Flossie. 'I've known this lad since he was a child, coming here every summer on his holidays,' she said. 'Hard to imagine he's old enough to be a married man. Time goes by so fast. Nice place for a honeymoon. Hope you have a nice time.' She scurried off.

'Was she alright?' Flossie asked. 'That was a bit over the top. You're hardly still a child at twenty-six years of age. Of course you're old enough to get married. Sure I'm only twenty and I'm old enough to be married.'

'Oh, pass no remarks of her. She's a bit funny,' John said, still glancing round him. Tiny beads of sweat glistened on his forehead.

Flossie said no more about Julie—or John's childhood holidays. Her thoughts returned to the tiny bedroom they had checked into earlier, and the book Mary had shown her all those years ago. And Frank Connolly.

§

Flossie was in bed before John, with the covers pulled up as far as her chin. It had been a long, unusual day, and her head was in turmoil. She'd drank far too much wine and she couldn't keep her eyes open; she just wanted to sleep. She kept her eyes closed when John slid in beside her. He turned out the light, leaving them in total darkness. *Did he think she was asleep?* He was so quiet—she couldn't even hear him breathing. Her heart thumped like the beat of a funeral drum. It echoed in her ears. She lay without moving a muscle, eyes wide open, willing him to do it. Touch her, kiss her, take what was his now and start loving her like a married man ought to love his wife. But John didn't move a muscle either.

CHAPTER SIXTEEN

Dear Mary,

It was great to see you last week. Did you think it was a nice wedding? Mammy said it was great. So it must have been alright. She's all delighted having John living with us. You'd nearly think it was her who's after getting married the way she carries on.

The Grand Hotel was beautiful. The fanciest place I've ever been to. We got the nicest wine you could ever have, Mary. It was French. I drank too much of it though and had an awful headache on Saturday.

The beach was lovely and the water wasn't too cold, so we went swimming on Sunday morning before we packed for home. I wish we had stayed longer than two nights. I know you're dying to know all about... you know what. Well, I'm not telling you, Miss Nosey Parker because I'm a lady now. Ha-ha. But you're still my best friend in the whole world!!

I'll send you a photo of the wedding and one of us in the Grand Hotel—Frederick lent us his camera. He didn't get them developed yet so I'll send them in my next letter.

It's a pity I didn't get to see much of Maureen. Miss Dunne was very good to mind her all day for you.

I started in the school last Monday. I was very nervous but as soon as I got talking to Miss Kennedy, I was okay. It's exactly the same as when I was teaching alongside her, except she's in with the bigger children and I'm with the infants. I know she's a strict teacher, Mary, and you didn't like her very much, but she's nice enough behind it all. I have no more news for now. Please write soon.

Love from your best friend, Flossie. 13/9/58

§

John O'Malley went to the phone box on Main Street. The operator put him through to the Dublin number he requested.

'Hello... Julie?'

'Yes?'

'It's me, John.'

'What the hell is going on John? Married?'

'Let me explain, Julie. I had to. Flossie's a friend, nothing more. I don't love her in that way.'

'You bloody married her.'

'Look, I know what it looks like, but she doesn't love me either. She's in love with another man, one she can't have. It's a marriage of convenience for both of us... I swear.'

'What about Alfie?'

'You know what he means to me. But my father...' A lump formed in John's throat.

'I know all that... but you have to tell him. I can't believe you hid this.'

'I'll be there next Wednesday, and I'll explain everything. See you then.'

'John...'

He hung up.

§

Dear Flossie,

Sorry I didn't write sooner. Maureen takes up all my time, running around and into everything. But she's a wee dote, so she is.

Jim's sister and her husband are coming up from Coventry to spend Christmas with us. Their little girl is a bit older than Maureen.

I'm wallpapering the sitting room and wish I hadn't started. I used to watch Mammy doing all the papering at home and it looked easy, but it's not one bit easy.

Did you hear that Alice is pregnant again? Due next March, Josey told me. Even though I was giving out the last time, I felt a wee bit bad that she had a miscarriage. I wouldn't have wished for that to happen.

Frank sounds happy about it, Josey said. Only for Josey, I'd hear nothing. Frank would never think of picking up a pen to write to me.

Will you be going to more fancy hotels now that you're one of the O'Malleys? And yes I did think your wedding was great. I was a bit drunk.

Not fair you won't tell me more about the honeymoon... aren't you even going to tell me if you liked 'it' or not? The book with this letter is your wedding present from me to you (not for John). Whatever you do... don't let your mammy read it or I'll be for the hanging. It's a love story with some bold parts, but you're a married woman now so you're allowed to read it. I think you'll like it.

Send me the photos please. I have to go for now.

Love from your best friend, Mary.

10/11/58

Flossie clenched her teeth so tight that her jaw hurt. Why was she so surprised that Alice was pregnant again? Somewhere in her fantasy world, that wasn't part of her vision. Maybe Frank did love Alice after all.

CHAPTER SEVENTEEN

Goretti Lynch had had a permanent smile on her face since John moved in. She fussed over him the same way she used to fuss over Danny.

Even though Flossie had quite enjoyed their weekend in Malahide, she knew John hadn't. He hadn't liked being in that hotel. He didn't like meeting that waitress woman, Julie, who they hadn't seen again after the first evening. Had John had a fling with her maybe? Back when he was a teenager? She was definitely at least ten years older than him. Flossie laughed to herself at the thoughts of him having a secret ex-girlfriend. A ridiculous thought.

Flossie observed as her mother sat in her chair beside the fire, knitting mittens for the neighbours' children. John sat on the opposite side reading *The Irish Times*. Now and again, they'd share their opinions on certain articles. Contented—the pair of them.

Flossie went to bed to read her book. She was half-way through the novel Mary had sent her. She had it kept well hidden from her mother. Mammy'd have a stroke if she read the scenes between the pages of this ordinary-looking romance novel.

Propped up against her headboard, Flossie traced her finger across the image of the young woman on the front cover. Was the picture meant to be of Kate, the nice girl? Or was it Lucille, the adulteress? She opened the page at her bookmark. Lucille was what some people would call a floozie. She was young and beautiful, and she was having an illicit affair with her married boss.

Flossie allowed herself to succumb to the sinful pages that made her insides shudder, lost in a world of forbidden love and sin; a world she wouldn't dare enter in real life.

As Lucille blatantly enticed her lover into her lonely bed, the familiar wave of warmth enveloped Flossie, and in her imagination, she became Lucille. As Spencer kissed his mistress, she felt Frank's lips on hers. She read steadily, absorbing every detail. Intoxicated by the words on the page, she felt every breath that Lucille took.

She closed the book and held it tight to her chest. Her heart pounded. A desire intense and urgent swelled up inside her. It tormented her, but she resisted. She refused to allow herself to think unholy thoughts.

She put Mary's book back under the mattress. She knew it was sinful, but it fascinated her. It unleashed sensations from deep within her that she hadn't known existed.

She wondered if women like Lucille ended up in hell. She wondered if she and John were to consummate their marriage, would it make them love each other like a husband and wife should? She wondered how many virgin wives existed. She closed her eyes and prayed the Our Father and the Act of Contrition.

§

Wednesday was Goretti's evening for her Legion of Mary meetings and for calling to Molly's afterwards.

John had himself geared up for an important conversation with his wife. With Goretti out until after ten, he had no excuse, he told himself. They'd been married three months now and things needed to be finalised. Night after night, he had intended to do what he should have done on their honeymoon, but in the end, he'd bottle out and sit up talking with Goretti instead.

A coal fire blazed in the grate, and John opened the curtains to watch the raindrops trickle down the window. He found it soothing. Flossie came in with two cups of tea and some custard creams. John closed the curtains and sat on the couch beside her. She told him about the concerns she had for a young child in school. He rarely brought lunch with him and he cried a lot. She saw him in the yard, in the shelters. And that Shaney Reilly, who's nothing but a little pup, had Miss Kennedy gone astray in the head. He brought one of his granny's hens to school in his bag. It dirtied all over the floor making a shocking mess. The headmaster nearly killed him—again.

'Will I throw a stick or two on that fire, John? Mammy will be freezing when she gets in and she'll be keeping you up with her usual gossip from Molly's.'

'I'll not be sitting up late tonight.' He pushed his glasses up his nose. 'We're married three months now, Flossie. Do you think maybe we should consummate our marriage?'

'What?' Flossie gaped.

'Well, I think it's about time.'

'Now?'

'Only if you want to... of course. But I was thinking that maybe we should.'

'I suppose we should. To be honest I was thinking the same thing myself.'

'Will you have a drink with me first? I have Jameson here and maybe you'd like a sherry?'

'Sure I'll have a Jameson with you. There's red lemonade in the press.'

'I have to tell you something important, Flossie,' John said. 'You probably know this already, but I'll say it anyway. I've never been with a woman before.'

She sat back down with her whiskey and red lemonade, the tea abandoned on the coffee table.

'What about Julie from the Grand Hotel? Is she not an old flame?'

He turned his head abruptly towards her. 'Christ, Flossie, no, absolutely not. What makes you think that?'

'The way she was when she saw us, and especially when you told her we were married.'

'I told you already. She's a bit funny in the way she goes on. She was surprised because she hadn't seen me in so long. Sure she's far too old for me anyway.' He laughed awkwardly.

'Okay. Let's forget about her then.' Flossie drank the whiskey quickly and poured another one, diluting it with less lemonade than before.

John watched her closely. She looked pleased. Her mood had brightened—like a dark veil had been lifted. Her eyes glistened like the raindrops on the window. She craved love and affection—the kind he couldn't give her. He could only promise himself that he would try harder to be a good husband.

'I'll go on up then,' Flossie said. She breezed out the door. John waited five minutes before following her.

§

The next morning John whistled while he polished his shoes for work. Goretti hummed a different tune as she cut two thick slices of batch loaf and placed them on the centre of the table.

'Come on now, John. Your breakfast is ready. You don't want cold porridge.'

He sat at the table and clapped his hands together. 'You make the best porridge, Mrs Lynch. Not that your daughter doesn't, of course.'

Goretti flushed. 'Get away outta that.' She handed John the Anglo Celt newspaper. 'My Flossie makes grand porridge, although it would be nicer if she put a bit of sugar in like I do.' She winked.

John knew Flossie hated cooking and wasn't half as good at it as her mother was. 'I'm a lucky man indeed.'

'You must have been tired last night to be already gone to bed when I got home,' Goretti said.

'I was indeed and I slept like a baby.' He spooned out the last of his porridge and then opened up his newspaper.

She poured his tea from her Royal Albert teapot. She buttered his bread and put it on his side plate and sat opposite him, sipping from her dainty cup. John continued to read as he bit into the thick buttered slice.

'I told Flossie that when she starts her family, she'll have no need to leave the school. I'll look after my grandchildren so the two of you will have no worries there.'

John caught his breath just as he had the cup to his mouth. The hot tea scalded his lips and the doughy bread lodged in his throat. The china cup crashed to its saucer, splashing tea all over the white linen tablecloth. He coughed and spluttered, stuttering apologies through his hands. He sprang off his chair as Flossie entered the room.

'Are you alright, John? Is Mammy trying to poison you?' she asked in jest. She clapped him on the back as Goretti dabbed at her tablecloth with the skirt of her apron.

'It's okay, John, you're grand. Don't worry about it,' she said.

He cleared his throat and straightened his glasses, repeating his apologies to Goretti. 'I've to go now anyway. I'm a bit late.' He turned to look at Flossie. His beautiful legitimate wife. She had a playful smile on her lips. With his shoulders back and a gleam in his eyes, he strode over and kissed her on the cheek. 'Goodbye, Flossie. Have a good day.'

He was truly a married man now.

CHAPTER EIGHTEEN

Dear Mary,

I read the book and I can see why you told me to hide it from Mammy. (And John.) Have you got any more like it? Only if you have now. I don't really care. I have a few books that Auntie Bridgey gave me anyway.

Christmas will be nice for you—having Jim's sister there. Only two weeks to go and I haven't bought any presents yet. The children at school are talking about nothing else. Wee Tommy Mac said he got an orange from Santy last year, and he better bring him a toy this year or he'll cry. Then the others laughed and called him a cry baby—so then he cried. Veronica wants a new bell for a bike that isn't even hers, it belongs to her sister. Betty wants a yoyo, and Jack said he'll take anything at all. Poor Jack. He could do with a new coat.

How's Maureen? Mammy thinks me and John might soon be having our first child. She said she'll look after it when I'm at work. Can you imagine her and Ruth O'Malley fighting over the child? Each one thinking they're the best granny.

The hair band with this letter is for Maureen. I picked yellow because it will suit her dark hair.

I was talking to your Josey a few days ago. He was in town buying weaner feed and we stood for a chat. We talked about you and Maureen mostly, then about Christmas and turkeys. I wish you were coming home for it!

(Don't forget to send me another book, if you have one.)

Hope you, Jim and Maureen have a very happy Christmas. Write soon.

Love from your best friend, Flossie. 12/12/58

§

Flossie posted Mary's Christmas card and letter first thing on Saturday morning. Next, she had to get a few groceries for one of the Legion of Mary women, Mrs Deignan, who lived on the Cavan Road. She usually walked or cycled to town for her own messages, but the frosty weather was detrimental, especially for a seventy-year-old woman.

'Good morning, Mrs O'Malley,' Mr Reilly greeted from behind his counter.

'Hello, Mr Reilly. I want to pick up a few groceries for Mrs Deignan. She's afraid to come out in the frost.'

'I wouldn't blame her—she's not getting any younger. I'll put together the usual for her,' he said.

'I'll drop them into her on me way past if you like.' Frank Connolly approached the counter carrying an armful of shopping.

She hadn't talked to him since her wedding. She'd spotted him in town a few times but stayed out of his way. And she saw him at Mass on Sundays.

'Not at all. Sure you have your own to carry,' Flossie said.

Mr Reilly had the groceries ready within minutes. 'Here you go, Mrs O'Malley. Tell her I have it down in the book and we'll see her next week if the weather gets better.'

'Thank you.' Flossie put her gloves back on and tightened her scarf. She lifted the box off the counter.

'Sure I'll be out the road with you,' said Frank after he'd paid for his groceries.

They walked down the street in silence. It wasn't like him to be so quiet.

'Here, swap boxes. Mine's lighter,' Frank said.

'Okay. Thanks.' *Dare she ask him?*

'How's Alice?'

'She's alright.'

'Are you nervous? You know, after what happened the last time.'

She expected a smart answer, but hugging the box close to his chest, he kept his gaze straight ahead.

'I think everything should be alright at this stage. The baby's due in March sometime.'

'Yes, Mary told me in her last letter.'

'Is that all she told you? She loves to gossip that one.'

'Yes, that's all. She talks mostly about Jim and Maureen.' Their warm breath formed soft clouds in the icy air. Flossie imagined the two puffs joining together.

'She's delighted Maureen will have a new baby cousin, one from her own side of the family,' she said.

'Ah yea. Sure I can't wait myself. I don't know if I'll be any good at it, you know, being a father.'

'Aw sure you will, Frank. Weren't you great with all the wee ones when we were growing up? We were still children when you had grown into a handsome man, and you still had great patience for us all. Do you remember the day we all hid down the woods when you were minding us? And you started to panic because you thought we were lost.'

Out of the corner of her eye, she saw him glance at her.

'So you thought I was handsome, did ya?'

'I did. I remember the time you kissed me on my birthday.'

He laughed. 'I did that on purpose because I knew well that you had a notion of me.'

'What?' Flossie let her jaw drop dramatically. 'So you were lying when you asked me to go to the pictures with you? Saying you wouldn't have a girlfriend by the end of the week.'

'If you must know, I wasn't lying. I really was breaking it off with Alice that weekend, but then she told me she was pregnant. We had a hell of a fight that night. I told her she was a liar because I was always careful, y'know. She gave me a blistering slap across the face.'

'I heard before that your friend Tenny sticks needles in the "you-know-whats" before he gives them to the lads.'

'That's rubbish talk, Flossie. He gets them up in Armagh and doesn't touch them. Séanie McHale made that up because he got his girlfriend pregnant—and then dumped her.'

'I remember that. She was sent down the country for a few months. Of course she had no baby with her when she came home. Her father still won't let her out of his sight.'

They walked at a slow pace on the frosty road.

'Anyway, I had no choice then but to stay with her. I had to think of the child too.'

'I was jealous when you married her, you know.' She cringed after she said it.

The box seemed heavier. The smell of the fresh bread sitting on top made her hungry. She could see a bag of Tayto crisps in there too. *Probably for Alice.*

'We're both married now to someone else and that's the way it is, Flossie. John's a good man and you'll have a happy life with him.'

'I know that. He's a good husband. Is Alice a good wife?'

He didn't answer. They walked in silence until they got to Mrs Deignan's house. They swapped boxes again.

'Tell Mrs Deignan I'll call the next time I'm on my way to town, and I'll bring home anything she needs,' Frank said.

'Are you helping Josey with the turkeys at the market next week?' she asked. 'We're going to Ruth's for dinner and Mammy said we're in charge of the turkey. Maybe you'd put one aside for us?'

'What size?'

'Sure you know yourself, Frank... there's five of us. But we want leftovers for the days after.'

'Come out to Josey's tomorrow if you have time and take a look. We'll kill it for you and hang it there 'til Christmas Eve if you like.'

'Alright. I'll say it to Mammy first.'

'Come at about three o'clock and I'll be there.' Frank said. 'I'll help you pick out a decent one.'

'Okay. See you then.'

She watched for a minute as he dawdled in the narrow road that led to his house on the Wood Lane.

Mrs Deignan invited Flossie in for a bowl of soup, which

she accepted without a second thought. They had a cosy house; small but plenty big for two people.

Flossie removed her gloves and sat by the hot range to warm her hands.

'Take that coat off too or it'll be no good to ya when ya go back out,' Mrs Deignan said.

Her husband sat on the opposite side, cleaning out his pipe. He was older than his wife and of ill health. He rarely left the house, except to tend to the hens and their two sows in the backyard.

'I see ya were out the road with young Frank,' Mr Deignan said to Flossie without looking at her.

'Yes, we met in Reilly's and got chatting. About turkeys.'

'I can still see yas all playing in those fields across the road. It seems like yesterday and now yas are all grown up and married.' He pushed a pipe cleaner through the stem of his pipe. 'Give the lassie a bit of bread with that soup,' he said to his wife as she poured a generous bowl of thin vegetable broth for Flossie.

'He's a good lad, that Frank. As for that mad woman he married!'

'Ach now, don't be giving out about her,' Mrs Deignan said. 'She's a bit hot-headed, that's all. Frank can look after himself.'

Flossie moved to the table for her broth.

'There'll be war yet up there. Mark my words,' he said. 'The roars of her one day... him heading to town on his bicycle and her shouting after him. Like a demon was in her.'

Flossie blew gently on her spoonful of piping hot broth, as hot as the anger boiling up inside her. 'Great heat from that range, Mrs Deignan,' she said.

'If auld Pat Connolly were alive today, he'd have put a stop to that woman from day one.' Mr Deignan was on a roll. 'Her own mother doesn't want a bit of her. Always caused nothing but trouble at home. Her father used to say she was swapped by the fairies, and I'd say he was fecking right.'

Flossie listened with mixed feelings. *Surely Alice wasn't that bad.* She didn't want her soup now; her appetite was spoilt.

Mrs Deignan threw her eyes up to the heavens and shook her head. 'Leave the lassie alone, for God's sake. She didn't get a great start in life. It wasn't that the mother didn't want those children, she wasn't able for them. She had a lot to bear with that bully of a husband. They say he gave her a hard time when she gave birth to each of the girls. He only wanted sons, I heard.'

Mr Deignan filled his pipe with fresh tobacco and cracked a match on the range. He puffed swirls of smoke into the air. Flossie inhaled the sweetness of Golden Virginia while wondering about Alice's childhood. She knew from Mary that Alice had attended national school in Muff, a country school in the foothills of Loughanleagh mountains. She later attended the Tech in Bailieborough but left after her first year.

'Where exactly does her family live?' Flossie asked.

'Up the mountain way. Moyar. They don't come near Bailieborough at all. They do all their business in Kingscourt,' said Mrs Deignan. 'Now, enough about that. Was your mother at the last Legion of Mary meeting? I'm after missing two in a row.'

CHAPTER NINETEEN

Flossie scratched an opening in the icy floral pattern on her bedroom window. She peered out onto the frosty street, pulling her dressing gown tightly around her. Kennedy's dog chased after somebody's hens—probably Mrs Sullivan's again. Flossie banged on the window, but the terrier mongrel was too busy to heed her.

She yawned and gave herself a good stretch. She was glad John had stayed in Dublin for the night as she always slept better when he wasn't in the bed twisting and turning. Goretti had breakfast ready by the time Flossie made her way down the stairs.

'We'll see Ruth at Mass and we'll tell her about the turkey,' she said.

'What size should I order, Mammy?'

'A good big one anyway. We'll divide the leftovers with Ruth and Frederick. We'll want two or three days out of it at least.'

§

Flossie liked ten o'clock Mass, the same one Frank went to—sometimes with Alice. Flossie, John and Goretti always sat in the aisle on the far right, five rows from the front. Frank always sat about five rows from the back, on the same side.

Flossie fidgeted during the sermon, anxious for communion time, the part of Mass she looked forward to most.

Every Sunday she would go up to receive the holy bread, hands joined below her breast. On the way back to her seat, she would lift her eyes from the floor to catch a glimpse of the pew—five rows from the back. And there he would be, looking straight at her. She would hold his gaze for a split second. And that's when he would get up to receive. She would kneel and pray as the holy bread melted slowly on her tongue. When it would dissolve to almost nothing, she'd swallow it and then keep her head buried in her hands until the Concluding Rites.

And this Sunday was no different. There Frank sat beside his wife waiting for the right time to go up. But on this occasion, Flossie didn't bury her head in her hands after communion. Kneeling with her chin resting on her clasped hands, she watched Alice walk up to the priest ahead of Frank. Husband and wife, the same height as each other, hers a stockier build than his. She fitted snugly into the emerald-green wool coat that once hung loose. She had her hair pulled back in a tight ponytail. Frank kept his head down, his shoulders hunched.

Alice sauntered back to her seat with her head held high, her pursed lips the colour of red wine, matching her rouged cheeks. The penny-sized pearl studs clipped to her ears were more suitable for someone more ladylike, thought Flossie. She pictured Frank's child in Alice's womb, and jealousy consumed her.

Frank walked past without as much as a glance in her direction. With her head in her hands, Flossie prayed the Act of Contrition.

§

With Ruth happy about the turkey arrangement, Goretti gave Flossie some money to give Josey. 'If that's not enough, tell him to call here next time he's in town,' she said.

'He mightn't want the money yet.'

'Bring it anyway. Now, I'm leaving you to wash up because I've to go. Molly's waiting.'

Flossie sped through the dishes with only one thing on her mind. Still wearing her mass clothes, she decided she should change into something more suitable for cycling.

She sat at her dressing table and studied herself in the mirror. She compared herself to Alice. *What did he see in her all those years ago?*

She smudged a little cream blush on the balls of her cheeks and brushed her face with loose powder. Then she painted her full lips a pale shade of pink.

She grabbed her shoulder-length hair and tied it in a ponytail. Then she let it down. *Keep it down. Damn cow's lick. Maybe some more rouge.* She always looked so pale in the wintertime. *Maybe a darker lipstick.* Natural was better though (on a Sunday). A dab of Lily of the Valley behind her ears and she was ready—to look at turkeys.

§

The sun glistened on the frosty hedges and a sheet of ice on Town Lake had melted in parts. She slowed down, not wanting to be too early. Pangs of guilt taunted her, but she assured herself she was doing nothing wrong. She picked up speed again as she passed by the long terrace of houses in Drumbannon. At Deignan's house, she turned right onto the narrow road that led to the Wood Lane. She hadn't been on this road in years. Her heart raced as fast as the wheels on her bicycle.

She pedalled down the lane, zigzagging between the icy puddles. She checked her watch—ten to three. For a moment she contemplated turning back. She slowed down but kept on pedalling until she could see Josey's cottage.

Smoke swirled from the chimney. She got off her bicycle and walked the last few yards. She asked herself why she had really come. *It was wrong*.

Childhood memories flooded her mind as she walked in the short, narrow path of the cottage that once belonged to the Connolly children's grandmother, Lizzie. Many times she'd played in this garden with them. Josey kept the place in tiptop shape and looked after the shrubbery and flowerbeds just like Lizzie had. It was as though she was still there. The door opened before Flossie got to it.

Frank greeted her with a smile. 'Right on time,' he said.

'I was expecting Josey.'

'Were you?' He raised his eyebrows slightly.

A blush tingled her cold face. 'I brought some mince pies —for Josie—I made them.'

'Come in for tea, Flossie. It's very cold. There's a good fire on here.'

'Is Josey here?'

'No, he's gone shooting... for a couple of hours.'

'Okay, tea would be nice.' She held her breath as she gently brushed past him in the doorway. *They were alone.*

Flossie sat by the fire while Frank busied himself with the kettle.

'Josey hasn't made many changes to the house,' she said, scanning the room from top to bottom.

'Aye, it's as if Granny Lizzie were still alive,' Frank said.

'Where's Alice?' Flossie asked.

'At home.'

'Does she know you're here?'

'She won't come here, if that's what you mean.'

They were alone with little chance of being disturbed. Was this her chance to admit her true feelings to Frank? Would it change anything?

'What is Alice really like, Frank?'

'She's not like you,' he replied.

'What do you mean by that?'

'I don't want to talk about Alice.'

'I have to tell you something important. Well, I think it's important.'

'Do you want this tea?' he asked, holding up the teapot. Their eyes locked.

'No, I don't want the tea.'

'Tell me this important thing then.'

She took a deep breath. *It's now or never. What harm could it do?* She stood up, her heart pounding. 'I love you and I've always loved you, and since the day you kissed me when I was eighteen, I've wished nothing more than for you to do it again. I know you don't love Alice and I don't really love John... not in the right way. So now you know.' Her legs wobbled and she stumbled back into her chair, shocked at her own boldness. 'Are you going to say anything?'

He shook his head. He put the teapot on the range and folded his arms.

'Well, I'm glad I told you. I've been dying to tell you all my life.'

He grinned. 'All your life.'

'Don't start being smart, Frank.'

'Come here,' he said.

'Maybe we should go and get this turkey.'

'Come here... please.'

She took his hand and he led her into the sitting room.

'Just this once, Flossie,' he said. She nodded as she took off her coat.

He held her face in his hands, gently, as if she were made of china. When his lips touched hers, she tingled. The words in Mary's book flashed through her mind. *Adulteress, floozy, sinful.* His tongue brushed against hers, arousing familiar sensations. *Like Lucille.* Her head fell back as he smothered her neck with warm kisses. 'I love you so much,' she said. In her head she said it again and again.

She held her breath as she surrendered the one part of her that was only ever for Frank, the essence of her whole being. She closed her eyes and let her mind soar like a wild bird flying high in the sky. He took her to a place she didn't know existed, so far within the depths of her soul she didn't want to return.

She was a floozy, like Lucille, and she didn't care. She took what she had desperately wanted since she was eighteen.

Afterwards, Flossie lay in Frank's arms, afraid to open her

eyes in case she'd find that none of it had really happened. Afraid it might be a dream. She wanted to hold on to the moment for as long as possible because she knew she might never get a moment like it again.

So the book didn't lie. Lucille really did experience all those things. This was what she meant about floating on a cloud, sensations rippling through her body, surrendering. And the borrowed man.

Frank stroked her hair. 'We should have been together you know... years ago,' he whispered.

'I know.'

'It wasn't my intention to end up with Alice.'

'It wasn't my intention to end up with John.'

'He's a good man, Flossie. I know I laughed at first and teased you about him, but he'll look after you.'

'I'd rather have you looking after me.'

'We can't ever do this again, do you hear?'

'But nobody would have to know.' She knew she was being fanciful. 'I think about you all the time, Frank. I wake up every morning wishing it was you beside me in bed.'

He stroked her face. He had lines on his forehead, and his eyes were sad.

'It'll ruin your life if you don't forget about me. Imagine if Alice found out,' he said. 'Get on with your life and forget about us.'

She knew he was right. Any plans God may have had for them were gone. Or did God have any plans for them to begin with? She clenched her jaw, a heaviness weighing down on her.

'You're right. Christ, Frank, what am I thinking? What are we thinking? This is my fault. I made this happen.' Flossie released herself from his arms and sat up. 'What the hell is wrong with me?'

'Hey, it's as much my fault as yours.' He put his hand on the small of her back. 'Look, it's done now. I'm not proud either, but we won't let it happen again.'.

She took a deep breath, refusing to cry. Conflicting thoughts and emotions scrambled inside her head. She turned to face him. 'I've been here long enough... can you pick a turkey for us?'

Frank laughed as he buttoned his shirt. 'The turkey wasn't the reason I asked you here. They all look the same right now. I can't pick you one until they're killed and weighed.'

'Devious,' she said.

'And I don't think the turkey was the real reason you came here.'

'If I'm honest, no. We're both devious.'

'But you're smiling,' he said.

'I am.' Flossie wasn't smiling on the inside though. Something crumbled inside her: her self-worth. *Is this what she'd become? An adulteress.* A spark of shame ignited and burned inside her. 'I really have been here too long. I'd better go.'

'I'll walk you to the door,' Frank said.

Didn't he feel it too? Was he not even the tiniest bit ashamed? She stepped outside and the cold air hit her like a slap in the face.

'Wait one minute, Flossie. Stay there,' he said.

He disappeared through the gate leading to the garden. He returned with a small bunch of flowers. 'For you.'

'They're beautiful. What are they called?' she asked as she stroked the delicate petals.

'Christmas Roses.'

'Red roses... very romantic, Mr Connolly.'

Frank smiled. 'They're purple, not red.'

'I see red... so they're red.'

'Are you colour blind?'

'I'm most certainly not.'

'Maybe one day I'll give you a real red rose.'

'You can't say that unless you mean it.'

'I mean it.'

'In a different life maybe.'

Flossie walked down the path. When she reached the gate, she turned to wave at Frank, but he was gone. She placed the flowers in the front basket of her bicycle and, with a heavy heart, she cycled towards home.

CHAPTER TWENTY

Alice and Joyce sat in the smoke-filled snug in Law's pub, drinking bottles of stout. They were in the festive spirit and on the lookout for a free drink.

'Hey, Liam, any chance of a Christmas drink?' Alice asked the young barman through the hatch attached to the bar.

'Didn't the boss give you one the other night?'

Joyce begged. 'Aw, come on. Throw us up a wee half one. I'll make it worth your while.'

'Well now, young Liam, there's an offer ya can't refuse. G'wan... a quick one. We won't tell the boss,' Alice said.

Liam blushed and returned to serving his other customers at the bar.

'Hello, ladies. Mind if I join you?' A strange man stood at the door of the snug, the same man Alice had seen in McCabe's bar recently.

'Be our guest,' said Joyce as she shuffled across the seat, making space between herself and Alice.

'Sit your handsome-self down here.' Alice smiled.

'Did I hear a request for a couple of half ones?' he asked.

Alice and Joyce eyeballed each other.

'Are you asking or offering?' Joyce said.

'Offering of course.'

The stranger ordered three whiskeys through the hatch, and then settled himself between the two women.

Joyce narrowed her eyes. 'Haven't seen you around town before, Mr...?'

'Stanley. Peter Stanley,' he said. 'My new job has me here. I'm a salesman.'

'What do you sell?'

'Tobacco. So, what's two lovely girls like you doing in here looking all inviting?'

'Well, she's a married woman with a child on the way, but I'm free and single. Isn't that right, Alice?'

'Don't mind her. She's doing a line with a fella from Curkish. Straight Paddy, they call him.'

Joyce pulled a face at Alice. 'That eejit? When it suits him. I'm as free as a bird, Mr Stanley. I can come and go as I please.'

'Ya wouldn't say that if he was sitting right beside ya,' said Alice. Paddy used Joyce and everyone knew it, but she was mad about him and could never resist him.

'Are you jealous of me?'

'Don't be fecking stupid.' Alice knew Joyce spoke the truth. She looked her up and down, envious of her single life and slim figure. 'I've to powder me nose,' she said, grabbing her bag.

'Don't hurry back,' said Joyce as she moved closer to Peter.

Straight Paddy was sitting at the bar just as Alice expected.

'Well, Paddy.'

He looked down his nose at her.

'What do you want?'

'Nothing. Your woman's in the snug being chatted up by a handsome young salesman.'

'She's not my woman.'

Alice went to the toilet, feeling smug. Why should Joyce have all the fun? She rummaged through her handbag for her lipstick and hairbrush. She pulled the elastic band out of her ponytail and brushed her shoulder-length hair. Her reflection in the mirror reminded her of how much she had changed in the last few years. Her light brown hair that once bounced when she walked was now lank and dull, and always in a ponytail. Her face was ballooning out, just like her pregnant belly. Marriage wasn't at all what Alice had expected it to be. She thought it would make her feel loved and wanted, not like at her childhood home, where she was only ever a nuisance to them all. She hadn't wanted them as her family anymore. She'd wanted a new family. She'd known the only way to get Frank to marry her was to pretend she was pregnant. She thought she'd get pregnant for real soon into the marriage, and nobody would know any different.

But it didn't happen like that. Alice didn't get pregnant as soon as she married Frank. He started to get suspicious when her body shape didn't change. 'It must be a very small baby,' he'd said one day. A couple of weeks later he asked her, 'Are you sure you're right about the due date, Alice?' The time had come to end the pretence. When he arrived home from work one evening, she told him that she'd had a miscarriage that morning, and luckily, Joyce happened to be visiting her at the time and knew what to do. She said that Joyce went into town and got Doctor Donnelly. She told Joyce a similar story—Frank was with her when it happened and went for the doctor. Alice knew Frank wouldn't question Joyce about it because men just didn't talk about that kind of stuff. Bloody fools believed everything she told them!

Now he looked forward to the birth of this baby. Alice rubbed her tummy, struggling to visualise a tiny baby in there. *Would it be a boy?* Even when it moved, she found it hard to believe that a little human was growing inside her. Why wasn't she excited like Frank was? Why did she feel nothing but a dreadful heaviness bearing down on her? Why did she feel the urge to run far away from everyone? Alice wanted to run until she could run no more, but she knew there was nowhere she could run to.

She touched up her lipstick and put her husband and unborn child to the back of her mind as she returned to the snug.

'Paddy's looking for ya, Joycie.'

Joyce let out an exaggerated sigh. 'Why didn't you tell him I'm busy?'

Alice smirked. 'What do ya think I am?'

Joyce leaned towards Peter. 'Don't go away.'

Alice knew she wouldn't be back. Paddy would ply her with more drink and she'd go off out the road with him for a court—like she always did.

'You're a sly little madam,' Peter said.

'Aw, she gets annoying after a few whiskeys. We'll have peace without her. I'll keep you company.'

He offered Alice a cigarette and they lit up from the same

match. She inhaled deeply, and tilting her head back, she blew the smoke towards the brown, sticky ceiling.

'I saw you in town a few weeks ago, Mr Stanley. You were eyeing me up in McCabe's bar.'

'Maybe I was. Do you mind?'

'Like Joyce said… I'm a married woman with this on the way.' Alice pointed to her belly.

'I've been watching you for a while now, Mrs Connolly, if you must know.'

'Why's that? Are ya some sort of quare fella?'

He laughed. 'Not watching you for the reason you think.'

'So what then?'

'You like a bit of fun, don't you? And I bet you like money too.'

'Well, you can't have fun without money,' Alice said.

'I've a wee job to do and I need help.'

'What kind of job? I'm not helping ya to sell stuff. I wouldn't have time for that.'

'No, nothing like that. Are you any good at keeping secrets, Mrs Connolly?'

'Well, that all depends on the secret.'

'It would be fun—this secret—fun, with money.'

Alice drained her glass and pulled hard on her cigarette, her eyes glued to Peter Stanley's enticing gaze.

'Do you know John O'Malley?' he asked.

'I'll have another wee half one.' Alice grinned, holding up her empty glass. 'And call me Alice.'

§

The adrenaline rushing through Alice's veins minimized the fear and doubt that had built up inside her. But she had nothing to fear, she assured herself. It was John O'Malley who should be afraid. She always knew there was something funny about him. Too good to be wholesome, he was. And that stuck-up wife of his, going around thinking she was better than everyone else.

She waited patiently outside O'Malley's shop for John to come out, her headscarf tied tight under her chin, keeping her rollers in place. John was always running around the shops for his mother: the butcher's, the newspaper shop, the post office. Joyce said he even picked library books for her sometimes. *Come on, O'Malley, hurry up, I haven't all day.*

Alice darted towards John as soon as he left the shop.

'I've to talk to ya, O'Malley,' she said.

'About what?' John looked surprised but kept walking up the street.

'It's private.'

'Is it about money?'

'Ya could say that.'

'Well, spit it out. It's private enough here, there's nobody around. How much do you owe us?'

'I know the conditions of your father's will. And if ya don't want to be left penniless when he kicks the bucket, ya may start coughing up a few pounds to me... or I'll tell him everything.'

John came to a sudden stop. 'What the bloody hell are you talking about, you stupid bitch?'

Alice watched him go pale. He pulled at his collar and loosened his tie.

She moved closer to him. 'I'm talking about your shenanigans in Dublin.'

PART TWO

1964

CHAPTER TWENTY-ONE

Frank Connolly took out his pocket watch to check the time. He had a half day booked off for his daughter Rose's fifth birthday. He had a special present for her and her sister, Nancy, whose fourth birthday was a few days away. The morning dragged in the hot, smoky foundry, and the two Reilly brothers had been at each other's throats since nine o'clock, but the tense atmosphere didn't dampen Frank's mood.

The girls wrapped their arms around Frank's legs as soon as he entered the house.

'It's my birthday, Daddy. It's my birthday!' Rose said, smiling up at him.

Alice busied herself at the range, a cigarette dangling out of her mouth.

'Happy birthday to you. Happy birthday to you...' Frank sang.

'Can I be five too, Daddy? When will it be my birthday?' Nancy asked.

Frank laughed. 'Your birthday's the day after Easter

Sunday, Nancy, but you'll be four.'

'You can't be five until you're finished being four, silly billy,' Rose said.

Nancy stuck out her tongue. 'When will Easter be here, Daddy?'

'Your birthday is in five days. But guess what, you're getting your present today with Rose. It's one big present for you to share.'

The girls jumped up and down. 'Where is it, where is it?'

'Wait 'til I have my dinner,' he said.

'What age are you, Daddy?' asked Rose.

'Thirty.'

Nancy frowned. 'You're old.'

Alice plonked a plate of spuds and bacon on the table and sat by the range. Frank considered leaving it until later but thought back to the last time he did that.

Rose skipped around the kitchen, clapping her hands. 'Where is the present? Is it a dolly? Is it a new book? Where is it, Daddy? Can we have it now?'

'Keep guessing, but you'll never get it right.'

'Can't see why you took a half day,' Alice said.

'I wouldn't expect you to see why.' Frank kept his eyes on his plate. He wasn't going to let her ruin the day. He ate quickly, and then put his empty plate into the basin on top of all the others.

'Okay, girls, coats on and come outside. Remember, the present is for both of you.'

'Yes, Daddy. Come on, hurry. We need it now,' said Nancy. 'I think it's a kitten... two kittens.'

'I think it's a swing,' Rose said.

'Wrong again, both of you.' Frank helped Nancy with her coat. His big fingers fumbled with the small buttons.

'Look at me. I know how to close my own buttons,' said Rose.

'When I'm five, I'll be able to close my own buttons too,' said Nancy.

Frank brought the girls through the small field behind the house. Their dog, Max, followed behind, barking as he picked up on the excitement.

'Why are we in the field?' Rose's eyes widened. 'Is it a donkey like Kitty Maguire's?'

'No. Something much better than a donkey.'

As they neared the end of the field, Frank stopped and bent down beside his girls. Pointing towards the chestnut tree that stood tall and wide in the corner where the two ditches met, he whispered, 'Happy birthday to my two favourite girls!'

'Why is your old fort our present?' asked Rose.

'Look closer. It's all fixed up. Inside as well. Just for you two.'

The sisters beamed at each other. Max started barking again. 'When did you fix it, Daddy?' Rose asked.

'When you weren't watching.'

'Can we go in it now?'

'You sure can.'

They ran towards the chestnut tree and Frank followed.

'There's one important rule though: no adults allowed.'

'But you're an adult.' Rose frowned.

'But he's our daddy. You can come into our babby house any time you like, Daddy,' said Nancy.

'If I go in there, there'll be no room for anyone else.'

Frank hadn't replaced the old rope that he and Josey had used to swing in and out of the fort. Instead, he'd positioned two planks of wood across the shuck to make a bridge. He'd recovered the roof—two sheets of galvanize that lay buried and forgotten under the brambles. They were bent and rusty in parts but still strong enough to use for shelter. He'd tied them securely to the overhanging branches and covered them with a sheet of clear plastic. The original timber walls were slightly weather beaten but still in good condition. He'd nailed some tough clear plastic sheeting to the open window to provide extra protection against the elements.

Frank guided Rose and Nancy across the wooden plank to their new playhouse. Max yapped and pawed the ground, unsure as to whether or not he should follow them across. He decided to stay where he was and sit guard. The girls pushed through the door—a rectangular strip of tough plastic—and stepped inside their babby house for the first time. Laughing, Frank got on his hands and knees and squeezed his broad shoulders through.

The girls could move around freely inside, but Frank, at five foot six, had to stay stooped. They chattered and giggled, making plans for their new house.

'This is far better than Jenny McGuirk's treehouse. Can I bring her here, Daddy?'

'You sure can, Rose. How about you stay here and play and I'll go up the lane and see if Uncle Josey wants to come and have a look.'

Frank whistled his way back down the field and into the back yard. Alice was filling the wash basin from the barrel of rainwater and, without looking at Frank, she said, 'Tell those two to get in now. It's time to get washed.'

'It's not even six o'clock yet. Anyway, since when did you start caring about washing them?'

Alice continued scooping out the water with her saucepan. For a fleeting moment, he imagined himself shoving her head into the barrel.

'For God's sake, leave the childer alone and let them play. What's wrong with you?'

'Piss off, Frank.'

'When I come back with Josey, they better still be up there. Maybe you should use that basin of water to wash out your mouth.' Frank stormed up the lane, sucking the cool air through his clenched teeth. She went against everything he did for the children, but he wasn't letting her ruin this for them. They were the only good thing he had in his life. He sometimes thought that was the reason she was so mean to them.

§

Alice marched up the field, muttering to herself. 'They needn't think they'll be spending all their time up here. And I'll not be traipsing up this field every day looking for them. They can get that outta their heads.'

'Rose. Nancy. Come on. There's jobs for yas to do and it's getting dark,' she shouted out as she neared the chestnut tree.

Max rose to protect the children. He snarled, rooted to his spot at the bridge.

'Shut up, you mutt. I'll not be going into that pokey little place, if that's what you think.' Alice shivered at the thought of it, her brother's face flashing through her mind. She felt a tightness in her chest.

'Rose and Nancy, out here. Now!'

'We have a lamp, and Daddy said we had to stay here,' Rose said.

'I say what you do, not him.'

Max darted towards Alice and snapped at her pudgy ankles. She jumped back, flicking him with her tea towel. She strode back towards the house, mumbling to herself. She met Frank and Josey on their way up. She walked past the two men as if they were invisible.

§

When out of earshot, Josey asked, 'What's she like these days?'

'Same as always. Never happy, and full-time giving out to the childer.'

'Aw pass no remarks of her.' Josey stood in his tracks as they neared the babby house. 'Holy God, Frank! You made a mighty job of it. Come on, I'll race ya.' They laughed and ran towards their old fort like the schoolboys they once were.

'Was the doorway always this small?' asked Josey as he poked his head through.

'Yes... but we were too—twenty years ago,' Frank replied.

'Hello, Uncle Josey,' the girls said in unison.

'Hello, my favourite people,' Josey replied. 'So that's what you did with my old milking stools,' he said out to Frank.

'I didn't want to tell you 'til I was finished.'

Rose and Nancy sat on the wooden stools beside an old tea chest that had one of Josey's net curtains thrown across it.

Josey had never seen them looking so happy; it warmed his heart.

'Have fun, you two. See ya later.' He took his head out of the babby house and brushed himself down. 'Frank, this is brilliant. Looks a hell of a lot different though. Where's the bows and arrows that used to hang on the branches? Oh, and the old paint tins of penknives and sharp sticks?' Josey laughed. 'If Mary could see it now... she'd love it.'

The memories stirred feelings of melancholy in Frank. 'Do you remember when we'd never let her in?' he said.

'Sure we were only children. Knew no better.'

'I suppose.'

'I'll head back now. I might see you later,' Josey said.

'She's in one of those moods, so I'll probably not get up to you tonight,' Frank said, raising his eyebrows.

'See you tomorrow then.' Josey went on his way, leaving Frank reminiscing about days gone by.

CHAPTER TWENTY-TWO

John O'Malley whistled as he watched his mother and his son emerge from the back room of the shop. She looked after Benny every Tuesday and Thursday, and Goretti took care of him every Monday, Wednesday, and Friday.

Granny Malley—as Benny called her—brought him into the shop a lot, lest she miss out on any important news or gossip. Nobody minded having Benny in the shop because he kept himself occupied behind the counter, reading a book or playing with his Matchbox cars. His grandad took great pleasure in teaching him about the clothes trade in between serving his customers.

'You could be a tailor when you grow up, my son; not just a seamster like me and your daddy,' he told Benny.

'I'm going to have my own aeroplane when I'm big,' Benny said as Granny Malley perched him on the high stool behind the counter.

His grandad laughed, shaking his head.

'Your father used to say the same thing.'

'I'm still saving for it.' John laughed as he joined in. The excitement on Benny's plump little face made him happy. 'I'm going up for *The Celt*. Anyone need anything while I'm there?'

Benny ran out from behind the counter. 'Can I come too, Daddy?'

'Come on then,' he said, taking his son's hand.

Ruth stood in the doorway, performing her morning scan of the street to see who was about, or who might stop for a gossip on their way past. 'Get *Ireland's Own* if it's in,' she said as her boys squeezed past her.

John and Benny walked a few yards up the footpath to Law's pub and newsagent, Benny pleading for the *Beano* and crisps and a mineral and bubble gum.

'You'll have one or the other young man. I'm not made of money.'

'You've loads a money, Daddy.'

'When you start working in the house and in the shop, you'll earn your own money.'

'Granny Lynch said I don't have to, and Granny Malley said I'm not big enough.'

'Your grannies have you spoiled rotten,' John said.

The bell on Law's door jingled as Benny pushed it open. He marched straight to the counter to pick out his comic. Even on tiptoe, he had to stretch his neck to see across it. The smell of stale cigarettes and beer strayed out from behind the sliding door that provided customers access to the pub, masking the more favourable aroma of chocolate and inky newspapers.

Peggy Law opened up the counter flap as she sometimes did for her favourite children, depending on her mood.

'D'ya need a closer look, young fella?' she asked. He ran through without hesitation and flicked through the comics on the shelf, throwing his eyes towards the sweet rack at the same time.

Mr Law stood in the corner of the shop talking to a salesman. John nodded his head in their direction and picked up a copy of *The Celt* from the pile that sat on the floor beside the paper stand.

'Hello, John,' said Mr Law. John smiled and gave a swift nod in reply.

The salesman glanced at John but didn't speak. He lowered his eyes back to his invoice book. John and his father had no dealings with this particular salesman because he sold cigarettes and tobacco.

John turned his attention back to Mrs Law. 'I'll take *Ireland's Own* too please.'

'Not a bad day,' she replied, reaching round for the magazine. 'Giving heavy showers for tonight, though—according to Mr Stanley.' She looked to the salesman.

'The farmers won't complain,' said John.

Mrs Law ruffled Benny's dark mop of hair. 'Did you decide yet, young fella me lad?'

'I'll have the *Beano*,' he answered, looking at a box of King crisps. John shook his head. 'And a bag of King please.' Benny giggled as he came out from the behind the counter holding his comic and crisps.

The bell on the door jingled. Alice Connolly stepped inside, then stopped as she cast a look in the direction of the salesman and Mr Law. Her mouth fell open. All eyes in the shop rested upon her. She shot a glance from Stanley to John, then without saying a word, she left again. Peggy shook her head and sighed.

The Stanley man cleared his throat and leaned up against the wall. John sensed a shift in his demeanour. *They knew each other, and it certainly wasn't through selling tobacco.* People gossiped about Alice's flighty nature, but she didn't care. She was brazen enough to hold her head high, regardless of what she did. Alice didn't hide from gossip, she relished it.

So her reaction when she walked in that door had nothing to do with whether she was fooling around with Stanley or not.

The incident played on John's mind for the rest of the day. The way Alice looked at him that morning in Law's wasn't her usual style of acknowledgement. For more than five years, all he got from her were sly looks and flippant comments at every opportunity. He wasn't sure how he managed to resist the urge to smash her face into a brick wall half the time. It baffled him all these years how she knew things about him. Although, he wasn't sure how much she really did know. She spoke in riddles half the time, but John couldn't take any chances; he kept paying her, every fortnight. Someone somewhere was feeding her information. Julie and Alfie didn't know her. She never left town. She had few friends. She flirted with the local drunken scallywags, bargained at the stalls with the Dublin women, and argued with people who tried to help her. Who exactly was this Peter Stanley and could he be the connection John had been looking for all this time? Had it been under his nose all along?

CHAPTER TWENTY-THREE

Goretti Lynch had the place upside down with the cleaning spree she took into the week coming up to Easter. She had the three beds in the house stripped bare, sheets and blankets from each one washed and dried. All drawers and wardrobes were emptied, dusted and wiped inside and out with vinegar and water. The presses in the kitchen got the same treatment—emptied and scrubbed until they looked almost new. The net curtains got a good soak in a tin bath of water and bicarbonate of soda. Flossie got her usual job of cleaning the windows, although she didn't mind too much considering her mother did most of the housework. Since she'd married John, her mother had stopped exaggerating about how *wonderful* her daughter was.

John seemed content, in a funny sort of way. He had the shop, the little empire, the castle he'd be king of one day. He arrived home from work every evening to home comforts and the absence of his mother's grating voice.

The physical side of their marriage came to an end immediately after Flossie announced her pregnancy. John's paternal instincts exploded. His wife and unborn child were the most precious things to him during those few months. Flossie enjoyed the special treatment, the morning cups of tea in bed, cocoa in the evenings. She didn't mind when John insisted they abstain from sex at such a delicate time. It seemed the natural thing to do. However, it didn't resume after Benny was born and her aspirations for a normal sexual relationship with her husband gradually dissolved into a dreary life of celibacy. She didn't know which was more unbearable: a marriage of celibacy or dull, rigid sex between two people who shared no passion, no understanding of each other's bodies, and no desire for each other. But she didn't dwell on it; she had much to be grateful for, or so she told herself. There were worse inflictions in the world than not being loved. She could be on her own, with her mother. She could be like Catherine, living a life of solitude, never being allowed to marry a mere mortal or have children. She could be living unhappily in Dublin—or *happily*. The what-ifs played on her mind like a scratched record.

Sometimes she envied Catherine, tucked away from the rest of the world in her silent sanctuary, worrying only about who needed her prayers—the sick and dying, the poor and even the rich, all sinners and all lost souls in purgatory. Maybe she'd have prayed for Flossie too, down through the years, if Flossie had been honest with her about the kind of life she lived. Or maybe she prayed for her anyway. Yes, of course she did because that was the type of person she was. Kind, thoughtful, pure. Halfway to heaven, and Danny not far behind her.

She looked forward to Catherine's letters. They radiated her personality, bright and cheerful and earnest. She told humorous stories about her *sisters*. She mentioned a particular novice, Sister Mary, who she'd taken under her wing, in the same way Sister Anne did for her when she was new to the convent.

Flossie had written many letters to Catherine filled with all her woes. She wrote to her about John and their mundane life together. She wrote all about Frank Connolly and how she dreamed about him, how she wished he had never met Alice. She told her how she still felt ashamed of what she did, but wasn't certain she wouldn't do it again if given the chance. She confessed her sinful thoughts and desires to her sister, the nun, who might pray hard for her. She folded all those letters and kept them in a black and white striped box. Other letters she wrote to Sister Catherine—the ones she posted—were embellished with elaborations and untruths.

CHAPTER TWENTY-FOUR

Alice received scornful looks from the two women in Law's paper shop as she plodded past them and slid through the pub door. Mr Law whistled as he rattled empty bottles behind the bar. The late afternoon regulars sat on high stools in their cloud of smoke: Jemmie in his mucky wellies as usual, and a bag of shopping at his feet; Ned, sitting opposite, his back so bent that he faced the floor; Eddie the Crow, with his mop of jet-black hair and long pointy nose, puffing on his long draw pipe. The sweet aroma of Mellow Virginia mingled with the farmyard stench of Jemmie's wellies. They barely looked Alice's way as she snaked into the snug.

She plonked herself down on the long, narrow seat against the wall. Light streamed in from the backyard window above her. The small, shiny table smelled of lemon polish—a subtle hint that four o'clock was indeed too early to be sitting in a pub, especially on Holy Thursday. She shrugged, wondering why Peggy even bothered polishing the place because it took only one cigarette and one woman drenched in cheap perfume to eradicate the lemony scent. She lit up a cigarette and slowly inhaled the nicotine deep into her craving lungs. She opened her purse and took out a slim roll of money. She divided it equally, putting one half in her pocket and the other half back in her purse.

Mr Law came to the hatch.

'The usual?' he asked, holding up a bottle of stout.

'Yes, and a Jameson along with it,' she answered as she handed him a pound note.

He returned with the opened bottle and a measure of Jameson whiskey. He counted out her change. 'Don't spend it all in here now,' he said.

Alice waited, drumming her fingers on Peggy's polished table. She looked down at her new slip-on shoes, admiring the little bow on them. Then she heard the distinct nasal voice of Peter Stanley, ordering a rum and black. His shadowy frame sat at the bar directly behind the frosted window of the snug. Alice sipped her whiskey. She took a long pull of her cigarette, then rested it in the ashtray. She took her red lipstick out of her bag and, with no mirror for direction, she blindly applied a layer of it to her thin lips. She kept her gaze on the window until he moved to the door.

He pushed it open and stepped inside, closing it tight behind him. He put his drink on the table and sat down on a stool opposite Alice.

'We're not to meet here anymore,' he said as he clicked his fingers and opened his hand.

'Why not?' Alice pushed the roll of notes across the table.

'People are too nosey around here... that's why. And keep your voice down.'

'Where can we meet then?'

'You're ten shillings short here,' he said as he counted again.

'He wouldn't give it all this time. He said I owed him for stuff on tick.'

'Not my problem, Alice. Hand it over.'

She took out her purse and flicked his money across the table.

'Is that why you ran outta the shop like a bloody eejit last Friday? Because you owe him money?'

'Eh... yeah,' she said. She lifted her foot out from under the table. 'D'ya like me new shoes? I'm only after buying them for Easter.'

'Aye, they're lovely.'

'You didn't even look.'

'Haven't time. Gotta go.'

'What if some day he won't pay up? Then what?'

'He won't stop. Not as long as his auld fella's still alive.'

'When do I get to know everything? 'Tis not fair that I'm the one doing all the running.'

'Because I don't trust you enough to tell you everything.'

'You're a little dose,' she said.

'Oh, shut up.'

'Tell me more about auld O'Malley's will.'

'Maybe next time.'

It irritated Alice not knowing the full story. 'I think I should be getting more of a cut from this whole thing.'

'Don't get cocky, Alice, or you might get more than you bargained for.'

'Oh, keep your hair on. I'm only codding.'

'Good girl,' he replied, giving her a steely glare.

She leaned forward with her elbows on the table. She put

the cigarette to her flirtatious lips and gently pulled on it. 'Are you staying the night?' She blew the smoke provocatively in his face.

'Not tonight. Have to head home. I'm in Dublin tomorrow.' He downed his rum and stood up to button his coat.

'So when are we meeting again?'

'Don't know. You're to put the money in there behind the picture like the old arrangement we had. And if you see my car parked outside the hotel, it means I'm staying the night. Leave a note with the money if you can meet up.'

'But where can we meet?'

'Maybe down in the woods.'

'Sure loads of people would see us down there.'

'Not if we're careful. We don't have to go together, just meet there. Plenty of hiding places. I went down for a dander a couple of weeks ago to check it out.'

'Suppose.' *It was better than nothing.* Alice wanted more than the odd fumble with this man. She had a real hankering for him.

'Happy Easter, Mrs Connolly. See you soon.'

'Stop calling me that!' She watched him disappear through the snug door.

Alice put her hand through the hatch and rapped the counter. 'Is Peggy in the back?'

'Aye, go on in,' said Mr Law. 'And don't stay all day.'

§

'People'll start gossiping about you and that salesman, y'know,' said Peggy as she opened two bottles of Guinness.

'Gossip about what? Sure we're only talking.'

'Sitting in the snug with him in the middle of the day. Doesn't look right.'

'I said we're just talking. It's no one's business,' Alice said. 'Anyway, it won't be happening again.'

'You should be at home with those wee girls of yours, not in here boozing.'

'They're alright. They're on the farm with Josey.'

'That's not the point. We'll have this one drink and off you go.'

Peggy sat on her armchair beside the open log fire and Alice sat cross-legged on the rug in front. Alice liked conversations with Peggy. She listened to Alice, even when she complained about Frank and the children, and even though Peggy scolded her betimes, Alice didn't resent her for it. She felt that Peggy cared about her in a way, but she didn't know why. Maybe because she had known her mother when they were in national school. She told Alice that her mother was a timid child, cried at the slightest thing, and because of that, she got picked on and teased. Alice couldn't understand why her mother didn't grow up to be a strong woman. Why she never stood up for her children, protected them. Instead, she took tablets that made her sleep. When she was asleep, she couldn't keep Alice safe. Why couldn't she have been more like Peggy?

'Why had you no childer, Peggy?' Alice asked.

'God's will.'

'I think you would've been a good mother.'

'I think so too.'

'I'm shite at it,' said Alice. 'My mother once said that having boys was easier. Maybe if Rose and Nancy were boys, I'd be better.'

Peggy's eyes softened. 'If you want to be a better mother, start off by staying out of the pubs. And try not to get so mad all the time.'

'I can't help it. I can't do anything right for them. I go to the pub to get away from them because they're better without me.'

'If every mother did that every time the child drove them mad, the pubs would be full of women with no room for the men.'

'The funny thing is, when I'm away from them I can feel them, in here,' Alice pressed her hand against her tummy, 'like they're back inside me. Then I try not to think about them. Why's that, Peggy?'

'Because deep down you love them. I think maybe you're afraid of that. Afraid of being a mother and all the work it takes. Think about that the next time you get mad at them. Don't run away.'

Caving in her chest, Alice picked at the label on her Guinness bottle. She spoke quietly. 'He despises me.'

'Who?' asked Peggy.

'Frank. I think if I'd given him sons, he'd be happier.'

'Frank dotes on those girls.'

'Well, he doesn't dote on me, does he?'

Peggy poked at the smouldering wood in the grate. 'The courtship is when the doting and all that malarky takes place. You've a good husband there, Alice. Think of your poor mother and the brute she ended up with.'

Alice did think about her mother, but frustration and bitterness blighted any feelings of empathy she may have had towards her.

CHAPTER TWENTY-FIVE

Rose and Nancy spent as much time as possible playing in the babby house. They had it all done up to their liking. The hollows in the tree had become shelves, where they kept old food tins and jars filled with shiny red and green haws. A broken clock hung on the stub of a branch, and two rusty enamel mugs sat on their stove, which consisted of four red bricks stacked into a square.

Max sat guard at the plank while the girls played inside. He growled at Alice whenever she came near, so she hollered out their names from the yard when she needed them.

On Easter Saturday evening, Rose and Nancy looked forward to attending the Easter Cludog the following day. Josey gave them two eggs to take with them for cooking on the fire. They had to keep them hidden from their mother as she didn't see the sense in an Easter Cludog. Max's barking turned to a disgruntled snarl as Alice yelled from the house.

'Rose. Nancy. Bath.'

'Let's go, Nancy. Leave the eggs here so Mammy won't see them.'

They wrapped their eggs in moss and hid them in the tea chest. Alice called again and the girls hurried. Rose smiled at her sister as they walked down the field. 'I can't wait until tomorrow.'

'Tell me again about the Easter Cludog,' Nancy said.

Rose laughed. 'Again?'

'But I forget.'

'Okay. Well, it'll be great fun. We'll cook our eggs on the big bonfire in Farrell's field, and everyone will be dancing and singing. Daddy wanted to bring you last year, but Mammy said he couldn't mind you properly.'

'Can he mind me now?'

'Course he can. Mammy's not coming because she thinks it's silly. I'm glad she's not coming.'

'I'm glad too,' said Nancy. 'She holds my hand too tight and makes me walk fast.'

'Imagine if we had a different mammy.'

'When will Daddy be home?' Nancy's pace slowed.

'I don't know. He's milking the cows with Uncle Josey.' Rose hated bath time, but Nancy feared it.

The tin bath sat on the kitchen floor, half filled with warm water. Alice knelt beside it, waiting. The girls shivered as they both got in together. Alice washed Rose's hair vigorously and rinsed it with jugs of the soiled water, unconcerned about getting soap in her eyes or water in her mouth. Rose had learned how to hold her breath and keep her eyes shut tight.

Nancy whined. 'I want Daddy to wash my hair.'

'Remember, Nancy,' said Rose. 'Close your eyes tight and hold your breath, like I showed you.'

Alice soaped Nancy's slight body with a bar of carbolic

soap, moving it up the back of her neck and onto her head. She rubbed the hard bar round and round until she had built up a thick pink lather. Then she scrubbed the child's scalp with the pads of her fingers, digging them in, pulling them through the knotty hair.

Rose kept her eyes on Nancy's screwed up face, willing her not to cry. Alice raised a jug of water above her head.

'Don't cry, Nancy,' Rose said softly.

'She won't cry. It's only water. Can't have you growing up to be a big softie,' Alice said.

She poured jug after jug of water over Nancy's head, holding it high in the air so that it splashed down with force. Nancy spluttered. Alice held one hand on the child's shoulder and continued to pour jugs of water over her. Nancy's rigid arms reached out to her sister. She cried out, 'Daddy!'

'Don't be such a baby,' Alice said and continued to drench the screaming child.

Frank burst in the door. 'What the hell are you doing, Alice? I could hear her screaming from the lane.'

Alice got up from her knees. 'Ah, she's being a big baby. I'm only washing her hair.'

'She is a baby, you stupid woman! She's bloody four years of age. Get out!'

'She needs to toughen up. You have them spoilt.' She whipped off her apron and stormed out the door, banging it hard behind her.

Frank lifted Nancy out of the bath and wrapped her in a towel. His whole body tensed as he hugged his little girl tight to his chest, consoling her with hush words to ease her sobs.

He felt like something was about to explode inside his throbbing head.

He sat with his girls until bedtime, and until his thumping headache subsided. He shuddered as he thought about the way Alice treated them—especially the children. *Why did he let her do it? Why didn't he stand up to her?*

'Sing the song about me, Daddy,' Rose said as he lay them both in their bed.

'*Red is the rose that yonder garden grows. Fair is the lily of the valley. Clear is the water that flows from the Boyne. But my love is fairer than any...*' He closed his eyes and thought about Flossie O'Malley.

CHAPTER TWENTY-SIX

Frank woke early on Easter Sunday morning. Alice wasn't in the bed and he wondered—but didn't care—where she'd gone after she left the house the previous evening. He shook off his sombre thoughts and leapt out of bed, forcing enthusiasm upon himself. He always loved Easter.

He pounded down the stairs and went into the sitting room to get his cigarettes. Alice lay on the couch still fully dressed, but missing a shoe. Thin strands of hair veiled her pasty face, her slightly parted lips speckled with bread-crumbs, a half-eaten slice of bread in her hand. She looked like a corpse, thought Frank. *Pity she wasn't.*

He got the girls up, fed and dressed them, and brought them to Mass. They were excited about the Cludog and chattered the whole way there.

§

Judgmental eyes bored into Frank as he took their usual seat at the back of the church. Easter Sunday and his wife didn't make it out to Mass—again. Not that he cared what people thought. At least, that was what he told himself.

He watched Flossie O'Malley, as he did every Sunday. Watching her was all he allowed himself to do. In over five years he hadn't spoken to her, or she to him. They avoided each other when possible. Any time they met unexpectedly, they behaved like strangers.

Every Sunday at Mass, Frank reminisced about the evening they'd made love in his brother's house. His spine would tingle as he'd remember how she took his breath away. He'd yearned to be with her every day since, but he knew he never could. She had a good life with the O'Malleys and her little son. He couldn't ruin things for her. They lived in the same town, but they were worlds apart.

Rose and Nancy always got restless towards the end of Mass. Frank welcomed communion time. He remained seated until Flossie received communion, as always. On the way back down to her seat she caught his eye, as she did every Sunday. He mentally stroked her peachy face and kissed her tender lips. He took pleasure in the way she tormented him in his fantasy affair—always in his head, during the day as he worked, in his dreams while he slept, and here at Mass.

§

Frank and the girls took their time walking home from Mass. Nancy asked the same questions about the Cludog as she did on the way there. Frank looked forward to getting away for the day, even if it was only to sit in a field full of children.

Alice had cooked up a pot of leek soup and roasted two lamb shanks for their Easter Sunday dinner. The room was filled with tension and the girls had even stopped talking about the Cludog. They ate their dinner quickly and disappeared up to the babby house to get their eggs.

§

The bonfire was blazing when Frank and the girls arrived at Farrell's field. The Daly boys danced round it, singing rebel songs and Father Tierney frowned, insisting that they sing something more appropriate for Easter.

'How about *Amazing Grace*?' he asked.

The Dalys, not impressed with the priest butting in, changed their tune from *Kevin Barry* to *God Save Ireland*. Father Tierney shook his fist at them and looked up to the heavens.

Frank took off his coat and lay it on the mossy ground. The girls discarded their own coats beside him. The sun shone, but the grey clouds threatened rain. Frank sat on his coat, watching Rose and Nancy playing with the other children, forgetting about his latest fight with Alice. He loved to see them laugh.

'Hello, Frank.' He recognised the soft voice. He turned his head, squinting as the sun blinded him.

'Hello,' he replied, standing up to get a better look.

'Flossie, how are you?'

'I'm okay. I came over to say hello. Maybe meet your wee girls, seeing as they're starting school in September,' she said. 'Benny here is starting too.'

His thumping heart echoed in his ears. He was certain she would hear it. He put his hand to his chest, as if to silence it, but it seemed louder. 'You're a grand little fella.' He offered Benny a handshake.

'I'm four and a half,' Benny replied.

'Well, what I meant to say was, you're a grand *big* fella.'

Benny grinned and shook the strange man's hand.

'That's Nancy over there. The wee, dark-haired one with the green cardigan. Can't see Rose; she's there somewhere.' Frank's face gleamed with pride as he pointed over at the group of children painting eggs. 'Are you sitting down?'

She looked back towards the people she came with. 'I better not abandon them yet. We've only just arrived. Wouldn't want to get into Miss Kennedy's bad books. I'll come back over in a while if that's okay?'

'Of course. See you in a while then.'

Her lily scent lingered. He inhaled it deep into his lungs, held it for a moment before slowly releasing it back into the air. He tried not to look in her direction, but he couldn't stop himself. She still looked so beautiful. Her hair reminded him of pale brown sugar, the way parts of it shimmered in the light, like tiny golden pearls.

After years of distant glimpses of her in town and stolen moments at Mass every Sunday, seeing her up so close reminded him of his teenage self, talking to his crush for the first time. His head spun with a jumble of thoughts: John O'-Malley, Alice, Rose, Nancy, kissing Flossie. *Cop yourself on, Connolly.*

When the fire died down, the children carefully placed their eggs into the red-hot embers for roasting. They sat around watching, some poking at the burning wood in a bid to hurry up the cooking process.

'Quit poking at it, Tessie McGuirk,' Pat Daly said.

'You're not the boss, Daly,' she replied. He lunged at her. She jumped up and ran round the fire screaming. He caught her, knocking her off-balance, and they both tumbled down the grassy hill, Daly laughing out loud and Tessie giggling.

Miss Kennedy tutted and scrambled after the pair. She pulled Tessie up by the arm. 'Stop that nonsense and get back up there. Wait until I tell your mother the carry-on of you. Have a bit of manners, especially on a Sunday,' she said.

'See ya tamarra, Messy Tessie,' Daly said

Tessie turned and stuck her tongue out at him, grinning. Miss Kennedy gave her another shove up the hill.

Frank laughed, remembering his school days and the fun he and Josey used to have flirting with the girls. They had the best fun with the ones who let on they had no interest, like Messy Tessie. The glint in her eyes showed that she fancied Pat Daly like mad, and he fancied her back. *Blind fools*, thought Frank.

§

Flossie was chatting with Miss Kennedy. The wind blew softly against her long flowing skirt, showing off the shape of her thighs. She turned her head swiftly, casting her eyes in Frank's direction. He wondered what went on in her mind. She turned back to Miss Kennedy, pulling her cardigan tight around her. Nancy ran towards her daddy with Tessie's little sister, Jenny.

'Daddy, can we have our spoon now? The eggs are ready. The man over there said they were.' She put her hand into Frank's shirt pocket, frantically seeking out the one spoon they had to share. 'Jenny has no spoon. Can she share ours too?'

'She sure can. Now, go get Rose and come straight back.'

The three girls sat on their coats, eagerly shelling their eggs.

'Jenny's big sister said that lady over there's going to be our teacher when we go to school,' Rose said.

'Her name's Mrs O'Malley and I think she looks nice. She smiled at me and I smiled back,' said Jenny.

Warmth spread through Frank, despite goosebumps prickling his skin since the sun disappeared behind a menacing grey cloud.

'So, Nancy, do you like the Cludog?'

'I like the big fire the best. I don't like Brenda 'cause she said I can't go to school 'cause I'm only three. And I said I can go 'cause I'll be four tomorrow and my mammy said I had to go anyway. I told Brenda I don't like her.'

'Never mind her. You're a clever wee girl and you'll pass her out in no time, so you will.'

'Why did I not go when I was four?' Rose asked.

Ignoring the question, Frank took a small brown paper bag from his coat pocket and shook it in the air. 'Guess what I have. Who's finished all their egg?'

The girls giggled. 'Guess what I have' always meant he had sweets.

'Uncle Josey sent a surprise. What's your favourite sweet in the whole world?'

'Penny bars!' Rose and Nancy said together and quickly dug into their roasted eggs.

'Hey, that's not fair. It's my turn to have the spoon,' Jenny said as Rose refused to hand it over. Nancy used her fingers to peel the eggshell away, as she had done many times before.

Frank gave the girls their chewy slabs of toffee, giving Jenny the one that was meant for him.

'Did you stay off sweets all during Lent, Jenny?'

'I did, but my sister didn't. I found her eating a Peggy's Leg up at the gooseberry bushes and she said she'd kill me if I told, so I didn't tell,' Jenny said firmly.

'Ah, you're a good girl.' Frank ruffled her short spiky hair.

'Daddy, the woman who's our teacher is coming over. I don't want to talk to her,' said Nancy.

'There's a boy holding her hand. Is he hers?' asked Rose.

'Yes and his name is Benny. He's around your age.'

Flossie smiled at the children. Nancy frowned.

'Hello, everybody, are you having fun?'

'You're going to be our teacher and I like you, but Nancy doesn't. She doesn't like anyone and cries all the time,' said Rose.

Nancy covered her face with her hands. Flossie moved closer to Nancy, still holding Benny's hand. 'This is Benny and he'll be going to your school.'

Nancy peeped through her fingers but stayed firmly rooted to the ground.

'Do you want the rest of my penny bar?' Rose offered Benny her last piece that looked like it had already been chewed. He refused and hid behind his mother. Rose popped it into her mouth and sat back down beside Jenny, who stared cautiously at the strange woman.

'Sorry about Nancy. She's a bit shy, that's all,' Frank said.

'Sure this fella's the same sometimes too. Don't worry. She'll settle in at school quick enough. It's still only March. A few months can make a big difference to a child.'

'I suppose you're right. I'm sure she'll be fine.'

'I'll take good care of them for you,' Flossie said.

'I'm sure you will.'

Flossie glanced at the children, who were sitting in a circle, engrossed in eating their toffee bars. 'Can we stop ignoring each other, Frank? It's been a long time.'

'Yes, too long. The past is in the past,' he said. 'You look well, Flossie.'

'Thanks.' She smiled. 'I'll see you around then?'

'See you around. Girls, say goodbye to Mrs O'Malley.'

Jenny and Rose said goodbye; Nancy gave a little wave. Benny jumped up and skipped towards his mother. She took his hand tenderly as she looked down on his smiling face, just as a mother would be expected to do. Frank wondered why motherly love didn't come easy to Alice. Did she know how to love at all? Could she be fixed? His heart sank for his daughters. They deserved so much more than the life he had brought them into.

The evening turned chilly and people were making a move towards home. The girls ran back to the fire as soon as Frank mentioned home time. He followed, carrying their coats.

'Can we please stay longer?' asked Rose.

'It'll soon be dark, everyone else is going too,' he said. 'Coats on please.'

The grey sky spat down droplets of rain. Frank hoped it wouldn't come on until they were home. He preferred when

Easter fell in the warmer month of April. He looked around the near empty field, hoping to steal another glimpse of Flossie before he left, but she was nowhere to be seen. He was pleased they were talking again and he knew he had to stop dwelling on what could have been.

§

Frank carried Nancy most of the way home. Rose preferred to walk alongside him, holding his hand, insisting she was too big to be carried. He whistled a tune as he dawdled in the Wood Lane, taking a deep breath as the sweet aroma of the damp soil hovered in the air. The sound of Flossie's silvery voice collided with every thought in his head. Nothing had changed as far as his feelings for her were concerned. He was still in love with her.

Nancy's grip tightened around her daddy's neck as they walked in the front gate of their house. Alice sat on the doorstep, swaying from side to side. She looked up with one eye closed and sniggered.

'Ah, look at the gypsies home at last. C'mere 'til I smell the smoke of yas,' she said.

'Come on girls, in we go,' Frank said, walking swiftly past Alice towards the back door. She flicked her cigarette butt after them, scattering red ash in their path. Her heavy steps loomed. 'Don't walk away from me,' she said as she picked up a piece of a broken clay flower pot. She fired it towards Frank.

He stumbled forward, startled by a sudden sharp pain in the back of his head. 'What the hell are you doing?' He turned to face Alice.

Another piece whizzed past, missing Rose by an inch.

Frank hurried the girls up the grassy field and ushered them into their babby house. 'Don't move from here,' he said. 'I'll be back in a minute.' Nancy sobbed and Rose wrapped her arms around her.

He took long strides back down the field, wiping a trickle of blood from behind his ear. His mouth was dry and his jaw was rigid. The dog barked furiously in the coal house, where Alice often put him. Frank unbolted the door and Max scampered up to the babby house. The wireless blared from the kitchen. He stormed into the smoky kitchen. The smell of alcohol stifled him. 'Where's the brats?' Alice said as she stumbled past him, making her way to the table.

'How dare you!' He gritted his teeth and pounded the table with his fist. 'What did they ever do to you?'

'They're all you ever think about. You do nothing for me and everything for them.'

'What kind of mother is jealous of her own children?'

'I am not jealous.'

He clenched his fists and paced the floor. 'I've been so patient with you, Alice. You get your own way all the time. I've always done everything I could for you, but you treat me like a dog, worse than a dog. I'm not putting up with it anymore.'

'Oh, shut up and don't be such a sissy,' she said.

'What the hell is wrong with you?' Frank lifted the empty whiskey bottle from the sideboard. 'Where did you get this from?'

Her glassy eyes pierced his.

'You're bloody mad. I rue the day I ever met ya.' Frank grabbed the kitchen towel to wipe the blood that trickled down the back of his neck, slamming the door on his way out.

'Coward!' she shouted after him, reaching for her Woodbines. 'All men are cowards,' she said, fumbling with the box of cigarettes.

CHAPTER TWENTY-SEVEN

July was Frank's favourite month. Bright fresh mornings made cycling to work easier and the long warm evenings meant more time away from the house. Just him and the girls, away from Alice.

They spent most evenings down in the woods. They played hide-and-seek in the trees and pretended to be bears or some other wild animal. Frank fished while they played. They stayed out until Nancy got tired, and Frank always had to carry her home. Rose always seemed to have more energy than her little sister.

Sometimes Alice was off visiting Joyce Rafferty or sitting in the back room of Law's pub with Peggy. When she had money, she went straight to one of the pubs. On those evenings, Frank always made sure he and the girls were in bed before she got home. The less he saw of Alice, the less rows they had.

Rose and Nancy spent a lot of time in Josey's, especially when there was a baby calf or newly hatched chicks to tend to. His orchard flourished during the summer months and after one or two belly aches, the girls learned the consequences of eating too many gooseberries and crab apples. Instead, Josey, who was a keen jam maker, promised them pocket money for gathering the fruit in basins when they were ripe enough for preserving. He sold his pots of jam to some of the grocers' shops in town, paying the girls from his small profit.

§

Rose scurried down the stairs and into the kitchen while Nancy dawdled behind. 'It's Saturday. Are we going fishing, Daddy?' Rose asked.

'We sure are. Is Nancy up? We need to get out nice and early if we want to get our favourite spot at the lake.'

'She's coming, with her eyes closed.'

Frank poured hot tea into a large lemonade bottle to have with their picnic. He covered it with a thick sock to keep it warm. He cut three generous slices of brown bread and spread them with plenty of Josey's rhubarb jam and wrapped them in brown paper. He had apples and gooseberries—also from Josey—a tin of spam and a tin opener. He packed them into an old biscuit tin.

Alice was outside checking on the sow and her two-week-old piglets. Frank watched her for a moment through the window. He couldn't imagine Flossie shuffling around in a pigsty the way Alice did, talking to them like they were puppies. She didn't stink of drink and cigarettes like Alice did either. She smelled like Josey's garden—roses and apples. He tried not to think too much about Flossie, but it was hard not to, especially on the days when Alice threw things at him, spat at him, and called him names.

Rose and Nancy skipped ahead of Frank as they headed down the lane towards the woods. Rose carried their two hazelwood fishing rods, while Nancy hugged the jar of worms. Frank drew a deep breath, welcoming the smell of freshly cocked hay in Josey's field. Only a few days ago, the same field was littered with shiny meadow buttercups, most of which would reappear when the grass grew again. He bent down and picked a buttercup from the grassy verge. He twirled it between his thumb and forefinger. Five heart-shaped petals created the illusion of a delicate little flower. The hard lump in the middle, hidden by tiny feathery spikes, showed that really it was a hardy little thing. Interesting and pretty to look at for a while, a buttercup, but toxic to the cattle. They knew to avoid the weed, but if there was nothing else available, they might be tempted to eat one.

Frank pulled off the petals one by one, and then he removed the feathery spikes, until the only thing left was a hard yellow ball on a wobbly little stem, naked and exposed for all to see. Frank threw the fragmented flower into the ditch. Alice was a buttercup. Frank preferred roses.

§

'I'll be the first to catch a fish,' Rose said as they set up their spot by the lake.

'I will,' said Nancy, handing the worms to her daddy.

'Mine will be bigger than yours anyway. I'm better than you are.'

'No, you're not! Daddy, Rose won't leave me alone.'

'Are yas trying to scare the fish away? Stop that fighting or we'll go home.'

The dew dried up as the sun got higher in the sky. Frank moved Nancy and Rose under some hanging branches where it was cooler; it was going to be a hot one. The fish were slow to take, but the girls weren't at all bothered. Being at the lake was enough for them. Soon they would abandon their rods and disappear into the trees.

Voices echoed around the woods. A lot of young boys fished in Castle Lake on Saturdays, some with their friends, others with their fathers. For the older ones, the lake was a place to take their girlfriends for a romantic picnic, usually followed by a walk through the secluded parts of the wood.

Frank emptied what was left of the worms into the palm of his hand. His heart wasn't in it today. The girls, bored already with their fishing rods, were paddling in the shallows nearby.

'Maybe your bait's not fat enough, Mr Connolly.'

'Well, if it isn't the schoolteacher. I didn't hear you creeping up on me.'

'I wasn't creeping at all. We couldn't pass by without saying hello, could we, Benny?'

'Hello there, young fellow. Do you want to have a go with the fishing rod?'

Benny nodded his head, taking the child-sized rod.

'First we have to put a worm on the hook,' Frank said. 'Then the fish will try to eat the worm, and when he does, he'll get caught on your hook.'

The girls kept their distance at first. 'Is it lunchtime, Daddy?' asked Rose.

'Yes, is it?' Nancy said.

They scurried over, looking the teacher and her boy up and down.

'Hello, girls. Nice to see you again,' said Flossie.

Nancy scurried behind her daddy, her wet toes peeping out from the side of his wellies. 'Hello, Miss,' Rose said. 'My tooth is wobbly, look.' Rose pushed her front tooth forward with her tongue.

'Oh, that'll soon fall out,' Flossie said.

'I have marbles in my pocket,' Benny said. He reached into the pocket of his shorts and took out two shiny green marbles. Nancy peered out from her hiding place, then slowly edged her way over to Benny, keeping her eyes on his open palm.

'Can I have one?' asked Rose.

'No!' He put them back in his pocket.

Rose picked up her fishing rod and took Benny by the hand. 'I'll show you how to go fishing. I'm the best at fishing and my daddy's the best fisherman in the world, so he is,' she said. Nancy followed them.

'Stay where I can see you, Benny,' Flossie said. 'He's not used to the water. Is it deep?'

'It's shallow there. We'll keep an eye on them,' Frank said.

'Okay.' She folded her arms and kept her eyes on the children.

Frank held up the bottle of tea. 'There might be an extra cup of tea in here, if you want to stay for a while. The girls don't take much.'

'Okay, if we're not in the way.'

'You're not in the way. Sit down beside that tree where it's shaded.'

Flossie folded her cardigan and placed it on the soft

ground at the base of the smooth tree trunk. The sun spiked through the willowy branches; there wasn't a breeze. Frank poured tea into his mug and gave it to her. She was as beautiful as ever. He struggled to keep his eyes off her. They were doing nothing wrong, he assured himself.

'It's far from a china cup, I'm afraid, but it's all I have.'

'It's grand.' They laughed and he relaxed.

The girls arrived back with Benny in tow.

'Benny can fish now, Mrs O'Malley. I showed him how. So he can come fishing with us any time he wants,' Rose said.

Flossie smiled. 'That didn't take long.'

'Oh, but we're not finished,' said Nancy.

'Mammy, I was fishing in the lake. The worm is gone now, can I have another one?' Benny looked to Frank, who lay on the grass, propped up on his elbows. He held the child's gaze for a moment; a strange sensation surged through him. Nancy interrupted.

'Can we have our picnic now?' she asked.

Frank's scalp tingled and a shiver ran through him. Benny looked to his mother.

'I need a drink, Mammy.'

'What do you say?'

'Please.'

Flossie took a bottle of diluted orange out of her handbag. 'Share with Rose and Nancy, that's the good boy.'

Frank gave his bread and jam to Benny and shared the gooseberries evenly between them.

'The woods are lovely. Do you come here every week?' Flossie asked.

'Loads and loads of times. Don't we, Daddy?' Nancy

seemed to be warming to Flossie. 'But sometimes Mammy doesn't let us.'

'Will you let Benny come fishing with us every time we go? He's my friend now,' said Rose.

Nancy moved closer to Benny. 'He's my friend too.'

'Well, maybe not every time but some of the time, yes,' Flossie said.

'Who's Benny's daddy?' Rose asked.

Benny answered. 'My daddy's at home in the shop.'

'What's his name?'

'John.' Benny wiped a bit of jam from the side of his mouth with his finger and then licked it off.

Frank glanced at Benny, then at Rose and Nancy. He looked to Flossie. That odd feeling swept over him again. Flossie stood up and handed Frank her empty mug, her face flushed. She clapped her hands as if she were in her classroom and they were all her pupils. 'Okay, everyone, will we play a game? I spy?'

'Flossie, they can't spell.'

She sat down again. She began poking through her handbag. Why was she uncomfortable all of a sudden? Was he overthinking? Surely he was. *Don't go down that road, Connolly.*

'We come here most Saturdays when the weather's good,' Frank answered her earlier question. 'The lad can come surely, if his daddy doesn't mind. I can make him a fishing rod. Plenty of hazel trees down here. They make good sturdy rods.'

Flossie put on a pair of sunglasses that she took from her handbag. 'Why would he mind? I'll bring him down next Saturday and pick him up after an hour or so.'

'I'll bring an extra bottle of tea.' Her smile gave him a feeling of optimism. She lifted his spirits and he would just enjoy it, and not go opening up cans of worms.

CHAPTER TWENTY-EIGHT

For several months, John watched out for Alice. He spent many hours outside the shop, rearranging the boxes of wares, clearing up windswept litter, washing the windows more often than they needed, so he could keep an eye on her movements. He knew what days she came to town, what shops she went to, who she talked to. He watched her dodge up Main Street, poking in display baskets outside shops, looking for bargains. He followed her further up the town a few times to watch her haggle with the Dublin women at their stalls, but she didn't consult with them for any other reason, as far as he could tell. He watched her on the days that he gave her money. Straight to Law's she went, which didn't surprise him.

He also watched Peter Stanley, every second Thursday when he came to town. Sometimes he stayed overnight in Graham's Hotel. Sometimes, he left town the same road he arrived. Other times, he drove out the Cavan Road. Occasionally, he went to Law's—on the same days that Alice got her blackmail money—but later than her, never at the same time. John couldn't connect Alice with Peter Stanley in any way. He couldn't connect her with anybody. Perhaps her ally was someone closer to home and he was barking up the wrong tree with this Stanley man. His jaw ached. His temples throbbed. He felt like leaving the shop and heading for Law's himself, but he wasn't a man for daytime drinking. And neither was he a frequent visitor in any of the pubs in town. He preferred to socialise in city pubs where people minded their own business.

A familiar, friendly voice greeted John and his father from the front door.

'Ah, good man, Roy,' said Frederick. 'Come on in.'

'Was passing through and sure I said I'd call,' Roy said.

Ruth bustled out from the back room. 'I knew I recognised that voice. Lovely to see you, Roy. How's Norah?'

'No bother on her at all.'

'You'll come up for tea?' She gestured towards the stairs.

'I'll not, but thanks.'

'Will I bring you down a cup, then?'

Roy shook his head.

'No, thanks. You might let this man out on Sunday for a round of golf.' He chuckled. 'Keeping him all to yourself, as usual.'

Ruth's face widened as her smile spread from ear to ear, then she burst out into disassembled laughter, well used to Roy's tongue-in-cheek banter. 'He's been busy, haven't you, Frederick?'

Roy squinted towards the open door. 'Well, would you look at who it is.' He darted to the window and peered across the street. 'Haven't seen him in a while.'

Frederick craned his neck as he joined Roy at the window. 'The tobacco man?' he said.

'Is he still at that?' Roy asked.

John walked the length of the counter and looked across the street where he saw Peter Stanley with a cigarette dangling from the side of his mouth, lifting boxes from the boot of his car.

'Do you know him?' John asked.

'I know *of* him. He's married to a daughter of Henry's,' Roy said, raising his eyebrows at Frederick.

'Who's Henry?' John asked.

'Your father and I play golf with him now and again.'

'Henry Butler? The solicitor?' asked John. His pulse quickened, and his eyes burned into Peter Stanley's back like hot pokers.

'Aye. Happy Henry, as they call him in Kells.' Roy laughed as he added, 'Because he's a grumpy auld fecker.'

Frederick mocked Happy Henry. 'Outta ma way, outta ma way.'

'He worked for Henry a few years back, but they had a big fall out,' Roy said, digging his hands into his trouser pockets. 'How long is he at this now?'

'Few years, would you say, John?'

'Six years,' replied John, watching Peter Stanley head into Clarke's with his delivery. 'Why did they fall out?' John tapped his foot on the wooden floor and crossed his arms.

'Don't know but I believe he's a bit of a boyo.'

'Is he now?' John kept his gaze on Stanley's car.

'Norah plays Badminton with a cousin of Henry's, Audrey. Around the time of Peter's wedding—sure, that must be seven or eight years ago—Audrey spoke of Henry's dislike for his new son-in-law. He called him a scrounger. He came round in the end though and even gave him a job in his office. Audrey said it was only so he could keep an eye on him. But after eighteen months or so, he fired him.'

'What did he do?' Frederick asked.

John held his breath and turned to Roy.

'That's the thing, Freddie, nobody knows. According to Audrey, the family's opinion of him changed after that, but that's all she knows about it.'

'No smoke without fire, eh, Roy?'

'I don't like the look of him,' Roy said when Peter Stanley returned to his car. 'There's a slyness in his walk. Wouldn't trust him as far as I'd throw him.'

'Does he live in Navan?' John asked.

'No, he lives outside Dunboyne, on the Dublin Road.'

'Well, thankfully we've no dealings with him here,' Frederick said.

John's heart raced and his limbs prickled as the blood rushed through him. *Dunboyne... Julie's hometown.* John picked up a pencil from the counter and snapped it in half.

CHAPTER TWENTY-NINE

Goretti was gone to one of her meetings, and Flossie was treating herself to a small glass of sherry. John sat at the table showing Benny a map of the United States from his old school atlas. He made it sound very exciting for the boy. He rummaged in the drawer of his writing desk and took out a picture of a Boeing 720.

'See this, Benny? This is an Aer Lingus aeroplane, and if you save up all your money, you'll go to New York in one of these when you grow up. You might even live there.'

Benny clapped and took the newspaper cutting. 'Can I keep it, Daddy?'

'Course you can, son. I'll stick it on your bedroom wall.'

'Grandad said I'll be his shopkeeper when I grow up. Does he not know I'll be going to America in the big aeroplane?'

Flossie didn't want to think about her son emigrating. In fact, she hoped that he would never have to emigrate. She would do her best to make sure he received a good education and got himself a good job, someplace not too far away.

Maybe Dublin. Maybe an accountant, like Jim, or he might even become a doctor. Her mind wandered. Or should he stay at home and be by her side forever? That would be nice. Like John and his mother. Since Benny had been born, she understood her mother-in-law a little better. She understood now why she still treated John like a child sometimes. She could see now how a mother's love for her son grew stronger with each passing day. Surely, that love and the need to protect and nurture continued to grow as the child did. Her own mother came to mind. What kind of love had she in her heart for Danny and Catherine? Did she not feel the desire to have them with her always? Flossie wanted to ask her so many times, but she knew the only thing she'd get from her mother would be a good scolding for being intrusive. Goretti Lynch was a closed book when it came to her feelings.

She turned her attention back to her husband and son, comparing John's fatherly ways to Frank's. John was a good father, teaching Benny the ways of the world, how to count money, how to read well, and often gave him the rundown of Irish history. She once heard him tutoring Benny about the importance of honesty and acceptance. *Remember never to hide from yourself, Benny, and treat everybody the same. And stand up for yourself if anyone ever says you're wrong when you know you're really right.* That conversation took place shortly after his fourth birthday, and the boy hadn't a clue what his daddy was on about. Sometimes John seemed to forget Benny was a child, not a miniature adult.

Frank talked to Rose and Nancy like most people talked to children. He played with them and took them on picnics. He took them fishing. Those wee girls didn't even know that life existed outside Bailieborough. They didn't know what history meant, that half the population had starved to death over a hundred years ago. They weren't told about the coffin ships. Money wasn't something they saw a lot of. Flossie wished for Benny to keep some childhood innocence, but John thought differently.

Flossie tapped her fingers on the side of her armchair. She took a gulp of sherry rather than her usual small sip. 'How was work today?'

'Same as usual.' John looked at her over the rim of his glasses. 'Why?'

'Just asking. We were in the woods today, Benny and me.'

'Daddy, are there fish in America?' Benny asked. 'The girl showed me how to go fishing today and her daddy's making me a fishing stick all of my own.'

'Yes, there's fish in America. Who's this man that's making you a fishing stick?' John kept his eyes on Benny.

Flossie answered, knowing the question was directed at her. 'We met Frank Connolly and his two wee girls. They were fishing, and the one who's the same age as Benny showed him how to use her fishing rod.'

John crossed his legs and cleared his throat.

'John, I'll be their teacher soon and their auntie is my best friend. It's nice that Benny has made friends with them.'

She wished John didn't squirm at every mention of the Connollys. Yes, he knew she'd held a torch for Frank before they were married, but that was all he knew. So, he had no real reason to dislike Frank. 'In fact, they invited him to go again next Saturday, and I said yes. I'll leave him there and then I'll go back and pick him up after a couple of hours.'

'I like fishing,' said Benny.

'Okay. I suppose it'll do him good. And by the way, I'll be in Dublin next Monday.'

'Again? But you were there on Wednesday.'

'You'll hardly miss me, will you?'

Flossie didn't answer.

CHAPTER THIRTY

It suited John that his father no longer had any interest in traipsing up and down to Dublin—especially in the winter months—dealing and haggling with the wholesalers. He said he'd done it for long enough and it was his son's role now. So he rarely questioned him about how often he did or didn't go. As long as John arrived back with stock for the shop, he could go as often as he liked. John also knew that if he took a box of shirts from the storeroom and put them into the boot of his car to pass them off as new stock, his father wouldn't notice.

So with the box of shirts in the boot, John didn't need to go near the city. He could go straight to Julie and Alfie's. He drove along Chapelizod Road with his windows down, a soft breeze fanning his clammy skin. A colourful gathering of parishioners mingled outside the Nativity of the Blessed Virgin Mary Church. The women behaved like excited children waiting for a parade, showing off their fancy frocks and high-styled hair and hats. Cars drove in the church gates with red ribbons tied across their bonnets. Weddings brought smiles and gaiety to all involved... usually.

John remembered his own wedding day. A day of mixed emotions. A day of lies—for both of them—but it had served its purpose. He got his wife because he needed one, and Flossie got a husband because the man she loved married another. He supposed he should be grateful to Alice for that much. He had no doubt in his mind that he'd still be looking for a wife if Flossie hadn't been available.

And little Benny happened sooner than he anticipated. He was the icing on the cake... until John began to suspect that he wasn't the boy's father at all. He'd heard Flossie talking to Benny in the garden when the boy was just a toddler. John had been on his way to join them but froze in the doorway when he heard her words.

'You have your daddy's eyes,' she told Benny as she tied his little blue bonnet under his chin. Then she kissed him on the forehead, and he giggled. John stepped back into the hallway and partially closed the door. *What was she talking about? Had his ears deceived him?* He took off his glasses and faced the mirror on the wall. His dark eyes, the colour of chocolate, protruded under thick black eyebrows. Benny's unfledged and innocent round eyes were blue like his mammy's.

John didn't confront Flossie and carried on loving Benny with every ounce of his heart. As the years passed, he studied the child's mannerisms, his personality, his hair, the shape of his face. He knew in his heart that Benny was Frank Connolly's son.

Since Benny's birth, the man's name hadn't been mentioned in their house. Until now! *Why is she back in*

Connolly's life? Why now? Does he know about Benny? Has she told him? Panic and dread filled John. Even if she didn't tell him, he'd guess. He'd see himself in the lad... sure he was getting more like him every day. Connolly wasn't stupid.

John had to be patient. Trying to stop Flossie from taking Benny fishing with the Connollys wasn't the answer—not yet, at least. He had a lot of thinking to do. He put it all to the back of his mind for the time being.

§

Although certain elements of Chapelizod reminded John of Bailieborough, he rarely thought of home when he was there. He wanted the urban Dublin village to be his home someday; it's where he preferred to be. Especially on days like this. Days when that dark cloud of deceit and lies hung over him. He pushed it away and slowed down a bit. It could almost be a perfect day. The sun shone and the villagers displayed a mood of blitheness as they went about their morning, in no hurry to get to wherever they were going. Little girls in short summer dresses, and boys in shorts and tee-shirts, squinted at each other as they licked ice lollies.

As John crossed the Anna Livia Bridge, he breathed in the pungent River Liffey and smiled. He remembered happy days with Alfie, sitting on the bank nestled among the bracken, a private place without interference from the outside world, where walkers walked on by, unconcerned about the lives of others.

He turned left at The Bridge Inn onto St. Laurence's Road. A small crowd gathered outside a narrow red brick house on Liffey Terrace where a young woman in a white lacy wedding dress emerged with her father. Her bouquet of red roses complimented her pink cheeks. She caught his eye. He recognised her as the assistant in the book shop two streets away. He smiled and she smiled back. He envied her, standing alongside her proud father, radiating happiness and optimism for the future with her prospective husband. He wished her well and hoped life treated her kindly. Of course, life wasn't that simple.

John pulled up outside Julie's house, a modest white-washed bungalow with a short set of steps leading up to the red door that was placed between two bulging bay windows. Neat little lawns on each side of the steps displayed an array of disorderly planted shrubs and flowers. Julie's bicycle balanced on its stand on the path in front of the black metal gate that led to the back yard. As he walked up the primrose-bordered steps, the window opened.

'You're early,' Julie called as she popped her head out the window.

'Can't keep away.' He smirked. Julie opened the door and John strode in.

'Tea?'

'Have you any lemonade? I'm parched.'

She took a bottle of red lemonade from the fridge and poured two glasses. 'Wanna sit out back?' she asked, handing him his drink.

They sat under the cherry blossom tree that shaded a small, round cast-iron table. Two matching chairs were made more comfortable with the addition of blue gingham cushions. John took a long drink from his glass, almost draining it in one go. He took a deep breath.

'So come on... tell me. What's wrong?' Julie rested her legs on an old wooden box, crossing one over the other.

He narrowed his eyes. 'Do you know a man called Peter Stanley?'

'Why?'

'It's important, Julie. Do you?' John crossed his legs and drummed his fingers on the table.

'I know a Peter Stanley from Dunboyne, if that's who you mean. Don't care much for him, if you want to know.'

'Why not?'

'Can you bloody tell me why you want to know?' Julie pushed the box away from her feet and stood up. She took a box of Carroll's cigarettes from the windowsill and lit one. She sat again, lying back in the chair with her legs crossed.

'Just asking. Do you know where he works?'

'John, I haven't seen him in a while. I have no idea where he works. I don't know him as well as I used to.'

'He's a tobacco salesman. He comes to Bailieborough every couple of weeks.'

'Did you have a run-in with him?'

'Julie, you know why I married Flossie. And Alfie knows why. Did you ever tell anyone about it? Did Alfie ever tell?'

'Jesus, John. Of course not.'

'There's a woman at home who's been blackmailing me. I'm not sure exactly how much she knows but enough to fuck up all our plans. She's a mad bitch and I don't trust her. I think this man Peter Stanley is behind it all because there's no way this woman could know anything about us. There's something about the two of them.'

Julie sat up straight. 'That's ridiculous. How the bloody hell would he know anything personal about us?'

'He used to work for his father-in-law, who happens to be Daddy's solicitor. Henry Butler. Daddy wouldn't use a solicitor from home—obviously.'

'And you think he saw the will and remembered? You're being paranoid now.'

'Come on, Julie, the conditions in Daddy's will wouldn't be easy to forget. But how does he know about Alfie? That's what I want to know.'

'Oh God.' Julie finished her lemonade and took a long pull on her cigarette. 'He was here.'

'What?' John put both hands to his head and shut his eyes. 'When?'

'Ages ago. I saw no reason to mention it at the time.'

'Why was he here?'

'I used to go with him in school, just casual, nothing serious. Don't know what I ever saw in him because he was such an arrogant bastard. But then I broke it off with him to go with someone else—who also happened to be a wrong one—no wonder I never got married,' she said, looking sideways at John. 'It was no big deal, but he made a big thing out of it. Called me all the names of the day in front of everyone. When I left home, I didn't think about him at all. Then a few years later, I was out in town with my friend, Ann, and we bumped into him. He charmed the socks off her and she ended up going with him for a few weeks. Soon after, I found out at work he was married so I told Ann. Another reason for him to be vexed with me.'

'When was he here?'

'Five or six years ago, maybe seven. I don't know, John. I haven't thought of him since.'

'So why did he call?'

Julie sighed. 'Do you want tea?'

'No. I want to know the reason he came here.'

'To get me to talk to Ann. Saying he loved her and all that shite. Then he picked up the photo of you and Alfie, the one at the zoo. He held it in his hand and gawked at it, in a funny kind of way. He said, "Well, well, would ya look at Mammy's boy... all grown up now. Is it true what they say about him?" He sniggered, the way he always did when he'd have one up on ya. I didn't answer him, the sanctimonious gobshite.'

'Did he mention me in the photo at all?'

'No. He left. It bugged me for a few hours afterwards, but then I forgot all about it. Haven't clapped eyes on him since.'

CHAPTER THIRTY-ONE

Every Saturday for the month of July, Flossie took Benny down to the Castle Lake to meet the Connollys. She would drop him there at eleven o'clock, and then cycle on through the woods to Corrie's shop. There she would buy biscuits and lemonade for their picnic. She would return to the lake and stay until about two o'clock. They found a new spot for fishing, more secluded than before. The children spent only part of the time fishing, and most of it playing in the trees. Frank made a swing from a rope and the seat of an old chair, which kept them occupied for ages.

One Saturday, while the children were exploring in the trees, Flossie saw the familiar glint in Frank's eyes.

'Close your eyes,' he whispered. She closed them without hesitation. 'Give me your hand.'

Velvety softness touched her skin; she opened her eyes. 'A red rose.'

'Definitely red this time, not purple.' Frank grinned and sang quietly. 'Come over the hills, my bonny Irish lass...'

Flossie smiled and sang with him, her eyes locked with his. 'You choose the rose, love, and I'll make the vow, and I'll be your true love forever...'

They laughed, but in their hearts, they wept.

'Can I have a flower too, Daddy?' Nancy asked.

Flossie quickly put the rose into her bag.

'Oh, hello there,' Frank said.

He took Nancy's hand and brought her over to the marshy bank. Wading barefoot through the lily pads and rushes, he bent down beside a bed of blue flowers. He picked one and handed it to her. 'This is the most important flower in the whole world and that's why I'm giving it to you. It's called a water forget-me-not.'

'That's a funny name,' said Nancy.

'It sure is, but it means we'll remember each other forever and ever.'

'Okay.' She smiled and threw her arms around his neck and kissed his cheek. Then she ran back to the others.

§

As the summer months passed, Flossie got to know a deeper side of Frank. She had always marvelled at his enthusiastic approach to life, his confident and charming wit. The years had changed him. The cheeky young lad didn't exist anymore. The impish glint in his eye was all but invisible now. The last smithereen of sparkle hung by a fine thread, kept intact only by his two little girls. He spoke in riddles about Alice, as if afraid to admit how unpleasant things had gotten. But Flossie looked deep, reading between the lines.

His young thirty-year-old face had pain etched in every crease. The grey that peppered his chestnut hair seemed more obvious—but perhaps only because she sat a bit closer to him each time they were together.

CHAPTER THIRTY-TWO

For weeks John watched Peter Stanley and Alice. Her routine stayed the same: into Law's straight after she picked up her money. Stayed about half an hour, then left. Stanley entered, stayed long enough to have one drink.

While watching one day, John took more notice of the young lad Liam who helped out around Law's. He was a quiet young lad who cycled in from the country every morning— hail, rain or shine. A reliable young man, John heard people say. Sometimes he came into the shop for messages for the Law's. Never engaged in much conversation. Spoke when spoken to and kept his head down. John could use this lad's eyes. He should have a chat with him, offer him a free shirt. His opportunity came not long after, when Liam arrived at the shop while Frederick was across the street talking to Mr Tierney.

CHAPTER THIRTY-THREE

Alice Connolly opened her purse to pay for her batch loaf and corned beef. That nosey Myles woman was there as usual, gossiping about the whole town, arms folded under her huge breasts. Alice caught her throwing a sly glance into her open purse.

'Ten woodbines as well,' Alice said, turning her back on the Myles woman.

'Hello, Mrs Connolly. How is everyone?' asked Mrs Myles.

Alice didn't answer.

'Saw your Frank down at the Castle Lake last Saturday. Grand wee lassies ya have, Alice.'

'Aye.'

'The wee O'Malley boy was with them too. Didn't know yas mixed with the townies.'

'Mind your own business and I'll mind mine.' Alice slammed the door on her way out. *What the hell is the O'Malley gasson doing, going fishing with her husband and her children? The fecking O'Malleys, of all people. The curse of God on you, Connolly. Fecking lick arse. You Connollys always had a notion of yourselves. That Mary one beyont in England thinks she's someone just because she married a lad with a few bob in the bank.*

Alice muttered the whole way out the Cavan Road on her way home, stopping briefly at Josey's to collect Rose and Nancy. The only times she took them anywhere was when Frank was at work and when Josey was too busy to mind them. They were a nuisance for her, and it wasn't as easy to sneak into the pub for a quick drink when they were with her.

'Is it home time for Daddy?' asked Rose as they sat at the table waiting for their tea.

'Who went fishing with you last Saturday?' Alice sawed through the loaf with the bread knife.

Pleased that she was interested in what they were doing, Rose answered with a smile. 'Benny O'Malley. He's my new friend and he'll be in our school.'

'He's my friend too,' said Nancy.

'I showed him how to go fishing.' Rose tilted her chin and looked down her nose at Nancy.

'Was his daddy with him?' Alice asked.

'No.'

'So how did he get there?'

'His mammy brings him. She's our teacher,' Rose answered.

'Once she stayed all day. She's nice.'

'I don't like boys—only Benny,' said Nancy, as she folded a slice of corned beef into her hungry mouth.

Alice's nostrils flared and her lips curled. *Nice? Is she now? That Flossie Lynch needn't think she can start hanging around with Frank just because she used to play in their house! Miss Law-Di-Daw, with her fancy hairdo and posh hats. Sitting at the front of the church like she was the Mother of God herself, sucking up to Father Tierney after Mass.*

The girls finished their tea and scurried up to the babby house. Alice lit the butt of a cigarette and poured more tea into her half-empty mug. She moved the pile of dirty clothes from the table to the threadbare armchair. *Sick of housework, sick of this place and everybody in it. Should've fecked off to England all those years ago, might've got in with someone decent. Someone with a bit of cop on—and a few pound. Stuck in this hole instead, with Connolly and the two whingers.*

She flicked ash on the floor and took a long pull of the tiny butt, the hot ash so close to the tip it almost burned her lips. She threw it in the pile of cinders that spilled out from the door of the range.

She peeled several potatoes and put them on the gas to boil. She lit up another cigarette. Pacing the sticky kitchen floor, Alice muttered away.

CHAPTER THIRTY-FOUR

Liam reported back to John several times over the coming weeks.

On the days that John paid Alice, she went into the snug and had a drink or two. About half an hour after she'd leave, Stanley would go in and write in one of his books while he had a drink. If other customers were in the snug, Alice would wait until they left. Stanley did the same.

'You have to go in there the next time, before Stanley gets there but after Alice leaves. Look around. She's hiding money there for him. If you find any, don't take it, come and see me.'

'There's somethin' else, Mr O'Malley,' Liam said.

'Yes?'

'I was going home the Cavan Road way one evening, on me bike, when he passed by me and drove in the wood gates. I followed him.'

'Go on,' said John, pushing his glasses up his nose.

'He drove in a good bit and walked the rest.'

'To where?'

'To the crossroads. He went way in then, in the trees,

where I couldn't see him. But I waited 'til he came out. Then Mrs Connolly came out after him. She went off up the back lane. Her house is up there, y'see.'

'Yes, I know that. So you're telling me Stanley and Alice were in the woods canoodling in the trees?'

Liam shrugged. 'I think so.'

'Good man, Liam. Don't tell this to anyone or it'll be the talk of the town.'

'Okay.'

'Could you follow them again?'

'Dunno when they'll be doing it again, Mr O'Malley.'

'You can try. Keep an eye out. See if they're giving messages to someone. How are they communicating? It's something to do with the snug, it has to be. You'll figure it out, Liam.'

'I'll try me best,' Liam said, sticking his chest out.

'When you think you're onto them again, come in here and let me know. Are you any good with a camera?'

'Better than me father with his.'

'I knew I picked the right man for the job. You'd make a great detective.'

John climbed to the second rung of his step ladder and took down a box of leather belts. 'Would you wear one of these?' He lifted the lid.

'I would.' Liam's eyes lit up.

'Take your pick then.'

Liam left the shop with his head held high, feeling very important, wearing his new bronze-buckled leather belt.

CHAPTER THIRTY-FIVE

'I'll make the dinner,' Rose said to Nancy as she gathered dandelion leaves in the field.

'I want to make it too,' Nancy said. 'It's my turn. It's not fair.'

'You have to put Jemima and Hannah to bed,' Rose said. 'Pick new rushes for the cot.' Nancy obeyed, preferring to be in charge of the dolls anyway. They had the babby house well-equipped with old, chipped plates, battered saucepans with no handles, bent spoons, and empty bottles.

Their dolls slept on a layer of withered rushes that lined the bottom of a wooden crate. Max sat in his usual spot at the entrance.

Rose busied herself preparing dinner. They were having cabbage, peas, and potatoes. She carefully tore the dandelion leaves to pieces and placed them into her warped saucepan. She added a handful of green haws and sprinkled her creation with white clover petals. The girls kept a collection of stones in the babby house which were used for potatoes or eggs.

'Bold girl, Hannah.' Nancy slapped the doll on the bottom.

'No dinner for you.' She put Hannah in her cot and took on the voice of Rose's doll, Jemima.

'*I'm a good girl, Mammy,*' Jemima said.

'You're a bold girl too,' Nancy said as she smacked the doll on the bottom.

Nancy squawked like a hungry fox.

'Why are you crying like that, Nancy?' Rose asked.

'I'm not crying. It's Hannah and Jemima. They're bold and I slapped them.'

Max barked sharply outside. Rose peered out the plastic window.

'Who's coming?' Nancy asked.

'Don't know.' Rose crawled out the door.

Max barked again. He was pacing over and back. Rose began to cross the little bridge, but Max nudged her back again. She could hear her mammy shouting from the house. Were they in trouble again? Then she heard her daddy yelling.

Rose crawled back into the babby house. She grabbed Jemima from the cot and hugged her tight to her chest.

'Who's coming?' Nancy whispered. Max barked continuously.

'Nobody. Mammy and Daddy are shouting.'

Nancy grabbed her doll and sat close to Rose.

'I need to do my pee,' Nancy whispered.

'Try to wait. We have to stay here.'

'But I'm dying; I have to go now.'

'No,' Rose said. Nancy pulled away; she stood up and cried. Urine dribbled down her legs.

The shouting continued. Cursing and swearing.

'Daddy's shouting very loud,' cried Nancy. A loud crashing noise travelled up the field and filtered through the thin walls of the babby house. Rose hugged her knees and threw her head into her lap. Nancy closed her eyes tight and clamped her hands against her ears, muffling the guttural cries of her father.

CHAPTER THIRTY-SIX

Flossie promised her mother she'd clean the inside of the windows. Benny was outside playing, so she'd fly through them without any interruptions.

The tedious task of window shining sent her mind into overdrive thinking about Frank. She and Benny had gone to the lake the previous Saturday to meet him and the girls, but they weren't there. Maybe he had to help Josey. But he hadn't been to Mass the following morning either. She scanned the streets for him every time she was over the town, but there was no sign of him.

By the time Flossie got to the last window upstairs, her arms ached. As much as she disliked the job, she always found herself rubbing vigorously to get rid of every last streak. She opened the sparkling clean window to let in some much-needed air, but there wasn't as much as a breeze outside.

She recognised a young man across the street, looking up at her. It was Tomás, Josey Connolly's farm helper. He looked around, shifting from one foot to the other, and then he beckoned to her. She rushed down the stairs. Why would Tomás want to see her?

He picked his bicycle off the ground and took long, awkward strides across the street and met Flossie at the door. 'Hello, miss. Mr Connolly told me to give you this.' He handed her a small brown envelope.

'Oh, okay, thank you, Tomás.' As he mounted his bicycle, Flossie asked, 'Which Mr Connolly?'

But he sped up Henry Street without looking back. She tore the envelope open. Untidy writing scrawled across the torn piece of brown paper.

Meet me at the lake at 7 on your own. Same place. Frank.

She kissed the letter and, smiling, stuffed it into her pocket.

§

When Flossie arrived at O'Malleys' to collect Benny, he was happily sitting at the kitchen table sticking magazine cut-outs into a scrapbook. Flossie was impressed—Granny Malley wasn't usually in favour of any projects that involved paint or glue.

'Now, Flossie. Mrs Ryan is retiring from teaching piano lessons. She asked about you and thinks you might like to take over from her,' Ruth said.

'Oh, I'd love to teach piano,' Flossie said. 'I've already started to teach Benny and he's picking it up nicely.'

'Good. Now, you go and see Mrs Ryan this evening—I told her you would—and sort it all out with her. She has about four or five pupils. She'll tell you all about them.'

'Thank you. And thanks for minding Benny.'

'He's a grand wee fella. No trouble.' She had a twinkle in her eye as she ruffled Benny's loose curly mop.

'He could do with a haircut,' she added as they were leaving. Flossie humoured her. 'Yes, next Friday.'

Mrs Ryan lived in Golbolie, a short cycle outside town. Perfect. She would call and see her, then cycle to the woods from there.

'That's great, Flossie. Sure you're brilliant on the piano and it'll be a few extra pennies in your pocket,' her mother said when she told her the news.

'I wonder does Mrs Ryan charge everyone the same?' Flossie said. 'I'm thinking about the people who can't afford piano lessons.'

Goretti sniffed. 'If they can't afford piano lessons, well, they'll hardly afford a piano.'

'Could we afford a piano?' Flossie asked with raised eyebrows.

'Just because Auntie Bridgey gave us her old piano doesn't mean we couldn't afford to buy one.'

Flossie knew that wasn't true, but she said no more. She would be the one to decide who paid for piano lessons and who didn't. Little Rose and Nancy might like to play, and she wouldn't charge them a penny.

'Will you look after Benny while I'm at Mrs Ryan's?'

'I will of course.'

§

Mrs Ryan's sitting room seemed smaller than Flossie remembered. Perhaps it was the larger coffee table, and the sideboard was also a new addition. Two tabby cats lazed on the same old couch with not a care in the world. Flossie sank into the red velvet-covered armchair that she'd always admired from the piano stool.

Mrs Ryan talked about each of her pupils as she sorted through a folder of music sheets. 'Ten-year old Lily Maguire comes at nine o'clock every Saturday morning—excellent pupil. Patrick Walsh is only a beginner and he's promising. He comes on Fridays at five o'clock. The two Farrell girls come together and they're hard work. Rosie McCabe only comes every second week because she's learning the fiddle as well.' Mrs Ryan admitted that she no longer had the patience for teaching, and she was pleased Flossie was to be her successor.

Flossie remembered her as a strict teacher, but always fair. She had long fingers, but Flossie didn't remember them being so crooked. Noticing how she stared at her hands, Mrs Ryan said, 'Arthritis. It's giving me a lot of trouble lately. I can't play my old Betsy like I used to.' She stroked her shiny walnut Blüthner like it was a prized pony.

Flossie put the thick folder of music sheets into the front basket of her bicycle and waved goodbye to Mrs Ryan. She pedalled as fast as she could out the Golbolie Road towards the back entrance to the woods. She wasn't sure how long it would take her to get to the lake from that side. She couldn't be late; Frank might not wait.

CHAPTER THIRTY-SEVEN

Rose and Nancy were playing snakes and ladders in their bedroom. Alice breezed in, clapping her hands.

'It's a lovely evening, you two. Why aren't yas out in that babby house instead of cooped up in here?'

Their mother's enthusiasm for playing in the babby house was unexpected.

'So come on, out you go, the pair of ya.' The girls jumped to their feet, abandoning the board game.

'Tell ya what. I'll make sandwiches for your tea and yas can eat them up there. And orange and biscuits.'

'Why?' Rose asked.

'Well, for being good girls today.'

'Where's Daddy?' Nancy asked.

'He's helping Uncle Josey. You're not to go up there looking for him now, d'ya hear? He said he'll be back in a couple of hours or so.'

'Come on, Nancy, let's go,' said Rose. They skipped through the field with Max close behind.

Alice hummed as she cut four slices of soda bread. She

checked the clock, calculating how long she could afford to be gone. She shouldn't be any longer than half an hour. She spread the bread thinly with margarine and strawberry jam and cut it into squares.

Her meetups with Stanley weren't as regular as they used to be. Since they stopped meeting in Law's, she had to make do with the occasional grope down the woods. She always knew he fancied her like mad—from that first day they met in the snug.

'You're a real woman, Alice,' he'd say. 'I dreamt about you last night.' Alice liked the idea of being the star in a man's dreams.

'Flattery will get you nowhere,' she'd reply. But it did and he kept the compliments flowing when he was in the mood for a bit of hanky-panky.

Unlike useless Frank Connolly who hadn't paid her a compliment since their wedding. All he ever did was make her feel stupid. And telling lies. Sneaking around down at the lake with yer one. Was it any wonder she had to accept the advances of a travelling salesman? A woman had needs, so she had. Frank didn't give her what she needed. He could feck off.

She poured some diluted orange into a lemonade bottle and put it into a small cardboard box, along with the jam sandwiches and several plain biscuits.

Max stood with his ears pricked as she approached the babby house. Rose stuck her head out the door.

'Here yas go,' said Alice, thrusting the box forward.

Rose crossed the plank. 'Thanks, Mammy.' She smiled.

'Now stay in there 'til I come back. I've cleaning to do and I don't want yas in the way.'

'Okay,' Rose said, scurrying back into the playhouse.

Alice hurried back down the field and into the house. She grabbed her cigarettes and matches off the table and put them into her handbag. Snowy mewed up at her. She picked him up and kissed his face. He purred and nuzzled into her neck.

'When did you get here? Only for me, Snowy, only for me. C'mon, I'll give ya a wee drop a milk. Let's find your saucer.' She took a bottle of milk from the fridge and peeled off the foil lid. An inch of cream plugged the top of the bottle. She scooped it out with her finger and sucked it. She filled Snowy's saucer with the cold fresh milk.

Alice opened her bag and took out a lipstick that was screwed up to the end. She pressed her little finger into what remained of her favourite red wine shade. With her mouth gaped open, she blindly rubbed it into her lips, smacking them together when she was done. She whipped the lid off her bottle of Tweed and spritzed her chest. She took a quick look down at her black knee-length skirt, deciding it'd do after she picked off some cat hair—not that Peter would notice anyway. She rolled up the sleeves of her blouse and flung her bag across her shoulder. She bent down to kiss Snowy, who had by now curled up on the chair beside the cold range. Alice made her way down the back lane that led to the woods.

CHAPTER THIRTY-EIGHT

Flossie had ten minutes to get to the lake. She pedalled hard, sweating in the dead heat. She had so much to tell Frank. She needed to be completely honest. Tell him everything. She loved John and he loved her, but it wasn't the kind of love she needed. Their life was good, but it wasn't enough. She could be with Frank in secret; it would be okay. Deep down she knew he loved her too.

Her heart thumped and she felt breathless, but she urged her aching legs to cycle faster. She wondered again where he had been the previous Saturday. The overcast sky mirrored her changed mood. What if he wanted to tell her they weren't to meet anymore? What if Alice had heard and wanted it to stop? What if he wasn't in love with her after all?

§

Flossie dropped her bicycle at the sycamore tree and walked along the bank that led to their secluded fishing spot. Her legs trembled and her head pulsed from the heat. She peered through the bushes and could see him, tucked away in their grassy little nook.

She rushed towards him, praying that he'd say what she desperately needed him to say. He turned to her and took off his cap.

Her smile disappeared as she came to a sudden halt. An icy force plunged her to the ground. Her exhausted body shuddered at the face in front of her. Black spots appeared before her eyes. The heat had gotten to her, she'd cycled too fast, and her eyes deceived her for sure.

Her mouth fell open as she stared at Frank's swollen, blistered face. Yellow gauze covered red raw skin across the left side, and an unsightly scab merged with his eyebrow. She tried to speak but all that came out was her breath. He dropped his cap to the ground and reached out to her.

'Hey, it's okay. It's not as bad as it looks.'

They sat together on the sun-scorched grass. He held her close to his chest and kissed her damp forehead.

'Frank, what happened?'

He took a deep breath. 'Alice heard about us. About us meeting here on Saturdays. She went stone mad, shouting and calling me names. She thinks we're having an affair.'

'But we're not. Didn't you tell her we're not?'

'Of course I told her. She doesn't listen when she's like that.'

'What did she do? Frank, it doesn't look good. Have you been to the doctor?'

'No. It's fine. Josey put ointment on it and he had this gauze in his medicine box. It looks worse than it is.'

'Frank, there's yellow stuff oozing from it. You should go to the doctor.'

'I know, but I don't want to take any more time off work. I've been off all week.'

'Go in the morning, please.'

'I might.'

'Was it the kettle?'

'No. A pot of boiling spuds. She threw a tin of peas first and got me right here.' He pointed at his eye. 'Then I felt the worst pain I've ever felt in my entire life. I thought I was on fire. I tried to get to the sink, but I kept slipping in the hot mush. I couldn't open my eyes. She laughed.'

'Where were Rose and Nancy during this?'

'In the babby house. Thank God for that place.'

'What are you going to do, Frank? Things can't go on like this.'

'I don't know what to do. Josey said I should get Alice locked up for what she did this time.'

'This isn't the first time, is it?'

'Oh, I got a few thumps and things thrown at me in the past, worse when she's drunk, but this is the worst ever. My head's all over the place. I can't sleep anymore.'

'What has she said since?'

'Not a word, and I haven't even looked at her since. I hate the sight of her.' He bit down on his bottom lip. 'What would happen to the girls if she ended up in the mental hospital?'

'I'm not sure, Frank. They might get taken away from you. I don't know. What does Josey think?'

'He thinks if he helps me to look after them, it'll be alright.'

'Do it, Frank. Go to the guards and tell them everything. What if she hurts Rose and Nancy?'

'That's what Josey said.'

Was now the right time to tell him about Benny? Would there ever be a right time?

'Flossie, can we meet again? I love you and I know you love me. You don't have to leave John, but maybe...'

She threw her arms around him. 'I want nothing more in the whole world. I've never stopped loving you, Frank. We can be together. Nobody needs to know.'

'Flossie, there's something else that's been bothering me. Something I've wanted to ask you for a very long time now.'

'Yes? What is it?'

A little Jack Russell appeared. He yapped in time with his wagging tail when he saw the embracing strangers.

'That's Finnegan's dog. You have to go,' Frank said.

'There's nobody with him. It's okay.'

'You better go anyway. And I need to get home too.' He helped her up.

'When will I see you again?'

'I don't know. I'll send another note with Tomás. Now go.'

'But you want to ask me something. Ask me quickly.'

'Next time. Go. I love you.'

He blew her a kiss as she got on her bicycle. Finnegan's dog scampered back to where he'd come from.

§

Frank watched until she was out of sight. He stood looking out onto the lake thinking about everything Flossie had said and wondering if she really could help him out of the hell he lived in. He worried about Rose and Nancy. What would people say? The lads at work.

He thought about Benny. The more time he spent with him, the more connected he felt to the lad. He had to know the truth. He had to hear it from Flossie. He knew in his heart that Benny was his son.

His head throbbed and his face hurt. The calm swish of tiny waves on the lake shore had a calming effect, tempting him to get in. But the sky darkened and time ticked by. *She* would be waiting. Things were already bad enough. The dead and murky air warned of a thunderstorm. *Five more minutes. A quick paddle.*

He slipped off his shoes and socks. He put his socks into the shoes and left them beside his cap. He rolled his trousers as far as his knees and hobbled across the stony surface.

Once in the water, he forgot about the sharp pebbles under him as the cool water caressed his hot sticky feet. He imagined how soothing it might feel on his festered face. He closed his eyes and imagined the water gently flowing all over his aching body. He took a deep breath and willed his turmoil into the dark waters, clearing it out of his tortured head to make space for what was to come. *It will come,* he told himself. *And everything will be okay.*

§

As Flossie cycled back towards town, adrenaline rushed through her veins. What would happen if Alice got put away? Would Frank and Josey really make it happen? *Beware the anger of a patient man! You've gone too far this time, Alice Ward.*

Conflicted thoughts spun round her head. She loved Frank more than ever, she felt sorry for Rose and Nancy, and she disliked Alice. But was she just as bad as Alice? *No, she wasn't to think like that.* Secrets and lies were one thing, but she would never hurt anybody. She would never do to John what Alice did to Frank.

She imagined what would happen if she were to leave John. *He'd be mortified. Disgraced. He'd never get over the shame. His parents would never forgive her. And to take Benny away from them?* Flossie shuddered at the thoughts of it. No, she could never do that. She'd almost confessed to Frank today; she didn't think things through properly. No, this wasn't the right time to tell him. Maybe when Benny was older, old enough to understand. For now, she and Frank would have to be careful. They mustn't be seen together.

CHAPTER THIRTY-NINE

Benny was playing on the street with friends and showed no sign of wanting to come in.

'Have you had your tea, Benny?' Flossie called as she jumped off her bicycle.

'Not yet, Mammy,' he shouted and carried on running. Flossie let him be for another while.

Her mother was in the kitchen, killing flies with the dish-cloth. 'This is the worst thing about the good weather. Is the fly spray all gone, Flossie?'

'Mammy, the smell of that stuff will kill us, never mind the flies,' Flossie said. 'Keep the windows closed.'

'I have to let air in. We'll suffocate in this heat.'

'There's going to be an awful shower. Look at that sky.' Flossie closed the kitchen window.

'It's thundery weather too. I've a headache all day.' Goretti flicked again at a bluebottle. 'How's Mrs Ryan?'

'She seems lonely. Crippled with pain, she said. Her fingers are very bent.'

'Ah bless her.' Goretti slammed the phone book down on the sideboard. 'Gotcha.'

Flossie yelped. 'Mammy! What are you doing?'

'The bluebottle. I think I only stunned him the last time, but he's as dead as a doornail now.'

Benny barged in, his red face beaming. 'It's raining and I'm hungry.'

'Time you were in anyway,' said Flossie. 'I don't know why John's so late home this evening. We'll have our tea without him, I'm starving. He'll not mind, Mam. It's already half eight.'

§

Soon after tea Flossie tucked a weary Benny into bed. As she tenderly kissed his flushed cheeks, she caught the faint smell of citrusy soap and minty toothpaste. She kissed him again.

'Night night, Mammy,' he whispered.

'Goodnight, my handsome little man.' Her heart swelled, but just as quick, it deflated again as familiar feelings of shame and guilt washed over her. She said a prayer over her sleepy little boy, asking God to tell her what to do, guide her, show her. And she asked Him—as she did every night since Benny was conceived—to forgive her.

Darkness had fallen and John still wasn't home. Flossie joined her mother, who sat in the corner of the sitting room close to the table lamp, reading a copy of *The Messenger*.

'If that husband of yours is waiting for the rain to stop, he'll be waiting a long time.'

'Doesn't seem to be easing at all, does it?' Flossie flicked through Mrs Ryan's folder of music notes. 'I can't wait to start the piano lessons.'

Suddenly a sheet of lightning lit up the room and a rattle of thunder boomed above them. Goretti leapt up and immediately began pulling out all the plugs.

Flossie jumped at the sound of three loud knocks on the front door.

'That must be him now,' she said on her way out the hall. 'Have you no key, John?' she muttered more to herself than to him.

A blast of wind and rain hit her in the face when she opened the door. The streetlights flickered, then went out. She grabbed a coat off the hook, threw it across her head, and stepped out into the night, calling for John. The waxing crescent moon gave little light to the dark, saturated street.

An icy shiver crawled down Flossie's spine and she scurried back into the house. She pushed the door closed. She stood for a minute in the pool of rainwater with her back against the door. Her heart hammered against her ribcage. Three knocks... definitely three knocks.

In the kitchen, Goretti had the Tilley lamp lit and Benny was out of bed, curled into a ball on the armchair beside the range, excited and scared at the same time.

'Janey Mac, Flossie, you're soaked. What are you doing?' Her mother pulled a towel from the line above the range.

'I thought that was John knocking on the door, but there's nobody there.'

'I heard nothing at the door. Don't be silly, Flossie. Sure John has a key so why would he knock?'

'He might have forgotten his keys.'

'He can't leave the shop without locking it, and for that, he needs his keys. Aren't they all on the one bunch?'

'Mammy, I heard three knocks at the door.'

'You're hearing things. Get out of those wet clothes. Where's all the mantles? I need one to light this other Tilley lamp.'

'Mammy! I'm not hearing things. You know what it means, don't you? Someone's dead.'

'Jesus, Mary and Joseph, you and your superstitions. It was the child getting out of bed you heard.'

'I hope John comes home soon.'

'Don't be worrying. Sure wasn't he this late before, a few months back, doing books or something with Frederick?'

Flossie squeezed into the armchair beside Benny, nudging him onto her lap. She put her arm around him and he rested his head on her bosom.

'I hate the thunder. I remember when an uncle of mine was struck by lightning. He was lucky he wasn't killed,' Goretti said, striking a match to light a candle.

'Shocking bad luck, y'know, to be hit by lightning,' replied Flossie.

'Nonsense! He hadn't a day of bad luck in his life.'

The front door banged shut.

'That's definitely him now,' said Flossie, blessing herself. 'Thank God.'

Another rattle vibrated through the house. The rain continued to belt the windows.

'That's fierce weather,' John said, handing his mother-in-law his dripping raincoat. 'At least it cooled the air a bit; it was very heavy all day.'

'I thought you'd never come home. I was worried,' Flossie said.

'I didn't think it was as late. Sorry. I was in the storeroom when the lights went out. Sure all I had was the end of a candle to guide me out.'

'You didn't tell us you had work to do in the store.'

'Ah, I was in the humour for it, so I got stuck in. I might have a wee Jameson.'

Flossie didn't mention the knocks. John always scoffed at her superstitious and ghostly beliefs.

'John, do you know where the mantles are?' Goretti lit another candle and held it up to John's face.

'There should be some in the same box as the shoe polish.'

After a few minutes of rummaging in the hardware press, Goretti found the mantles. 'Where would I be without you, John?'

John held up the bottle of whiskey. 'Will yas join me?'

'I'll not. Benny's half asleep here, so I'll take him to bed. I'll go myself then. I'm tired.' Flossie got to her feet with her son in her arms. 'Mammy might have one with you.'

John raised his glass of whiskey and swigged it all in one go. 'Here, I'll carry him up,' he said, gently lifting Benny from her.

'Here you go,' said Goretti, holding up the second Tilley lamp and a lit candle.

Flossie led the way up the stairs, holding the lamp as high as she could to light the way for John. She stood inside Benny's room and watched as John tucked him into bed. He stroked the boy's face affectionately and whispered, 'Sleep tight.'

Flossie turned the lamp down low and left it on top of Benny's chest of drawers. More thunder rumbled in the distance, but the child was sound asleep and deaf now to the outside world.

'Goodnight, Flossie. Sleep tight.' John left the room and went back downstairs.

§

Flossie sat up in her bed reflecting on the eventful day behind her. The candle flickered in the draught, giving her a sense of calm. Her eyes wanted to sleep, but her mind buzzed with everything that happened with Frank. She slipped her hand down the side of her mattress and felt for the small tear. She burrowed into it with her finger and pulled out the key of her wardrobe.

She had sins to confess, sins she couldn't bring herself to tell the priest in the confessional. Auntie Bridgey once told her that praying for forgiveness was as good as going to confession. Flossie often thought Bridgey had her own religion—making up her own rules as she went along. She wished she could be more like her, honest with herself, and not frightened to say what was on her mind, regardless of what people thought.

She went to her wardrobe and turned the key in the tiny keyhole. She kept her diaries in a box on the top shelf, her current one sitting on top. She took it down and got back into bed.

This was her favourite diary out of all her others. Pages filled with happy days at the lake with Frank and the children. Intimate conversations, touching against each other, pretending it meant nothing. Now they were both sure it had meant something. Flossie poured her deepest thoughts and feelings into the ink and let it flow onto the pages.

CHAPTER FORTY

The loud ring of the telephone woke Mary Fitzpatrick from a deep sleep. She elbowed her husband in the bed beside her to get up, but he didn't budge. She glanced at the clock. Almost seven. 'Time to get up anyway,' she said, pulling on her dressing gown. She could hear Maureen gabbling to herself as she passed her bedroom.

'I'm coming,' she shouted as she moved quickly down the stairs. She lifted the receiver, expecting the caller to ask for Jim. It was Sergeant Kennedy and his call was to Mary. She gripped the receiver with both hands and shook her head. 'What did you say?' She shook her head again. *There was a mistake.* 'Are you sure?'

A lorry rumbled past the house. Mary pressed a hand to her ear. 'I don't think I can hear you properly.' She switched on the lamp. The sun didn't come round to the front of the house until late morning and she wished she had put a brighter wallpaper in the hall. Sergeant Kennedy was still talking. She wound the receiver cord tight around her fingers until her knuckles turned white. 'I'll put Jim on,' she said.

Jim was half-way down the stairs with Maureen in his arms. 'Everything okay?' he asked.

'It's Sergeant Kennedy. Will you talk to him? We've to go home, Jim.' Mary took Maureen and brought her into the kitchen. It was a mess. She should've washed the floor. And the ironing. There was so much to do. Maureen began to cry. Mary gave her a rusk and put her into her playpen. She went to the sideboard and lifted the framed photo of Frank sitting on the lake wall with Rose and Nancy. Mary hugged it to her heavy chest and closed her eyes. *It can't be true.*

§

With Benny by her side, Flossie stepped out into the cool fresh morning air. They left Goretti sleeping; she had stayed up later than usual with John and the bottle of whiskey.

The storm had cleared the layer of overcast that dulled the air the previous day. The heaviness had lifted, but an uncomfortable silence lurked in the calm atmosphere.

The main street was busy, as it always was on a Friday, when many of the country people came in to do their weekly shopping. But it lacked the usual hustle and bustle. The men who usually engaged in friendly banter huddled in odd piddling groups instead. The mammies with their prams weren't smiling and laughing, or chatting about everything but nothing in particular. Instead, they whispered, their faces conveying shock and sadness. Mrs Deignan blessed herself and wiped the tears that flowed freely down her wrinkled cheeks.

Somebody died. It was always a bit like this when some-

body died. Flossie called out to Mrs Deignan. 'Are you okay? What's happened?'

'Oh, my dear Flossie. Haven't you heard? Those poor children,' Mrs Deignan said.

'What children? Who do you mean?' Flossie squeezed Benny's hand instinctively.

'The wee Connolly girls. Did ya not hear what happened?' she whispered, glancing at Benny, who was too busy drooling at the jars of sweets in the shop window to hear her anyway.

'Rose and Nancy? What happened? What do you mean?' She wrapped her arm around Benny, pulling him closer.

'Their father, Frank. He's dead. Isn't it shocking?'

'No, he's not.' Flossie frowned, shaking her head at Mrs Deignan.

Benny wriggled in her embrace. 'Mammy, let go.' She eased her grip. Benny fled to the shop window for a closer look at the sweets.

'Don't be silly, Mrs Deignan. I saw him yesterday and he's very alive.'

'Flossie, he's dead. Drowned in Castle Lake. Mick Murphy was out fishing, early this morning, and found him.'

'That's not true, Mrs Deignan. It's gossip. It must be somebody else.' Flossie turned to go. Where would she go? She might go home. Faces stared at her. Father Tierney crossed the street with Sergeant Kennedy.

The sun got hotter in the sky, blinding her. She turned again to Mrs Deignan, who was babbling. *Where's Benny?* She couldn't see him. She swayed, seeing only a haze around Mrs Deignan's head. Father Tierney's voice hummed in her ears. *More voices... fading away.* Sergeant Kennedy's black gloved hands reached towards her like two giant black tongs, but he didn't get to her. Her heavy body fell, as if into a black hole, into the depths of her own body. She fell into a silent heap on the dusty footpath.

§

'Flossie... Flossie... can you hear me?'

John's voice loomed in the near distance. Droplets of cool water fell on Flossie's dry lips. A wet cloth slid off her damp forehead; it stank of mothballs. She heard Benny crying.

'Take a drink, Flossie. You're okay,' John said.

She sat up amid a crowd of onlookers looking down at her, blathering and insinuating. *Is she in the family way? Is it the heat? She grew up with the Connollys, y'know! Her wee lad is friends with them wee girls, y'know. His sister is her best friend.*

They were talking about Frank. It must be true. How could he drown? He was a strong swimmer. This wasn't right. The sun beamed in the sky, yet she shivered with the cold. *Should she cry? She didn't feel like crying. Why wasn't she crying?*

John helped her up and took her across the road to the shop.

'I'm sorry, Flossie. I should've went home and told you as soon as I heard, but Dad wasn't here. He was up the town and I couldn't leave the shop. You're out earlier than usual anyway.'

Frederick handed her a cup of sweet tea. 'Shocking business, so it is,' he said, shaking his head. 'Do you want to ring Mary?'

Flossie shook her head slowly. 'Maybe later.'

'They're saying it wasn't an accident, y'know,' said Frederick.

'Who's saying that?' Flossie asked.

'Sure, everyone knows that man was a good swimmer. Reared in the lakes, he was. Meant to do it, they're saying.'

'Frank wouldn't do that. That's an awful thing to say,' Flossie said. 'He must've got tired. Or got a cramp. Yes, that's probably what happened. He got a cramp and couldn't make it back in.'

'It's not the safest lake for swimming though. It's possible he got into trouble, alright,' John said throwing his father a cautionary look. 'Let's not speculate.'

Benny came out from the back room with Ruth. He ran to his mother's arms.

'Were you dead, Mammy?'

'No. No, Benny. It was a little faint, that's all.'

'I was afraid and I was crying.'

Flossie hugged him tight. So small and vulnerable. So innocent. *Rose and Nancy. Frank would never have left them... not with Alice.* 'I should go and see Josey. Is Benny okay here?'

'Of course he is. He can help me shell beans,' said Ruth.

'Sit there for another while and finish your tea. What's your hurry?' John asked.

'I'm alright, John. I'll go home first and make a bit of breakfast. That's all that's wrong, and the heat.' Flossie left her half-empty cup on the counter and left.

§

'That fella's swimming in lakes since he was a gasson. He'd know the dangers. All very sinister if you ask me,' Frederick said when Flossie had left.

'He wasn't at work all last week, I heard, so God knows what was going on,' John said.

'Aw, sure, poor Flossie. Didn't she grow up with the Connollys? I hope I didn't upset her by saying what I did, but she'll hear it again from others anyway. And poor Mary; she'll be heartbroken.' Frederick sighed.

Mrs Deignan arrived into the shop. 'I'm after hearing that the poor divil got a cramp and couldn't swim back to shore.'

Frederick opened his mouth wide and looked up to the heavens.

'He had his clothes on. If he was out for a swim, he'd have taken his clothes off now, wouldn't he?' He shook his head.

'I'm only saying what I heard,' she said.

'What can I get you, Mrs Deignan?' John asked as he came out from behind the counter, trying to distract her from his father's rudeness.

'I don't want anything, thank you!' She scowled at Frederick and walked out.

§

Flossie walked across Anne Street. She had to get home. The gossipmongers stared and whispered, but she didn't care. They knew nothing. *Did she care if they did know? Yes, she'd care if they knew the truth.* She wanted to scream. Her head was on the verge of exploding. *God had a cruel way of disciplining his people, of punishing them. Wasn't there another way? Hadn't she sacrificed herself enough?* She clenched her fists. Tears welled up in her burning eyelids, but she held them in until she was behind her front door.

And there she sat on the cold tiled floor in the hall, with her knees to her chest, sobbing into her hands.

Goretti appeared at the top of the stairs. 'Flossie?'

Flossie looked up, wiping her face with her skirt. Goretti rushed down, tying the belt of her dressing gown. 'Christ of Almighty, what's happened?' She bent over and helped Flossie up off the floor. 'Come into the kitchen. Where's Benny? Tell me.' She dipped her finger into the holy water font that hung on the wall and blessed herself.

'Frank Connolly's dead. He drowned in the lake. That's what people are saying but I don't know if it's true.'

Goretti blessed herself again. 'Jesus, Mary and Joseph. Who told you that?'

'I think it's true, Mammy. But they're saying things about him that's lies. He wouldn't leave Rose and Nancy, I know he wouldn't.'

'What things?'

'That he did it on purpose.'

'Where's Benny?'

'With Ruth. I've to go and see Josey. Find out what happened.'

'That's shocking news. My God.'

'I'll have to ring Mary too. Oh, Mammy... the poor wee girls.'

'Yes, yes, I know.' Goretti pulled the rollers out of her hair and gathered them into her hairnet. 'I better get dressed. I'll go for Benny. You go on to Josey's.'

Flossie left but she didn't go to Josey's. She couldn't face going near the place. Instead, she walked up the Kells Road to the graveyard. There she sat alongside her father's grave and cried until her tears had dried up.

§

John took long strides up the town. The subdued atmosphere had lifted slightly, people getting on with their business, but he knew Frank Connolly's untimely death would be the main topic of conversation for many days to come. He went down the side entrance of Law's, where he expected to find Liam dutifully tidying the yard. He called out his name.

'He's not here,' Mr Law shouted as he poked his head out a window. 'Can I be of help?'

'No, it's okay. I'll catch him later.'

'He's never been late, not even once, so he'll hardly be in at all,' Mr Law said.

John clicked his fingers, thinking to himself. *Sounded like Liam alright. Never late for work.*

'Sure I'll get him tomorrow. He borrowed something that I need back.'

John chewed on his lip as he marched back to work.

CHAPTER FORTY-ONE

Josey cracked open his boiled egg with the back of a spoon, not sure if he could stomach it. He went to the window as he heard a car drive into the yard. Sergeant Kennedy and one of those new guards stepped out of the squad car.

He took two mugs from the press. The sergeant's voice carried in through the kitchen as the latch lifted on the door.

'You in, Josey?'

'Come on ahead, sergeant.'

'Sorry for your troubles, Josey.' Sergeant Kennedy gave him a confident handshake. 'This is Garda McCarthy.'

The young guard followed his superior's lead and shook Josey's hand dutifully. 'Sorry about your brother,' he said sincerely, looking him in the eyes.

'Thanks.'

'How're you faring?' Sergeant Kennedy asked.

'Aw, now. Sure y'know yourself.' Josey half-filled two mugs with tea. 'I'll make more,' he said as he drained the teapot.

'You're grand, Josey, sit down.'

For a minute, the three men sat quietly at the table. The sergeant added two heaped teaspoons of sugar and a dollop of milk to his tea. Garda McCarthy barely coloured his with a drop of milk. Max barked outside, breaking the silence.

'He's looking for him,' Josey said.

'When did you last see Frank?' the sergeant asked.

The young guard took a small notebook and a red pencil out of his breast pocket.

'Yesterday. Do yas know what happened to him yet? Ones in the town are saying he drowned himself, but I'm telling you now, sergeant, I know that's not the case.' Josey pointed his finger at the sergeant.

'Calm down now, Josey. At the moment that's just pure talk. We'll wait and see.'

'Wait for what?' Josey asked, shaking his head.

'We found Frank's shoes and socks alongside his cap, a good distance away from where his body was recovered. I can imagine the water would've been fairly rough with that storm we had. Now tell me, Josey, did you ever know of him to swim in that lake?'

Josey rubbed his temples. 'No. Years ago maybe, but he never liked it. He always said it wasn't safe. He swam in Town Lake a lot and in Corrie's River.'

'It's highly likely the cause of death was drowning. He also had bruises on the front of his body... not unusual when a body is found in shallow water. The rough waters would've dragged him along the bottom. But his face was an awful mess. And the back of his head.'

Josey paled and got up from the table. He paced the floor. 'Alice did that.'

The young guard wrote in his book.

'Alice Connolly, his wife?' Sergeant Kennedy said.

'Yes, his wife.'

'So, what exactly are you saying she did?'

'I'm saying she did that to his face.'

'When?'

'This time last week. They weren't getting along. Things got out of hand lately.'

'There's no record of a doctor's visit.'

'Sergeant, he was ashamed of how bad things had got between them. He didn't even go to work last week. He didn't want anyone to know, not even the doctor. She's a horrid, jealous woman. Couldn't leave him alone for a minute, always accusing him of having affairs and what not.'

'So maybe he suffered a bit of depression?'

'So, you do think he drowned himself?'

'Trying to get all the facts here, Josey. Was there anyone else he didn't get along with?'

'Frank had only friends—no enemies.'

'Okay. Can you tell me exactly the extent of the injuries Frank had the last time you saw him?'

'A bad cut above his eye and his face was blistered. She threw things at him, at his head. She scalded him.' Josey's voice trembled.

'What was that row about?'

'I don't know.' Josey shrugged, avoiding the sergeant's eyes.

'And did they row yesterday?'

'All seemed fine when I was talking to him, but that was in the morning time. I didn't see him after that.'

'Did he ever mention headaches or dizziness?'

'My brother has had a headache since the day he married that woman!' Josey slammed his open palm on the table. 'Write that down in yer notebook.' He glared at the young guard.

'Now, Mr Connolly, I understand your frustration. We're trying to rule out some possibilities here.'

'I'll kill her if she's the cause of this, I swear to God I will.'

Garda McCarthy eyed the sergeant as he bit the top of his pencil. He lowered it to his notebook.

'*Don't* write that down,' the sergeant said.

§

John O'Malley watched his wife with interest. She was devastated, grieving for her childhood memories and her best friend Mary. And, of course, the two wee girls. But John knew she mostly grieved for the loss of Connolly himself—the love of her life.

But she'd get over him in time and carry on being his perfectly suitable wife with their perfectly suitable son. John had never wished the man any harm, but he never had any sympathy for him. Frank Connolly instigated his own fate! It was his fault he ended up with Alice. Then to be carrying on with Flossie behind his back all those years ago and sitting at Mass every Sunday looking as innocent as Jesus Christ himself. He should have been ashamed of himself. Well, now that he was out of the picture, John wouldn't have to worry about him trying to rekindle his love affair with Flossie—if he hadn't already done so—and more importantly, Connolly could never claim his son. The Lord worked in mysterious ways.

John loved Flossie in his own way. He didn't feel guilty about marrying her out of necessity because she only married him when she couldn't have Connolly. They were evens as far as he was concerned.

§

Flossie walked around in limbo. It was almost like losing her father all over again, but her emotional state was on a different level. She didn't know that pain could run so deep, that it could drag her down into the core of the earth. She screamed inside, where nobody could hear her. She screamed at Frank for swimming in the lake so late in the evening, asking him over and over again if he meant to drown like people said. *Were you really only swimming? Why were you in the lake with your clothes on? Did you fall? Why did you not go straight home after I left you?*

She fought with God for taking him away from her just as they were about to sort themselves out. She would have left John for him in the end. Was this God's way of punishing her? The adulteress! *What about his children? What's your plan for them? How could you leave them to fend for themselves against Alice? Surely you can see that if she's capable of violence against a man, she's more than capable of doing the same to her children.* She wondered if God even listened. If he ever really listened, or if he even existed at all.

§

Goretti and Molly bustled into the house looking like two fried tomatoes. They plonked themselves at the table, gasping with thirst. Flossie took a jug of diluted barley water from the fridge and poured two glasses.

'Why didn't you get a lift out, Mammy?'

'Aw, we thought the walk would do us good. I didn't think it was as warm as it is.' Goretti took a long drink of the ice-cold water.

'Was Mary there?' Flossie asked.

'She arrived not long before we left,' Goretti said.

'Poor lassie,' said Molly.

Flossie moved around the kitchen looking for things to do. Her eyes stung and her throat had felt raw since the previous day. 'Are Jim and Maureen with her?'

'No. She came alone.'

'She came by air... in an aeroplane,' said Molly.

'How is she?'

'Heartbroken. It's a closed coffin, so all she has to kiss goodbye is a wooden box.' Goretti blessed herself. 'She lay across the top of it, sobbing her heart out.'

Molly nodded. 'God help them all.'

'Josey said it was better that Mary didn't see the body. It was enough for him and Alice to see. He said he didn't look the same, y'know, with him being in that muggy lake for hours,' said Goretti.

Flossie shuddered, imagining his festered, scalded face. She shook the thought from her mind. She preferred to remember him as he used to be, with his mischievous grin and soulful eyes. She wondered if Josey told Mary about his face. Probably not. If Mary were to find out about that, there'd be another death in the family. 'And what about Alice?'

'She's still in shock and not saying very much to anyone. When Sergeant Kennedy informally identified the body, he told Alice immediately. She left him standing at the front door and ran to Josey's house, roaring and crying.'

'What about the girls?'

'They're in Father Tierney's house. Miss Dunne's minding them,' Goretti said.

'When are you heading out there yourself, Flossie?' Molly asked.

'Later this evening. John's coming with me.'

§

Dread and panic swelled in Flossie's throat as she and John drove out the Cavan Road in Frederick's car. She'd have to sympathise with Alice. She'd have to shake Alice's hand and tell her how sorry she was for her troubles. She'd have to look into her face and say how terrible it was that Alice had lost her husband. Everyone feeling sorry for Alice and pitying her because she would have loved her husband dearly, and now she was left on her own to care for two children.

She imagined Alice's eyes boring into her, accusingly: *You are the woman who was having an affair with my husband. You are the reason I threw a saucepan of boiling mush into his face.* A huge weight bore down on Flossie's shoulders. Everything inside her shrivelled up and formed into a tangled knot. She wanted to jump out of the car and run home. But she knew she had to face it all whether she wanted to or not.

People spilled out of Frank's house. Men he worked with, relations, neighbours, town folk and strangers. Flossie felt exposed and vulnerable as soon as she got out of the car. She wondered if people talked about her and Frank. *Did anyone know? Did he ever tell anyone?* She kept her head down and stayed behind John.

§

The smoke-filled kitchen smelled like a pub. Neighbour women busied themselves making tea and sandwiches. Mrs Deignan offered John and Flossie a drink as soon as they entered; they both declined.

'Have some tea then,' she said. 'Get up, yous, and get outside,' she said to two teenage lads as she clipped one of them on the ear. 'Sit down there now, Mr and Mrs O'Malley.'

She was back with tea and a plate of sandwiches and biscuits within a minute.

Flossie looked the place up and down. Childhood memories of her time there flooded back. Fun and games, laughter, the sight of Josey chasing a sassy hen from the scullery, and the smell of baking. It was a different house now. The net curtains were the same except they were grey and frayed, not snow white and pristine as they once were. The red paint peeled in patches on the dresser that was once filled with odd pieces of vibrant pottery.

Everyone was talking about Frank; some were laughing, some crying, and some doing both at the same time. The sombre atmosphere was fraught with speculation and disbelief. The wide-eyed busybodies, hungry for the latest gossip, were whispering and watching, listening to everything that was being said. Some were only there for the drink; others were there out of genuine concern.

Flossie sipped at her tea, but she couldn't face a sandwich. She took a Marietta instead. It would keep her hands busy. John chatted to the man who stood next to him.

Flossie thought back to the last time she had seen Frank. She doubted everything now, nothing seemed clear anymore. Maybe he did take his own life. He was in such despair that day and perhaps he couldn't see a way out. *No...*

She shook herself and took a deep breath. She refused to think like the rest of them. Frank wouldn't leave Rose and Nancy like that, she was certain of it. And he loved her. He really did love her. When she'd left him at the lake, he was happier. He had a flicker of hope and determination in his eyes. He hadn't killed himself. *What happened to you, Frank? In the name of God, what happened?*

John nudged her with his elbow. 'We should go on in.'

All the chairs in the mourning room were occupied, mostly with strangers—relations probably—and a few men who worked in Corrie's. Those men he worked with, did they know what went on in this house? Did he ever tell any of them? Even one of them? No, of course he didn't. That would've been a great laugh for them. Flossie knew how they carried on, how they teased and ribbed each other. They were the last people Frank would tell about the mental torture he'd had to endure in his own home. The same house that had been his home since the day he was born. His happy childhood home!

A gentle breeze from an open window flickered the tiny flames on the candles that surrounded the coffin. The smell of incense brought Flossie back to her father's funeral, and she remembered gazing at him, laid out in his best suit, coins sitting on his closed eyelids, and Auntie Bridgey pulling her away. She'd thought it was the strangest thing, the coins.

She would touch the coffin and she would say a prayer. She was glad it was closed because then she could pretend it was merely an empty box. *A big brown wooden box with nothing in it.*

Josey and Mary were sat together. Mary looked pale and her eyes were red raw.

Alice looked dreadful and, for a brief moment, Flossie pitied her. She sat lamenting by the coffin, rocking back and forth. She seemed oblivious of the people coming and going. They uttered sympathetic words of comfort as they shook her limp hand, but she looked right through them, nodding in response.

Flossie's heart pounded and her hands shook as she sympathised with the relations one by one. A cold, clammy sweat prickled the back of her neck as she came face to face with Alice. She reached out to shake her hand. Although warm to touch, it sent a shiver down her spine. Flossie kept her head down. She barely managed a whisper. 'I'm sorry for your troubles.' She dared to glance up at Alice's face.

Her glassy eyes looked like those of a Crolly doll. Alice tightened her handshake and their eyes locked. Flossie stiffened as the threat oozed from the menacing face, inches from hers. Alice opened her mouth as if to speak but instead expelled a puff of breath into Flossie's face. Flossie tugged her hand away and recoiled at the hot, putrid stench of cigarettes and sour alcohol. She turned her back and walked to the coffin, still conscious of Alice's eyes boring into her.

'Sorry for your loss, Mrs Connolly,' she heard John say.

Flossie stood beside the coffin. She blessed herself and silently prayed the Hail Mary. She touched the coffin and walked away. Tears blurred her eyes as she kept them firmly fixed on the floor. She didn't stop to talk to Mary. She had to get out as quickly as possible, away from that house and everyone in it.

§

Flossie went to see Mary the night before she went back to England. They hadn't seen much of each other around the time of the funeral. She had so much to say to her friend, and now it would all have to wait.

Her parting words pressed into Flossie's heart. 'Please look out for Rose and Nancy for me. Promise me you will.'

'I promise you, Mary. With all my heart.'

They hugged each other tight, holding on longer than they ever had before. Josey walked Flossie out to the door. 'You'll get home before dark,' he said.

'They're getting shorter now... the evenings,' said Flossie.

'He thought a lot of you,' Josey said.

'Did he?'

'I could see right through that fella.'

She squeezed the handlebars of her bicycle and managed a grim smile.

'When did you last see him, Flossie?'

'Why do you ask?'

'What do you think happened?'

'I don't know, Josey. But I know what didn't happen.'

'There's something funny about the whole thing. She gave him an awful doing a few weeks back, y'know. Yer one above.' Josey tilted his head in the direction of Frank's house. 'Accusing him of something or other, as usual. Sure the man couldn't walk the same side of the street as another woman, but she was at him. Shocking jealous woman. She couldn't even bear to see him having fun with his wee girls. She's not right, I'm telling ya.'

'Josey, I'd better go because this lamp is dim and it's getting dark.'

'Mind yourself now. Goodnight.' He stood at the gate until she was out of sight.

Flossie let her pent-up tears fall freely as she cycled back into town. The cool evening breeze carried her piteous cries up to the heavens. Every bone in her body trembled. Every vein throbbed as harrowing sobs etched their scars into her broken heart.

CHAPTER FORTY-TWO

Dear Mary,

I hope you're well. I had so much to say to you when you were home for the funeral but now I don't know what to say.

Rose and Nancy seem to be getting on okay. They come to school every day, anyway. They sit beside each other and they're very quiet.

Master Dunphy is awful hard to like (I don't think I'll ever like him). He speaks to me as if I'm still only a helper, and not a proper teacher with proper training. He still shouts a lot at the children, especially the boys. I think his voice is even louder than it used to be (if that's possible). But at least Miss Kennedy is still nice. I know you're looking to the heavens reading that part, but she is nice. I promise.

Did Josey write to you lately? I wonder how he is. I haven't seen him in a while. I might call to see him so I can tell him Rose and Nancy are doing good in school. He'll be happy to hear that.

I hope Maureen and Jim are keeping well. John is fine and

Benny is getting big. Mammy is as happy as Larry these days. Has been since Benny was born. She loves being his granny and loves it more when Benny chooses her over his granny Malley. It's only because he can twist her round his little finger.

Write soon, Mary. Do you think you'll come home for Christmas this year?

Love from your best friend, Flossie. 25/9/64

§

Flossie hadn't been entirely honest with Mary. Rose and Nancy weren't getting on okay. They stuck to each other like glue and wouldn't play with the other children in the yard. Nancy cried every day for the first week and spent most of her time staring out the window. But it was only six weeks since the funeral—so still early days—and Flossie didn't want Mary to worry. *However long the day, the evening will come,* Flossie reminded herself.

The rapport Flossie had built with Rose and Nancy back in July now seemed muddied. It was as if they no longer knew her. She was their schoolteacher and nothing more. Did their memories of the picnics, the games and laugher, all die with their father?

Miss Dunne, who took care of them during the wake, called to see Alice and the girls a few times after the funeral. Other neighbours called with groceries, and bags of clothes. When Alice berated Nuala Roe one day for being an interfering old biddy, people stopped feeling sorry for her. They only had sympathy for the children. After a month or so, they stopped calling.

Nancy arrived at school one day with a new haircut. Short, uneven spikes replaced the shoulder-length wavy hair that once framed her innocent face. She wore short trousers and a brown woolly jumper, clothes more suitable for a boy. *Where did she get them?* Flossie hadn't spoken to Josey since the night before Mary went back to England. She needed to see him.

§

'This is the Gospel of the Lord.' Flossie paid little attention to the priest's words. She questioned God's intentions. One thought in conflict with the next. She flicked through her small black prayer book, stopping randomly on odd pages. 'Forgive us our trespasses, as we forgive those who trespass against us. Lead us not into temptation. Forgive me, Father, for I have sinned.' *I was tempted and I was weak; so where were you when I needed you?*

Flossie thumbed through the pages. 'I believe that your divine Son became man and died for our sins.' *Jesus died for us. Did Frank die for his sins? What about my sins? I could have saved him. I would have given him everything.*

The altar boy shook the daylights out of the Sanctus bells as Father Tierney called upon the Holy Spirit to bless the Eucharistic bread. Benny muffled a giggle; he loved the bells. She knelt and closed her eyes to prepare for communion. *Oh my God, I am very sorry for all my sins...*

§

When Mass ended, Goretti took Benny outside. Flossie remained seated. She wanted to catch Josey at the votive stand. Since Frank had died, he lit a candle after Mass every Sunday. She waited until he finished saying his prayers before approaching him.

'Hello, Josey.'

He smiled, and for the first time Flossie saw a resemblance between the two brothers, a glimpse of something behind Josey's grave expression. Or had she imagined it? They weren't very alike at all. Josey's blue eyes didn't sparkle like Frank's.

'How are ya, Flossie?'

'I'm fine. Can I have a word with you about Rose and Nancy?'

'Are they doing okay in school?' Josey led them out the side door into the cool crisp air.

'I'm not sure. They're very quiet—Nancy quieter than Rose. Who cut her hair?'

'That Alice is a funny one, by God she is. She scalped the poor child, and she went into the town and bought boy's clothes from the Dublin women.'

'If it was a decent cut itself, it wouldn't be so bad,' said Flossie.

'Sure ya'd swear she took the scythe to it, the state of it.'

'They hardly ever have lunch either, Josey. Sometimes just a bit of bread and jam, and milk in a Magnesia bottle to share between them. I don't mind bringing a bit in for them, but she's getting the widow's pension and people were helping her out—maybe they still are—so what's going on?'

Josey shook his head slowly. 'She's full-time drinking.'

'Look, say nothing to her. She'll only fight with us. I'll bring a bit of lunch in for them every day.'

'Okay. That's good of ya, Flossie. Thanks. I'll give ya some money.'

'You will not!' she said. 'Does she listen to you at all?'

'Ah, sometimes. She leaves the girls with me every chance she gets. Once, she landed them into the byre with me and went off into town. She wasn't back 'til after ten that night.'

'What about her family? I saw them at the funeral, but they might as well have been strangers.'

'Ya can say that again. It was shocking strained, so it was. Myself and Mary got a handshake with a few words of sympathy and that was about it. The mother kept to herself the whole time, in a world of her own. The brothers hardly spoke to Alice. Quare-looking lads they are too. The Mattie lad, a head on him like a ferret. The older sister or the father didn't turn up at all.'

'I heard that alright,' said Flossie.

'The other one, Nellie, was there. She seems normal enough. Spoke to us and to Rose and Nancy. The others all left soon after the burial and didn't show one bit of concern for the wee gershas.'

'If I get a few bits and pieces, clothes and things, can you pass them on? You can let on you got them on the stalls, maybe. Sure she won't know.'

'Yea, sure. No bother.'

'I'll meet you in town next Saturday morning. It'll be after twelve because I have piano lessons before that.'

'Aye, that's grand. See ya then.'

After that, Flossie and Josey met in town once a fortnight to talk about Rose and Nancy's progress in school.

§

Dear Flossie,

Can you believe it's nearly Christmas again? I have two bits of news for you. First of all... guess what Jim brought home last Saturday. A dog! He's beautiful, Maureen loves him so much. He's a black collie with little white flecks all over him, so we named him Fleck.

I think Jim only got him to cheer me up because I can't stop thinking about Frank and I can't stop wondering how he ended up in the lake. I keep going over it in my head. I'm driving myself mad thinking about it and I know I have to stop.

How's Rose and Nancy? I got a very short letter from Josey. He said that you were taking good care of the girls during school. Thank you, Flossie. I wish I was there. He also said he'd make sure they get a good Christmas dinner. Not sure what he meant by that.

Guess what Jim said I should do, now that Maureen is at school half the day? He said I should get a part-time job. I told him no way at first but then when I thought about it, I decided I might like it. I'm excited about it now.

I'm afraid we won't be home for Christmas because we want to go home next Easter instead. Maureen wants to go on an Easter Cludog, nobody does them over here, and there's no place really suitable to do it anyway. We'd look horrid funny lighting a big fire in the middle of the front garden.

Thanks for being so kind to Rose and Nancy. You really are my best friend, Flossie.

Love, Mary.

2/11/1964

§

By the end of October, the girls were still turning up at school without coats. They arrived late one morning wearing buttoned-up cardigans, their jaws quivering, and their lips blue from the chilling easterly winds. Flossie allowed them to sit beside the fire until break time.

The following Saturday, Flossie got the bus to Dublin. She walked from the bus station to the Anglesea Market and rummaged through the second-hand clothes. She came across a beautiful red wool coat that would bring a bit of colour to Rose's pasty complexion. Flossie pictured her beige-blonde hair in neat little pigtails resting on the black fur collar—not that Alice ever put the child's hair in pigtails. Apart from a slight tear on the sleeve, the coat looked brand new. Five shiny gold buttons set it off.

She spent longer trying to find a coat for Nancy, one that wasn't too worn or drab looking. After a couple of hours rifling through bundles of used clothing, a striking emerald-green colour caught her eye. A swing-style wool coat with a thick band of velvet around the collar and cuffs—it had Nancy written all over it. A little big maybe, but she'd grow into it and maybe get a couple of winters out of it.

She passed the coats on to Josey, and he gave them to Alice, telling her they were an early Christmas present from their Auntie Mary.

§

The mid-winter months brought hard frost as early as November. Goretti knitted several pairs of mittens for the neighbour's children, and some for Flossie to take to school. Flossie gave a pair each to Rose and Nancy.

A few days later, Nancy arrived to school without her mittens. Flossie knelt beside the child and held her purple hands in hers.

'You're freezing, Nancy. Why aren't you wearing your mittens?'

'Can't find them, Miss.'

'Why didn't you keep your hands in your pockets where it's nice and warm? It's very cold out, you know.' Flossie rubbed Nancy's hands to warm the blood in them.

'They're broken, Miss.'

'What's broken?'

'My pockets.'

'Don't be silly, they can't be broken.'

Flossie tried to slip her fingers into one of the pockets. A wave of pity swept over her when she realised the pockets on Nancy's coat had been sewn up with crooked black stitches. 'Your lovely new coat...' With all her strength, Flossie kept her seething thoughts to herself. What a horrible thing to do! She sat through the rest of the morning simmering with anger.

At play time she took a pair of mittens from her drawer and gave them to Nancy.

'Now, Nancy, you wear these outside and when you come back in, give them to me and I'll keep them safe in my drawer.'

'Me and Nancy were picking sticks in the field this morning,' Rose said.

'Picking sticks? For what?'

'For the fire. Mammy said we had to.'

'Oh... did she help you?'

'No, we did it all by our own selves,' answered Rose.

'Have you lunch with you today?'

'No, Miss.'

Flossie gave them cream crackers with cheese inside. 'Now, off you go. Put your mittens on too, Rose.'

'Yes, Miss.'

CHAPTER FORTY-THREE

By December, the girls had settled in at school. Rose made friends with Kathleen McKeon. This pleased Flossie because Kathleen was a happy little girl and made Rose laugh. Nancy followed them around the yard like a lost lamb.

Flossie told Josey she could no longer keep quiet to Mary about the welfare of the girls. 'I promised Mary I'd look out for them,' she told him.

'She can be hot-headed, y'know,' Josey said.

'But she might have ideas, advice maybe.'

'I'd rather you didn't. We'll wait another while and see how things go.'

§

Dear Mary,

I hope this letter finds you all well. Everything is well over here.

Josey and I are keeping an eye on Rose and Nancy so you

have no need to worry about them. They're doing fine in school.

I got them two lovely coats for the winter and Josey gave them to Alice. He pretended they were from you (I hope you don't mind). If she knew I got them, she'd say I was interfering for sure. I bring extra lunch to school every day for them, because sometimes they don't have much.

They're fine so don't worry about them. A strange thing happened though, that I must tell you. Alice cut Nancy's hair very short. She used to have lovely hair so I don't know why she cut it. She dresses her like a boy and now with the short hair... well, she gets teased by the other children. I know this is a funny thing to say, Mary, but I think she likes Rose more than she likes Nancy.

Did Josey write to you lately? He's cooking the Christmas dinner for Alice and the girls. He's very good. I'll send a few things out to them. Mince pies and a box of sweets maybe.

Mammy is fine. She doesn't treat me like a child anymore. I think it's because she has Benny to concentrate on. As well as that, I stand up to her more than I used to. I used to think she didn't love me but now, I realise it's just the way she is and she'll probably never change.

John is fine too. He was in a terrible humour last week when he didn't get going to Dublin because of the frost. As if someone in town will be badly stuck someday for a spool of green thread, or a pair of long johns! Ha-ha!

I think he likes going to Dublin just to get away. Sometimes he meets up with old friends from school. One of the O'Neil lads, he mentioned a few times.

I didn't finish the last book you gave me. I might give up reading stories about love and things like that. It's a sin anyway, I think. The adultery part I mean, not the love part. Maybe I should read books about mystery and murder. But murder is a sin too!

Do you believe in true love, Mary? Do you truly love Jim? Is that a nosey question?

I bet Maureen can't wait until Christmas comes. Give her lots of kisses from me.

Happy Christmas.

Love from your best friend, Flossie. 18/12/64

§

The artificial Christmas tree in the corner of the Connollys' small sitting room had seen better days, but Rose and Nancy proudly hung their homemade decorations on its spindly green branches.

'When will it be dark?' asked Nancy.

'Not for ages yet. I hope you know it's my turn to switch the lights on,' Rose said.

'I don't care. Why are they called fairy lights anyway?' Nancy struggled to keep her red crepe paper chain on the tree.

'Because when the fairy is on the top of the tree, she's the boss of the lights,' Rose said while positioning Nancy's decoration firmly in place.

'We have no fairy, Rose.'

'I know. Let's make one.'

Rose spread out a sheet of white crepe paper and drew a fairy with her green crayon.

'Can I make the wings?' Nancy asked.

'No, you won't do them properly and she has to be a proper fairy.'

'Can I cut her out then?'

'No, because you're not allowed to have scissors. Only I'm allowed because I'm bigger than you.'

'It's not fair. What can I do?'

Alice stuck her head round the door. 'You two stay in the house 'til I get back. I won't be long.'

'Are you going to town, Mammy?' Nancy asked.

'Yes, and no, yas can't come before you ask, I'm in a hurry.'

'Will you buy a fairy for the Christmas tree?'

'Do ya think I'm made of money?'

Nancy knew not to ask a second time.

'Rose, when I'm gone, you're to sweep the kitchen floor. Nancy, you've to do the washing-up.'

Nancy ran to the window and peered through the cracked pane until her mother was out of sight. 'Can we put the fairy lights on now?' She reached for the plug.

'No! Get away from it, Nancy.'

The coloured lights twinkled on the skinny Christmas tree.

Rose reached for the plug. 'Mammy'll kill us.'

'I hate you, Rose. You're mean like Mammy. I want Daddy here.'

'I'm not mean. You're bold.'

Nancy lifted a tennis ball and threw it at Rose. It missed her head by an inch and shot through the glass door of the china cabinet, leaving a gaping jagged hole. Rose screamed as the crash of breaking glass rang through her ears. Nancy sat silent with her mouth open, then burst out crying.

'You're in trouble now, Nancy. Mammy's gonna kill you, so she is.'

Nancy ran from the house, stumbling through grassy sods and damp rushes to get to the secure galvanised walls of the babby house. Max scampered across the field from Josey's farm, meeting Nancy with licks and whines.

She crossed the short plank and entered her safe place. Spiders dangled on strings of wispy webs, and slaters scurried in all directions to avoid being crushed by Nancy's knees as she knelt down on the old linoleum. The coldness from the hard ground penetrated her trousers.

Nancy lifted Raggy Ann and Hannah from their wooden crate and hugged them close to her chest as she sobbed. In the dim light, she held the dolls out in front of her. She didn't notice their stale smell or that their clothes had started to turn mouldy from the damp surroundings, nor did she care that cobwebs clung to their hair.

Nancy played at being a puppeteer.

'Bold girl, Hannah,' said Raggy Ann.

Hannah replied in a determined tone, *'I didn't do it. It wasn't me.'*

'Who broke the glass?'

'Rose did it... Rose did it... Rose did it,' Hannah said.

Nancy placed Hannah back in the crate and lifted Jemima out. She manipulated Raggy Ann to pick up a twig from the linoleum-covered ground and made her beat Jemima across her head.

'Bold girl, Rose. You have to get slapped now. You're a nuisance.' Raggy Ann slapped Jemima across the head several times.

Jemima cried. Nancy threw the dolls into the crate.

CHAPTER FORTY-FOUR

O'Malley's shop was busy with Christmas shoppers. Ruth was more of a hindrance than a help to John and Frederick, chattering to whoever had time to listen. They had one of the young Daly lads, Phil, helping out for a few days.

'I've a bit of Christmas shopping to do in Dublin on Tuesday, Dad. Will you manage without me? Phil will be here. I'd be back before two o'clock.'

'You're always in Dublin. What is it you can't buy here at home?'

'Sure, I only go once a month and that's shop business. And Benny wants an aeroplane from Santy and I saw the perfect one in Clery's Toytown.'

'Maybe you'll take your mother with you for the spin,' Frederick said with a smirk.

'Take me where?' Ruth came in from the back room, carrying a box of tinsel.

'Nowhere at all, Mammy! Dad, it's quiet at the minute... I'm heading over to the house for a few minutes.'

'Okay, son. Aw, Ruth, you're not hanging more of that stuff!'

John smiled on his way up the street. His mother had so many decorations hanging in the shop, Frederick was tripping across them.

§

Benny left the sitting room and his jigsaw when he heard his father's voice in the kitchen.

'Are you home for good, Daddy?'

'I'm afraid not, sonny. Just having this quick cuppa and I've to go back.'

'Can I come and help you and Grandad?'

'It's very busy, y'know. You stay here with Mammy and finish that big jigsaw, and if you get it finished today before six o'clock, Mammy might take you over to Francey's for Black Jacks.'

'Mammy doesn't like me having Black Jacks.'

'She might let you have them today if you finish the jigsaw.' John gave Flossie a pleading look.

'We'll see,' she said. Benny had built the same jigsaw several times before, he'd have it finished in no time. She didn't like to give Benny everything he wanted though. She wanted him to grow up knowing the difference between being deserving and being entitled. Benny cheered and scurried back into the sitting room.

'Why can't you wait until Wednesday? I'd be able to go with you,' Flossie said when John told her about his plans for Dublin.

'Tuesday's a better day and anyway, I can't bring you because then you'll see what I'm buying you for Christmas.'

'Can't we get the rest of what we need here in town?'

'I can't get Benny's aeroplane here,' he whispered. 'I saw some great ones in Toytown the last time I was in Dublin.'

'Fine,' she said. She opened up the ironing board and plugged in the iron.

'Where's your mother?' asked John.

'Getting her hair done with Nan.'

John cut out a triangle of Goretti's apple tart.

'If I did that, she'd give out to me.' Flossie laughed.

'Mmm, it's still warm. Tell her I'll be late home for tea this evening, so I'm having my piece now,' he said.

'Did I tell you Mary won't be home for Christmas?' Flossie said, keeping her eyes on the iron as she pressed it hard onto the collar of the blouse.

'You were saying that alright.' John took his empty mug to the sink.

'She asks a lot about wee Rose and Nancy, in her letters. She worries, you see.'

'So how are they?' John filled a mug of water from the tap and drank it down in one go. With his back against the sink, he folded his arms the way Master Dunphy did when he was about to scold or cane one of his pupils.

'John, I know you haven't much time for the Connollys, but Mary is my best friend and I'm in charge of those wee girls while they're in school. I'm their teacher and I'm very worried about them.'

'You can't be attached to them because that's all you are, Flossie, their teacher.'

'Mary's my friend, the family are my friends. I promised Mary I'd help.'

'Why are you worried?' John's expression softened, making it easier for Flossie to open up.

'Well, I told you before that they don't always bring lunch to school. I'll be honest, John, I often bring extra from here to give them. But it's not only them, mind you, sometimes the wee Flynn lad doesn't have lunch either, and God knows he's scrawny enough.'

'Flossie, we can't be feeding the whole town.'

'It's not the whole town, and sure one piano lesson on a Saturday morning would more than cover the wee bits I give them.' She didn't tell him about the coats or that she often bought frocks and jumpers from the Dublin women. 'Anyway, I'm not talking about the lunches. I think Alice is cruel to Nancy. I'm not sure about Rose.'

'What kind of cruel?' John filled his mug with more water and sat at the table.

'Mary sent home good winter coats to them, and Alice sewed up the pockets on Nancy's—at least it had to be her. Who else would?'

'Why the hell would she do that?'

'I gave them mittens too, and Nancy lost hers on the first day, but I know Alice took them.'

'How do you know? You don't know that.'

'I know damn well.' Flossie unplugged the hot iron and placed it on the worktop. She sat at the table. 'Yesterday, I noticed marks on the back of her knees. I asked her what happened, and she said Josey's cat scratched her.'

'Sure maybe it did,' John said.

'I know a cat scratch when I see one. Sure didn't I get

scratched many times when I was a child. Anyway, last Monday when Nancy was ages at the toilet, I sent Kathleen out for her. When she came back, she told me Nancy had a sore arm and was crying. When I went out to check on her, she wouldn't show me at first. I bribed her with the promise of an orange. She had a burn on the inside of her arm and I don't care what anybody says, John, but I know it's a cigarette burn.'

'Would you not mention it to Miss Kennedy? If you're certain, that is.'

'I don't know what to do. I've spoken to Josey a few times about them. But I didn't mention the burns.'

'Are you ever talking to Alice?'

'I have no intentions of going near that woman. I wouldn't trust her as far as I could throw her.'

'Well, I agree with you there. Do they go to school every day?'

'Most days. She leaves them as far as Drumbannon and they walk the rest of the way with the children from there. They walk most of the way home by themselves.'

'Shhh, Benny's coming,' John whispered.

'Mammy, can we go to Francey's first, then I'll finish my jigsaw?'

'Absolutely not, mister.'

'How many more days 'til Santy's coming? Benny took his aeroplane book from the dresser and sat on John's knee.

'Not many now, sonny. Were you a good boy in school today?'

'Yes. But Shaney wasn't. He was spitting at everyone outside. Michael told on him, so he got slapped, but he didn't cry.'

'Santy mightn't bring him anything then.'

'He'll bring my aeroplane, won't he?'

'We'll have to wait and see.' He ruffled Benny's hair.

Flossie liked seeing them together. Benny was lucky to have such a good father. She'd picked a good husband.

'Okay, young man. I've to get back to the shop. It's very busy over there and Grandad will be sending Granny looking for me.' He lifted Benny down off his knee. 'Flossie, we'll talk tonight.'

§

Nancy peeped out of the babby house door as soon as Max started barking. It was Rose.

'Nancy, it's getting dark and Mammy will soon be home.' Rose joined her sister in the babby house.

'I'm staying here forever.' Nancy pressed her finger on a wriggling earwig.

'We didn't do our jobs yet, come on.'

'Are you going to tell on me?'

'No. Let's pretend we don't know how the cabinet got broken. Mammy won't even see it for ages, she stays in the kitchen most of the time.' Rose shivered. 'Come on, Nancy, it's cold in here.' Rose wafted a dangling spider from her face. She nudged her sister out the door in front of her.

The girls stayed quiet as they did their jobs. Nancy filled the basin with cold water from the barrel outside. She added a handful of clothes detergent and filled it with the dirty dishes.

Rose swept until there wasn't as much as a crumb left on the kitchen floor. She put a shovelful of coal on the fire and then took a tea towel from the clothesline that hung above the range. As she dried the dishes, she complained. 'For God's sake, Nancy, you're no good at washing the dishes. They're not done properly.'

'Yes, they are. This was my job, Rose, 'tis not fair.'

Rose ignored her, scrubbing the hardened potatoes off the saucepan with a wire scrub. 'Give that out to the pigs,' she said, handing Nancy a bowl of scraps.

'Mammy didn't say I had to, so I'm not.'

'Mammy said to Joyce she should've drowned you the day you were born because you're only a nuisance.'

With her shoulders drooped and a frown between her eyebrows, Nancy took the enamel bowl and brought it out to the pigsty in the back yard. Tears rolled down her cheeks. *Why did Rose say that? Her daddy drowned and he was never coming back. He was gone to heaven because he drowned. Why did her mammy want her to go there too and never come back?*

§

Alice bustled around the gable of the house carrying two bags of messages, one in each hand. She collided with Max, lost her balance and toppled down on top of him. Max yelped and snarled as he wriggled and twisted himself out from under her heavy body. She rolled onto her back, still holding the bags to protect her groceries—in particular her naggin of vodka.

'Bastard of a dog!' She drew a kick towards him. He turned and stripped his teeth as her foot missed his head by less than an inch. Acting on the instinct that Alice posed a danger to him and the children, Max darted at her and sunk his sharp yellow teeth into her ankle.

'You'll pay for that, ya bloody mongrel.' She fired a handful of stones after him as he bolted up the field.

Nancy watched from the pigsty, ignoring the hungry grunts from the pigs waiting on their scraps. The sight of her mother tumbling down on top of Max amused her. And when he bit into her ankle, her tummy fluttered. Nancy felt warm all over! She held her hands to her mouth to stifle her giggles.

§

Rose watched her mother bathing her ankle in a basin of salty water, muttering to herself about Max; how he was only a nuisance, and that she'd be getting rid of him for once and for all. Rose kept busy dusting the dresser, praying her mother would have forgotten about it by morning and not really give Max away. She also prayed she wouldn't go into the sitting room to turn on the Christmas tree lights. She wondered how long it would be before she'd discover the broken cabinet.

The rest of the weekend passed without another word about the dog or the china cabinet.

CHAPTER FORTY-FIVE

Alice hated Christmas. Everything about it reminded her of her family, all of whom she detested—except Nellie, who wasn't too bad. As for Carol, she left home when she was sixteen, a week before Christmas. She promised Alice in a note that she'd come back for her, but she never did.

She wished other people would keep their excitement to themselves. What was there to enjoy anyway? Busyness, spending money they probably couldn't afford, telling lies to children about a big fat jolly man who magically called to every child in the world with a present.

He hadn't come to her when she was a child. Her father had made it quite clear that there was no such man, and if they had money to spend on them at Christmas, they might get a present. If they had no money, it was tough luck. One year she got an orange that she had to share with her sister Carol, but Carol got most of it.

It was the Christmas after her ninth birthday that she remembered most, the Christmas when they all got a present. Alice got a porcelain doll. She had scratches on her face and her clothes were tatty. Alice didn't care that she wasn't brand new; she belonged to her now and that was all that mattered.

It would have been the happiest Christmas ever if her mother and father hadn't drunk so much and passed out on the couch, leaving her to the mercy of her two older brothers, Mattie and Pete.

She tried to keep out of their way, she really did. But there weren't many places to hide in their small house. They took her doll and played tug ó war with her. They pulled off her arms and legs. Alice screamed and wailed as she tried to pull the doll from them. It made them tease her even more. They taunted her and threw the doll back and forth like it was a ball.

'Smelly Alice can't catch the smelly doll,' they sang. She pleaded with Carol for help, but she went upstairs to see to the crying baby, Nellie.

Mattie bounced the doll off the ceiling. He caught it before it hit the floor and smacked it against the cement wall. Then he threw it at Alice's feet.

Alice sobbed as she picked her dolly off the floor. Her beautiful porcelain face was gone, replaced with a black hole.

Her father's slurred voice boomed in from the sitting room telling them to shut up. She tried to pick up the broken pieces, but Mattie and Pete dragged her across the floor and pushed her into the cubby hole. The door slammed shut and the key clicked in the lock, making Alice scream again. She banged on the door with her small bunched up fists until she had no energy left. Thin shards of light knifed their way through the cracks in the door. Her eyes adjusted to the darkness and her breathing settled. She leaned her back against the iron mangle, recoiling at the sudden feeling of coldness on her skin. The back door of the house slammed shut, and the boys' laughter faded into the distance.

The damp coats that hung on the wall smelled like their shaggy, old mongrel. She hated that awful dog because he knocked her to the ground every time he came in contact with her. The cold soggy mat under Alice's bare legs squished as she shuffled on her knees towards the door. She peered out through the keyhole. She called for Carol in a voice too low for her sister to hear her.

The tiny hole of light at the keyhole darkened. Alice shrunk back into the corner, on top of a pile of dirty washing. She held her faceless doll to her chest, the sharp broken edges sticking into her. Mattie's low husky voice filtered through the keyhole. 'D'ya want me to come in, Alice?' Alice shook her head vigorously and closed her eyes tight. 'No, no. I'm alright,' she said. She smelled his tobacco breath through the door; like before. Mattie turned the key and joined his shivering nine-year-old sister in the cubby hole.

§

Alice's ankle throbbed as she hobbled across the street. She cursed the dog; she couldn't do a thing all day Sunday because of him. *He'll not do it again, and that's for sure.* She sniggered to herself.

She stood queuing in the butcher's, gingerly stamping her feet on the sawdust-covered floor, in a bid to warm them. The women in front gabbled about Christmas things. Turkeys, cakes, and trifle. Auntie this and Uncle that, coming for the dinner. *They'd sicken ya!*

She was glad they were going to Josey's for the dinner on Christmas Day. He wasn't a bad auld craythur. He told her about the tricycle he was doing up for Nancy. He got it from one of Frank's friends in the foundry. It had flat tyres and rusty wheels, but he'd make it look brand new. He was fairly good with things like that. He said he had a present for Rose as well. Maybe she'd buy them a few sweets from Francey's.

Mary had sent over a couple of frocks and tights. Fancy tights they were too—very Englishy. Busybody that Mary one, but at least she sent stuff.

'All set for Christmas, Mrs Connolly?' the butcher asked.

'Half a pound a liver and a good big bone for the dog,' Alice replied and looked out the window.

The shopkeepers in town were used to her rude and abrupt manner. They paid little attention to her moods.

'Thanks,' she said taking her wrapped bone and liver.

'No bother, Mrs Connolly. You're welcome.' The butcher nodded his head, smiling as he added, 'Have a nice Christmas now.'

She left the shop, her thoughts focused on more important matters.

She decided to visit Joyce, knowing she'd get a grand cuppa tea and a nice bit of batch bread.

Alice found Joyce to be a bit odd lately, not as much fun as she used to be. The youngest in her family, Joyce was the only one left living at home. Her brothers and sisters were scattered all over the place: America, Dublin, London.

Alice knocked once on Rafferty's door, then she turned the key to let herself in. 'Hello, are ya in?'

Joyce and her mother sat each side of the scorching hot range drinking mugs of steaming Bovril. Above them, wet sheets and pillow slips were hung on timber slats suspended from the ceiling.

'God, it's lovely and warm in here,' Alice said, holding her hands in front of the fire.

'It's needed on a day like this,' Joyce's mother said. Alice knew Mrs Rafferty didn't like her, but she didn't care.

'The kettle's boiling. Will you take tea or Bovril?' Joyce used the tea towel to lift the hot kettle.

'I don't want that horrible stuff. Give me the tea.' Alice scrunched up her face in disgust.

'Have you all your Christmas shopping done? What's wee Rose and Nancy getting from Santy?' Mrs Rafferty asked.

'They're getting new bikes and we're going to Josey's for the Christmas dinner, so I haven't much to do at all.'

'Good man, Josey.'

'Aye, he's not a bad auld divil,' Alice said.

'Was there many in the butcher's?' asked Mrs Rafferty, eyeing up Alice's brown paper package.

'A few.' Alice pulled a chair out from the table and hung her coat on the back of it.

'That's a big lump of meat.'

'It's a leg-a-lamb.'

'The dog'll enjoy that,' Mrs Rafferty said and before Alice could answer, she added, 'Saw Josey coming out of the Parochial House yesterday, whatever he was doing up there.'

'Mam. Never mind,' said Joyce as she put sugar and milk in Alice's tea.

'Maybe Father Tierney's buying one of his turkeys, or

maybe his housekeeper is,' said Alice, knowing too well the priest or Miss Dunne never bought turkeys from Josey. They both went to her sister's house in Moynalty every Christmas. *What business did Josey have up at the Parochial House? And what's it got to do with you, Mrs Rafferty?*

'Are the girls getting their school holidays today?' Joyce asked.

'Indeed they are.'

'I've a wee Christmas cake for you,' said Mrs Rafferty. 'I iced it too... for the children.'

'Oh, thanks. There was no need.' *Suppose she wasn't a bad auld biddy at all. And she did bring loads of food to Frank's wake that time.*

Mrs Rafferty disappeared into the sitting room and returned with the cake wrapped in tin foil. 'Sure isn't it the season of good will and all that,' she said.

Alice blew into her cold hands. 'Ah, you're shocking good, Mrs Rafferty. Will ya put it in a bag for me, along with me leg-a-lamb?'

Mrs Rafferty stiffened as she opened a drawer and pulled out a thick paper bag with handles on it. She placed it on the table in front of Alice. 'Okay, Joyce, I'm heading down to Tierney's with these eggs. Bye, Alice. See you after the Christmas.'

'Yeah, see ya. Any bread, Joycie? Batch?' Alice asked.

'We've only soda bread.'

'That'll do. Put jam on it.'

Joyce sighed. She left the bread, butter and marmalade on the table in front of Alice. 'Sure you'll manage it yourself,' she said.

Alice didn't notice Joyce's irritation. She cut a thick slice of bread and dug the knife into the cold slab of butter. 'Jesus, your butter's shocking hard, Joycie.'

'Scrape it off the top.' Joyce gritted her teeth and poured herself a cup of tea. She sat at the opposite end of the table.

'Will we go to the pub on Christmas Eve?' asked Alice.

'And who'll mind Rose and Nancy if you're in the pub?'

'Josey will.'

'On Christmas Eve?'

'So what?'

'Well, maybe Josey might want to go to the pub himself.'

'Sure I'll ask him.' Alice cut another slice of bread; skipping the butter, she piled marmalade on top.

'You know what, Joycie, you're so lucky you've no children. They're a fecking nuisance. You can do what ya like and go where ya want, without any brats hanging outta ya.'

'Surely they're not that bad. There's never a peep out of them wee girls whenever I see them,' said Joyce.

'Aye. Outside angels and inside devils. That's what they are. Especially that Nancy one.'

'Jesus, Alice. You never knew how lucky you were. You got the catch of the town when you got Frank Connolly and all you ever did was give out about him. And now all you ever do is give out about the children. You're nearly thirty, you're a widow with two children, and look at me, heading for thirty-two with not a sign of getting a decent man.'

Alice's jaw stopped, and she swallowed her half-chewed bread.

'It's not my fault you couldn't keep a man.'

'I'll tell you why I couldn't keep a man. Because of hanging around with you! Everyone calls us two tramps. Do you know that?' Joyce was spitting with every word. 'Two bikes. Well, I'm fed up carrying on like a tramp. I'm not going to the pub any more nights with you, or getting off with those salesmen, thinking every bloody time one of them will marry me.' Joyce's voice trembled. 'Even Paddy hardly looks at me anymore.' She pushed her shoulders back, proud at having stood up to Alice. 'And if you must know, I'm going over to London to my sister after Christmas. She's getting me a job. Mammy and Daddy said I should and I think I should too.' Joyce leaned against the dresser with her arms folded, her lips pressed so tight they were almost invisible.

Alice laughed while stuffing the last piece of bread into her mouth. She held up her cup.

'Put another spout in there for me, will ya?'

'Do it yourself, Alice.'

Alice's face turned crimson. 'Who the hell d'ya think ya are?'

'Get out. I've had enough of you. You're mad!' Joyce flung her arm towards the door.

'So ya were jealous of me, were ya?' Alice put on her coat and stuffed her bone and liver into the bag along with the cake. 'Catch of the town, my arse. Frank Connolly was nothing but a flirt. Did yas all think I was stupid? Did he think I was stupid? I knew all about him and that stuck-up cow, Flossie Lynch.'

'See... you're talking rubbish, Alice. Frank wasn't a flirt. He was just nice to people. That's all! He talked to everyone. And he had fun—at least he did before he married you.'

'What's that supposed to mean?'

'Are you forgetting *why* he married you?'

'Shut up, Joycie!'

'How stupid do you think I am? I know you weren't really

pregnant, Alice. There was never any baby. And your miscarriage was a lie!'

'You stupid little bitch, Joycie.' Alice stood up and darted towards her. Joyce was just as quick and squared up to Alice with hands on her hips. 'I'll call Daddy if you don't feck off, Alice.'

'Hope you haven't been going around telling lies about me.'

'What lies? It's not lies. And Frank knew too. He asked me questions. Sure the doctor told him you hadn't been to see him about any pregnancy. Frank was likely too embarrassed to admit what he really knew deep down.'

'Oh, so what? He tried to get rid of me. Who cares anyway?'

Joyce knew it no longer mattered and that Alice held no remorse. It was like talking to the wall.

'I'll come to London with ya.'

Joyce shook her head in disbelief. 'How the hell can you even think about coming to London with two children?'

'I suppose,' she said.

'Get a job while they're at school. Take my job in Tierney's.'

'I don't want your stupid job.'

'Stop drinking, Alice. And give up them fags. You've an awful cough, like an auld one.'

'Are you becoming a nun, Joycie? Because you fucking sound like one.'

'I'll write to you.'

'Oh, don't bother your arse.' Alice grabbed her bag off the table and stomped towards the door. She stuck up her two fingers at Joyce as she left.

§

Alice's thoughts sped through her mind like wildfire. She mumbled to herself as she limped down Main Street. *Catch of the town indeed. Well, he's not here now, is he? Never should have got with him in the first place. Look at me now, stuck with two ungrateful little brats. How dare Joycie call me a liar and then feck off to London.* Alice's eyes stung as she thought of her sister, Carol, who fecked off too, to God knows where. She may never have left home if Alice hadn't told her what Mattie had been doing to her. She wished she had kept her mouth shut... wished Carol had kept her mouth shut too.

'Don't tell, Carol, or he'll take me to the bog and put me in a black hole,' Alice had said.

Carol's face tightened, as if someone had squeezed it. She walked round in circles in their tiny bedroom, biting her closed fist. She took several deep breaths. 'We'll tell Mammy,' she said. 'It's not right.'

Alice pleaded with her sister. 'No, you can't. Please don't.'

Carol placed her hands on Alice's shoulders. 'It's okay. Stay here, I'll be back in a minute.' Carol left the room. The muffled voices in the kitchen below fell silent—just for a moment. Alice went to the window and looked up at the starlit sky. She heard laughter from Mattie. Carol's voice got louder. Alice tried to count the stars. She strained her eyes to see the Seven Sisters. There they were, small and twinkling, in their little cluster. She shivered at the sound of Mattie's voice coming through the ceiling. 'She's a liar. Nothing but a little liar.' Her father said it too. 'Liar.' Alice's vision blurred and she lost sight of the Seven Sisters. She wiped her wet face with the curtain. 'Troublemakers, the pair a ya, filthy liars,' her father said. Alice knew by her sister's pitiful cries that she was suffering a beating. The bedroom door opened slowly. Her mother's skeletal figure stepped inside. The Tilley lamp cast shadows over her ashen features. Alice peered into her mother's eyes, searching for a sign that everything was going to be okay, but she saw nothing.

Her mother spoke placidly. 'Just stay out of their way, can't you?' Then she left. Alice buried her head in her pillow until everything went silent again. A week later, just before Christmas, Carol left a note under Alice's pillow. *I'll come back for you,* it said. She never did.

Alice wiped away her tears and went into O'Malley's shop.

'What can I do for you today, Mrs Connolly?' said Frederick, approaching her with a smile.

'A roll of elastic. John knows the kind I get,' she said, staring at John who remained focused on serving Molly Fagin. Alice stayed near the door until Molly left. Frederick carried on hanging up shirts on a display rack.

'Will I give you the usual, Alice?' asked John as he took a box of elastics from a shelf.

Alice approached the counter. 'Aye, the thick stuff.'

With his hands under the counter, John rolled up a five-pound note and wound a yard of cheap elastic around it.

'We have to meet,' she whispered.

John gave a wry smile and leaned closer to Alice. 'We do indeed.'

'I need more money, O'Malley.'

'You sure do, Alice.'

She recoiled at his tone. His narrowed eyes stabbed at her

through the thick black rims of his glasses. He wrapped the roll of elastic in a piece of paper. 'There's a wee love letter in there for you too.'

She snapped it out of his hand and left. She had John O'Malley all figured out. He'd do anything for her rather than let his family know all his dirty little secrets. She wasn't afraid of him. *Weak little man.* She took the roll of elastic out her pocket and peeled the note from it. She read it and smiled. 'That's the good boy, Johnnie,' she said.

Alice thumbed a lift on her way home, but no one stopped for her. Hobbling in her back yard she went to the coal house. She climbed a step ladder to reach the top shelf where a tub of rat poison was kept.

CHAPTER FORTY-SIX

'N*o more Irish, no more French, no more sitting on a hard wooden bench...'* Nancy and Rose sang merrily with the Drumbannon children on their way home from school.

They were all excited getting their Christmas holidays, chattering over each other about what they hoped to get from Santy. Roisin Rogers had the longest list as usual, with Joey Farrelly telling her she was greedy and would get nothing.

Rose and Nancy left them arguing and carried on down the road towards the Wood Lane. When passing Josey's house, they talked about Christmas Day, Santy, cake, snow, and their daddy.

'Do you like Mrs O'Malley?' Nancy asked.

'Yes, she's nice. She was Daddy's friend, y'know.'

'I like her a bit. But sometimes she gives out.'

'Only when you're bold, Nancy. She likes good girls.'

'I try to be good,' said Nancy.

Their mother met them at the back door.

'We have our Christmas holidays now, Mammy.' Nancy

smiled up at her.

'Get in there,' Alice said.

The girls scurried past her.

'Get up to your bedroom, now!'

Nancy tensed and ran up the stairs behind Rose. Halfway up, she stumbled. She let out a cry but swiftly gathered herself up. She heard Rose close behind and her mother's heavy steps.

Nancy jumped on the bed and pressed her scrawny body against the cold stone wall. Her breath quickened as her heart hammered against her bony chest. Rose followed, her spindly legs like jelly. She tripped on the chamber pot, knocking it over. Stale putrid urine splashed her tights.

'Now look what ya done,' Alice said.

'Sorry, Mammy, it was an accident.' Rose jumped up beside Nancy.

'Who broke the cabinet?' Alice asked as she stood over the bed with her hands on her hips.

'It was Rose. She did it, not me,' said Nancy.

'Stop telling lies.' Rose tightened her fists, her nails digging into her palms.

'I don't care who did it, but there's no Santy coming to this house. And we'll not be going to Josey's for the Christmas dinner either.'

Alice's vexed face glistened and her chest heaved as she released her raspy breath. Nancy stared up at her mother's eyes; she imagined they might fall out of her head and roll across the floor like Benny O'Malley's marbles.

'Don't leave this room until morning,' Alice said.

When Alice closed the door behind her, Nancy shut her eyes tight. She hugged her knees and rocked back and forth.

She searched her mind for her daddy's face, his kind face. Other faces appeared instead: Uncle Josey, Mrs O'Malley, her friend Kathleen in school, Father Tierney. Then she found him—her daddy. He put his arms around her. His soft voice whispered in her ear, '*There, there. Poor wee Snipey, wet and drukey, out in the rain all night. Poor Snipey, poor Snipey.*' She felt his hands stroke her face. The tears gushed through her closed eyelids like a burst dam as she whimpered in her daddy's arms.

§

The cold room darkened as the hours passed, but Rose and Nancy didn't notice. They ignored the grumbling in their bellies, not daring to venture down to the kitchen. Rose stroked Nancy's short spikey hair, wishing it was still long and wavy so she could pull the hairbrush through it to make it shine, like she used to. She pulled the bedcovers over both of them.

'I didn't mean to throw the ball,' Nancy whispered.

'Doesn't matter. I think Santy will come anyway. She can't stop him. And Uncle Josey will bring us to his house for dinner,' Rose said. 'I promise I won't be horrible to you ever again, Nancy.'

'I won't be bold ever again.'

'And you can't tell lies either... or you'll go to hell.'

'I won't tell lies ever again.'

'I'll mind you forever,' Rose told her.

'Can we live with Uncle Josey?' Nancy whispered.

'I don't think so.' They huddled together and eventually fell asleep.

CHAPTER FORTY-SEVEN

Everything reminded Josey of Frank: working on the farm, being with his nieces, dark frosty mornings—like this one—when he'd call in for tea before heading to the foundry.

Even with two pairs of thick wool socks, the cold shot up Josey's legs when he pulled on his wellies. Icy mist invaded his nostrils as soon as he stepped outside. He popped a clove drop into his mouth. A skein of ice on the barrel of water outside the door caused Josey's insides to shiver as he remembered how Frank used to break the ice, fill his mug with the freezing water and drink it down in one go. Always fancied himself as the hardier of the two—which he was, Josey admitted.

Walking through the two fields that separated his home from Frank's, he expected Max to meet him along the way. Alice probably had him locked in the coal house. With the house still in darkness, Josey assumed they were all still in bed. He went straight to the byre where Tomás had already started milking the cows.

Tomás was a quiet young man who rarely started a conversation but chatted away when encouraged. He worked hard for Josey, never complained, and never missed a day's work. He cycled in from Galbolie every morning in all kinds of weather. Josey was grateful for Tomás, especially now that he didn't have Frank's help in the evenings.

'There's a few small jobs Rose and Nancy can help with later,' Josey said.

Tomás smiled. 'No bother. Sure they love helping. Wee Nancy's a great worker for only the size of her.'

'She's a tough one, alright! I'll call for them when we get this byre cleaned out.'

'Josey,' Tomás said as he kept shovelling into the wheelbarrow.

'Yeah?'

'You know the way Frank used to help you on the farm in the evenings?'

'I do. I miss him for that.'

'Well, I was thinking, I could stay longer every day and help you.'

'You must be a mind reader because I was thinking the same thing. I'll give you a rise of course, and you don't have to stay on every evening. Not Fridays. Take Fridays off.'

'Ah, I'll stay every day.'

'Tomás, you should go out places. The pictures, or the dances. You'll never get a woman if you're not out places.'

Tomás blushed, and still he shovelled the dung. 'I'm fine, boss.'

'Whatever ya think, young lad.'

They worked themselves warm for a couple of hours and after the foddering, they were ready for their morning tea.

'I'll head down for the girls and we'll meet you at the house. Will ya put a match to the fire? I've it set,' Josey said.

Still no smoke from Alice's chimney, although Josey had seen days when she wouldn't have it lit until dinnertime, even on a hard frosty day.

He whistled softly as he crossed the hedge into her back yard. The pigs snuffled around in the sty, and his cat, Snowy, sat on the post looking in at them. Josey was surprised to see the coal house door wide open.

'Max. Here boy,' he called as he peered into the dimness. The lazy dog lay in the corner. 'Hey boy... you're quiet this morning.' Max stretched himself, yawned and followed Josey. 'You must be getting old. Any sign of these ones today?'

Josey rapped on the door, lifted the latch and entered. He expected to hear the wireless and the chattering of Rose and Nancy. He expected to see Alice sitting at the table in a cloud of cigarette smoke and a mug of tea in her hand. Instead, he walked into a silent, empty kitchen.

He went into the hall and stood at the foot of the stairs and called out. 'Alice?'

'Uncle Josey,' two small voices answered.

'Oh, there you are. I was starting to think the fairies ran off with yas,' he said.

'Can we come down?' Nancy asked.

'Of course you can.'

'Rose said we had to wait till Mammy calls us, and I'm hungry,' Nancy said as she led the way down.

'Where's your mammy?'

'Don't know, somewhere,' said Rose.

'Well, the door wasn't locked so maybe she's down at the well. Come on, I'll make tea,' Josey said.

'The bucket's here so she's not at the well,' said Rose.

Josey rummaged in the presses. *Porridge, eggs, anything.* He found half a loaf. He turned to the table, letting out a string of curses.

'Can we live with you, Uncle Josey?' Nancy asked.

He bent down beside her and looked into her puffy eyes. He traced his finger across her pink cracked lips. 'Were you crying?'

She nodded. He held her cold hands in his. The smell of urine stifled him. 'Did you go to bed in your clothes?'

Rose nodded, hanging her head low. 'Uncle Josey, we didn't mean to. Mammy got mad 'cause Nancy broke the glass and we stayed in bed all day.'

'The whole day?'

'Yes. Then it got dark and we went to sleep.'

'Did you get dinner?'

'No, because Mammy said we had to stay in our room.' Rose dabbed at her bruised knee.

'What happened to your knee?' Josey asked.

'I fell.'

'I'm taking you and Rose up to the farm for the day. Would you like that?'

'Are we allowed?' Rose asked as she huddled close to the cold range.

'Yes.' Rage engulfed Josey. He pulled a shopping bag from the cubby hole and stomped up the stairs and into the girls' bedroom. A urine-soaked towel lay on the floor beside the chamber pot. The place stank of staleness and dirty clothes. When it was Mary's room, it smelled of books and soap. Their mother had it decorated in bright colours that radiated joy.

Josey shook his head. He had let his brother down by not interfering, and he wasn't prepared to let his nieces down too. He packed some clothes into the bag—clean and dirty. He needed to call Mary.

§

Tomás had the fire lit and the kettle on the gas. He gave the girls his usual welcoming smile. 'Ah, here they are. The best wee farmers in the country,' he said. His smile faded when he sensed that all wasn't well. Josey looked mad and mumbled something about *that woman*.

'Tomás, will you do me a favour?' Josey pulled a notepad from the dresser drawer. 'Go to Flossie O'Malley and give her this note, please.' Josey wrote only a couple of words on the sheet of paper, folded it in half, and gave it to Tomás.

'Boss, will I go to her house?'

'Yea, but don't give the note to anyone. Only her. If she's not home, you'll find her in town somewhere.'

Tomás ran his bicycle out the path, then mounted the saddle after it gathered up speed. The cold wind blew in his face, the dampness of the December air chilled him to the bone, but he was so used to being out in all weathers, it didn't bother him.

§

'It's that young lad from Connolly's at the door. He wants you,' Goretti said.

Flossie remembered back to the last time Tomás came looking for her. 'Bring him in, Mammy.'

'He won't come in. He wants you at the door.'

Goretti sniffed the air. She followed her daughter to the front door.

'It's private, Miss,' Tomás said.

'Mammy, will you go in please?'

'I've to see to my scones anyway,' Goretti said. She didn't like to be kept in the dark about anything.

'I have a note from Mr Connolly. Not Frank, Josey.' Tomás blushed. 'Sorry, miss.'

'It's okay, Tomás. Give me the note.'

He spoke in a hurried loud whisper. 'I promise I didn't read it, miss, but I think it's about the two wee girls, Rose and Nancy. Mr Connolly has them in his house and he's mad at the mother.'

Flossie read the note.

'Okay, Tomás. Thank you. Tell Josey I'll be there as soon as I can.'

'Mammy. I'm going out to Josey Connolly's. I won't be long.'

'Why are you going out there? What's going on?'

'I don't really know 'til I get there. Probably nothing much. See you later.'

'Will I come with you?'

'No, Mammy, of course not.' Flossie wasted no time cycling down the Cavan Road; she would do anything for Frank's children.

§

Rose and Nancy sat at the table eating boiled eggs and brown bread. They looked pitiful even though they smiled when

Flossie walked in. A tightness in her throat brought her out in a cold sweat.

'You going to help Uncle Josey today?' she asked, whipping off her hat and scarf.

'Yes, miss.' Rose beamed. 'We've to help clean the hen house.'

Nancy nodded, her mouth too full to speak.

'It's nice and warm in here, but wrap up well going outside because it's bitter cold today,' Flossie said.

'I have to talk to Mrs O'Malley in the sitting room for a minute,' Josey said. He beckoned at Flossie to follow him.

Flossie hadn't been in the sitting room in exactly six years. Mixed emotions welled up inside her. Bitterness, an urge to run from the place where she'd declared her love for Frank, a desire to touch him, tormented by the memories and a yearning for memories she didn't get to make. Regret gnawed at her psyche knowing Benny would never know his real father. She shivered. 'What's going on, Josey?'

'Ya hardly saw Alice in town, did ya?'

'Well, no. But I wasn't out and about today. I came straight here when Tomás gave me your note.'

'God knows where she is. I called to the house to pick the girls up and they were on their own.'

'Wouldn't be the first time,' Flossie said.

'True. But I've a feeling she's gone since last night. No signs that she was even in the kitchen this morning. Sure she'd have two or three fags smoked and a couple of mugs of tea in her before getting dressed. Not only that, she also wasn't in the habit of leaving the girls in bed 'til near mid-day. Up scrubbing floors and gathering sticks in the hedges, be more like it.'

'Jesus. Are you sure, Josey?'

'They slept in their clothes. Rose said they're in bed since early yesterday.'

'So where the hell is she?'

'No idea. They were sitting in wee-soaked clothes. They stink.'

'I'll sort them out for you, Josey.'

'Thanks, Flossie. There was no one else I could ask. I'm calling Mary. Today!'

'And tell her what?'

'Tell her what's been going on. She might have some idea what to do. Apart from fecking killing Alice!'

'Have you got all their Christmas stuff sorted?'

'More or less.'

'That's good.'

'I went to see Father Tierney about them. I told him Alice wasn't fit to look after them. I told him out straight she was mad in the head.'

'Ah, Josey. We can't have the girls getting sent into a home. He could have Alice locked up and Rose and Nancy taken away. You'd never see them again.'

'No. He said as long as someone could take them in, that'd be grand. So Mary might take them.'

'Over to England? You'd never see them, Josey.'

'Well, it'd be a hell of a lot better than watching that woman treating them like stray dogs on the streets.'

'I'll take them.'

'What? Are you serious? You couldn't!'

Flossie plonked herself on the couch. Her head was exhausted thinking about Frank, and the girls. Not to mention the strain of constantly pretending at life, hiding her grief from everyone. 'I would, you know. If John would let me.'

'Something was going on with you and Frank. Am I right?' Josey turned his back to Flossie, embarrassed by his question.

She almost denied it, but what did it matter now? She trusted Josey. 'We almost got together before he married Alice. And again, just before he died. We were in love. I saw what she did to him. He talked about signing her in, but he didn't know what to do.'

'I would have helped him. He should have come to me,' Josey said. 'I'd suspected for a long time, things weren't good, and then when she scalded him...'

'He was embarrassed.'

'That's why you care about these wee girls, isn't it?'

'They're the closest thing to him, I suppose.'

'And Benny?' Josey asked, and in the same breath, he added, 'Sorry, forget I said that.'

Flossie looked Josey in the eye, dismissing his embarrassment. 'I'll bathe the girls if you show me where things are. Have you clean clothes for them?'

'I brought whatever I could find from the house. Their clothes need a wash.'

'I'll do that,' she said. 'When do you think she'll be back?'

Josey raised his voice. 'Alice can feck off if she comes here looking for them. I'll tell her I'll get the guards out.'

Flossie understood Josey's anger.

'I'm going to town to ring Mary. Have you time to stay?'

'Of course, you go on. I'll see to the girls.'

'Thanks, Flossie.'

'Josey.' Flossie took the biggest breath she ever took in her life. 'I'm glad you asked about Benny. The answer is yes. He's Frank's son.'

'Jesus, Flossie.' Josey pressed the tips of his fingers into his creased forehead.

'Please don't think bad of us. Yes, we did a terrible thing and I feel so ashamed.'

'So you've been together all these years?'

'No, God no. We were together like that only once and then we avoided each other all down the years.'

'Did he know about Benny?'

Flossie's shoulders dropped. 'I don't know. He may have suspected, but we didn't talk about it.'

'And John?'

'No, he doesn't know. I can't tell him, Josey. How can I?'

Rose called out from the kitchen.

'We'll talk about it again,' Josey said.

'Please don't be mad at us, Josey.'

Josey didn't reply, but Flossie saw the disappointment in his eyes.

§

Rose and Nancy were excited at having a bath in Josey's. He'd had a proper bathroom put into the cottage: a toilet, a sink and a huge bath. Flossie half filled it with warm water and squirted some shampoo in to make it bubbly. The girls giggled as they stepped into the pool of white foam. The shampoo smelled fresh and clean, like the trees in the woods.

Nancy tensed when Flossie poured a jug of water over her head. 'If you lean back a little bit, Nancy, and look up to the ceiling, it will be easier. Close your eyes and think about your most favourite thing in the world,' Flossie said.

She shampooed Nancy's short hair twice until the suds were snow white. She made little white spikes and let her see in a mirror. 'You look like one of Molly Fagin's meringues.'

The girls laughed and Nancy said, 'I like you, miss.'

'And I like you too Nancy—very much.' Flossie held the child's face in her hands and scanned her features. She looked so much like Frank. Sallow skin, and eyes like little droplets from the ocean.

'It's my turn now, miss,' said Rose.

When the girls' fingers began to resemble dried prunes, Flossie wrapped them in towels and sat them on the armchair in front of the fire. She dressed them as appropriately as she could. There wasn't much to choose from in the bag of clothes Josey brought from the house. Pants, but no vests. Trousers, light summery frocks and a couple of woolly jumpers.

The day turned wet and Josey decided against taking the girls out to the farm. He asked Flossie if she could stay until evening time, when he'd be finished work. Tomás had messages to get in town and Flossie gave him a note to give Goretti.

I'm in Josey's minding Rose and Nancy for a little while. I'll be home this evening. Flossie.

Throughout the day, Josey called to the house every hour to check if Alice had returned. When it got dark, he became concerned.

'I don't think she ever stayed away this long,' he said.

'Did Tomás check Joyce's house?' Flossie asked.

'Yea. Joyce said they had an argument yesterday and she

hasn't seen her since. He checked all the pubs too, but no one's seen her.'

'I have to be off now. I'll call back tomorrow morning.'

'Okay. Thanks, Flossie,' Josey said.

§

'You took your time.' Goretti had the front door open before Flossie had the key out of her bag.

'Did you not get my note?'

'I did. What's going on out there at Connollys'?'

'I can't tell you because you'll only spread it around town and it's nothing much anyway.'

Her mother snorted, her eyes wide in disbelief. 'As if I'd do any such thing.'

'Mammy, it's nothing much. Rose and Nancy miss their father, especially with Christmas here, and because I'm their teacher, Josey thought I could talk to them.'

'Sure why didn't you say that in the first place? Acting like it's some big secret.'

'Do you know if John's home from Dublin?' Flossie asked.

'Well, I saw the car outside the shop around dinnertime.'

'Dinnertime?'

'Sure he left at cockcrow this morning. I'd say he was at Clery's before it even opened,' Goretti said.

CHAPTER FORTY-EIGHT

John and Frederick worked late every evening coming up to Christmas. The Widow Johnson had finished all her cleaning jobs for the week and she stood inside the door of the shop waiting for her wages. 'There's a bit extra in there for you,' said Ruth as she handed her an envelope.

'I heard Alice Connolly is gone missing and nobody knows where she is,' Mrs Johnson said.

Ruth's mouth gaped open. 'What?' she asked.

'Not been seen since Monday. Josey's looked everywhere.'

'How come I didn't hear about this? Frederick? Did you know about this?'

'Eh, I forgot to mention it, dear. But I only heard about it this morning, from John.'

'What about the two wee girls?'

'Josey has them, as usual,' said Mrs Johnson.

'Poor divils. But it's Christmas in two days.' Ruth shook her head and sighed. 'No father and mother at a time like this. God help them.'

'Well, a happy Christmas to all of ye,' said Mrs Johnson as she tightened her scarf and pulled her hat down over her ears.

§

Flossie and her mother had a lot to do. Goretti started on icing the Christmas cake while Flossie took out the good delft and glasses from the cabinet to wash them for Christmas Day. Everything had to be immaculate, especially with John's parents coming for dinner.

The word had spread about Alice going missing. John arrived home from work with several versions of the gossip. Some believed she ran away. Probably with a man, some said. Billy Rafferty said the fairies took her back and it wasn't before time.

Goretti didn't speak to Flossie for hours for not telling her the true reason she was out at Connolly's the previous day.

'Josey said to say nothing until he was sure where Alice was. He thought she'd be back by lunchtime. Anyway, I bet she's back already. You know what people are like, making a mountain out of a molehill.'

'No smoke without fire,' said Goretti.

'I'm calling back out to Josey's later. I'm going to the graveyard first. I have a holly wreath for Daddy's grave.'

'Do you really think she's back?'

'I haven't a clue. Funny for her to disappear for the whole day though. I'll collect Benny on my way back from the graveyard. Is that okay, Mam?'

'Yes, yes, of course.'

§

Flossie stood beside Frank's grave; the cold ground numbed the soles of her feet. Icy wind blew in her face. The graveyard was the coldest place on earth, even on a summer's day. She cried more these days than she did when he first died. Only now was she able to visit the grave. Only now, she fully realised that she would never see him again, never have the chance to make a life with him. Never leave John.

The emptiness inside her would stay empty forever. Nothing would ever fill the gaping hole, the black mass of nothingness that would sometimes expand in her chest and spread up to her neck, blocking the back of her throat so she couldn't breathe properly.

Flossie stared at the mound of hard clay and the patches of stubborn frost that refused to melt in the soft sun. The dead flowers had all been removed. All that remained was an artificial wreath put there by Josey. Tears rolled down her cold cheeks. She let them flow; they soothed her.

'What is the soul?' she whispered, looking to God above. 'What is it all about? What is it really all about? We die, earth to earth, ashes to ashes, dust to dust. We return to our Father in Heaven. But what if the soul dies too? Like the body. Nothing left. No Heaven at all, no Hell.' Flossie blessed herself and prayed for Frank's soul—and begged forgiveness for doubting her faith.

The darkness gnawed inside her. She had to believe she would see him again. She would go to Heaven at her time of death. Why was life so unfair? She should have been his wife and the mother of his children. Alice wasn't a good wife or mother. Now she was gone, and they had no mother.

'I'll take care of your children, Frank, don't you worry about that. I promise you. I will love them the way I love my Benny—with every ounce of my heart.' She blessed herself and made her way to her father's grave with the holly.

§

When Rose answered the door of Josey's cottage, Flossie's heart bounced; *Alice still wasn't back.* The girls were happy to see Benny and the three of them went into the sitting room to play. Josey made tea for himself and Flossie.

'Any sign of her yet?'

Josey looked stressed. 'No. I'll have to go to the guards. God knows where she is. What if something happened to her? If someone harmed her?'

'I'd say she ran off,' Flossie said.

'Well, that wouldn't surprise me either.'

'You have to tell the guards either way, I suppose.'

'Mary gave out yards about her on the phone. She reckons she'll come crawling back when whoever she's with gets sick of her,' said Josey.

'Josey, would you and the girls come to our house on Christmas Day?'

'For the dinner?'

'Yes, for dinner. I'll check with John and Mammy of course, but I'm sure they'd be fine with it.'

'But they don't know us as well as you do. Especially John. I can't expect that, Flossie.'

'What are you talking about? Mammy has known your family for years. And John knows you're a good man.

Mammy feels sorry for Rose and Nancy, and she knows Benny gets on great with them. They'll be happy about it.'

'Well now, we'll be grand here on our own anyway.' Josey lowered his voice. 'Did I tell you I done up an old bike for Rose? It's as good as new. They'll have a grand day.'

'At least think about it. Will I take the girls home with me and you can get on with your work?'

'Are you sure you can?'

'Of course. They can play with Benny. There'll not be a bother on them.'

§

Goretti wasn't surprised when Flossie and Benny returned with Rose and Nancy. She knew her daughter had been attached to that family since childhood, and she'd promised Mary she'd look out for them.

'Benny, take Rose and Nancy out to the back garden to play on the swing. Leave your coats on,' Flossie said.

'Is the mother back?' Goretti asked as soon as the children ran out the back door.

'No sign of her. Josey's going to the guards. She could be dead in the woods for all we know.'

'Jesus, Mary and Joseph, don't be saying things like that.' Goretti faced the Sacred Heart picture and blessed herself.

'They're as good as orphans anyway, Mammy,' Flossie said.

'Sure God help them.'

'Can they come here on Christmas Day, with Josey?'

'Oh God, I don't know about that now.' Goretti recoiled.

'Why not? You're always preaching about doing good and helping those in need.'

'What about the O'Malleys? They're coming too, remember,' Goretti said.

'Sure we've plenty of room. It won't be for what they'll eat. Rose and Nancy can sit at the coffee table in the sitting room with Benny. There'll be plenty of room for the rest of us here in the kitchen. The Legion of Mary women would talk about how kind you are to take in the Connolly orphans.'

'Flossie, they're not orphans! Stop calling them that.'

'They might as well be. They've no parents, so they're orphans.' Flossie chewed on a broken fingernail. 'And wouldn't they be great company for Benny? Someone to show his new toys to, someone to play with.'

'I suppose so,' Goretti said.

'So is that a yes?'

'Oh, I suppose it would be a nice thing to do.' Goretti imagined telling her friends about the good deed she had done for Christmas. She'd be the saint of the town.

'Mammy, I think it would be better if you mention it to John. It's your house and everything.'

'Sure John's a good man, he'll not mind at all.'

Flossie plamaused her mother some more. 'Ah I know, but he has a soft spot for you.'

Goretti blushed and bobbed her head from side to side.

CHAPTER FORTY-NINE

'What else did he say?' Mary asked Jim as she dished out his tea.

'That she hasn't been seen since Monday. Disappeared into thin air. He was going to the guards as well.'

'And he definitely said the girls are alright?' asked Mary.

'Yes. Sort of.'

'What do you mean… sort of?' She paused half-way through pouring milk into a jug.

'Josey said she's horrid mean to them, especially wee Nancy. They were starving and filthy when he picked them up from the house. Flossie sorted them out for him.'

Mary's eyes widened. 'What?' She put down the milk bottle. Then her nostrils flared. 'I'll kill Alice if I ever get my hands on her. Our Frank would turn in his grave.' She paced the kitchen floor. 'What if they want to take the girls away? To a children's home.'

'Josey said he'll do what he can.' Jim loved Mary and he knew what she was thinking even before she knew herself.

She drummed her fingers on the worktop. 'Josey's not the outspoken type. Does he even have a plan?'

'He said Flossie was helping him too. She's very good to them in school, you know.'

'Yes, I know that. And Goretti's well in with the guards—and Father Tierney.'

'Flossie won't see them taken away, so don't you be worrying,' Jim said.

'She had a mad notion of our Frank, you know.' Mary lifted Frank's photo off the sideboard. 'She thought I didn't know, but I saw the way those two looked at each other. Long before Alice came around the place, and after Alice. But I never said anything.'

'Well, I didn't know that,' Jim said.

'Sure I'd say she only married John because she didn't get Frank.'

'Jesus, Mary, don't say things like that. I think they're well matched, her and John.'

'Will ya go away outta that,' Mary said. 'He's as dry as anything, odd as two left feet.'

'Ah, he's not that bad.'

'Anyway, it doesn't matter now. She married him and now she's stuck with him.'

'Mary,' Jim gestured towards the chair beside him, 'sit down for a minute.'

Mary blew her nose with her cotton hankie and sat down.

Jim looked at her earnestly. 'Before Frank died, we talked about going back home to Ireland. I know you haven't settled in here properly, and to be honest, I'm not sure I have either. Would yourself and Maureen make your way back after

Christmas and as soon as I have myself sorted with a job there, I'll follow? And the dog of course.'

'Really, Jim? Do you think we could do that?' Mary's eyes lit up the room and Jim's heart swelled a little.

'I've been making enquiries already if you want to know, and there's a few positions coming up near home.'

'Jim, I'd love that. We'll help Josey to look after Rose and Nancy, and if that cow does come back...'

'Never mind her, Mary. Of course she'll be back, but at least we'll be there to look out for the girls. We can stay with my mother until we get our own place.'

'I'm going home Jim, to my own house. She'll not be back.'

'And if she does come back?' he asked.

'I'll deal with that if it happens.'

CHAPTER FIFTY

Rose and Nancy liked playing with Benny. He had jigsaws and board games. He had more toys than anyone else in the whole world. Benny took out a box of marbles, to the amazement of Nancy. The small colourful balls rolled across the floor, making a melodious chink as they bounced off each other. Benny divided his collection of marbles into three piles, explaining how his game would be played. He enjoyed being the master of all the toys.

At six o'clock, the bells of the Angelus called from the wireless and Goretti called on the children to say their prayers. Rose and Nancy weren't familiar with the routine of evening prayer. They knelt on the mat beside Benny, copying everything he did.

Flossie watched them closely, admiring her son and his manners. Rose was a good child too, but she wasn't sure what to make of Nancy. She couldn't decide whether the child was shy or afraid. She seemed alert and attentive to everything that went on around her, just like in school. She'd say very little most of the time, but when she did, she was straight to the point.

The Angelus was quick, so the children didn't have time to get bored. As soon as Benny said 'Amen', he was up off the mat, followed by Rose and Nancy.

'Tea will be ready soon,' Flossie said.

'When are we going back to Uncle Josey's?' asked Rose.

'We're staying here all Christmas,' said Nancy.

Flossie stared at the child, and her mother nudged her from behind.

'Aren't we, Mrs O'Malley? I heard you saying it.'

'Well, we don't know yet, Nancy. You have to go back to Uncle Josey's after tea and then we'll see,' Flossie said.

Nancy narrowed her eyes, pursed her lips, and folded her arms, keeping her gaze on Flossie.

'Off you go now, back to the toys,' Goretti said. 'How did that child hear us talking about Christmas? Wasn't she in the garden with the other two?' Goretti hissed when they were out of earshot.

'Christ, Mammy, I don't know. She must've been standing outside the door. And with the wireless blaring in here too.'

'There's nothing wrong with her hearing anyway, I'll say that much,' said Goretti. 'I need a cup of sweet tea after that.'

§

John was glad to get home. His feet ached, running up and down to the storeroom all day, looking for this, that and the other for people who couldn't make up their minds what they wanted. He couldn't wait to see the back of Christmas.

His chicken casserole stayed warm over a saucepan of hot water on the range. Benny didn't run to meet him as he usually did.

'Where's my Benny?' he called.

'The Connolly children are here, John,' Goretti whispered.

'Oh, right. Why are you whispering?'

'Because,' she whispered again.

He looked at Flossie. 'So why are they here?'

'Josey asked me to help. Alice didn't come home, and poor Josey has to work and...'

'Okay, Flossie, fine.' John sat at the table eager to have his tea. 'Thank God tomorrow's Christmas Eve. I'll be glad of the rest,' he said. 'Tell Benny I'm home.'

Flossie opened the hall door and called for her son.

'John, could you take the girls home in Frederick's car?' asked Goretti.

He felt like saying no. He was tired. 'I suppose I could.'

The children ran into the kitchen.

'Daddy, my friends are here.' Benny smiled, showing a gap where his two front teeth used to be. 'We played marbles and I won. I won all the games, because Rose and Nancy haven't got any games like me, so they don't know how to play.'

'Well now, I'm sure they have some games,' said John.

'We have dolls and books,' Nancy said. 'We're orphans, so we are.'

'What's orphans?' asked Benny and Rose at the same time.

'No, you're not orphans. Your mammy will be back soon;

she went away for a wee holiday,' Goretti said as she took their coats off the hook.

Flossie tensed when Nancy moved closer to John.

'She's gone and we have nowhere to go at Christmas.'

'That's not true, Nancy. We're going to Uncle Josey's.' Rose scowled and smacked Nancy on the back of her hand. Nancy squealed.

'Rose! Don't slap your sister. Say sorry,' said Flossie.

'But why?'

'Because you have no need to slap her like that. Now, tell her you're sorry.'

Rose looked at the floor. 'Sorry.'

'Granny said they can stay with us for Christmas Day,' Benny said.

'Well, maybe I said something like that. Let's wait and see, please.' Goretti was flustered. 'Now put these coats on and John'll take you home.'

'Can I finish my tea?'

'Whenever you're ready,' Goretti said, oblivious to John's sarcasm.

John sighed heavily and glanced at the Connolly children. *Weren't they better off without their mother? If they ended up in an orphanage, they'd be fed at least.* He imagined Benny in an orphanage. His chicken casserole churned in his stomach.

§

Flossie went with John and the girls. He didn't speak the whole way there. The Garda car pulled out of Josey's yard as they arrived.

'I'll go in with them and see what's happening now,' said Flossie.

'Don't be long.'

'Bye, Mr O'Malley,' said Nancy, too cheerfully for John's liking.

'Goodnight now,' he said.

Rose and Nancy ran ahead of Flossie, one more eager than the other to be first. Josey's outside light came on and he appeared in the doorway. The smell of frying sausages wafted out past him.

'Hello, Josey. No bother on these two. Sure they had a great day playing with Benny. And they had their tea so you've nothing to worry about.'

'Thanks, Flossie. You two, go on upstairs and get ready for bed.' The girls were tired and obeyed him without argument.

'I see the guards were here. What did they say?'

'Asked a lot of questions about Alice and took down names of people who knew her well. They want to talk to the girls tomorrow. They searched the house inside out; they're in it all day. They can't really tell if anything is gone from the house, like clothes or anything. If she brought anything with her, it was very little, they said.'

'They were asking around town today as well. Mammy had a few visitors in and out all day—the usual nosey parkers. Molly Fagin said the guards went round all the pubs asking questions. The whole town's gossiping about it.'

'I can't find Max either. He's not below at the house, and he hasn't been following me around the fields the last couple of days either.'

'He was on the lane yesterday. I'm sure it was him, further down, between here and Frank's,' said Flossie.

'I'll check around again. I left food in his bowl; it's gone but sure any old dog or fox could have eaten it.'

'I was talking to Goretti about Christmas, and Nancy was listening outside the door, so now she thinks they're coming to our house, but we didn't get a chance to mention it to John.'

'She's a funny wee one sometimes,' said Josey.

'She heard me calling them orphans too.'

'Sure they might as well be,' he said.

'Oh, I know, Josey, but I was mad that she heard me saying it.'

'Ah, don't be fretting.'

'I'll come back out some time in the morning. And I'll go to Father Tierney to tell him we'll help with the girls. I'm afraid they'd take them away.'

'We'll have to make sure they won't. Thanks again, Flossie.'

§

'Sure isn't it the season of goodwill and all that?' said John as they drove back into town.

'What d'you mean by that?' Flossie asked.

'You looking after them children. Because Mary's your best friend.'

'I'm friends with all the family. I remember feeling very sad when their mother died in the hospital. I was only ten, but it frightened me.'

'It was a brain haemorrhage, wasn't it?' said John.

'Yes, and I didn't understand what that even meant at the

time, but I remember watching their father crying like a child. He looked sad every time I saw him after that. He was gone himself less than two years later. I heard Mammy and Molly saying he died of a broken heart. I remember lying in bed at night, worrying that I might break my heart someday, and then drop dead because of it. It was only when Daddy died I understood the meaning of a broken heart. And yes, I did feel like I would die. My heart broke into a thousand pieces, and Daddy took one of those pieces with him, leaving a gaping hole. Ever since, all these fragments of my heart move around trying to fill the hole, but it will never be filled.' She put her hand to her chest. An intense ache burned inside her. Yes, her father broke her heart when he died, and Frank broke it again, taking a bigger piece, leaving a bigger hole.

'I'm sorry, Flossie. You're so young and you've had a lot of grief in your life.' John turned the car at Town Lake and drove back out the Cavan Road.

'John, what are you doing?'

'We're going back to Josey's, and you're going to tell him he has to come to us for Christmas Day, with those wee girls. Sure nothing is their fault, is it?'

Tears pricked the back of Flossie's eyes, and a grin spread across her face. John was such a good man indeed. Yet again, guilt plunged through her. She didn't deserve him.

CHAPTER FIFTY-ONE

Rose and Nancy woke early, excited at the thoughts of Santy coming. Mrs O'Malley got them new pyjamas and said they weren't to wear them until Christmas Eve night. They got dressed into the clothes they'd worn the previous day, and then went down to have breakfast with Josey and Tomás.

'Is he really coming tonight?' Nancy asked.

'He really is,' Tomás answered.

'I have something to tell you, girls,' said Josey.

Rose clapped her hands, excited by the look on Josey's face.

'We're going to O'Malleys' house tomorrow for Christmas dinner.'

'I know that,' said Nancy.

'You didn't really know,' Rose said.

'I did.'

'Right. Eat up your eggs and then get your wellies on. You've to help me and Tomás for a while.'

'Uncle Josey, I've to get my Raggy Ann from the babby house.'

'Okay, we have to go down there to see to the pigs anyway.'

'I have to take Raggy Ann to Mrs O'Malley's house 'cause Benny said I had no toys.'

'Well now, we can't have him thinking that.'

§

Josey threw the scraps into the pigsty, and then he let himself in the back door of Frank's. Still no sign of Alice, just as he expected. He lit a fire in the kitchen and in the sitting room to prevent dampness setting in. The house already smelled fusty, and the coldness penetrated through the thick stone walls. Rain leaked through a small crack in the window, leaving a pool of grimy water on the windowsill. The place was a far cry from what he remembered it to be when he was a child. His mother used to keep the place spick-and-span, her home-baking and lavender-scented polish harmonising with the smell of his father's pipe tobacco. He still missed them.

§

Nancy crouched down and pushed through the plastic flap of the babby house entrance. 'Oh, hello, Max.' The dog lay motionless against the tree trunk. Nancy crawled towards him and stroked his wet body. She took Raggy Ann's cold stiff blanket from the floppy cardboard cot and put it across Max.

'Now you'll be warm.' She lifted Raggy Ann from her

damp sleeping place. The cardboard box wasn't as durable as the wooden crate they once had. It had been the perfect cot, until Alice cut it up for firewood.

'I forgot to bring you with me, Raggy Ann,' said Nancy. 'Look what I have.' She took a handful of marbles from her coat pocket. 'I got them at Benny's house, but you can't tell anyone.'

'I won't tell,' squeaked Nancy in her *Raggy Ann* voice.

'Good, because I'll beat you if you tell. I only took five and Benny has too many marbles anyway.'

'Benny is mean,' said Raggy Ann.

'Yes, he is. Now come on, we have to go.'

Nancy kept an old Mick McQuaid tobacco tin hidden under the straw bedding of the cot. She liked the shape of the tin—a perfect circle. She didn't like the old man's face on the lid, but she did like the sweet smell inside it. She dropped her new marbles into it, one by one. The tin was shiny, and all her things inside it were shiny too. The ring she took from Pauline O'Meara in school, a green glassy stone she found on a grave, a broken spoon which her daddy once used for fishing. She didn't know the purpose of the spoon, but she had seen it in his fishing box, so she took it after he died. She heard Josey call out her name. She put her trinket tin back under the straw and tucked Raggy Ann under her arm. 'Bye, Max.'

§

They went back through the fields to Josey's cottage. He took out his pocket watch. Ten o'clock. The guards were due to call with an update on the search for Alice. Josey and the girls crossed the sty from the field into the yard. The squad car was parked and the sergeant was nosing around the yard. Josey was glad to see Flossie's bicycle parked against the wall.

'Hello, sergeant, come on in,' said Josey.

'Morning.' Sergeant Kennedy followed him into the house.

Flossie had the table laid with cups, milk and sugar. A fresh soda bread waited to be sliced. The teapot sat in the centre of the table, covered in a blue knitted tea cosy that Josey didn't recognise.

'You know Mrs O'Malley, Sergeant?' Josey gestured towards Flossie.

'I do indeed. You're helping out, I hear,' he said as he took off his hat.

'You'll have tea, sergeant? she said. 'Take a seat here at the table.'

'I will indeed. That bread smells good.'

Flossie gave Rose and Nancy a lollipop each.

'We're orphans,' Nancy said, looking at Sergeant Kennedy.

'Are you indeed?'

'Yes, because Daddy is dead and our Mammy is gone somewhere and she won't be back.'

'That doesn't mean you're an orphan, Nancy, and your mammy will be back,' Josey said.

'She said we're orphans.' Nancy pointed at Flossie but kept her eyes on Sergeant Kennedy.

Flossie flushed and turned her focus to cutting more bread.

'Did she tell you she was going?' the sergeant asked Nancy.

'No, and she didn't give us orange and biscuits like she always does when she goes out without us.'

'You're not allowed to tell about the orange and biscuits,' whispered Rose.

Josey shook his head. 'Their dog Max is missing too.'

Nancy yanked the lolly out of her mouth with a loud pop. 'No, he's not. He's asleep in the babby house.'

'Are ya sure?'

'I saw him when I was getting Raggy Ann. I put the blanket on him 'cause he was very cold.'

Josey's shoulders dropped. 'I'll go down in a while and have a look. He's normally a lively dog, sergeant. Follows these childer everywhere.'

Sergeant Kennedy caught Flossie's eye and raised his eyebrows. He gave a slight nod to the girls and then to the door.

'Come into the sitting room with me girls 'til you see what I have in there for you,' Flossie said.

They jumped up without hesitation and followed her out the door with a skip.

'Nice new frocks for tomorrow,' she said.

§

'Did you get to speak with Alice's family?' Josey asked the sergeant.

'We did indeed. None of them have seen her since Frank's funeral. One or two haven't seen her in years.'

'A funny bunch they are,' Josey said.

'We've no reason to think she has come to any harm. It appears that she isn't a very reliable sort, and maybe things got the better of her and she's scarpered. It happens, you know.'

'But where would she go? How would she survive? She doesn't know anybody anywhere—that I know of.'

'There must be someone,' the sergeant replied.

'What about that tobacco salesman she used to be friendly with? Heard rumours about them months ago.'

'Aye, Peggy Law put us wise to him. He works a different region now, down the south of the country. He hasn't seen Alice in weeks.'

§

'There's something about that child that bugs me, Flossie. I don't know what it is.'

'Aw, John.'

'It's the way she stares, saying nothing, just stares at me. And then when she starts talking, she won't stop. I feel sorry for them and everything, but I'll be glad when tomorrow's over.'

'It'll be fine. She'll be too busy playing to bother you, and the day will fly by.'

'And how could she think the dog was sleeping? Sure he was stone cold and stiff as a poker.'

'John, she's four. She never saw a dead dog before. Leave her alone.'

John turned on his side and said goodnight.

Flossie lay awake, mulling things over in her mind. Nancy was a bit odd, alright, but she'd grow out of it. Rose was the opposite: quiet, pleasing, obedient. She could hardly believe that John had agreed to have them for Christmas dinner. He might eventually agree to them moving in permanently. It was hard not to pity them, even though some people didn't. Awful things were being said about them in town. *They'll end up like the mother. They carry diseases. They'll never be much good. Something's wrong with the younger one. Couldn't blame the mother for running away.* She prayed that wherever Frank was, he couldn't hear what they were saying. Flossie closed her eyes and gave in to the tiredness.

CHAPTER FIFTY-TWO

On Christmas morning, Josey drove into town on the tractor with Rose and Nancy in the cab beside him. He carried Rose's tricycle and Nancy's new Crolly doll in the transport box. He dropped the toys off with Ruth and then brought the girls to half-eleven Mass.

When they returned to O'Malleys' after Mass, Benny showed off his new aeroplane and wouldn't allow Rose or Nancy to play with it—because it was only for boys. Nancy boasted about her new doll. 'She came in a box and her name is Suzy.'

Everyone admired Suzy's glossy blonde ringlets, and her navy hot pants and pink blouse.

'Sorry about the tricycle; it's a bit clunky, but Rose wanted to bring it,' said Josey. 'I hope it won't be a nuisance.'

'Not at all,' Goretti said. 'She can go out the back on it for a wee while if she wants.'

The tricycle looked brand new; Josey had made a mighty job of it. He'd painted it red and white and attached a new bell on the handlebar.

Ruth and Frederick arrived not long after them. Ruth seemed put out by the presence of the Connollys, but she came off her high horse after a few pre-dinner sherries and her voice box went into overdrive.

She gave herself top marks for her sage and onion stuffing. 'A turkey's nothing without it,' she said. She lectured Goretti on the importance of perfect timing when it came to Brussel sprouts as she mashed one with the back of her fork. The sting of her criticism eased when she later praised Goretti's *deliciously rich* Christmas pudding.

Ruth fell asleep after dinner, giving Frederick and John a chance to relax over a game of draughts. Josey contentedly helped Benny build his new jigsaw. Goretti had given the girls a child's embroidery set each. Rose began stitching straight away, but Nancy showed no interest in hers; instead, she made a camp behind the couch, and played on her own with Suzy and Raggy Ann.

The evening ended with tears when Benny discovered one of the lights was missing from his aeroplane. Every corner of the room was searched but the light couldn't be found. The noise disturbed Ruth and she woke complaining of a headache. Soon after, she and Frederick gathered their belongings and left for home. Josey decided he and the girls should make tracks too. Goretti wrapped some turkey and ham for him to take home.

'You're very good, Mrs Lynch. Thank you very much for today. You've made the Christmas for these two,' he said, tilting his head towards Rose and Nancy.

'No trouble at all, Josey. Take care now.'

Flossie walked them out to the door. 'I'll call to see you tomorrow.'

'God no. You've done more than enough for us already.'

'Well, you know where I am if you need anything.'

'Thanks very much for everything, Flossie.'

Josey lifted the tired girls into the cab of the tractor and secured the toys into the transport box.

§

Flossie retired early, shattered after the long day. She flicked through the pages of her diary. 1964 had been a year full of promise and optimism—for the most part at least. She took her Biro from her locker drawer and penned her last entry of the year.

Frank, seeing how happy the girls were today would have made you smile. They had a wonderful Christmas Day. When they're with me, I feel you with me too, guiding me. So in a way, Frank, we can be together. In spirit. Josey is a great uncle, but they need a proper family. I can give them that. Two parents and a brother. I hope Alice never comes home, even if she does, no one will want her. John and I will adopt the girls and they will never want for anything. And you always said John was a good man, so I know you'd approve.

She returned the diary to the box in her wardrobe. She locked it and put the key back inside the hole in the mattress.

CHAPTER FIFTY-THREE

The first week into the New Year brought frost and bitter winds from the East. Christmas trees stood limp in front windows, stripped of their withered needles. The artificial ones now lost their appeal, the novelty of fairy lights and tinsel worn off. Goretti was treated like a saint at her Legion of Mary meetings because of her act of charity towards the Connollys on Christmas Day. Flossie was happy to let her take all the glory.

While Josey worked on his farm, Flossie took care of Rose and Nancy. Every day they expected the guards or the priest to call for the girls, but no one did. Flossie presumed that they could see how she and Josey were managing fine. She prayed Alice would never return. Rose and Nancy had a new mother now.

Soon, she'd talk to John about the girls living with them—and then convince Josey. She wanted everything organised before school started again. She had phone calls to make, people to see. She wrote to Mary to let her know she was taking care of everything. She'd contact Auntie Bridgey too. She'd know some things about the adoption process.

§

Flossie wore her fur-lined boots, duffle coat and thick woolly hat. 'I'll see you later, Mam. Benny, be a good boy for Granny. I won't be too long.'

He nodded, eagerly spooning sweet porridge into his mouth. Flossie kissed his forehead before stepping out into the crisp morning air.

She posted her letter to Mary, and then bought a fresh loaf and a bunch of bananas in Tierney's. Rose and Nancy liked banana sandwiches. She knew everything a mother needed to know about them. She felt light inside; happy.

Flossie liked walking in frosty weather, especially when she had things on her mind, although it pleased her to think that if Rose and Nancy were to live with her, she wouldn't have to go traipsing out the Cavan Road every day.

Mrs Deignan stood at her gate waving to Flossie as she approached Connollys' lane. 'Will you come in for tea, Mrs O'Malley?'

'I would if I had time.'

'Are the wee Connollys getting on alright?'

'They're fine, so they are.'

'Come here for a wee minute.' Mrs Deignan held up a bag. 'Will you give this to them? Two cardigans I knitted over the Christmas. Good Aran wool that, not the pretend stuff.'

'That's awful good of you. Thank you.'

'No sign of her?'

'No. It seems like she abandoned them.'

Mrs Deignan shook her head. 'Shocking troubled she was anyway. I felt sorry for her, you know.' She folded her arms and straightened herself. 'There went a car in that lane late last night... 'bout ten o'clock.'

'Well, I wouldn't know anything about that,' said Flossie. 'I'm heading there now to pick up Rose and Nancy. I often take them home for a wee while, you see, so Josey can work.'

'I know you do. 'Tis very decent of you.'

'Thanks again for these. They'll love them. I better head on if you don't mind.'

'I don't think that car came out again, y'know, unless it left during the night,' Mrs Deignan continued.

Flossie walked on. *Is it Alice back? With someone who owns a car? Never!*

The strange car was parked in Josey's yard. Flossie's heart beat erratically. Surely it wasn't someone coming to take the girls, the authorities. No, they wouldn't have stayed all night.

The key was in the cottage door, but Flossie knocked anyway. She heard laughter coming from behind the door as she waited for it to open. A woman's voice, one she knew.

'Hello, Flossie.' Mary beamed at her friend as the door swung open.

'Mary! What are you doing here?'

'Home sweet home.' Mary threw her arms around Flossie. Flossie stiffened.

'Jesus, are you surprised or just disappointed?' Mary laughed. 'Come in, will you.'

'Surprised, of course! I thought you weren't coming home until Easter.' Flossie followed Mary into the kitchen.

'That was until *she* fecked off.'

'But Mary, you know I've been helping Josey with the girls. We're doing a grand job, you know.'

'Josey told me all about how good you are, Flossie, and Christmas was special for them. Thanks very much.'

'They're unfortunate, so they are.' Flossie feigned a smile. 'How long will you be staying?'

'Forever.'

'What do you mean, forever?'

'Jim knew I couldn't settle over there, and since Frank died, I've been even more unsettled. My heart is here in Bailieborough, Flossie. Alice leaving was the last straw. Jim and I had a good talk at Christmas and he had already been thinking of coming home. There's a good chance he'll get a job somewhere close.'

Flossie's insides hardened, her breathing faltered, as if she'd just been punched. 'Where's Jim now?'

'Below in Frank's. Lighting the fire and getting it sorted out. We're moving in. Like I said Flossie, home sweet home.'

'Jesus,' said Flossie.

'Jim's not staying yet. He'll head back to Manchester to sort everything out and he'll be back in a few weeks with the dog.'

'Where's Maureen? Is she home too?'

'Of course she is. I hardly left her behind. I'm not Alice!'

'I know. Sorry.'

'She's with Rose and Nancy outside somewhere. Probably in that old fort behind their house.' Mary pulled on a pair of rubber gloves.

Flossie thought how motherly and busy she looked in her apron, vigorously washing the breakfast dishes, in a hurry to tackle her next chore. Three children to see to now, and too busy to fix her wispy strands of hair that hung from her loosely weaved plait. *She came home to be Rose and Nancy's mother.* 'What if Alice comes home and finds you living in her house?'

'Well, for a start, it's not her house. That house was left to Frank and me. Now that Frank's gone—Lord have mercy on him—it's mine.'

'Oh, I see. I didn't know that. But isn't she entitled to part of it? As his wife?'

'Entitled? She walked out and is entitled to nothing. How dare she ever come back here,' replied Mary as she yanked off her rubber gloves.

'But what if she does?'

'She can feck off. I'll have her locked up. That's what.'

'Here, Mrs Deignan sent these for Rose and Nancy.'

Mary took the bag and peered inside. 'Ah, wasn't that nice of her! She was always a great woman for the Aran. Plain and purl is all I can manage.'

'She was dying to know who owned the car. I think they sat up half the night, watching for it to leave again.'

Mary sat beside her friend at the table, lit up a long cigarette, and drew heavily on it.

'My God, Mary, the length of that fag.' Flossie lifted the box of cigarettes to inspect its contents.

'*Rothmans King size*. Fancy!' Flossie took a cigarette and puffed on it. 'Are they English?'

'Here, will I light it for you?' Mary said.

'You'll not. I'm fine.'

'I might give them up. Jim hates them.'

'So you'll be busy getting the home place back to what it used to be,' Flossie said.

'I haven't been down there yet. But it wasn't in great shape the time of the funeral.' Mary shook her head despairingly.

'It needs a good cleaning, Mary. It's grand otherwise.'

'There's stuff missing from the house, stuff that was there when Frank married her. My mother had lovely wee ornaments in the china cabinet; they're gone. The delft is in bits, the net curtains are pure yellow and tattered. Mammy would turn in her grave, so she would.'

Flossie reminded herself of the children's welfare. Mary would be a better mother for them surely, and it's what Frank would have wanted. She tapped her fingernails lightly on the table. 'I'll help you make it lovely again, Mary. We'll make your old room beautiful like it used to be, for Rose and Nancy. They'll love it. And they'll love having a wee cousin to play with. They get on grand with Benny, most of the time, but they'll love Maureen more, I'm sure.'

Mary took a long pull of her cigarette. 'Josey's certain that Max died of poisoning.' She narrowed her eyes. 'It wouldn't surprise me if that mad bitch poisoned him.'

'Jesus, don't let the girls hear you saying things like that.' Flossie got up and sighed heavily. 'I'd better head on home. It's great that you're back, Mary. It'll be like old times.'

'There's no place like home and that's for sure.'

'I have to call down to Frank's. I lost one of my good gloves and I might have left it there when I was picking up stuff for the girls. I can say a quick hello to Jim when I'm there.'

'Okay. See you soon.'

§

A strong smell of Jeyes Fluid met Flossie as she entered the back door of Frank's. A stinking bag of rubbish sat on the scullery floor ready for dumping. Jim had his sleeves rolled up, sweeping around the fireplace. He had a pile of sticks stacked beside the range, and the fire roaring. Flossie shivered and folded her arms tight. 'Hello, Jim.'

'Ah, Flossie. Nice to see you.' He put the broom down and took a deep breath. 'Janey Mac, I wouldn't like to be doing this kind of thing every day,' he said.

'I can stay and help if you want.'

'Ah sure I'm nearly done. The main thing is to get the place warmed up.'

'Jim, when you go back to Manchester, you'll find a letter there, from me to Mary. You see, I wrote it before I knew about the move and it contains silly plans I had. Do me a favour and burn it. There's no point giving it to Mary.'

'If that's what you want,' said Jim. 'Is everything okay, Flossie?'

'Of course. Yes. You see I planned on visiting Mary in Manchester but now she's here and I don't want to embarrass her or make her think I'm embarrassed.'

'Sure you know Mary, she'd laugh,' said Jim, smiling. 'But that's grand. I'll get rid of it,' he added, noting Flossie's grim expression.

'Thanks, Jim.'

§

'She's a saint, that woman. Giving up the good life in Manchester to come home for those wee urchins,' said Goretti.

'They're not exactly urchins,' John remarked without taking his eyes off his book.

'She didn't like England that much anyway,' Flossie said.

'Better life there than here. Why wouldn't she like it?' Goretti said.

Flossie tutted as she looked up to the heavens. 'She was homesick *she said*.'

John closed his book and pushed his glasses up his nose. 'You don't sound too happy that your best friend is home.'

'Of course I'm happy. Don't be silly.'

He clenched his jaw. 'Well, at least now you won't be worrying about those girls and spending all your spare time running in and out the Wood Lane.'

Goretti rambled on. 'Well, that Mary one's a saint...'

§

Flossie knelt beside her bed and blessed herself. Her thoughts rambled as she tried to focus on her prayers. *Annoyed at Mary for coming home like that. No warning. But isn't it best for Rose and Nancy? I had plans for them. I wanted to be their mother.*

She penned her thoughts into her diary, damning Mary and Jim for ruining her plans. She asked God for guidance; she couldn't fall out with her best friend. As she poured her frustrations onto the page, she felt calmer, and her words swayed in a more positive direction. She could still be part of Rose and Nancy's lives, like she'd promised Frank. Mary's return didn't have to change things. She promised herself she'd support her friend and let go of what could have been.

CHAPTER FIFTY-FOUR

Cheerful golden daffodils bloomed in neglected flower beds in Frank's garden—now Mary and Jim's. The old rockery, once a mass of colour and oddly positioned stones, was now covered in moss and weeds. *No doubt Mary and Jim will have it back to what it once was.* She cycled past the small front garden, and through the yard to the back of the house. She parked her bicycle on its stand beside the coal shed and let herself in the door. 'Hello?' she shouted as she went through the scullery and peered into the kitchen.

'Yes, I'm in here.' Mary had the mop in one hand and a bucket in the other.

Flossie tiptoed across the wet linoleum.

Mary had the house looking well again. She had steeped the net curtains in bluing and sewn the torn bits. She'd repainted the table and chairs to their former glossy white. Josey had helped her to put up new wallpaper in the sitting room. The dresser looked as pretty as ever, with Mary's crockery and ornaments that she'd brought home from England neatly arranged on it, colourful and non-matching, just like Mrs Connolly's. Flossie smiled at the memory. 'Where's the girls?'

'With Josey, feeding the calves.'

'Don't make tea for me. I'm not staying long,' Flossie said as Mary lifted the kettle.

'I'm making it for myself anyway. I'm on the go all morning. I'd forgotten about the extra work involved with a family of five.'

'Can I do anything for you?'

'No, you're grand. Sit down there.'

'It's great that Jim's back now too. How does Fleck like his new home?'

'It's better for him here than our house in Manchester. Rose loves him. Not sure about Nancy. She keeps on about Max.'

Flossie eyed up the sally rod on top of the dresser. 'You wouldn't use the rod on them, would you, Mary?'

'Ah, that's only a threat. I only ever used it once on Maureen and that was for telling lies in the confessional. I heard her telling Rose that she tells the same sins every week because she doesn't know what else to say.'

'Sure when you think of it, there's no need for them to be going every week if they've no sins. I only go every three weeks.'

Mary laughed. 'I don't need to go at all.' Flossie laughed along with her; it felt good. It seemed like an age since she'd had fun and laughter in her life.

'I was thinking I might go to Auntie Bridgey's some weekend,' Flossie said.

'Lovely. Will you take Benny too?'

'Ah no, I'd leave him with Mammy. I'd like to visit Sheila and George when I'm there.'

'Oh, I didn't know you three kept in touch.'

'Mostly Christmas cards. Sheila writes sometimes. She's teaching in Portobello and lives there with a friend. George still lives at home with his parents. That's all I know, really.'

'Am I still your best friend?' asked Mary with raised eyebrows and a sheepish grin.

'You'll always be my best friend.'

Mary laughed and spooned tea leaves into the teapot. 'Are you sure you won't take tea?'

Flossie glanced at the clock above the table. 'I'll not, thanks. I've a wee lassie coming for a piano lesson at twelve, so I'd better head back.'

'Sure it wasn't worth your while calling.'

'I'll call again tomorrow, after mass.'

'Flossie, there's no need to call every day. Sure, we're doing grand with Jim back home and everything. You've enough to be doing yourself.'

'But I like helping.'

'I know you do, but really we're fine, so we are.'

'Okay. Let me know if there's anything you or the girls need.'

'I will of course.'

Flossie cycled home with a heavy heart. They didn't need her.

§

Mary kept a strict regime with the girls, and Flossie noticed changes in them as the months went by. Rose and Maureen developed a close bond and didn't like being in different classrooms. At break times, they stuck to each other like glue, along with Kathleen, while Nancy wandered around on her own. The other children were in awe of Maureen because of her English twang and her relaxed attitude towards schoolwork. She enjoyed the attention, and Rose assumed a new air of confidence being the new girl's cousin.

A steel railing separated the boys from the girls in the yard. Flossie walked up and down the length of it, watching the children in their different clusters. As usual she kept a particular eye on Dottie Conway and her friends, who had a reputation for bothering some of the younger children, Nancy included. Earlier that morning, she'd watched as Maureen rescued Nancy from their taunts.

'You need to stand up for yourself, Nancy,' Maureen told her. 'Give her a good slap the next time she calls you an orphan, you hear me?'

Now Nancy sat alone in the shelter, her unopened lunch box on her lap. Flossie slowly made her way over. 'What's for your lunch today, Nancy?'

'Miss, I wanna go home. I want Auntie Mary.'

Flossie crouched down beside her.

'But you have me, Nancy. I'll look after you.'

'Can I come live with you then?'

'I'm afraid not, but I'll mind you here in school.'

'Rose doesn't like me anymore and Maureen said I have to slap Dottie.'

'You leave Dottie to me. Why don't we go over and see what Jenny's doing? She's on her own too. You can eat your lunch together.'

Nancy agreed and sat alongside Jenny McGuirk further

up the shelter. Flossie gave them two sticks of chalk to play with.

Dottie was the most spoiled child Flossie had ever met, and she knew there was no point discussing her bullying antics with Miss Kennedy. Dottie's family were regarded as valuable members of the community, therefore she rarely got punished. At the slightest scolding, Dottie's mother would arrive at the school to complain because Dottie was a good little girl who did nothing wrong. In a way, Maureen was right. Nancy did need to toughen up in order to get through her school days with the likes of Dottie Conway lurking around the corner.

§

Rose spent less time in the babby house since Maureen arrived. Maureen didn't care much for it. It stank, she said. Nancy played there alone most of the time, with her dolls, talking to them and lending them her voice.

'Let's play a game. Suzy, you can be Mrs O'Malley 'cause you're the biggest, and Raggy Ann can be me,' Nancy told her dolls.

'Hello, Nancy,' said Mrs O'Malley Doll.

'Hello, Mrs O'Malley,' answered Nancy Doll.

'You're an orphan and you're going to live with me, Nancy.'

'Just me and not Rose?'

'Yes, just you.' The dolls hugged. Nancy lifted the other doll, Hannah, from the crate.

'Hello. I'm Auntie Mary and I'm your new mammy.' Nancy walked Hannah towards Suzy and Raggy Ann. She

manipulated the dolls to wrestle each other and then she threw Hannah against the galvanised wall.

'Come along, Nancy, come live with me in town beside the shops,' Mrs O'Malley Doll squeaked.

'And Nancy lived happy ever after,' said Nancy as she placed her dolls into their cot. She hummed *Hush, Little Baby* as she rocked them to sleep.

CHAPTER FIFTY-FIVE

Smiling faces said goodbye to Flossie as she finished her classes for the week. She welcomed Fridays as much as the children did. She tidied her desk, switched off the lights and closed the door behind her. On her way up the corridor, she saw Mary talking with Miss Kennedy outside her classroom. As Flossie got closer, Mary's voice got louder. Before Flossie reached the two women, Mary turned and stormed out the main door. Miss Kennedy glared at Flossie, shaking her head.

'Is everything okay, Miss Kennedy?'

'Yes, fine!' She stepped back inside her classroom and closed the door behind her.

Flossie met Benny outside. She grabbed his hand and rushed to catch up with Mary. 'Come on, Benny, hurry up.' Benny took into a trot beside her.

Flossie called out, 'Mary, wait!' Mary marched on towards the school gates with the three girls scurrying to keep up with her. 'Mary!' she called again. 'Mary, are you alright?'

'I'm highly insulted, that's what I am,' said Mary.

'What happened? And please slow down,' Flossie said as Mary picked up speed again.

'That woman sent a note home yesterday with my Maureen, telling me I need to get her elocution lessons. She said the child can't speak properly. She said it would teach her how to pronounce her words properly. Who the fecking hell does she think she is?'

'Oh God, Mary. What did you say to her?'

'I told her she needed to go and get her ears tested and I told her where to stick her elocution lessons.'

Flossie burst out laughing. Mary glared at her, her face blood red. 'It's not funny, so it's not.'

'It is funny. You've been dying to speak to her like that since you left school.'

Mary smirked. 'Not really. But it did give me pleasure, I have to say. You should've seen her face.'

'I did. She was as white as a ghost when I left.'

'Well, she better not start picking on any of these three, I'll tell you that now.'

'Come in for tea,' said Flossie as they reached her house.

'Oh, can we please?' said Nancy.

'A quick cup then,' Mary said.

§

The sweet smell of hot strawberry jam filled Goretti's kitchen. She stood at the range singing like she was Doris Day, stirring her big pot of bubbling fruit and sugar. Benny and the girls were immediately drawn to the tray of freshly filled jam pots on the table.

'Don't touch them, they're mad hot.'

'Holy God, Mrs Lynch. That's a lot of jam,' said Mary.

'You can bring a pot with you. Bring one for Josey too,' said Goretti.

Flossie shooed the children into the sitting room with a small bag of jelly babies. 'Mammy, I told you I'd make the jam.'

'Ach now, Flossie. Remember the last time you tried making jam; you know well it's better when I do it.'

Flossie rolled her eyes to the heavens. Mary held in a giggle and shook her head.

'How's the Irish dancing going for the girls?' asked Goretti.

'Maureen and Rose love going, but Nancy hates it. The teacher told her she was too heavy on her feet to be a dancer,' said Mary. 'So now she doesn't want to do it.'

'I heard she's shocking strict that one,' said Goretti. 'But it makes them dance better, y'know.'

'Nancy likes singing in class,' said Flossie. 'I think she has good rhythm.'

'She got that from Frank. He was a lovely singer like Daddy,' said Mary with a slight smile. 'Do you remember all the céilís we used to have in our house?'

Goretti lifted her hot jam jars out of the oven. She turned to the two young women at the table. 'Ah Mary, they were great memories of your mammy and daddy. I remember one night, there must have been fifty in the house. And everyone had a song or a story to tell. It was the best céilí house in town.'

A familiar ache pressed at Flossie's heart. 'I have an idea, Mary! How about I give Nancy piano lessons? She could come when Rose and Maureen are at dance classes.'

'Aw, I don't know. Would she need her own piano to practice? Because we don't have money for that kind of thing, or the space for that matter.'

'No, Mary, calm down,' said Flossie. 'She can come here to practice as often as she wants. After school maybe.'

Goretti's eyes widened as big as the lids of her jam pots. She opened her mouth to speak but Flossie cut in. 'Mammy, here, is a beautiful singer and she might like to guide Nancy with her harmonies and all that. Mammy, you could get her ready for joining the choir. The best woman to teach her.' Flossie beamed. 'Imagine if Nancy became the best choir singer in the parish and everyone knew you were her singing teacher.'

Goretti chuckled and wiped her brow with the tea towel. 'Well, I suppose I could help the child. Not every day, mind you.'

'One or two days, Mammy. She can practice at home every other day,' said Flossie.

'Well, it seems you have it all worked out,' said Mary.

'Sure it'll keep her occupied,' said Flossie.

'I suppose. It'll get her out of that babby house, so it will.'

'She can start this Saturday if she wants.'

When Mary left, Flossie beamed with satisfaction.

Goretti went through the post; two for John, one for herself, and one for Flossie. 'Looks like Bridgey's writing.' She handed a pale blue envelope to her daughter.

'She hasn't written in a while,' said Flossie, slicing the letter open with a knife.

'Too busy at those meetings and protesting on the streets.'

'Ach, Mammy, stop. Sure someone has to do it.'

'I'm not saying she shouldn't, Flossie, but...'

'She said she's coming for a visit next Saturday.'

'Why is she telling you and not me?'

'Because I'm the one who writes to her.'

'Well, I'll be visiting Catherine on Saturday. Molly's coming with me and we're making a day of it. Oh, what a pity I'll miss her,' Goretti said.

Flossie shook her head. Her mother could be so unsociable sometimes. 'It's good she's coming because I want to ask her if I can stay with her for a weekend soon. If I go, will you mind Benny for me?' she asked Goretti.

'And why can't you bring him?'

'Why can't you mind him?'

Goretti huffed and shook out her apron before tying it round her waist. 'Of course I'll mind the child.'

'Thank you. I hope to spend some time with Sheila and George when I'm there.'

'Sure that's all you had to say in the first place.'

§

Nancy turned up on Saturday morning for her first piano lesson. Goretti and Molly had already left for Dublin on the early bus, and Bridgey was expected to arrive on the mid-day one. 'Good girl, Nancy, you're very good for a beginner,' said Flossie as she finished up the lesson.

'Do you think Auntie Mary might buy me a piano now?'

'Oh, I don't think so. But I have an idea. How about I ask

John to put a wee advert in The Celt asking has anyone got an old one for sale? You could do wee jobs for me around the house and your payment could be the piano. I'd buy it for you.'

'Mrs O'Malley, that would be amazing.'

'Amazing...' Flossie grinned.

'That's what Maureen says all the time. It means really, really great.'

This was the happiest Flossie had seen Nancy in ages. She hoped Mary would agree to the arrangement.

'I could come some days after school to practice.' Nancy buttoned up her coat.

'Hood up, it's raining,' said Flossie. 'Let's wait and see what Auntie Mary has to say first. That's her at the door now.'

'Okay. I can't wait to get my new piano.'

As soon as the door opened, Nancy spouted her news to Mary. 'I'm getting a new piano, so I am. I have to help Mrs O'Malley in her house for her to buy me one.'

Mary glared at Flossie, who blushed at her friend's scornful expression.

'Sorry, Mary. I should have asked you first, but the thought came to me out of the blue and I had it said before I knew it.'

'Yes, you should have.' Mary took Nancy's hand and positioned her umbrella behind them as she rushed away.

By the time Bridgey arrived, Flossie had a small dinner of potatoes, cabbage and bacon ready. Since their time together in Dublin and regular exchange of letters, the two women had become very fond of each other. Flossie strived to make her aunt proud. She wanted her to see that her guidance and generosity were appreciated.

Bridgey brought a fresh cream sponge cake and a bag of dolly mixtures for Benny. Flossie put the cake in the fridge and the sweets in the press, until after dinner.

'Mary's not impressed with me at the minute,' Flossie said.

'What did you do?'

Flossie told her aunt about the piano.

'You need to think before you act, Flossie. You can't make promises like that to a small child without discussing it first with her mother.'

'Well, for a start, she's not her mother. But yes, I know you're right. I just want to help. Rose seems to be so tied up with Maureen, and Nancy's being forgotten about.'

'I'm sure the novelty of Maureen will soon wear off and things will go back to the way they were for Rose and Nancy.' Bridgey set the table. 'I bumped into your friend Sheila last Saturday.'

'Oh really? I wanted to ask you if I could stay with you some weekend, to visit her and George.'

'Yes, of course. We'll choose a weekend I'm not working.'

'I'll wait until May when the weather's a bit warmer.'

Benny watched his mammy from the table as she mashed the potatoes much slower than Granny Lynch did. He glanced at the press where his dolly mixtures were. 'Can I be first, Mammy?'

'Manners, Benny,' said Flossie.

'But I'm starving, and I don't want cabbage.'

'You'll get no sweets if you're bold.'

He sighed heavily and buried his head in his folded arms on the table.

Bridgey poured milk for each of them. 'How's your mother?'

'Fine. Happy to be seeing Catherine.'

'Why don't you ever visit her?'

'Come on, Benny, lift your head. It's ready.' Flossie put the plate in front of him. 'I don't like going there. It's like talking to a stranger.'

'I visit her sometimes, you know. She talks about you.'

'Damn, this white sauce is awful. Sorry.' Flossie promptly lifted the jug off the table.

'It's only a few lumps. Here, give it to me.' Bridgey got up and took a sieve from the drawer. 'Are you alright, Flossie?' Bridgey pushed the thick lumpy sauce through the sieve.

'The last time I went to see Catherine, I told her lies and I felt bad.'

'Come on, let's eat and tell me all about these lies. I came here today to have an important talk with you, Flossie. You need to tell me what's bothering you.'

'What kind of important talk?'

'What lies?'

'Small lies. Catherine asks too many questions. *How are you? Are you happy? How's John?*'

'Sure why does that annoy you? Everyone says they're fine even when they're not.'

'But she's a nun and I shouldn't lie to her.'

'Well then, the next time you visit her, make sure it's on a day when you're feeling on top of the world.'

Flossie sensed sarcasm in her aunt's voice. Now she felt childish. She hadn't wanted to visit Catherine when Frank died, afraid she'd ask too much. Her guilty conscience intensified when she visited the convent. The eyes of the statues bored into her soul, knowing what she was, reading her mind, her secrets. A sinner among the holy nuns; she didn't deserve to sit there among them.

After dinner, Flossie gave Benny his sweets and he scarpered off into the sitting room.

'So, Bridgey, what's the important thing you want to talk to me about?'

Bridgey cleared her throat and glanced at the hall door. 'Is that door shut tight?' she asked. Flossie nodded. 'Is something wrong?'

'I was helping the society deliver leaflets around Chapelizod... a couple of weeks ago. I saw a familiar face there.'

Images of Alice flashed through Flossie's mind. 'Alice Connolly?'

Bridgey frowned. 'No. Not Alice Connolly. God knows where that woman is.'

'The girls are better off without her anyway,' said Flossie.

'Well, never mind her for now. I saw John there.'

'My John? In Chapelizod?'

'I would've passed no remarks, thinking he was on business, but the thing is, Flossie...' Bridgey's voice lowered to a whisper, 'he was with a woman.'

'What d'you mean, a woman?'

'I can't be sure what this woman means to him, but she's no stranger. She greeted him with a hug and a kiss on the cheek. Then they went into a house together.'

'What did she look like?' Flossie asked calmly.

'Older than John, that's for sure. At least forty. Fairish red hair.'

A lump grated the back of Flossie's throat. So she hadn't imagined it all this time. She pushed her near empty plate away.

'I'm sorry, Flossie, I truly am, but I had to tell you.'

Flossie opened the sideboard press and took out Goretti's bottle of gin and two highball glasses. As she poured, she took a deep breath. 'Her name is Julie.'

PART THREE

1976

CHAPTER FIFTY-SIX

B*e My Baby* by the Bay City Rollers blasted from the record player in nineteen-year-old Maureen Fitzpatrick's bedroom. She lay on her front across the bed, flicking through a *Jackie* magazine.

'Isn't he gorgeous?' said Rose.

Maureen traced her fingers across the image of Bryan Ferry. 'He is, but not as gorgeous as my Dougie' she sighed.

'What does it feel like?' asked Rose.

'It feels amazing.' Maureen turned on her back to look up at the ceiling.

Nancy barged into the room. 'What feels amazing?'

'Out, Nancy,' Rose said.

'I kissed a lad,' Maureen said.

Nancy sneered. 'So what?'

'Well, if you must know, smarty pants, she *French* kissed him,' Rose said.

'Out, Nancy.' Maureen leapt off the bed and shoved her out the door. Nancy stuck out her tongue.

'There's something wrong with that one.' Maureen

pressed her back up against the closed door. 'Why did you tell her about the French kissing? That's a secret.'

'Can it make you pregnant?' Rose whispered, glancing at the door.

'No, of course not.' Maureen laughed.

'You know that other thing you told me about getting pregnant?'

'What about it?' Maureen propped herself up on one elbow.

'Did you do that with Dougie?'

'Rose Connolly! What do you think I am?'

Rose blushed. 'Just asking.'

'But I might.' Maureen chuckled and Rose covered her face with a cushion.

CHAPTER FIFTY-SEVEN

Why were Mondays worse than any other school day? Dottie Conway seemed like a bigger bully on Mondays, waiting outside the convent gates, sneering at those less fortunate than her, sticking out her chest when the lads came along.

Nancy hated her. Someday she'll tell her that too—but not today. This morning, Dottie and her friends were busy taunting two first years. The Maguire twins were quiet girls from a small country school outside of town. Freckle-faced and thin, they both wore glasses. Patsy had a patch covering one eye, and Josephine's ears stuck out from under her straggly lank hair.

The nuns didn't let Dottie away with anything. Not like the teachers did in national school. Sister Kieran, the principal of Lourdesville Convent, had a spite on her, much to Nancy's satisfaction. *That skirt's too short. You're not wearing your tie. Close your top button. Straighten yourself. Look at me when I'm talking to you, madam.* Every day she criticised Dottie. When Sister Kieran didn't care much for someone, she addressed them as 'madam'. Nancy liked Sister Kieran.

Dottie discarded the twins as Nancy approached. 'Here's the oddball coming.' She blew cigarette smoke in Nancy's face as she passed her. Nancy spluttered and walked faster.

'Thought you'd be used to smoke... coming from hell.' Dottie and her friends laughed, then turned their attention to the school bus pulling up.

Nancy mentally made the sign of the cross as she made her way to class. The one thing she did like about Mondays was home economics, especially cooking. Her cooking partner most days was Jenny—her only friend.

Jenny went from being a shy child in national school to an outgoing teenager who got on with everyone. She grew tall and burly and took no nonsense from anyone. One day, she overheard Pat Daly calling her Big Jugs Jenny. She got him in a headlock and nearly squeezed the eyes out of his head. She reduced him to tears and he'd stayed out of her way since.

Jenny played camogie and played to win. She'd thunder up the pitch like a raging bull, putting fear in the hearts of her opponents. She's often asked Nancy to join the team, but Nancy couldn't imagine being any good at it.

'Maybe someday I will,' she'd say.

§

Mrs Flanagan, the home economics teacher, stood by Nancy and Jenny's work station.

'Nancy, explain to me why it takes less time to cook fish compared to meat,' Mrs Flanagan said.

'Don't know, Miss.'

'What type of fish is a herring?'

'Oily fish, miss.'

'What fish are you using today?'

'Don't know, miss. Jenny brought the fish.'

Miss Flanagan looked to the plate of fish. 'Who cut it up like that? I didn't tell anyone to cut up their fish,' she said, looking from Nancy to Jenny.

'I did, miss,' replied Jenny.

'So do you not know what it is by looking at it, Miss Connolly?'

Nancy gaped at the chopped pieces of white fish. *It could be anything.* Miss Flanagan drummed her fingers on the countertop and sighed.

'White fish, miss,' whispered Nancy. Her face burned and a cold sweat pricked her skin. Laughter erupted, Dottie Conway's cackle louder than the rest. Nancy screamed inside, clenched her fists and gritted her teeth so tight her jaw hurt. She opened her mouth to release the pent-up frustration, like a young child plunging into a tantrum. Instead of a scream, a deep, desperate moan escaped her stifled body.

Dottie laughed louder. 'Oh look, it's the Devil himself trying to escape. Told yas the Devil was in her. And he wants out!'

Miss Flanagan glared at Dottie. 'How dare you! Stand outside that door until I tell you to come back in.'

Dottie stomped across the room, giving Nancy a dirty glance on her way past. Jenny raised her hand.

'Yes, Jenny,' said Miss Flanagan.

'She doesn't know, miss, because it's all cut up. I didn't mean to cut it, miss.'

Miss Flanagan ignored her and turned to Nancy. 'Sit

down and pull yourself together.' She shook her head and moved on to the next work station. Dottie was left in the corridor and all was forgotten about within minutes. But not for Nancy; she felt suffocated, drowning in her own body. She was going to say 'plaice' but didn't because it might be wrong—she'd look silly. If she'd been asked to write the answer in her copy, she'd have gotten it right. She hated when teachers asked her questions in front of everyone else. Tears blurred her vision, her eyes stung, she wanted to go home. She wished she was already in the secretarial class and nearly finished with school—like Maureen.

§

Auntie Mary had beef stew on the table when the girls got home from school. Nancy fished the parsnips out of hers and dropped them into Rose's bowl. Maureen and Rose chatted as they ate. Nancy's thoughts were still in school.

'That's the best idea ever,' Maureen said.

'Right. Nancy, that's settled,' said Rose.

'What?' Nancy mopped up the last bit of gravy with a slice of bread, then left her bowl in the sink.

'I'm moving into Maureen's room with her. So you can have a bedroom all to yourself.'

'Why?'

'Because me and Maureen have more in common and you talk in your sleep and keep me awake sometimes.'

'You never said before that I talk in my sleep.'

'Well, you do. And I'm moving into Maureen's room. Today!'

Nancy looked at Auntie Mary, expecting her to disagree.

'Don't be going moving any beds up there until Jim gets home,' Mary said.

'Are you letting them do it?'

'Sure what's the harm? Aren't you the lucky one, getting a room all to yourself?'

'Some people are never happy,' Rose said. 'Come on, Maureen. Let's start with my clothes.'

§

Still feeling sensitive from Dottie's taunts earlier, Nancy sought comfort in the babby house and her dolls.

She squeezed through the tiny doorway and sat on her three-legged stool. She inhaled deeply. The earthy smell and damp wood reminded her of her father. Empty food containers still sat on the kitchen side of the babby house. Rose and Maureen had stopped coming in. Rose had abandoned Jemima in her cardboard cot soon after her fourteenth birthday, the way Alice had abandoned them when she got fed up of being a mother. Nancy took care of Jemima, like Aunty Mary took care of them.

'Let's play school today,' Nancy said. 'Jemima, you're Dottie, because you're the smallest.' She lifted the rag dolls from the cot. 'And Hannah, you're Miss Flanagan.'

'Is it a sin to be mean to others, Dottie?' said Miss Flanagan Doll.

'Yes, miss,' Dottie Doll replied.

'Is it a sin to tell someone they have the Devil in them?'

'Yes, miss.'

'Is it a sin to call people horrible names?'

'Yes, miss.'

'Are you sorry, Dottie?'

'Yes, miss.'

'It's lunchtime, Dottie. You stay here and I'll get your lunch.'

Nancy took a spoon and a rusty old can from her shelf on the tree trunk. She crawled outside. She dug a small hole and filled the can with soil. She spooned water out from the shuck and stirred it into the can of soil as she hummed to herself. 'I hope you're hungry, Dottie Conway,' Nancy said, back inside the babby house.

'I'm starving,' replied Dottie Doll.

'Oh, goody.'

Nancy filled the spoon with the sticky mud from her tin can. She smeared it across the doll's mouth. She peered into the can, then lifted out a worm with her fingers. Placing it on a flat stone, she chopped it into pieces with a sharp stick. 'Here, Dottie, eat up all your lunch.' She made a small incision in the rag doll's mouth and shoved the minced worms into it. 'Do you like it, Dottie?' Nancy smiled.

The doll stayed silent.

'Do you like it? Answer me, you bad, horrible girl.'

She shook the rag doll violently, then threw her up against the tree trunk.

CHAPTER FIFTY-EIGHT

Nancy got ready for school quicker than usual. She retrieved an empty jam jar from the bin and washed it out. 'I'll give the pigs these scraps before I go, Auntie Mary.'

'What are you up to?' Mary asked, squinting her eyes.

'Nothing. Sure I won't feed them if you don't want me to.'

'Go on with you.' Mary carried on loading the clothes into the twin tub.

Nancy threw the basin of scraps into the sty on top of the squealing pigs. She went behind the coal shed and dug the soft earth with a stick. Her eyes widened at the sight of the black-headed worms.

'Nice and juicy,' she said, dropping a fat one into her jam jar. She poked deeper, filling the jar with worms of all sizes.

§

Dottie Conway leaned against the wall at the main door of the school, chewing gum. Her sickly-sweet perfume wafted through the air. Her friend Lily Connors had got a new watch from her American uncle. She had her sleeves rolled up, showing it off, and bragging about how rich he was. They stood to attention as Nancy approached.

'Isn't it funny, Dottie, how some people are so rich and others are so poor?' Lily said.

'Speaking of poor people, here's the orphan coming,' said Dottie.

'Do you like my new watch?' Lily held up her wrist close to Nancy's face as she walked by.

Nancy looked ahead and kept walking. Dottie leapt forward, blocking her path. 'Lily asked you a question,' she said.

'Fuck off, Dottie,' Nancy said.

Sister Kieran appeared at the door. She clapped her hands, noticing the altercation between the girls. 'Come on, girls. In you go, the clock's ticking.'

Dottie hissed through gritted teeth. 'See ya later, *orphan*.'

Nancy's chest hurt. Her earlier feelings of empowerment wavered. She knew they'd get her later for that. She had to stick to her plan. Don't be afraid. Fight back. *Do it once, Connolly, and they'll not bother you again.* Jenny's voice swirled in her head.

§

Nancy sat through the morning classes unable to focus on her lessons, Dottie's face embedded in her mind and her hiss echoing in her ears. Nancy's anger bubbled inside her, like Goretti Lynch's hot jam. It smothered any fear she had in her. She held it there, in her belly and in her mind.

The bell rang at eleven o'clock. She knew Dottie and her sidekicks would go round the back of the school for their quick smoke as soon as they got out. This would give her time to prepare. She waited by the prefabs, watching Jenny and her team practicing camogie. The clicking of their wooden sticks and cheering echoed across the school grounds. Their legs were purple from the cold, but it didn't seem to bother them. At that moment, Nancy wished she was among them. Part of what they were. She could almost see the fire in them as they yelled at each other in camaraderie. The next time Jenny asked her to play, she'd say yes.

A hover of crows perched on the prefab roof. The convent was like a crow sanctuary; hundreds of them nested in the thicket of trees that surrounded the place. In her first year at school, Nancy hated them. When her father was being buried, the foreboding caws of the crows echoed off the headstones and they frightened her. She heard them in her sleep for months afterwards. Now, she relished in their gravelly calls. She wasn't afraid of them anymore. They had never harmed her and she knew they never would.

They were coming, the three of them—Dottie, Lily, and Barbara. Nancy buttoned up her duffle coat as an icy blast of wind swiped at her. It whipped up her skirt, smarting her bare legs.

'Where's Sister Kieran now?' Dottie asked. Lily and Barbara stood behind her—always behind her—with hands on hips, chewing their bubble gum like cows chewing their cud. They laughed when Dottie expected them to, moved when she said. For the first time, Nancy saw them for what they really were—puppets. Just like the dolls in the babby house. Two puppets, nothing without their leader. And as for

Dottie, she was nothing without them. Nancy sniggered at the realisation.

'What's so funny, orphan?' Dottie asked.

Nancy kept her hand in her coat pocket, the worms wriggling through her fingers.

'Don't call me orphan again.'

'But that's what you are, you and your gangly sister.'

Nancy took a step closer, her eyes firmly fixed on Dottie's face. Dottie took a step back, less confident. 'Say that again, Conway.'

Dottie turned to her puppets for a sign of alliance. Lily shrugged. 'Oh, leave her. She's not worth the hassle.'

Barbara's jaw muscles churned the gum round and round like it was acid, her wide eyes staring at Nancy.

'She can't get away with talking to me like that! Smelly little bitch,' Dottie said.

The cold worms filled Nancy's hand. The fire in her belly flared, the anger bubbled up until it reached the back of her throat. Growling like a feral cat, she lunged at Dottie, knocking her to the ground. Nancy straddled her, and before Dottie had time to register what was happening, Nancy pressed both knees down on her arms, pinning her to the gritty ground. She shoved a handful of worms into Dottie's mouth as soon as she opened it to scream. She pushed the clay-covered blackheads deeper and deeper until Dottie could scream no more. She smeared the dirt all over her perfect peachy skin. Her muffled cry was the most harmonious sound Nancy had ever heard. 'I hate you,' Nancy said. 'Everyone hates you. You're a horrible little bitch, and if you hassle me again, I'll kill you.'

As the worms slid down Dottie's neck, Nancy swept

them back towards her dirty mouth, prising her lips apart with her mucky fingers. She dug into her coat pocket, feeling the few remaining worms, with sticky and bloody fingers; she stuffed them down Dottie's bra.

Lily and Barbara screamed hysterically, afraid to touch Nancy, too afraid to help their friend. Lily pulled at her own hair. 'Oh my God... the Devil really is in her.'

The crows circled above them, like hawks waiting for the kill. Their loud rattling caws delighted Nancy. She pressed her knees harder on Dottie's arms.

'You're mad in the head,' Barbara said.

The camogie girls gathered round, cheering and waving their sticks in the air.

'That's the girl, Nancy. Teach her a lesson she'll not forget,' Jenny shouted.

They're cheering me on... They like me... They like what I'm doing.

Master Dunphy's loud bellows shook the trees. His huge hands grabbed Nancy's shoulders, lifting her off a distressed Dottie. 'What the hell is going on here? A *disgrace,* Miss Connolly! *That's* what you are!'

Nancy panted; adrenaline surged through her veins. No remorse—only satisfaction.

Master Dunphy helped Dottie up. Tears rolled down her clay-streaked face. Her whole body shook, worms fell from her hair as she jumped up and down, pulling the slimy creatures out of her bra. She heaved several times before throwing up. Undigested cheese and onion crisps splattered to the ground, spraying Master Dunphy's shoes.

Marcus Jones gagged. 'Uh, that's rotten.'

'Were they King or Tayto?' said his friend Justin. The

two boys gathered the worms and threw them at Jenny and the others. The thrill of being chased by a gang of angry girls waving camogie sticks was the highlight of their morning.

Sister Kieran appeared. 'What in the name of all that's good and holy is going on here?'

'She attacked me,' Nancy shouted, pointing at Dottie.

'I might have known you'd be involved, Miss Conway.'

Dottie was too distraught to answer. Master Dunphy explained the scene he'd come across, and Sister Kieran poked Nancy in the ribs with her pale bony finger. 'Get into my office right now, you.' She glared at Dottie, pursing her lips in disgust. 'And you too, madam, after you've cleaned yourself up. And calm yourself down; don't be so ridiculous. Such carry-on.'

'Maybe she should go home for now, Sister... the state of her,' Master Dunphy said.

'Go on then, but I want you in my office first thing in the morning.'

Rose and Maureen turned the corner as Nancy was being led into the school by Sister Kieran. 'Where are you going?' Rose asked, following them.

'She's coming to my office, that's where she's going.'

'What's wrong?' Rose gripped Nancy's arm and walked alongside her.

'Why do you want to know?' Nancy yanked her arm away.

'That's enough now. Go to your class, Rose Connolly. There's the bell,' Sister Kieran said.

The students moseyed back to their classes, some still laughing about the altercation between the two girls. Rose spotted Jenny in the crowd. She called out, rushing towards her, Maureen close behind. 'What happened with Nancy? She's gone to Sister Kieran's office.'

'There was a fight between her and Dottie,' Jenny said.

'What?' Rose stuck her neck out, her mouth wide open. 'That bloody Dottie Conway. And why wasn't she sent to the head as well?'

Jenny laughed. 'Because she got sick all over herself, and Master Dunphy said she could go home. Nancy stuffed a load of worms into her mouth and down her blouse.'

'Wait 'til Mammy hears about this,' Maureen said.

Jenny curled her lip. 'Is that all you can say?'

'She finally stood up to her.' Rose grinned. 'I can't believe it.'

'She sure did. Conway won't go anywhere near her again, and that's for sure,' Jenny said.

§

This was Nancy's first time in Sister Kieran's office. It was small and cluttered, not like she expected. A statue of the Virgin Mary stood in the window, the perfect size, as if the window had been built specially to accommodate Our Lady. Huge wooden rosary beads hung on the wall behind Sister Kieran's desk. Nancy couldn't understand the point of such huge beads. How on earth could anyone hold them to say their rosary?

'Now tell me what happened.'

'She started it, Sister.'

'Well, I have no doubt about that. But the worms, where did they appear from?'

'My pocket, Sister.'

'Do you always keep worms in your pocket?'

'No, Sister.'

'It's bad enough catching the boys fighting, but when two girls are found on the ground, pulling the heads of each other, well, it's disgraceful. That's what it is.'

'Sorry, Sister.'

'I understand you were only standing up for yourself, but that's not the way to do it. It won't be tolerated. I've a good mind to suspend you—and her!' She looked up to the statue of Our Lady. 'Your grandmother, Annie Connolly, was a lady, you know. A holy woman, kind and dutiful. She'd be hurt and disappointed if she were alive to see all this carry-on.'

'I never knew her.'

'And that's such a pity. Now, come to me in future if Dottie Conway bothers you. No doubt her parents will have something to say about this.' Sister Kieran shook her head. 'Off with you.'

'Yes, Sister. Thank you, Sister.'

Nancy left the office, feeling exhilarated. She'd expected a thousand lines and a decade of the rosary. Sister hadn't even made her say the Act of Contrition.

CHAPTER FIFTY-NINE

Nancy loved Tuesdays. It was her day for going to Benny's house after school for a piano lesson and to do the housework. She liked being with Benny and liked getting away from Rose and Maureen—mostly Maureen. Some days, she had very little housework to do because Granny Lynch did most of it herself. One afternoon, she overheard her telling Mrs O'Malley they didn't need a cleaner, and the arrangement wasn't meant to be long-term. And Auntie Mary kept telling Mrs O'Malley that a pound was too much for a couple of hours cleaning, especially with free piano lessons. But Mrs O'Malley disagreed with both of them.

Nancy used her own key to let herself in. Mrs O'Malley was playing the piano and singing a song. She had a soothing voice, but it sounded sad, maybe because the song she was singing was a sad song. *That once he was truly my lover… Red is the rose…*

Nancy put the kettle on. The words of the song pulled at her, stilled her, as if they should mean something. She listened closer. *Red is the rose.* Nancy hummed along, and then found herself singing the words. *It's all for the loss of my bonny Irish lad, that my heart is broken forever*. Her daddy used to sing it! That's where she'd heard it before. He sang that song for Rose, she recalled. Nancy rubbed her chest and filled her cup with water to quench the sudden onset of thirst.

She sat at the table, thinking about her mother. Most memories were vague, but others appeared in her mind as fresh as if they'd happened only yesterday. She tried not to think about her, but sometimes she couldn't stop herself. The hiss of the steaming kettle brought her out of her daydream.

§

Maureen sat on the bed writing a letter to her American pen-pal. Rose had convinced her not to mention the Dottie incident to Auntie Mary.

'If you tell on her, she'll tell on you,' Rose said.

'I'm not even sure I care, Rose. I'm going to marry Dougie no matter what anyone says.' Maureen twirled the pen through her hair.

'You won't be allowed.'

'I'm nineteen, I can do what I want, and if I want to marry a protestant, I will.'

'What about Father Tierney? Aren't you afraid of him?'

'Why would I be afraid of him?'

'It's a sin to French kiss a boy unless you're married, you know,' said Rose.

'It's none of his business who I kiss or who I marry. I'll go back to England if I have to. It's different over there. And no, Rose, it's not a sin. Grow up.'

'Will you become one of them?'

'I might.'

Rose sat on the bed beside Maureen. 'Are you not afraid that, y'know, you mightn't go to heaven?'

'A bit.' Maureen shrugged her shoulders. 'Anyway, Nancy doesn't know about Dougie, does she?'

'She only knows you French kissed a boy, but I don't think she knows who he is,' said Rose.

'I saw her creeping out of that babby house one day. Does she still play with those creepy dolls? They're disgusting, covered in mildew.'

'Don't know, but you wouldn't catch me going in there anymore. It stinks and it's full of creepy crawlies.' Rose screwed up her face.

A grin spread across Nancy's face as she crept away from the bedroom door. She tiptoed downstairs, skipping the creaky step.

Her piano sat in the sitting room directly under Maureen's bedroom. She flicked through her music copybook. *The Old Orange Flute.* Nancy flexed her fingers and sat down. She banged the keys and sang as loud as she could, looking towards the ceiling as she did so. 'T'was the old flute still a-whistlin *The Protestant Boys.*'

Mary sat knitting beside the fire. She chuckled to herself as she remembered back to when Flossie first suggested Nancy should learn piano. She didn't think the child had any music in her at all. After two years of piano lessons, Flossie and John bought Nancy a second-hand piano. They managed to squeeze it into the room with a bit of furniture re-arranging. It was the best thing anyone could have done for that child, Mary thought. Nancy was proud to remind everyone that she earned the money all by herself by doing jobs for the O'Malleys. Even after the piano was paid for, they kept Nancy on as their little helper. She knew Flossie liked having the girl around. Lord knew why because Mary found Nancy harder work than her placid and obedient sister.

CHAPTER SIXTY

Nancy smiled as she left the Post Office. She tucked her green savings book safely into her handbag. She had nearly one hundred and thirty pounds saved up now.

A woman whom she recognised from up the town walked towards her, smiling. She'd seen the same woman outside Benny's house one day, but Mrs O'Malley didn't seem happy to see her. She didn't let her in.

'Hello, Nancy,' the woman said.

'Hello.'

'My name is Joyce. You don't know me.'

'What do you want?'

'I have something for you.' Joyce reached into her coat pocket. 'It's a letter. From your mammy.' She held out a white envelope.

'My mother's dead.'

'She's not dead, Nancy.'

'Who are you? How do you know anything about her?'

'I was her friend when she lived here. Sometimes she writes to me.'

'Where is she?' Nancy asked in a whisper.

'Dublin. She sent me this letter to give you.' Joyce pointed up the street. 'I live up there, on the Institute Road, in the grey house. Come and see me any time you want... if you have questions.'

'I have to go,' Nancy said. She stuffed the letter in her pocket and hurried down the street. *Should she tell Auntie Mary? Rose had said their mother was dead. Did she lie? Or is that what she really believed? Should she tell Rose their mother was alive?* Nancy walked faster.

She went straight into the babby house when she got home. Sweating and out of breath, she tugged at her scarf to loosen it. She threw her hat and gloves on the old, rotted tea chest and took the letter from her pocket. No one ever spoke about her mother; only about her father. Nancy knew she'd left them; she remembered it. She beat Nancy that day, and then ran away. Nancy often wondered if that was the reason she left them all. She had asked Rose once if that was why she left, but Rose told her not to talk about their mother.

She rubbed her aching belly. Her mouth felt as dry as dust, like it always did when thoughts of her mother crept into her mind. She got the same feeling of needing the toilet and wanting Rose's arms around her to protect her. That's what Rose used to say, before Maureen came into their lives. *We'll protect each other, Nancy.* Resentment simmered inside her. If only her father was still alive, Maureen wouldn't be here at all. And damn Joyce for giving her the letter. She should have let things be. Nancy was happy to believe she'd never see her mother again.

She took a deep breath, the cold damp air lodging itself in the back of her raw throat. She opened the envelope slowly, as if its contents posed a threat. Her heart sped up again as she read the pencilled words on the fine lined paper.

Later that evening, she walked back into town, duffle coat buttoned up and her new red woolly hat pulled tight below her ears. She knocked on Joyce Rafferty's front door.

§

The yew trees surrounding the graveyard were barely visible behind the fog. The scene before her eyes reminded Flossie of a painting she'd once seen, the grey headstones like smudges on the canvas, and the ambling figure below, a casual flick of his brush.

Flossie placed a bunch of daffodils on Frank's grave. She had gently twisted the stem of a snowdrop around each one. She said a prayer, and then told Frank all the latest news.

A murder of noisy crows made their way to the tress where they'd settle for the night; darkness was almost upon them. The chill penetrated her bones. She couldn't stand still for the cold creeping up through the soles of her boots, paining her legs. She glanced around, looking for the person she had noticed earlier; it was difficult to see through the hazy twilight. She saw them again... closer... a few graves across from Frank's. A woman... in an emerald-green coat and a red hat. Flossie's throat tightened and the hairs stood on the back of her neck.

The woman moved closer. Flossie's body froze, her heart-beat quickened, and she held her breath. Then the face emerged from the veil of fog that surrounded her.

'Hello, Mrs O'Malley.'

Flossie flung her hand to her chest. 'My God! Nancy! I thought you were someone else.'

'Sorry. Are you disappointed?'

'No, God no.'

'Who did you think I was?'

'You're wearing your mother's coat, so for a minute...' Flossie's heart raced.

'Daddy bought her this coat for her birthday once. Rose told me. That's why Auntie Mary kept it, because Daddy bought it. Auntie Mary said that Mammy didn't wear it after she had me because she stayed fat.'

The coat was a perfect fit for Nancy. She had indeed grown from a scrawny girl into a strong sturdy young woman, the same cut as her mother was when she was younger. Nancy never talked or asked about her mother, and she rarely visited her father's grave.

'That's a nice little bouquet there on Daddy's grave.' Nancy touched the arrangement of daffodils and snowdrops with the toe of her shoe. Icy tendrils of mist swirled up Flossie's nostrils, catching in the back of her dry throat as her breath quickened.

'Did you put them there?'

'Yes. Josey picked them from his garden. I put some on his grandmother's grave too... like he said.'

'Do you visit Daddy's grave often?' asked Nancy.

'When I come to my father's grave, I pray at other graves too. Your dad's, your grandparents', Mr Rafferty's and one or two others, people you wouldn't know.'

'It's important to pray for dead people, isn't it?'

'Yes, we all want to be remembered after we die.'

'Who remembers Daddy?' Nancy pushed her hands deep into her pockets.

'Everyone. His family and all his friends from work.'

'Tell me their names. I'd like to know.'

'Well, you and Rose of course. Josey, Mary, Jim, and his friends from work—I couldn't tell you all their names.'

'What about you?'

'Well, yes, me too. We all grew up together, y'know, me and the Connollys. We were all friends.'

'I know that,' said Nancy.

'Look, I really have to go now. It's getting dark and you should be getting off too. Walk with me,' said Flossie.

'No thanks. I'll stay for a little while longer, I'm fine.'

'Okay, see you tomorrow after school for piano.'

As Flossie faded into the fog, Nancy called out, 'Do you think my mother's dead, Mrs O'Malley?'

Flossie looked back at the misty shape. 'I'm sorry, Nancy, I have no idea what happened your mother. Everyone believes she ran away... for whatever reason. Nobody knows.'

§

Dottie, Lily and Barbara stood outside the convent gates. Nancy approached, almost regretting the worm incident. She held her head in the air and pushed her shoulders as far back as she could manage. She looked straight ahead as she walked past the three troublemakers.

'Don't even look at her, she's not worth the time of day,' Barbara said.

Nancy's heart pounded and the hairs prickled her scalp, but she kept going. A somewhat familiar sensation stirred inside her. It was as if her insides were smiling, laughing even, at Dottie and her stupid friends, the same feeling she'd had when she found out that Maureen had a protestant boyfriend. She hummed her way into class, with a spring in her step. *Red is the rose*. She couldn't shift that song out of her head.

At lunchtime, Nancy sat with Jenny. 'Hey, Jenny. I was thinking maybe I'll try a game of camogie today. Would that be alright?'

'Sure aren't I asking you to play this ages?'

'I don't have a camogie stick.'

'Don't worry, I'll sort ya out,' said Jenny.

'Thanks, Jenny.'

'What does this fella want?' Jenny said as Séan O'Shea strutted towards them.

'Well, girls.'

'What d'you want?' asked Jenny.

'To ask Nancy something.'

Nancy frowned at O'Shea, who'd never bade her the time of day before. 'Ask me what?'

'D'ya wanna come out with me some night?'

'I do not,' Nancy answered looking him up and down. She knew enough about him to know he could charm honey from a bear. She also knew Dottie Conway had a notion of him and she most certainly didn't have the same taste in men as her. Dottie was welcome to stocky little O'Shea.

'G'wan, Nancy. We'd have a great time,' he said.

'I have a boyfriend already.' Out of the corner of her eye she saw Jenny's head swivel round.

'Who? I never see ya with anyone,' O'Shea said.

'You wouldn't know him. He goes to the Tech.'

'Sure let me know when he breaks your heart and I'll fix it for ya.' He swaggered back to the lads, hands in pockets, whistling a catchy tune.

'That fella thinks he's great.'

'So, do you?' asked Jenny.

'Do I what?'

'Have a boyfriend.'

'Maybe.'

'You're telling lies. You only said that to get rid of him. Sure why didn't you tell him yes?'

'Do you think I want to be going with someone Dottie Conway fancies? I have far better taste than her.'

'Why care about her? Sure loads of girls fancy him. Look at them,' Jenny said nodding towards a group of giggling girls who had gathered around O'Shea and his friends. But Séan O'Shea only had eyes for one girl: Nancy Connolly.

CHAPTER SIXTY-ONE

As Nancy walked along the Virginia Road towards town, she saw Benny on his way down from the Tech. She often wished she had gone to the Tech instead of Lourdesville, but Auntie Mary insisted the convent was the best school for girls.

She thought about her mother's letter. She'd said the O'Malleys forced her to go away and stole her family. Joyce said she didn't understand what Alice meant by that. She forced it to the back of her mind, for now.

Benny was good fun... and handsome too. Loads of girls were mad after him, including Rose. Nancy hoped he wouldn't be bothered with a girlfriend because then he might not have time for her. He strolled towards her like he hadn't a care in the world.

'Hiya, Nancy. Who did you beat up today?'

'Shut up.' Nancy shoved him across the footpath. 'Do you want to know a secret?' she asked as they walked together.

'Depends.'

'On what?'

'If it's really a secret or if it's something stupid that no one cares about.'

'It's about Maureen and her secret boyfriend.'

'Secret boyfriend?'

'And I know who he is. He's a protestant.'

Benny slowed down. 'Jesus, are you sure? Who is he? Does Mary and Jim know?'

'No, not yet. It's Dougie Taylor.'

'One of the Taylors from Killan?'

'Yeah. He's far older than her too. Twenty-five. I found out weeks ago.'

'There'll be war when her ones find out about that.' Benny let out a long whistle.

'You won't tell anyone, will you?'

'I don't gossip,' he replied with a wry smile.

Nancy knew that wasn't true, and that Benny would be mouthing his latest news to his buddies in the Tech.

§

Benny picked up the note from the kitchen table and read it out loud.

Benny - I'll be home late this evening. Will you light the fire before you go to Gaelic training please? Granny is at Molly's.

Nancy - sorry we have to miss your piano lesson today. You can carry on with the usual chores. I knocked over a vase of flowers in my bedroom this morning. Will you see to it for me, please? I had to rush. Thank you.

They made jam sandwiches and Benny had his gobbled down before Nancy half-finished her first one. He lit the fire, grabbed his football gear from his bedroom—washed and packed by Granny Lynch—and filled a bottle with tap water.

'Keep an eye on the fire there, Nancy, and knock her back when she lights up.'

Nancy bowed her head. 'Yes, master.'

After he left, Nancy sat at the piano and played one of the first tunes she ever learned. *Happy Birthday.* She sang the words with the same enthusiasm as she'd sing at a funeral. The thirtieth of March and no one remembered. Not Auntie Mary or Maureen or even her sister. Mrs O'Malley remembered every other year. She always gave her a nice card and present. Now, on her sixteenth birthday, not one person cared.

Nancy opened the drawer beside the piano, where Mrs O'Malley kept all her music manuscripts. She sifted through the folder labelled *Classical Music. The Blue Danube, Swan Lake, Clair de Lune, Moonlight Sonata.* Nancy's fingers were immediately drawn to the keys. She closed her eyes and played with ease.

She took out the *Irish Ballads* folder. Mrs O'Malley was passionate about Irish music. She said it was in our souls and had pieces of our hearts sprinkled through it. She told Nancy, 'No matter what mood you are in, or whatever emotion you are feeling, there's an Irish song for it. *The Last Rose of Summer, Boulavogue, The Lark in the Morning,* and many others tell stories about everyone.' She came out with some quare stuff sometimes, Nancy thought.

She picked up the last one in the pile. *Red is the Rose.* It was old and tattered, brown at the edges, like the others at the bottom of the pile. The urge to learn the words of this song nagged at her. She folded it and put it in her school bag. She hummed the tune as she made her way upstairs and across the landing.

Benny's bedroom door was open. Nancy stopped and peered in, as she often did. She liked the way his room smelled, like the fresh air and her daddy's hair.

She moved on to the end of the hall to Mr and Mrs O'Malley's bedroom. She hardly ever went into their bedroom because it wasn't on her chore list. She had ventured in a few times when she was a child. She liked to smell the perfumes and talcum powder, and often pouched curiously through the drawers and one of the wardrobes that had Mr O'Malley's clothes in it. The other wardrobe was always locked.

When Nancy lifted the vase from the floor, she noticed that the other wardrobe was slightly open, with the key still in the lock. She opened it. It smelled like a garden, sweet and summery. Soft cardigans and jumpers in pastel shades of pink, blue and lilac were neatly folded on the top shelf alongside three colourful boxes. Summer dresses hung one side and winter skirts and trousers on the other. She sure did keep everything very tidy, unlike Auntie Mary, whose things were higgledy-piggledy.

Nancy ran her hand across the line of hanging dresses, soft and fragrant. She took down a yellow summer dress, midi-length with short sleeves. The thick cotton was lined with smooth satin. The dress brought Nancy back to a childhood memory, fishing with her daddy at the Castle Lake. Mrs

O'Malley was there. Rose and Benny too. She closed her eyes to capture a vision of his smiling face. She didn't have many memories of her father, but his smile was the one part of him she remembered so clearly. Then the vision of his smile faded, expelled by images of a bruised and sorrowful face; the bad memories trying to dominate the good ones—as always. She focused harder on the image of his smile. His kind eyes... sad eyes. *Why was he sad? Did she ever make him sad?* She couldn't remember. Tears built up, stinging her eyelids. She blinked them away and took a deep breath. She knew that if her daddy was still alive he would have remembered her birthday.

She closed her eyes again. *Mrs O'Malley in her yellow dress, holding a red rose... Daddy giving her the rose... she's smiling... they're both smiling. He's singing that song, the same song he often sang to her and Rose at bedtime.* She twisted the dress tight around her closed fingers. Her skin prickled from the top of her head to the tips of her toes. She looked at the crumpled dress in her hands. *The song wasn't for Rose at all. It was for Mrs O'Malley.*

Nancy put the dress back on its hanger, closed the wardrobe, and cleaned up the broken vase. She mopped the soggy carpet, took the flowers into the kitchen and threw them in the bin.

She returned to the bedroom with a chair. She wanted to see inside the boxes. She took them down one by one and lay them on the floor. A layer of dust covered the lid of the one on top, a black and white stripy round one. It looked the most interesting.

A thrilling sensation surged through Nancy as she lifted

the lid. She liked private things. Invading the privacy of another person excited her, but she knew it was wrong.

Bundles of letters tied with string filled the box. Each bundle had a label. Mary, Auntie Bridgey, Danny, Catherine. She took out an envelope labelled *Notes from Frank*. Little flutters gently vibrated behind her breastbone. Her temples pulsed; her hands trembled slightly. *Her father, Frank? Why was he sending Mrs O'Malley notes?* She put them to one side. She took out the bundle labelled *Mary* and put it with *Frank's* notes. There was also a bundle labelled, *Letters to Sister Catherine*. Her sister the nun? Why write so many letters and then not send them? Nancy had often posted letters to Sister Catherine for Mrs O'Malley, but why not these? All of them were sealed. Dare she open one? *No*. She put them to one side with the others.

She opened a Milk Tray box. It contained birthday cards, memory cards of dead people and other uninteresting things. She pushed it to one side. The next box was more familiar to Nancy, a bright orange shoe box with a black cat on it. She'd had a quick look in this one before, many years ago.

She'd been hiding under the bed from Benny during a game of hide-and-seek. She opened the lid thinking she'd find a box full of black cats, but instead a shiny silver heart glinted in the dim light. When she heard Benny coming, she closed the box and crawled out from under the bed, with the shiny locket in her tight fist. It wasn't until she got home she opened the locket. The silver heart framed her daddy's face. At that time and ever since, she didn't question why Mrs O'Malley would have a photo of her daddy—they were, after all, childhood friends.

Nancy liked the black cat box. It contained holy medals,

tarnished jewellery, and two photos of Frank. Nancy had heard many stories from Auntie Mary about their childhood and growing up with Flossie Lynch (as her aunt still called her). But this was more than a friendship, this went deeper. It appeared to Nancy that Mrs O'Malley had a closer relationship with her father than she had with her Auntie Mary.

The last box was bigger and heavier than the others. Nancy ran her fingers across the handwritten words on the lid. *May you never forget what is worth remembering, nor ever remember what is best forgotten.*

The cardboard box harboured a stack of black hardback notebooks. She took one out and flipped it open. A diary. She opened another. They were all diaries. Mrs O'Malley's diaries. Nancy knew in her heart she was crossing a line, but the menace in her couldn't stop. Adrenaline rushed through her veins as she opened the 1958.

Leaving Auntie Bridgey... missing Dad, Catherine and Danny... bumped into Frank Connolly at the lake... still in love... shotgun wedding... waiting for Mary to come home... wedding dresses... imagined it was Frank standing there... living will be rich and fine.

Nancy suffocated in the words. She flipped the pages one after the other, searching for things she wasn't sure she even wanted to know. She grabbed the envelope of notes off the floor and tore it open. *Meet me at the lake.* She could only reach one conclusion: her father was a cheater. So was Flossie O'Malley. Adulterers. Her mother wasn't lying.

The hotel was beautiful, but as far as honeymoons go, it wasn't exactly what I had always wished for. Not that I thought it would be anything different, unless Frank had been my new husband. But I did expect John to consummate the marriage at least. That Julie one didn't help things. I'm certain John is hiding something. Old friends indeed. Oh God, I'm a hypocrite to expect John not to have secrets when I have so many of my own. John is a good man... I mustn't forget that.

Nancy closed the diary, grabbed two more and scanned the pages, searching for answers, trying to make sense of it all. But she didn't have time just then. She replaced the boxes neatly on the top shelf and left the bedroom cradling Flossie O'Malley's books of secrets in her arms, along with the letters to Sister Catherine.

§

Almost five o'clock. At least it would still be bright by the time she'd get home. Nancy hated walking home from town in the dark, especially down the Wood Lane. Josey told ghost stories about the headless horseman who travelled the back lane at night, wearing a black cloak, galloping on his black horse. Nancy was afraid of her life she might meet him and end up headless too.

She took her hat from her school bag and pulled it down over her ears. She walked fast to keep warm. Her mouth watered at the thoughts of dipping a slice of heavily buttered batch loaf into her favourite vegetable soup. *Please don't let it be oxtail.*

The weight of the diaries in Nancy's schoolbag pained her shoulders, as if silently accusing her of what she had done. Stealing bits of jewellery and money was one thing, a sin of course, but taking Mrs O'Malley's diaries was surely a mortal sin. But wasn't adultery and telling lies a bigger sin? Maybe she had read it all wrong. Maybe her father didn't even know Mrs O'Malley was in love with him. Yes. That was probably it. He probably knew nothing about it. It was all her. Her secrets.

She would return the diaries on Friday and forget about them. She'd ask for forgiveness at confessions on Saturday—and never steal again!

§

As she passed Uncle Josey's house, his two cats jumped out at her, spitting. She hated his cats... they were as nasty as the wild briars in the hedges. Auntie Mary threw cups of water at them whenever she caught them in her garden. Nancy wondered why they ever went back.

Uncle Jim's car was parked in the yard in puddles of suds. He paid Rose and Maureen to wash it once a week for two reasons: he liked having a clean shiny car and they moaned constantly that Nancy always had money and they didn't. Nancy liked Uncle Jim. He was kind, always left discipline up to Auntie Mary. When the girls were younger, he sometimes gave them money in secret. Five pence each, to spend on sweets. 'Don't tell Mary,' he'd whisper with a wink.

The warmth of the house enveloped Nancy as soon as she stepped inside the front door, but a curious vibe hovered, a silence unusual for the time of day, and unfamiliar smells blurred her senses. She ran upstairs and shoved her heavy schoolbag under the bed.

'Hello?' she called as she came back downstairs.

Rose shouted from the kitchen. 'In here!'

Nancy sauntered into the kitchen and a loud cheer blasted her, followed by a bubbly chorus of *Happy Birthday*.

She stood gaping, not sure who to look at... Rose, Maureen, Jim or Auntie Mary. Mrs O'Malley and Benny were there too. And of course Uncle Josey, and even Jenny. An array of colourful balloons decorated every corner, and a huge pink poster spelled out the words 'Happy 16th Birthday Nancy'.

Everyone clapped. Nancy's cheeks burned. She became aware that she was smiling possibly the biggest smile ever. They were all laughing, happy for her. They hadn't forgotten after all. The heaviness she'd been carrying around all day lifted. Her tummy felt light and airy, her eyes burned as they filled up. She swallowed hard and blurted out, 'I didn't think anyone remembered.'

Benny winked; she looked away. 'Sweet sixteen now, Nancy,' he said and everyone laughed.

'Open your presents, Nancy' Auntie Mary said.

'Can we eat first?' asked Maureen.

'I can eat and open presents at the same time,' said Nancy. She hung her coat on the back of a chair.

'Marvellous,' said Benny, clapping his hands and grabbing a sausage roll.

'You're at the head of the table today, Sweet Sixteen,' said Uncle Jim as he held his chair out for Nancy.

A warm sensation spread through her. She caught Benny's eye, and he gave her another wink. She pulled her hair over her tingling ears. 'Thanks, Jim.' Nancy grabbed the nearest sandwich, not caring what was inside. No boy ever winked at her before. *But she looked awful, scruffy, hair not brushed.* There was no point in thinking about that now. She looked around. Everything was beautiful and perfect. Each chair had a balloon tied to it—even the armchair by the range.

A sandwich cake oozing with jam and cream sat in the centre of the table, dusted with icing sugar. Hopefully, Auntie Mary baked it, not Maureen, because she covered everything with icing sugar to hide the burnt bits. Sixteen candles waited to be lit. What would she wish for?

She looked across at Benny. He was deep in conversation with Rose, who had her chair pulled right up beside him; so close, she was millimetres from touching him. Her body leaned towards his. Since when was Rose interested in hearing about a football match? She had a notion of him alright. Surely, she didn't think he fancied her.

Nancy grabbed another sandwich, biting into it without realising it was corned beef and brown sauce. She gagged as soon as the spicy sauce hit the back of her throat. She swallowed and washed it down with red lemonade. Uncle Josey always put brown sauce on his meat sandwiches; she hated it. She always hated it. Her mother smothered it all over their sandwiches once, and when Nancy refused to eat it, Alice forced it into her, holding her hand across her mouth until she swallowed it. Two minutes later, she vomited it across the table. She slapped her across the legs that day, making Rose clean up the vomit.

'Will you open ours first?' said Auntie Mary, handing Nancy a small box wrapped in silver paper. She peeled the Sellotape carefully, trying her best to protect the nice paper, which she then folded neatly and put on the table.

Maureen laughed. 'Bloody hell, Nancy... whatever's in the box is your present, not the fecking paper.' Everyone else laughed along with her.

Ignoring them all, Nancy opened the grey velvet box to

reveal a gold Claddagh chain. Nancy smiled. 'It's beautiful. I hope it fits me.'

'Don't be silly, it's a chain, Nancy. They don't come in sizes,' said Maureen.

'Some of them do actually,' Mrs O'Malley said.

Nancy didn't know if that was true, but it shut Maureen up anyway.

'Happy birthday, Nancy. This is from me.'

'Thanks, Mrs O'Malley.'

'And one thing you have to do from now on is please call me Flossie. You're not a child in my school anymore. You're my friend.'

'Okay.' Nancy pushed her shoulders back, feeling grown up.

'Can I call you Flossie as well? Sure I'm older than her,' said Benny.

'No, you can't, cheeky!' Flossie threw a jelly sweet at her son. He laughed.

Rose still sat close to him, gawking into his face, twirling her beige-blonde hair around her fingers.

'It's from both of us,' said Flossie, nodding towards Benny.

'Is it not from John too?' asked Nancy.

'Well, yes of course.' Flossie smiled stiffly, glancing around the room.

Nancy picked the Sellotape with her thumb nail, but still the green glossy paper tore. *Why was Mrs O'Malley so good to her and Rose? Was it because she had been in love with their father? Did she feel sorry for them? No one ever told them exactly what happened to their parents. Daddy drowned, but how? Alice disappeared, and why did she say in her letter it was because of the O'Malleys?*

The last piece of Sellotape came off and the paper opened up. It was a bottle of Charlie perfume. She really did feel like a grown-up today.

'Thanks, Mrs O'Malley.' Nancy opened the bottle and dabbed a bit behind her ears. 'It smells lovely.'

'She said you can call her Flossie,' said Maureen.

Auntie Mary frowned at Maureen. 'What's wrong with you today?'

'Nothing.'

'Keep your smart comments to yourself, please.'

Jenny gave Maureen a sideways look. 'I didn't get you a present, Nancy, but next Saturday, if you come to our camogie match, I'll buy you a bag of chips on the way home.'

'Sounds like a good idea. Thanks, Jenny.'

Josey's present—a pair of Claddagh earrings to match the necklace from Mary—wasn't wrapped, but Nancy didn't mind. She was enjoying the attention. Having a surprise birthday party made her feel important. Maureen was spoiling it though, and Rose... hanging out of Benny like he was her boyfriend.

Uncle Jim started the singsong. Benny played the spoons while Rose and Maureen joined in with their tin whistles. Everyone sang the chorus. After a few tunes, Auntie Mary opened a bottle of sherry, pouring one for everyone. She handed a glass to Nancy. 'Only because it's your birthday.' She smiled.

Flossie stopped singing. 'Mary, she's only sixteen!'

'Ach, it's only one. Sure it's her birthday. Rose and

Maureen had a wee sherry on their sixteenth birthdays, and it didn't do them any harm,' Mary said.

'Well, we were far more mature than her when we were sixteen,' Maureen said.

Rose laughed. Nancy blushed, and anger burned the back of her throat. 'I'll hardly become a drunk with just one.' Nancy glared at Flossie. 'Like my mother.'

Mary gasped. Silence shrouded the room.

'That's not what I'm saying,' said Flossie.

'So I can have one. Thanks, Auntie Mary.'

Mary poured the sherry into Nancy's glass and she drank it all in one go.

'Them glasses are very small... I'll have another one.'

'They're small for a reason,' said Maureen.

Mary chuckled and poured more sherry for Nancy.

Flossie frowned. 'Jesus, Mary, you said one. She's a child, for God's sake.'

'It isn't even any of your business,' said Nancy. 'And I'm not a child. You said I wasn't a child anymore and I should call you Flossie. Was that a lie?' She felt like a child at that moment—a small bold child. Not special anymore. No more important than anyone else in the room. She wanted to leave, run and hide in her babby house, away from everyone. But still she lashed out. She craned her neck towards Flossie. 'Are you trying to ruin my party?' she cried.

'I care about you, that's all. You don't need alcohol to enjoy your party.'

'Why do you care about me?'

'Okay, everyone, can we go back to having fun?' said Uncle Jim, frowning at his wife for causing the situation.

Jenny moved nearer to Nancy, pleading with her eyes.

Nancy looked at Benny, who wasn't smiling anymore. Rose crouched into her chair, the tops of her fingers white like her face as they pressed tight on the holes of her tin whistle.

Glancing at the door, Nancy tapped her foot on the floor. Running would only make her look more foolish. She put her glass of sherry down. The bottle of red lemonade suddenly seemed more appealing. 'I'm sorry. Let's sing again.'

Jim took his fiddle from its case and tuned up. His forehead was creased, his smile strained. Nancy hadn't mean to upset Uncle Jim... she loved him. She loved Rose too and didn't want to upset her. Jenny was her friend, she didn't want to lose her.

The uncomfortable atmosphere disappeared soon after Jim started playing his fiddle. Everyone relaxed again. Soon after, Benny announced it was time to light the candles on the cake, so Mary made another pot of tea. The spotlight was on the birthday girl again. Benny lit the candles.

Nancy closed her eyes, willing herself to make a wish. But she couldn't because what was the point? *Her wishes never came true.*

'Did you make it?' said Jenny.

'Yes.'

'You have to blow them all out if you want your wish to come true, y'know,' said Maureen.

'I know that.'

'And you also have to believe it'll come true,' said Benny.

'Do you need help?' asked Maureen.

Nancy filled her lungs with air. She held her breath for a moment. Repeating her wish in her head, she blew hard on the candles, until all sixteen yellow flickering flames disappeared into thin waves of grey smoke. Everyone clapped as they sang another chorus of *Happy Birthday*.

'Flossie, will you play the piano for us?' asked Nancy.

'Oh, yes, Flossie, please do,' said Mary, beckoning towards the sitting room.

'Okay, why not?' Flossie said. 'What would you like me to play?'

'Something lively, Mam. None of that boring ole Mozart stuff,' said Benny.

'*Whiskey in the Jar*,' said Jim with a clap.

'Not on the piano. Don't be silly, Jim,' said Mary.

'Why not? Grey Fagin used to play it on the piano accordion. Sure isn't it the same thing?' Jim said.

'I can play it if they want, Mary.'

'What about *Red is the Rose*?' said Nancy.

Flossie stalled. 'I don't think I know that one.'

'Yes, you do. I heard you playing it once. I'll sing a bit of it to jog your memory,' said Nancy. 'T'was down by Killarney's green woods that we strayed...'

'That's the song Daddy used to sing for me,' said Rose. 'Yes, please play that, Flossie. It was mine and Daddy's favourite song.'

'I don't think it was for you, Rose. It's a love song,' said Nancy.

'How would you know? You can't even remember your father,' Maureen said.

'Yes, I can,' said Nancy as she lunged towards her. She clawed at her hair and Maureen clawed back.

'Jesus, Mary and Joseph, what has got into you two?' Josey said as he pulled the girls apart.

'Tell Rose the song wasn't for her... go on, tell her.' Nancy glared at Flossie, her eyes brimming with tears.

Rose covered her face with her hands. Benny put his arm around her shoulder, giving Nancy an angry look.

'What's the matter with you, Nancy?' Jim asked.

Mary began to clear the table. 'I think the party's over,' she said.

Nancy grabbed her coat and stormed out the back door, slamming it hard behind her.

CHAPTER SIXTY-TWO

'No chance of squeezing in an extra five minutes around here,' said Rose, pulling the blankets over her head. 'Maureen, why is your mother shouting?'

Maureen sat preening herself at the dressing table. 'She said Daddy didn't close the coop properly last night, and a fox killed two hens... from what I can hear. He's saying he did close it.'

Jim's car revved out the yard.

'I'd better get up and not have her coming in roaring at me. She's probably still mad at Nancy for making a show of herself yesterday,' said Rose.

'Jesus, she has an awful temper that Nancy one.'

'It wasn't all her fault though.' Rose yawned and pushed the blankets off, shivering at the thoughts of leaving her warm bed.

'Why was she so horrible to Flossie? And everything she does for her, organising the surprise party and everything.'

'You weren't that nice yourself, Maureen.'

'What d'you mean?'

'You know well what I mean.'

'You can't talk. You know she has a wee notion of Benny, and you were all over him.'

'Sure who hasn't got a notion of Benny?' Rose said, throwing her head back.

Maureen gasped. 'So you are after him!'

'Well, I think he likes me. He couldn't take his eyes off me all day.'

'Oh, I don't know about that. I saw him winking at Nancy.'

'Only because it was her birthday. They're just friends.'

Maureen weaved her long frizzy hair into a plait. 'Do you think Mammy and Flossie ever fell out before?'

'Don't know. They were really mad at each other last night, that's for sure.'

'I don't think Flossie had any right to tell Mammy she was irresponsible. All over a glass of sherry.'

'Sometimes you'd think she was Nancy's mother the way she carries on,' Rose said.

'I once heard Mammy saying to Daddy that Flossie interfered too much. That she was very bossy and acted like she knew everything about children, just because she's a schoolteacher.' Maureen slipped on her shoes and flung her schoolbag over her shoulder. 'I'm ready. You'd better hurry up or Mammy'll be up, giving out.'

Rose finished dressing and dawdled into the bathroom. As she brushed her teeth, she peered out the open frost-tinted window, hoping to see a blue sky instead of the usual watery grey clouds. She pushed the window open further so she could see the babby house. She had distinct memories of the day her father showed her and Nancy his old fort he'd worked so hard to refurbish for them. He'd been so proud of it.

In her head she heard him singing their song. It probably was a love song, if you'd like it to be. But wasn't every song? Why had Nancy said it wasn't her song when it absolutely was?

CHAPTER SIXTY-THREE

'What sins will you tell today, Maureen?'

'You ask me that every time, and I keep telling you it's none of your business.'

'No, you don't. You always say you have no sins, that you only go to try and listen to other people's.' Rose laughed.

'And what about you? Will you be confessing your sinful thoughts today?'

'You must be joking. Not after what Maisie Brady told me about the time the priest said, "Goodbye, Maisie", as he handed out her penance. She said she nearly fainted in the confession box. Not that she had any mortal sins to confess, she said, but it was the thoughts of him knowing who she was.'

They lowered their voices as they entered the church. Maureen dipped her fingers in the holy water font and flicked it at Rose. Sister Patricia turned to scowl at them. They scurried past the row of kneeling nuns and sat in queue for the confession box half-way up the aisle. Nancy was sitting at the end of the pew in front, next in line to tell her sins.

'She'll be a while in there,' whispered Maureen, stifling a giggle.

Nancy got up from her seat and, as she approached the confession box, she turned and glanced at Maureen. She smirked before she disappeared into the darkness. Maureen shifted uneasily in her seat.

§

Nancy could hear her heart thumping inside her chest. She hated this part, waiting in the dark for the priest to finish with the person in the opposite booth, mumbling and whispering. Her eyes soon adjusted to the darkness; she took deep breaths, repeating her sins over and over in her head. *Disobedient, unkind, cursing, bad thoughts.* Yes, the bad thoughts especially.

She decided not to mention stealing the pound from Uncle Jim. She intended on paying it back anyway, so it wasn't really stealing. She wondered if a priest ever reported anyone to the guards for stealing.

Mrs Rafferty, who was in before Nancy, had left a smell of TCP behind her. Nancy could hear the priest's whispers behind the closed grid and the mumbles from the opposite booth. Then it was her turn. The wire grid slid open.

'Bless me, Father, for I have sinned. It's been three weeks since my last confession. I was disobedient, I was unkind, I told lies. And the other thing is, Father...'

'Yes?'

'Well, I'm thinking terrible things, Father, about all the Catholics, and how I should become a Protestant.'

Father Tierney's head swerved round. 'And what would you want to be doing a thing like that for?' he asked, in a loud raspy whisper.

'You see, Father, it's my cousin Maureen who told me I should be like her and change into a Protestant. Her boyfriend, who she's going to marry, is a Protestant, and she says they're better than Catholics.'

His breath invaded her small space, more so with each word she spoke. *It was him who stank of TCP, not Mrs Rafferty.*

'Does her mother and father know all this?' he asked.

'No, Father. It's a big secret, and I can't tell because she'd kill me, I swear she would.'

'Say two "Our Fathers" and three "Hail Marys", and keep saying them until those ugly thoughts are gone from your mind.'

'Yes, Father. Oh, and Father, don't tell her I told you. She'll be in here in a few minutes. You'll know it's her because she has an Englishy accent. Sure maybe you could talk her out of marrying him.'

Nancy separated herself from the huddle of sinners and sat nearer the altar. She knelt down and crossed herself. She began her penance, slowly, in no hurry to leave the church. She might even light a candle for Maureen before she left.

§

Rose sat in the small dark booth, turning her nose up at the stench of TCP. She opened the door slightly to let in some air. Maureen occupied the opposite one. Rose felt a sense of disharmony between her cousin and the priest.

Her murmurs developed into a high-pitched whisper, and the priest shuffled in the tiny cubicle, like a caged bear. Through the crack in her door, Rose could see the wide eyes of the other penitents staring at the confession box. Maureen sounded the same as she did when she argued with Auntie Mary. *Things weren't good.*

Father's Tierney's voice got louder. 'Get out,' he said.

Rose froze, crouching in the dimness. *Who was he talking to?*

'I said, get out.'

Rose bolted out of the booth just as she heard Maureen shouting, 'You're not supposed to know who I am!'

Father Tierney's door flew open. 'You're the Devil's child,' he said as he pulled Maureen out of the booth. He gripped her arm and dragged her to the font of holy water at the back of the church.

'I'm going to be a Protestant and you can't stop me. I hate you,' Maureen said.

The nuns in the back pew stopped praying, expressions of horror on their faces. Sister Michael blessed herself several times, shaking her head, her eyes closed.

Father Tierney scooped up a handful of holy water and threw it in Maureen's face. 'This is the house of God. How dare you! Now get out and don't come back.'

Nancy came and stood beside Rose, grinning. 'I wonder what that was all about.'

'Why are you smiling?' Rose asked.

'Because it's the funniest thing I've ever seen in my whole life.'

'It's not funny at all, Nancy. What's the matter with you?' Rose curled her lip and walked away from her sister.

Rose caught sight of Maureen sprinting out the church gates onto Virginia Road. She ran after her. What the hell had she told the priest in there? What sin could be that bad? She felt a stitch in her side and slowed down. She hadn't a hope of catching up with Maureen anyway. She was gone like a scalded cat.

§

Rose walked around town in the hope of finding Maureen. She met Maisie Mac coming out of Byrne's shop, sucking on a liquorice stick. 'What's the matter with your Maureen?'

'What d'you mean?'

'I met her down the town bawling her eyes out.'

'Where did she go?'

'Well, I didn't see because I went into the pub to...'

'Yes, Maisie, to look for your father to send him home for the dinner.' Rose hurried down the street.

§

Auntie Mary had warned them to be home no later than one on the dot, because she had to go away in the afternoon. Rose prayed the whole way home that Maureen was already there.

The smell of frying drifted from the open kitchen window. Rose visualised fat sausages and streaky bacon in the pan, their usual Saturday dinner. She licked her lips and forgot for a moment about Maureen and Father Tierney.

'Where's the other one?' asked Mary when Rose walked in.

Rose feigned a surprised look. 'Is she not home yet?'

'Would I be asking if she was?'

'She left before me. She must be in town.'

'I told yas all not to be late.' Mary pounded the pot of spuds with the masher. Nancy sat at the table concentrating on the bowl of soup in front of her, her face glowing with satisfaction. She glanced at her sister as she blew gently on the spoon of hot broth.

'What happened at confession?' asked Mary.

Rose glanced at Nancy. 'I... I don't know. Nothing.'

'Don't nothing me, miss. Nancy told me all about Father Tierney pulling my Maureen out of the confession box.'

'Then why are you asking me?' Rose immediately regretted answering back.

Mary threw the masher in the sink, grabbed the tea towel and made a swipe across the table at Rose.

'Sorry, Auntie Mary. I'm sorry. I really don't know why Father Tierney gave out to Maureen. I can't find her. She ran into town and I couldn't catch her. I swear.' Rose made for the scullery to dodge being whipped by the tea towel. When she opened the back door to escape, a shower of hailstones pelted her in the face.

Jim had pulled up in the yard and was dragging a roll of chicken wire out of the boot. Mary pushed past Rose in the doorway, cursing as the icy hail hopped off her. 'Where the fecking hell did that shower come from? The sun was shining this morning. Jim, come in here.' She shoved Rose back into the kitchen. 'You, sit down and eat your dinner or I'll give it to the pigs.'

Rose didn't need to be told twice. She scurried to the table and glared at Nancy, who was shoving a forkful of turnips into her mouth. 'Why did you tell?' Rose said as she stabbed a sausage with her fork.

Nancy screwed up her nose. A lump formed in the back of Rose's throat, tears stung her eyes. She knew Nancy was mad at Maureen, but she didn't think she'd tell tales. Auntie Mary hadn't been this mad in a very long time. *Poor Maureen is for it now. Dougie should leave her alone and find someone else. Maureen would get over him and meet a nice Catholic man to fall in love with, then no one would be mad at her.*

§

Jim left his boots inside the scullery door and hung his heavy wet overcoat on the coat hook. 'I'll get that wire on after the spuds, Mary.'

'Never mind that. Maureen's not home from confession yet. Nancy said Father Tierney pulled her out of the confession box and called her a Devil's child.'

Jim's eyes opened as wide as his mouth.

'This one here said she knows nothing about it, but I don't believe her.'

'Why did he call her that?' asked Jim. His face paled as he paced over and back, looking from Nancy to Rose. Nancy avoided his eyes. Rose wanted to be sick. Mary reached across the sink to close the window. 'Oh Christ! Look who's coming now,' she said.

Father Tierney stepped into the scullery without knocking. He towered in the kitchen doorway.

'Good afternoon, Father,' Jim said coldly.

'Rose, run down to Josey's with *The Celt*. We're finished with it.' Mary handed her the folded newspaper.

'But I'm not finished my dinner. Why can't Nancy go?'

'I'll keep it in the oven. Nancy has polishing to do upstairs.'

'But it's lashing out there.'

Mary gritted her teeth. 'What d'ya think coats are for?'

Rose obeyed. Nancy didn't argue at all and bolted out the door with a tin of polish and a cloth.

Rose pulled on her wellies and stuffed the newspaper inside her coat. She cursed her way down the lane, plodding through all the puddles. She saw how Nancy turned as red as a beetroot when the priest walked in; she couldn't get out quick enough. She'd told him! She had bloody told him about Maureen and Dougie. Rose was sure of it because if Father Tierney had known about it before confession, he would have called to see Auntie Mary immediately.

§

Tomás drove into Josey's yard as Rose lifted the flowerpot looking for the key.

'The door's not locked, miss.'

'Is Josey in there?'

'No, he's getting ready for the milking. But Maureen's there.'

Rose pushed open the door and removed her wet coat and boots. Maureen sat huddled beside the range, blowing her nose into a hankie. Her eyes were red and puffy.

'God, Maureen.'

'I'm for it now.'

'What happened in confession? Father Tierney's up at the house.'

'Oh, Jesus, he's not, is he? Did he tell them what happened?'

'I don't know. Your mother sent me and Nancy off.'

'I phoned Dougie's house earlier. His mother answered so I hung up. Will you phone for me, Rose?'

'Sure what am I supposed to say to his mother if she answers again?'

'Pretend you're someone else.'

'You still didn't tell me why the priest banned you from the church and called you a Devil's child.'

'Someone told him about me and Dougie. Sure I told him all my sins and I sat waiting for my penance. The next thing he said was, "Are you sure there's nothing else you need to confess?" When I told him no, he said, "That's not what I heard." And I told him he heard wrong.' Maureen blew her nose into her hankie. 'I got so mad then that I told him it was nobody's business what I did, not even his.'

'Jesus, Maureen, you and that accent. I've told you before to change your voice in confession.'

'That's when he said I had no respect for the Catholic Church or for the confessional. I told him I'd rather be a Protestant. Then I told him to go to Hell. I didn't mean it!'

'Lord bless us and save us,' said Rose, making the sign of the cross at lightning speed. 'Is it any wonder he threw you out?'

'I can't go home. They'll kill me.'

'It won't be that bad. Probably a lot of shouting and you won't be allowed out for a month. And you'll have to break it off with Dougie and find yourself a Catholic to marry.'

'Well, I'm surely not going home if that's the case. I'd rather die.'

'Are you really going to turn into a Protestant?'

The door closed behind them. Josey stood ashen-faced. 'Tomás said ye were here. What's going on?'

'Maureen wants to be a Protestant so she can marry Dougie Taylor. Father Tierney said she was the Devil's child and he's up at our house now telling Auntie Mary all about it.'

Josey scratched his head and inhaled deeply through his teeth. 'Maureen, I think you should go home and sort it out there.'

Maureen gave her uncle a pleading look. 'Will you go and find out what they're saying? God knows what Father Tierney's telling them.'

'Look, we'll wait until he leaves and we'll all go. In the meantime, sit back down and tell me exactly what's going on and all about this Dougie fella.'

CHAPTER SIXTY-FOUR

Flossie spent another weekend wondering what her husband was getting up to in Dublin with his mistress Julie. Even though she tried not to dwell on it, she couldn't help obsessing over it sometimes. She almost asked him several times about Julie, but deep down she didn't want to know. She didn't want to know if Julie was his friend as well as his lover. She had no right to judge him, after all; her heart lay elsewhere too, even if it was with a dead man. But his real place was here, at home with his wife and son.

Auntie Bridgey had given up trying to talk her into leaving him. She stopped asking about him in her letters. Flossie had no intention of giving up her safe, cosy life with John to start as a struggling single woman in Dublin city.

Bridgey said Benny would leave home soon—fly the nest, she said—and God knew where he'd end up going. He might emigrate like all the other young lads, like John wanted him to. Flossie could see that Benny had no interest in pursuing his childhood dream of becoming a pilot because that's all it was, a dream, passed on to him by his father. She preferred for Benny to stay at home and inherit the shop, marry a nice girl and have children. She didn't want to think about him ever leaving home.

Bridgey also pointed out that Goretti was getting on in years, and did Flossie really want to be left with boring old John when her mother died? Or he might eventually throw her out and move his other woman in. Flossie told her not to be so ridiculous. She shook herself and gathered her thoughts. She had more important things to think about at that moment.

Nancy! What was going on in that girl's mind? She'd been rude and spiteful last Friday. Mary didn't help by giving her alcohol. And the song—her and Frank's song. Shivers ran down Flossie's spine. She hadn't known he sang it for Rose too. Melancholy consumed her like a dark shroud. She didn't want to fall out with Mary. They may have had one or two disagreements in the past, but they never fell out, not like this. She had to go and make things up with her.

Over a week had passed now since Nancy's party, and none of the Connollys had been to see her, nor had she been to visit them. Even Nancy didn't call during the week to do the cleaning.

Benny said everyone in school was talking about what Maureen did at confession. Goretti came home from Molly's on Monday night saying the same thing. 'Mary Connolly's Maureen ran away with a Protestant after Father Tierney threw her out of confession. She's the talk of the town. They say she might be pregnant too. Is that true, Flossie?'

'Mammy, I have no idea. I didn't see any of them since last Friday.'

'Well, you should call out and see what's going on,' she

said.

'Of course it's not true, Granny.' Benny laughed and shook his head. 'I saw Rose after school and she said Maureen is banned from leaving the house.'

'Is she pregnant?' asked Flossie.

He looked to the heavens and shook his head. 'Of course not. Father Tierney went there and told Mr and Mrs Fitzpatrick what Maureen said in confession. They were mortified. He put her out but if she goes to see him about the whole thing, they'll sort it out. That's what Rose said anyway.' Benny whistled as he slung his football bag across his shoulder and left.

'I'm sure there's not a word about it, Mammy. You know what people are like,' Flossie said.

Goretti arched her eyebrows. 'There's no smoke without fire.'

§

Nancy removed the shabby net curtain from Raggy Ann's cot. She cut it into four pieces and wrapped each of Flossie O'Malley's diaries separately. She placed them into a battered shoebox and buried them under a pile of stones. She knew she should return them, but she wasn't finished with them. Perhaps she'd misread the whole thing. Next time, she'd read them more thoroughly, get the full picture. Her father did no wrong.

Raggy Ann smelled of mildew, and Hannah was almost bald; her red painted lips and rosy cheeks had faded to the same peachy colour as the rest of her face. Suzy, the Crolly doll, still wore the hot pants and pink blouse she came in. Her hair, that once shone like a pearl, was now a matted yellow mop. Nancy imagined the dolls had shrunk. They were smaller in her hands now, delicate even.

Nancy sat Suzy on her knee and hummed a made-up tune as she cut off her hair. 'Suzy, you look like a hedgehog now. You can be a boy in my game. Your name is Benny.' She sat her down beside Raggy Ann.

'Hello, Benny,' said Nancy Doll.

'Hello, Nancy,' said Benny Doll.

'Is Rose your girlfriend?'

'Rose is O'Shea's girlfriend. I don't need a girlfriend, Nancy.'

§

A mixture of nerves and excitement kept Nancy awake for most of the night before her first camogie match. She played the match a million times over during the night, telling herself what to do and what not to do.

She met Jenny in town, and they walked out the Shercock Road to get to the park. The excitement had by this stage outweighed her nervousness. *Playing in a real camogie match, on a proper pitch.*

'Did you have a boiled egg for breakfast like I told you to?' asked Jenny.

'I did.'

'So, you're the new girl,' the coach said as they approached the dressing rooms.

'Yes. I'm Nancy Connolly.'

'Have you played much up 'til now?'

'A bit, in school. But I've watched the girls playing every

day since first year and I know all the rules.'

'She's well fit, coach,' Jenny said.

'Off you go then. Right corner forward.'

The two teams warmed up, ignoring the blasts of wind and rain that whipped their bare legs. As soon as the game started, Nancy couldn't wait to get at the ball. Visions of her mother flashed through her mind. The day she banged her head against the wall—lots of times—until the room went black. Memories of Rose in the babby house saying she'd take care of her forever. Maureen ruining everything, taking Rose from her. Her father. Flossie O'Malley's diaries.

Nancy faced her opponents with gumption and hit the ball with all her might, harder than she ever hit it in school. Her head opened like a tap and all her thoughts spilled onto the pitch. An unfamiliar buzz gushed through her veins. She ran again for the ball, barely noticing the wooden sticks whacking off her, oblivious to the imminent bruises on her shins.

'You're fearless, Connolly, quick as lightening too. You'd make a great defender,' the coach told Nancy after the match. 'I'll keep my eye on you.'

Nancy smiled inside and out as she sprinted towards the dressing rooms.

'Good match.' Séan O'Shea leaned against the bonnet of a car. His denim jacket, the same dark blue as his jeans, made him look cool. Or was it the way the cigarette hung from the corner of his mouth?

'We lost,' Nancy said.

'Only by a point.'

Nancy slowed to a stop. 'What are you doing here anyway?'

O'Shea knocked on the bonnet with his knuckles. 'Spinning about in the auld fella's car.'

'I was thinking about you this morning if you want to know,' said Nancy.

'Thinking about kissing me?'

'Not really. I need a favour.'

'What's it worth?'

'Stay there. I'll be back in a minute,' she said.

'I won't move. Don't be long.'

Nancy changed quickly into her cords and jumper, stuffed her jacket into her bag, and slung it across her shoulder. The dressing room buzzed with excited chatter, but Nancy had more important things to do than join in.

Séan waited as he said he would. 'You're getting good at it, the camogie,' he said.

Nancy had caught him watching her before, in school. It made her play harder.

'I'm not too bad, I suppose.'

'So what's the favour?'

'I don't know exactly yet.'

'You're a funny one, Connolly.'

'So will you?'

'What's it worth?'

'Ten pounds.'

'Where would you get ten pounds.'

'In the Post Office. Will you or not?'

'Is that all I'll get?'

'You'll have to wait and see.'

'Must be a big favour.'

'Big enough.'

'Anything for you.' He grinned.

CHAPTER SIXTY-FIVE

Nancy missed going to O'Malleys'. She'd done nothing wrong and had no reason to stay away, she decided. She needed to go back; she had to see Benny. She had hoped to walk there after school with him, but Mrs Rooney kept them back an extra ten minutes to lecture them about the no-alcohol policy at the upcoming school disco. She promised that anyone caught drinking would be in trouble. Few were ruffled by her threat.

Before she got to O'Malleys', Nancy popped a stick of spearmint gum into her mouth. The key was in the door, but she knocked. Flossie opened the door. 'Oh, hello, Nancy. Nice to see you.'

'Hello.' Nancy held up her music folder, indicating why she was there.

'The key's in the door. Why didn't you come on in? Sure you know you're one of the family.'

'Well, I'm not really.' Nancy strode past her.

'You smell nice today.' Flossie followed her into the kitchen.

'Thanks.'

'Will you do your wee bit of cleaning before piano? I have to run across to Frederick's for a minute.'

'Yea, okay.' Nancy was glad there was no mention of the party; she hoped it would never be mentioned again.

She made a start on polishing the furniture in the sitting room, where Benny sat watching television. 'What's on?' she asked.

'Nothing much.' He got up and switched off the television. Nancy sprayed it liberally with polish and glided her cloth across the screen.

'So is Maureen allowed out again?' he asked.

'Not yet. She's going mad at home. Auntie Mary won't let her out of her sight. She walks her to school and picks her up at home time. And Sister Kieran keeps her in at break times.'

'They can't keep that up forever,' Benny said. 'So she'll not be at the disco Friday night then, I take it.'

'No.'

'Will Rose be going?'

'Probably.' Nancy polished harder. Then she started on the china cabinet, even though it didn't need doing.

Benny whistled softly as he lifted his school bag off the floor. 'Hey, Nancy, will you give this book to Rose?' Benny handed her a paperback book. *The Mill on the Floss* by George Elliot.

'Who's George Elliot?'

'The woman who wrote this book.'

'Woman?'

'Yes. Mary Ann Evans is her real name.'

Nancy laughed as she took the book. 'Rose reads Mills

and Boon. I bet she doesn't even know who George Elliot is, or Mary Ann Evans.'

'Well, if she didn't know before, she knows now. Anyway, reading is reading, whatever it's about.'

'So will you be going to the disco?' Nancy asked.

'Maybe. I'll see.' Benny returned to his homework. Nancy finished the polishing in silence, but the voices in her head chattered away, plotting and planning.

§

Nancy stood at the doorway of Flossie's bedroom. She could see her wardrobe, its doors closed tight, guarding her sins and secrets. Bile crept up the back of her throat as she remembered the words in one of the diaries.

All good things come to those who wait. They do indeed. Well, I've waited long enough and today was worth waiting for! Only I can hear the songs in my tainted soul. I hate Alice Ward, and isn't that a sin? Is it hate? Contempt? I still feel it, whatever it is, even now that she's gone. That's all I've wanted, her to be gone, so then my pain can go with her and I can stop drifting from day to day. I can stop dreaming about her burning in hell, calling to God for help but God doesn't hear her. (*Dec 1958*)

Why did she hate Nancy's mother so much? Nancy yearned to get another rummage through those boxes. Questions bounced around inside her head. She liked Flossie O'Malley, even more than she liked Auntie Mary. But now, she didn't know her. She ran down the stairs, grabbed her coat and bag. She called out to Benny. 'Tell your mam I've a pain in my head so I'll skip the lesson today.'

'Okay,' he shouted back.

She paused. 'See you after school tomorrow?'

Benny didn't answer. Nancy left, closing the door harder than was necessary. 'George Elliot, my arse,' she said, flinging her bag across her shoulder.

§

As Nancy turned onto Main Street to go to the Post Office, a voice called out. 'Nancy, Nancy!'

Joyce. Nancy carried on walking.

'Nancy, wait!' Joyce scurried across the street. 'I thought I'd see you after school, but I missed you.'

'I was late getting out today.'

'I have something to tell you.' Joyce stood close to Nancy. 'She's home.'

'Who?'

'Your mother. She's back and she wants to meet with you.'

Nancy stiffened. *Home? Why? Meet me?* Her gut tightened as her mother's angry voice echoed in her head and her sweaty face flashed before her eyes. 'I can't. Tell her no.'

'I think she's changed, Nancy. She was delighted that you replied to her letter.'

Nancy rubbed her chest with a tight fist. 'I have to go to the Post Office before it closes,' Nancy said, walking away.

'Call up to my house, please. We'll talk properly there,' Joyce said. 'Your mother's not there, she's staying up at Uncle Billy's old house.'

'Where's that?'

'Further up the Institute Road, past my house.'

Nancy didn't answer. She went into the Post Office and withdrew ten pounds from her savings account. Could she trust that Joyce one? She knew nothing about her.

Joyce approached her again when she came out. 'Will you come? For five minutes?'

'Okay. Only five minutes.'

§

The atmosphere was almost back to normal in the Fitzpatrick house. Maureen seemed more accepting of her punishment and was being extra polite to everyone. At least the whole thing took the spotlight away from Nancy and the disastrous party.

'You went to O'Malleys' after school I suppose,' said Mary.

'Yeah.'

'Everyone well?'

'Yeah.'

'That's good.' Mary held her warm cup in both hands. 'Did she ask about me?'

'Who?' asked Nancy, her thoughts on her mother.

'Flossie.'

'No, she didn't.'

Mary's face fell. She got up and started clearing the table, reminding Rose it was her day to help. Nancy escaped to her room. Sucking on a bonbon, she took a copy book out of her bag. Benny's copy, filled with his neatly joined handwriting, all in black ink. He had tidy writing, for a boy. All the lads in her class had untidy scrawls, awash with scribbled-out spelling mistakes in dog-eared copies.

Nancy opened a new page in her own copy. She practiced writing like Benny, line after line, slow and meticulous, in black ink, until it looked identical to his. She surprised herself at how easy it was to forge someone's writing. She tore a clean page out of the back of her copy.

Hello, Rose. I'll be at the disco on Friday night. I hope you'll be there. Meet me at the back of the hall, at the boiler house steps at 10 o'clock. I have something to show you. I think you'll like it. Benny.

Nancy put the note inside the centre pages of *The Mill on the Floss*. She replaced the book in her schoolbag. She opened the door wide and made a start on her homework.

Maureen and Rose whispered as they crossed the landing to their bedroom. They both looked through Nancy's door as they passed. Giggling—*always bloody giggling.*

'Rose,' Nancy called. 'Come here.'

'Yes?' Rose poked her head through the door.

'Benny gave me a book for you.'

Rose's eyes widened and she flushed slightly. 'What book?'

'Oh, some book ye were talking about last week, or something,' Nancy said without looking up. 'It's still in my bag, there on the floor.'

Rose searched through the bag, took the book and scurried out the door.

§

'What's that all about?' Maureen asked.

'All what?' Rose clutched the book in folded arms and looked straight ahead, aiming for her bed.

'What are you up to?'

'I'm not up to anything. What's wrong with borrowing a book?' Rose flopped onto her bed and put the book under her pillow.

'Whatever you say.' Maureen peered at her through slanted eye.

When Maureen left, Rose took Benny's book from under her pillow. She smelled it first, rubbed the cover softly, imagining Benny holding it in his hands. She held it to her chest and closed her eyes. She laughed inwardly at herself, feeling silly because she'd told him she liked George Elliot. *The Mill on the Floss.* She would have to read it now so they could talk about it. She flicked through the pages. Something caught her eye. She flicked through again, stopping at the centre page. A bookmark? Reading the tidy black handwriting, Rose held her breath. A tingling sensation swept through her like a tidal wave. He wanted to meet. Benny wanted to meet her and it could only be for one reason. She swooned back on the bed, her insides puffed like her feather pillow. This was the best day of her life. How romantic, using the book to smuggle a note to her!

CHAPTER SIXTY-SIX

Alice Connolly looked around Billy Rafferty's old house with her nose turned up. 'It's not great, is it?'

'It's better than nothing. It'll do you for now,' Joyce replied.

'Yea, thanks, Joycie.'

'Why now, Alice?'

'Why what?'

'Why are you back?'

'I told you. To make up with my girls. To explain a few things.'

'You could've done that years ago. They thought you were dead.'

Alice scowled. 'And who the hell told them that?' she said. 'Probably that busybody, Mary.'

'If you go out there fighting with her, then you've lost, straight away,' Joyce said.

'I don't want to fight with her. I only want my life back, here, where I belong. With Rose and Nancy.'

'I met Nancy today. I think I can talk her round.'

Alice lit up a cigarette. 'And Rose?'

'She's always with Maureen when I see her. Can't get near her.'

'I've changed. I'll prove it to Nancy and she'll sweet talk Rose.'

'Did you give up the drink?'

'I said I've changed, Joycie, not that I've become a fecking saint.' Alice rolled her eyes to the heavens. 'I'm only having ya on. I don't drink that much anymore. The odd night. I quit all that other carry-on.'

'I have sticks and coal there. You can light the fire. I had it lit yesterday to get the place warmed up a bit. There's food in the fridge and bread and stuff in the press.'

'Aw, good woman yourself,' Alice said.

'Uncle Billy's old tom cat still sleeps out in the coal shed. I feed him when he comes calling down to us, but you can give him any scraps you have.'

'He'll keep me company. I had a cat in Liverpool, but she went missing a few months ago.'

'Have you money to keep you going? I can't bring food here every day.'

'I've a bit, aye.' Alice moved around the spacious kitchen —sparsely furnished but heavily cluttered. Cardboard boxes were stacked against one wall, and old paint tins against another. Empty food packaging littered the worktop at the sink. A dresser designed for crockery was packed with books and newspapers half hidden behind thick cobwebs.

'Would ya not do the place up and rent it out?'

'I might, sometime,' said Joyce.

'I could be your tenant.'

'So you think you might stay?'

'Why wouldn't I? I'll get meself a job in the boot factory. Have experience now, y'know. I was sewing knickers and bras in a factory in England. I've a letter and all from the manager saying I was a great one on the sewing machine.'

'Looks like you're on the right track so.'

'So will ya?'

'I'll think about it. We'll see how you get on. I'm promising nothing, Alice.'

'Good girl, Joycie. My best friend.' Alice smacked a kiss on her hand and blew it over to Joyce.

§

The Bitter End Road Show was the best disco ever. They played all the latest music and plenty of slow sets. The disco was the main topic of conversation in school all week, along with lengthy discussions about who'd be wearing what and who'd be getting off with who.

Some of the girls brought in clothes and make-up to swap with each other. Rose lent Kathleen her denim bell bottoms in return for her sequined skirt and boob tube top—which she daren't put on until she got to the toilets in the community centre, or Auntie Mary would have a heart attack.

Maddie Smith, and several other Bay City Rollers' fans, swapped all sorts of tartan bits and pieces.

Finn Murphy took orders for small bottles of poitín, that he would fill from his father's illegal stash in an outhouse on their farm.

Rose spent longer than usual getting ready. She carefully put on some eyeshadow under the scrutiny of make-up fanatic Maureen. 'I wish you were coming too, Maureen. It's not fair.'

Maureen closed the door tight. 'Can I tell you the biggest secret ever?'

Rose put down her eyeshadow and jumped on the bed, her eyes as wide as saucers. 'Who is it about?' she asked.

'Dougie has been phoning me at work. We're running away together,' Maureen whispered.

Rose stared, mouth open, craning her neck towards Maureen.

'Please don't scream, Rose!'

'Jesus, Maureen. You can't do that. Your mam and dad will go mad.'

'I don't care. I love Dougie and they won't let me marry him. They won't even let me see him, so we're going.'

'But where? You've no money.'

'Dougie has money and he knows people in Dublin. We're going there.'

'But what about me?'

'You can come and visit, or come and live with us when you leave school. You can get a job there. It'll be great.'

Excitement bubbled inside Rose. *She'd love to live in Dublin.* 'When are you going?'

'In the middle of the night. Dougie is borrowing his brother's car and picking me up outside Daly's.'

'Oh my God, Maureen, tonight?'

'Yes. I'm so sorry I didn't tell you sooner, but I couldn't.'

'It's okay. You were probably right because I don't know how I would've acted normal if I'd known.'

'Thanks, Rose.'

'Are you excited? Are you scared?'

'I'm everything. I can hardly sleep these nights.'

'Are you sure everything will be okay? My heart is flying now.' Rose grabbed Maureen's hand and held it on her chest.

'You're not to worry about me. I know what I'm doing. I'll leave a note for Mammy. You're to pretend you had no idea.' The girls hugged each other tight.

Maureen had her case under the bed, packed to its fullest. 'You can keep everything else in there,' she said, opening her wardrobe door.

'Really? Are you sure?'

'Of course. It's not much.'

'I have something to tell you too,' Rose said. She took Benny's note from her school bag and handed it to Maureen.

'How come you didn't tell me about this?'

'I don't know. Afraid, maybe. Sure it might be nothing much at all.'

'I think it is something much. You're mad after him, aren't you?'

Rose turned pink and covered her face with both hands.

'What about Nancy?'

'All's fair in love and war! Isn't that what they say?'

'Well, maybe it's you he's fancied all along.' Maureen took her favourite lipstick out of her handbag. 'Here, have this. It stays on for ages. Bring it with you and when you come home tonight, put it straight back into my bag.'

'I will, I promise.'

'I'll miss you, Rose.'

'I'll miss you even more.' Rose tightened her lips and tears welled up in her eyes.

'Stop right now or you'll ruin your make-up.' Maureen pulled up the corner of the bedsheet and dabbed Rose's eyes with it. 'You go and get Benny O'Malley and kiss the face off him.'

Rose laughed. The thought of kissing Benny gave her butterflies.

'Be careful, Maureen. Write to me as soon as you can.'

'I promise I will. I'll post it to Kathleen's for you. Remember what I said. No talking when you come home tonight. I won't be asleep, but you have to act as if I am. I'll be gone when you wake up.'

§

Josey picked up Rose and Nancy to drop them into town.

'Have manners at that disco, you two,' said Mary as they left.

'I'll be outside at twelve to collect ye,' said Jim.

Rose sat in the front seat of Josey's Morris Minor and Nancy sat in the back. Josey chatted about the weather, school, the farm. Neither Nancy nor Rose was listening—both were lost in their own thoughts.

'Are you two not talking?' Josey said.

'We are,' Rose replied. She couldn't stop thinking about Maureen. Her best friend was leaving and that made her feel sad. She wished there was another way. Benny occupied another part of her mind. Her gut had turned itself into a knot. What if he wanted to French kiss her? She was kissing a boy from Shercock one night behind the blue house in Lourdesville, and when he tried to put his tongue inside her mouth, she slapped his face. Even though he apologised, she couldn't go with him again. She was mortified when Maureen told her later that it was normal to kiss like that and she should get used to it. The second fella she went with didn't try to French kiss her but slobbered all over her face and groped at her breasts. She told him she was dying to go to the toilet, and she returned to the disco and avoided him for the rest of the night. She'd be happy to kiss Benny though. *And if he wanted to French kiss her, he could.*

§

It was already half nine when they arrived at the community centre. The hall was packed with locals and youngsters from Shercock and Kingscourt, who came on a bus. Rose looked out for Benny as soon as she walked in. All the boys sat on the right; the girls took over the seats on the left. She saw some girls from school, so she joined them. The scent of cheap perfume and aftershave filled the hall. Cigarette smoke swirled and puffed from teenage mouths, and strips of Wrigley's and Juicy Fruit chewing gum were being handed out like lives depended on them. The more confident girls and the ones who had vodka inside them were dancing, eagerly awaiting the first slow set of the night.

Benny sat high up on the back of a long wooden seat. He looked Rose's way and smiled when she caught his eye. She wanted to smile back, but instead she looked away, nervous, excited. She joined in the talk with the girls, yet she had no idea what they were discussing. She laughed when they laughed, nodded when they nodded.

The lights dimmed as Cliff Richard sang out *Miss You Nights*. The gum-chewing jaws sped up. Rose's heart beat faster than ever. Soon it would be ten o'clock. Surely Benny wouldn't ask her to dance if he planned on meeting her outside in ten minutes. He walked towards her. Her palms moistened, and her face flushed right down as far as her neckline. Séan O'Shea appeared from behind him and scurried towards her. 'The gorgeous Rose Connolly. C'mon and dance with me.' Séan pulled her onto the dance floor, putting both hands around her waist.

'Séan, thanks, but I was about to dance with someone else,' she shouted across the music.

'What? Can't hear you.'

'You can hear me damn rightly,' she yelled. 'Stop acting the Mickey.'

He laughed and held her tighter, swaying her further up the hall like a mannequin on wheels. She couldn't see Benny in the crowd. She didn't know if he went outside or not. She checked her watch. It was five to ten. Her stomach churned, not helped by the smell of stale body odour coming from the group of sweaty boys leaning against the stage.

When the song finished, Séan let her go. He bowed before her. 'Thank you, Rose.'

'Welcome,' she snapped as she stormed through the crowd.

§

Nancy kept her eyes on Benny. He sat halfway down the hall. She joined him. She stood in front of him making sure to block his view. At a glance, she saw Rose storming down the dance floor, heading for the door, Séan following close behind her.

'Guess what I have in my bag,' said Nancy.

Benny narrowed his eyes and smiled. 'What have you?'

'Poitín.'

'From Finn?'

Nancy winked. 'Only the best.'

'You're mad.' Benny laughed. 'Have you got a mixer?'

'A wee bottle of red lemonade.'

'Come on then, let's go.'

Nancy followed Benny outside. 'We'll go round the back, to the steps,' she said.

The waxing moonlight cast shadows in the dark corners down the side alleyway of the community centre. Couples huddled together, hiding from their supervising teachers, where they could smoke, drink and kiss in peace.

'I hope no one sees us and thinks we're getting off with each other,' Benny said.

'You'd better stay quiet then.'

As they approached the end of the building, close to the steps, Nancy stopped. 'Shh... I think someone got there before us,' she whispered. Two figures huddled in the shadows at the corner, close together. Their chatter muffled, laughter from him, tones of irritation from her.

'Sure we'll stay here,' Nancy said as she leaned up against the wall of the building. Benny moved with her and stood rubbing his palms together, looking forward to the sneaky tipple.

She took the half-full bottle of poitín from her bag and topped it up with red lemonade.

'I'd rather vodka,' said Benny.

'I couldn't get any vodka.' Nancy punched him playfully on the arm.

'I wonder who it is, over there shifting each other? She's doing a lot of yapping,' Benny said.

'Who cares?' Nancy took a swig from the bottle, then handed it to Benny.

He put the bottle to his mouth and took a long guzzle of the lemon-flavoured poitín. Then he took a deep husky breath as the strong liquid burned his throat. 'Here, top that up with more lemonade,' he said, handing her the bottle.

The couple from the corner walked towards them, making their way back inside.

'Jesus, I'm freezing. Warm me up, Benny.' Nancy stood in front of him.

The poitín gave Benny a dreamy look. He smiled at Nancy and put his arms around her waist. As the couple walked past, Nancy wrapped her arms around him and pulled him closer. He loosened his embrace at the sound of a click.

'Good evening, Mr O'Malley... and Nancy,' said Séan O'Shea, holding a cigarette lighter close to the couple.

Benny pulled away from Nancy. Looking across her shoulder, his eyes widened when he saw Rose. Her fair hair gleamed in the moonlight as she stood facing them. O'Shea put a cigarette to the lighter in his cupped hands, its flame casting a flickering light across Rose's face. She didn't speak; she turned and fled, O'Shea close behind.

'Well, this is just marvellous, isn't it?'

'What's the matter?' Nancy asked.

'If I'd known it was your sister over there, I'd have gone somewhere else,' said Benny, taking the bottle from Nancy. He swigged the poitín, screwing up his face as he swallowed.

'Why do you care?'

'What if she tells... that we're drinking?'

'She won't.'

'I didn't know she was going with O'Shea. How long is that going on?'

'She's mad about him. They're always together in school. I saw them behind the blue house once or twice.'

'He's not really her type, is he?'

'She's not as prim and proper as everyone thinks.' A heaviness weighed down on Nancy. Benny would never speak to her again if he knew what she had just done. She knew she was selfish not wanting to share him with Rose—or any girl—but Rose had Maureen.

Benny handed her the bottle. 'Here, I've enough.'

§

Back inside the hall, O'Shea hung around, dancing with Rose and her friends, acting like they were together. When he had tried to kiss her outside, she pushed him away; she could only think about Benny. Now the thoughts of Benny embarrassed her. *Why did he arrange for her to be at the back of the hall? So she could see him getting off with Nancy? Why did he think that would please her?* She mentally ripped his note to shreds. *How could she have been so stupid?*

Nancy and Benny returned to the hall just as the lights dimmed. The single lads looked around for single girls to dance with, some hoping for a girlfriend, others happy to get a one-night stand, a kiss and a grope before the night ended. O'Shea put his arms around Rose. She rested her forehead on his shoulder rather than look at her sister with Benny. She wished she could run away with Maureen.

§

Nancy sat in the back of the car on the way home. Rose sat in the front. Small talk from Uncle Jim broke the uncomfortable silence between them. Rose's head buzzed from the loud music, her thoughts a mix of confusing flashing images. She wished Uncle Jim would stop talking and asking questions.

Nancy went straight to bed when they got home. Rose made tea for herself and Uncle Jim. She prayed he wouldn't talk about Maureen because she didn't trust herself to appear oblivious to her plans.

'Why are you two not talking?'

'We are. We're tired after dancing half the night, that's all.'

'Is there anything up with your sister?'

'To tell the truth, I don't know.'

'You and Maureen never include her in things. I'll have a word with Maureen. She can be a bit inconsiderate sometimes.'

'Well, Nancy can be a bit like that herself, y'know.' Rose had a lump in her throat. 'I've to go to bed now. See you in the morning.' Rose kissed Uncle Jim on the cheek and made a quick exit with her cup of tea. She crept up the stairs, skipping the fifth creaky one. Auntie Mary's snores shook the cobwebs that hung from the ceiling. Nothing but silence emerged from behind Nancy's door.

Maureen was in bed, curled up like a kitten. Rose cleaned off her eyeshadow and blusher. Examining her reflection in the dressing table mirror, her heart sank. She let her tears fall freely down her pasty face, holding in her sobs—something she'd learnt how to do easily when she was a child. She knew Maureen wasn't asleep because her breathing was light and she always slept flat on her back with her arms sprawled and her mouth open. They often joked that she looked like Jesus on the cross while she slept. Rose put the borrowed lipstick into Maureen's bag, then got into bed. She stayed awake for as long as she could, looking across at Maureen because she knew she wouldn't see her again for a very long time.

CHAPTER SIXTY-SEVEN

'Go and tell those two it's time to get up,' Mary said as she loaded the washing into the twin tub. 'And bring the clothes basket down from the bathroom,' she shouted after Nancy.

Nancy knocked on the girls' door three times with the palm of her hand. 'Up,' she called.

The door opened, and Rose pushed past Nancy in the doorway.

'Jesus, you're in a hurry,' Nancy said. 'Maureen, up!' She peered into an empty bedroom and then went to the bathroom. 'Are you in there?'

When she got no reply, she reached in for the clothes basket, then sped down the stairs. The washing machine shook noisily as it spun the heavy load of clothes. Auntie Mary waved a letter in the air as she and Rose argued.

'What's wrong? Has something happened?' asked Nancy.

'If you knew about this Rose, I'll kill you.' Mary unplugged the washing machine and left the house.

'What's wrong? Where's she going?' Nancy asked.

'Maureen ran away.'

'What d'you mean, ran away? Where?'

'This is all your fault, you know,' Rose said.

'What are you on about?'

'I know you told Father Tierney about Rose and Dougie. Because of that they're gone. Ran away to Dublin, forever.'

The blood drained from Nancy's face. 'How was I supposed to know they'd run away?'

'Why did you tell?'

Nancy hung her head, unable to look her sister in the eye.

§

The telephone rang in the hallway. Before John could excuse himself from his customer, Ruth bustled into the shop. 'John, phone call for you. I'll look after Mrs Johnson.'

He was expecting a call from a supplier and so brought his notebook with him. His mother had the dinner cooking in the kitchen upstairs. The savoury smell of roast chicken wafted up John's nostrils, making his mouth water. He lifted the receiver, expecting to hear Foy's secretary on the other end.

'O'Malley, it's me.'

John gripped the telephone receiver so tight his knuckles whitened. Hoarser than she used to be, he recognised the aggressive tone of Alice Connolly. 'What the hell are you calling me for?'

'I'm in town and we have to meet.'

'No way, Alice. You can piss off.'

'O'Malley, you listen to me. I need money and if ya know what's good for ya, ya'll meet me.'

'You're forgetting something,' John hissed down the phone.

'You've no real proof, O'Malley. 'Tis only a photograph; it could've been taken any day of the year. Not a soul will believe a word ya say, especially when they all find out what you're really like.'

'You should've stayed away, Alice. There's nothing for you here.'

'I have my girls. I'm their mother. Not that Mary one or your interfering wife.'

'Those girls don't want you. You left them, remember?'

'Shut up, O'Malley, ya big mammy's boy.'

'Go away, Alice. You're not getting another penny from me.'

'I was talking to a certain Mr Stanley a few weeks back. He filled me in on one or two details that he forgot to mention before—details about a will.'

John hung up. The smell of roast chicken no longer appealed to his senses. He loosened his tie and took a deep breath. He went back through to the shop, where his father was busy fitting out a young boy for a suit for his upcoming confirmation. Ruth was chatting to the boy's mother about the persistent April showers.

'Mam, I've to head home to see Flossie for a few minutes,' said John.

'Okay. Don't be long, the dinner's soon ready.'

'A great son you have there, Mrs O'Malley,' the boy's mother said.

John hated when people said things like that to his

parents. They thought they knew everything about everyone, when they knew damn all.

The cold spell of weather didn't stop the usual Saturday shoppers from leaving their homes to come into town. For some of the country folk, it was the only day of the week they got to leave the house—except for Mass on Sundays—to chat and catch up on all the news. John hurried across the street towards The Green, his fists clenched and his jaw tensed.

A young piano student left his house as John approached. He didn't reply when she said hello, his head buzzing with thoughts of Alice, Peter Stanley, Frank Connolly, and Alfie.

§

Flossie could tell as soon as she saw John's face that something had happened. His glasses steamed up as soon as he entered the kitchen. His hands shook as he took them off to wipe them and he dropped them to the floor. 'Bloody hell,' he said, bending down to retrieve them.

'John, what's wrong? Did something happen?'

'Where's Benny? And your mother? Where's your mother?'

'Football. Mammy's getting her hair done. Why? What's the matter?'

'I'm sick of the whole thing. This place, you, the Connollys.'

'What d'you mean? What did I do?'

'Alice Connolly is back.'

'Here? Back here in Bailieborough?'

'Yes. Back here.'

Everything inside her somersaulted. Every follicle on her

body stung like she had been whipped with a bunch of nettles. For a fleeting moment she could smell Alice—weeds and stale cigarettes. And cats. She smelt like cats. *What about Rose and Nancy? They won't want her back. And Mary... she'd kill her.*

John paced over and back the kitchen floor, his hands jingling loose change in his trouser pocket, his agitation not fully making sense to Flossie. *He had no grievances with Alice Connolly.*

'Why are you so... so... like this?' Flossie asked.

'There's things you need to know. I should've told you long ago. Sit down.' John dragged a chair out from the table.

'What's going on?' She raised her eyebrows and sat down reluctantly.

John sat on a chair opposite. 'Alice was blackmailing me for years.'

'What? When? For money?'

'More or less since we got married. Right up until she left. Yes, for money.'

'Blackmailing you over what?'

'I can't tell you that part.' John massaged his temples and drew a deep anxious breath.

He leaned back in his chair. 'I wish I could tell you, Flossie. You mean the world to me...'

'But you don't love me.'

'I do love you, as a matter of fact.'

'Is all this about Julie?'

His wide eyes shot across the table at her. He swallowed, as if to disperse the unanticipated question. Before he could answer, Flossie continued.

'I know about Julie. I know you go to her when you're in

Dublin. In fact, that's probably the reason you go there most of the time. I know you've always loved her and she makes you happier than I ever have. You get restless when it's time to go to her, and when you come back from her, you radiate a certain something, like a blitheness and serenity.'

'Flossie, I don't know what to say.' John's face paled. He went to the tap and poured a glass of water. He gulped it down like a ravenous suck calf. A pang of guilt swept over Flossie. She shouldn't have married him. They weren't meant to be. He sat down again.

'Who told you?' he asked.

'Auntie Bridgey saw you together. Going into a house. Julie's, I presume.'

'I can't believe you didn't say something. Were you not angry?'

'Not angry, disappointed maybe. I didn't really know how I felt at the time. I had no right to feel anything. It would have been hypocritical of me. But yes, I was hurt. Jealous, I think. I wanted to ask you about her so many times but the coward in me prevailed. That coward in me didn't want to hear the truth. Sometimes the truth carries consequences. It was no more than I deserved. I married you while I was in love with someone else. And I haven't stopped loving him, if truth be told.' Flossie's voice quivered. Sentiments of the past washed over her.

'I tried to make you happy, Flossie. I really thought we'd learn to love each other and you'd forget Frank. I'm so sorry. I've failed you in more ways than one.' John slouched in his chair.

'You've been a good husband to me and you're the best father Benny could ask for.'

John's brow furrowed and he sat up straight. He studied the Sacred Heart picture for a moment. He then looked directly at Flossie. 'Yes, I am.'

'Good. So that's that all sorted then. Alice can go back to whatever hole she crawled out of.'

John shuffled his feet. 'Em...'

'Wait a minute,' Flossie said. 'How did Alice know about Julie? I didn't tell anyone and I'm quite certain Bridgey didn't tell her.'

'A man called Peter Stanley used to sell tobacco in the town—you'd hardly know him—he knows Julie from childhood. He had Alice doing his dirty work... and other things I suspect.'

'So why did she run away?' Flossie asked. 'If she was getting money on the sly, and all the help she could ask for with those children, why did she go?'

'I paid her to go.'

'Jesus, John. Why?'

'To get rid of her, of course. She was demented. She could have dropped me in it at any time.'

'Would it really have been that bad? I found out anyway.'

'And what about my parents finding out? And the whole town?'

Flossie switched on the kettle. 'Is that all you care about?'

'You can talk. You're as bad. Don't pretend otherwise. And don't pretend you were sorry that Alice disappeared.'

She knew there was truth in what he said. She liked her comforts and the good name that came with the O'Malleys. Alice leaving was the best thing that had ever happened to Rose and Nancy.

'So she buggered off... just like that. How much bloody

money did you give her?'

'That's not the point.'

'And what about the Stanley man? Did you pay him off too?'

'No.'

Flossie's temples throbbed. 'I've a feeling she's been in touch with Nancy. I met her at the graveyard one day and she was acting a bit strange and asking questions about Alice.' The kettle hissed and Flossie wet the tea in the pot.

'What kind of questions?'

'Normal stuff, but it's the way she was behaving that wasn't normal. And she was wearing Alice's old coat—one Mary kept.' She put the teapot and cups on the table with the milk and sugar, then sat back down in her chair. She folded her arms. 'So, the Stanley man?'

John said nothing but took a deep breath and exhaled slowly. He poured the tea. His grip on the teapot whitened his knuckles. The last time Flossie had seen John this anxious was the time they met Julie in The Grand Hotel.

'When I was absolutely certain that Alice and Stanley were in cahoots, I gave young Liam my camera to catch evidence of them together. He'd been watching them for a couple of months and got to learn their routine. He followed them to the Castle Lake one Thursday evening.' John stopped stirring his tea. He put the wet spoon into the sugar bowl. At that moment he pitied his wife as she looked straight at him. 'You were there.'

A sour-tasting lump swelled in Flossie's throat. She swallowed and it travelled to the pit of her stomach. She instinctively put her hands to her ears to block out the silent alarm bells that rang in her head. 'What did you say?'

John kept his eyes on the Sacred Heart. 'Liam followed Stanley as far as the crossroads in the woods. Alice was there waiting. Almost immediately, Stanley pulled her into the trees and that's when Liam saw you coming on your bicycle, up from the lake. They were hiding from you. He said you were pedalling hard, in a real big hurry.'

'Which Thursday, John?' Flossie asked.

'When you were out of sight, Alice stormed off towards the lake, with Stanley hot on her heels. Liam followed through the weeds close to the bank. Then he heard Frank's voice and a lot of shouting between him and Alice. Stanley stayed back, out of sight. At first Frank just stood there, knee deep in the water, letting her shout and rant. Then he exploded and grabbed her by the shoulders. He said he hated her and was getting her locked up so he could be with someone else.'

'How did she know he was there... at the lake?'

'Alice may be a lot of things but she's not completely stupid, or blind.'

'I wasn't going to leave you. We only wanted to be together. Like you and Julie.'

John continued. 'Frank let go of her shoulders and turned his back. Alice picked up a rock the size of a turnip and lunged at him. When he turned his head, she bashed him in the face. He stumbled, his head in his hands, blood pouring through his fingers, Liam said. Then he went down like a ton of bricks, fell face down in the water.'

Flossie went to the sink and heaved. John carried on, heedless of her distress. 'Alice shouted out to him, yelling at him to get up. Stanley ran to them then, roaring and cursing at her. He turned Frank round and dragged him in. He must have been dead because, seconds later, Stanley dragged him back into the water, further out. Then they took off, him and Alice. Liam couldn't see Frank then, gone, disappeared into the murky waters.'

Flossie stared into the sink, trying to comprehend John's words. She couldn't get them to register in her brain. She looked out the window, into the garden. The cherry blossoms flourished on the tree. *They were so pretty.*

John drummed his fingers on the table. 'So now you know.'

She turned to face him. 'Alice did it. Someone else did it, which means he didn't do it to himself. And you let her go. She fucking murdered him, John!'

'Shh… I know and I'm sorry.'

'Why did you let everyone think Frank drowned himself?' Tears streamed down Flossie's face. All the pain she held deep inside her resurfaced. Her breastbone burned like it had split in half. 'I can't believe you didn't tell all this to the guards. Why didn't you tell? People think Frank took his own life.' She sobbed.

'Everything would've come out.'

'Everything? Julie? I can't believe that's all you care about. Someone died and all you're worried about is people knowing about your infidelity?'

'It's not like that.'

Contempt for her husband smothered every other emotion that poured out of her. 'She killed Frank and you let her go. What kind of a man are you? Do you even know where she went?'

'When Liam returned my camera and told me what happened at the lake, I saw it as my chance to get rid of her. I met her with a bag of clothes and an envelope of money. As soon as I showed her the photographs, she panicked and got into the waiting car. She got dropped off at Holyhead and was met there by an uncle of Julie's and brought to Liverpool where she was to live happily ever after. One call to Peter Stanley made sure he didn't darken the streets of Bailieborough again.'

Every muscle in her body quivered. Her chest stung as if it had turned to acid. She glared at him. 'Christ of Almighty, I don't know who you are anymore. Did I ever know you at all?'

'Well, that's an easy question to answer.'

Flossie reached out and picked up the first thing her hand touched. She hopped it off John's head; lucky for him it was only a plastic jug.

'Now, there's no need for that.' He rubbed the top of his head.

'This is murder! You lied all these years.'

'Keep your voice down, for God's sake.'

'Why is she back?'

'She's looking for more money. She reckons a photo can't prove anything and I have more to lose than she does. She's right.'

'I'll go to her and tell her I know everything so she can feck off and find some other idiot to threaten.'

'No way, Flossie. You're not to go near her. Mammy would have a stroke at the thoughts of a scandal.'

'Is it really that bad, anyway? So what if people gossip that you're having an affair? You're hardly the first. That bitch is getting away with murder.' She paced the floor, over and back, up and down, around the table, taking short, shallow breaths. 'I can't believe this.' She stabbed a finger at John. 'You could get into big trouble for this, y'know. You're a witness to a murder. And you blackmailed them. You blackmailed two killers.'

'I know. I bloody know all that, Flossie.'

'Jesus Christ, wait 'til Mary and Josey hear about this.'

'They're not going to hear about it!' John slammed his fist on the table. 'I'll pay her another lump and she'll go again.' He checked his watch. 'I've to get back to the shop or they'll be out looking for me.'

'Does Mary know she's back? Who knows?'

'I don't know and I don't care, Flossie.'

'I have to go to Mary and find out.'

'Who's back?' asked Benny as he walked in.

'I have to get back to the shop. We'll talk later,' said John.

'Who are you on about, Mam? Is Maureen back?'

'No, son. It's nobody you know.'

'Were you crying?' Benny frowned, peering into her face.

'Your mother's fine... women problems,' John said as he left. Benny shrugged his shoulders.

'I've to go somewhere, Benny. I won't be long,' Flossie said.

Benny lifted the bottle of milk off the table and put it to his thirsty mouth. Flossie couldn't be bothered to chastise him yet again for not using a glass. Instead, she reached out to him and hugged him tight.

'Jesus, Mam. I'm a bit old for that.' He pushed her away gently, grinning.

She dipped her fingers in the holy water font and blessed herself on the way out the door. Joyce Rafferty would surely know all there was to know about why Alice was back.

CHAPTER SIXTY-EIGHT

Mary rarely missed Mass. She couldn't face leaving the house, people talking. Jim took Rose to Mass and made Nancy stay at home. She brought a cup of tea and a slice of soda bread up to her aunt's bedroom.

'You should've gone to Mass with Jim and Rose,' Mary said as she sat up in the bed. Nancy's heart ached at the sorrowful sight of her aunt. Her eyes looked sore and her mouth drooped. Nancy had only wanted to get back at Maureen; she didn't mean to hurt Auntie Mary. 'She might come back.'

'She won't.' Mary swung her legs out the side of the bed and put on her dressing gown. 'Lucky I have you two.'

Nancy looked down at the floor, ashamed of herself. She'd ruined everything. Maybe her mother was right: she should've been drowned at birth. 'Can I go to the park with Jenny later to practice camogie?'

'I suppose so. I've to have a bath. Is the fire lit yet?'

'No, but I'll do it now.'

'Thanks, Nancy.'

§

Nancy knelt beside the range, watching the flickering flames struggling to stay lit in the smoke-filled fire box. She willed the wispy yellow flames to stay strong, to dominate the smoke. She gazed at the burning sticks, the growing blaze licking the lumps of coal. The smoky smell filled the room. When the fire roared up the chimney, she closed it off and put the matches in her trouser pocket. She took her mother's green coat from the hanger in the scullery. She put it on along with her hat and scarf. She walked across the field to her safe place.

A row of daffodils bloomed outside the babby house. They brightened it up, but it was still damp and dim inside. Nancy looked forward to summer, when the earth warmed and the chestnuts sprouted on the babby house tree. Her cushion stank of mould, and the dolls had had black spots on their faces so long now that she barely remembered what they looked like before.

Nancy took a box of Major out of her coat pocket. She put one between her lips and lit a match. As she held the tiny flame to the end of the cigarette, she pulled hard on it. The smoke hit the back of her throat, making her cough. Her eyes watered, but she persevered. She stared into the corner where she had Flossie's diaries buried. The cigarette made her feel warm, and older.

She unearthed the old shoebox from under the pile of stones. She unwrapped the year *1964* from the square of Josey's old net curtain. She flicked through the pages scanning for relevant entries. *Nancy, Rose, Alice, Frank.* Their names were scattered all over the diary. Everything about them. So many Saturdays fishing at the Castle Lake. *Frank is sad. Alice the alcoholic, the tramp, the bad mother. In love with Frank. Alice scalded Frank with the pot of spuds while Rose and Nancy hid in the babby house.*

That day mustered up one memory Nancy didn't need reminding of: the sound of her daddy roaring, merged with her mother's sardonic laughter. She often heard it in the walls of the babby house. Then she'd sing a song, as loud as she could to drown out the voices. She sometimes needed reminding of what her daddy looked like, but she always remembered what he sounded like.

13th August - At last we're to be together. In secret is better than not at all. My prayers have been answered. The next time we meet I'll tell him about Benny. He'll be pleased I'm sure. We're a family.

Nancy dropped the diary as if it had stabbed her. *Tell him what? What about Benny? Did he do something wrong?* Her head spun. She imagined the blood draining from her, dripping from her pores and seeping into the damp earth, pulling her down with it. She lit another cigarette. *What has Benny got to do with anything?* She lay on her back, her head turned to one side, squinting out through the dirty plastic window. Hailstones clipped against it, like the ticking of a clock—tick... tock... tick... tock. Then they sped up—tick, tick, tick, tick, tick—battering the roof so hard Nancy though it would cave in on her. She pulled gently on the cigarette. It made her feel dizzy. Tears flowed down the back of her neck. She liked the coolness on her skin. She sat up, took off her hat and pulled her hair until it hurt. She touched her green sleeve with the lit end of her cigarette. A perfect little black circle formed, she made another one, and another. She opened the diary again.

The funeral, loveless marriages, Alice leaving, adopting Rose and Nancy. *My best friend is Mary, yet I can't tell her my sorrows, my regrets, or my worries. Perhaps one day, she can read these diaries, and understand. Perhaps one day Catherine will read the letters that I'm too cowardly to send.*

Nancy hurled the diaries back into the mucky hole. She threw the clay and stones on top, wishing she'd never read them. Wishing they'd never been written.

§

After Mass, Flossie made a beeline for Jim and Rose. She might have known Mary wouldn't come out today. The town buzzed with the gossip about Maureen and Dougie running away together, exaggerated versions of the story. Some still insisted she was pregnant, and her parents had thrown her out. Others said they sent her to a mother and baby home down south. *No smoke without fire,* they said.

'Flossie, how are you?' Jim greeted her as soon as she was within hearing distance.

'I'm fine, thanks.'

Rose scarpered off after a brief hello, to chat with a girl from school.

'How's Mary? I'd like to go see her.'

Jim scratched his head. 'You two falling out like that. She misses you, especially with all this Maureen business.'

'I miss her too. I'm so sorry about what happened.'

'I know she is too. Stubborn as each other,' Jim said.

Flossie smiled. 'Jim, there's something you should know.

And Mary should know too.'

'Is everything alright?' Jim asked, gauging Flossie's grave expression.

'Alice is back.'

Jim's mouth fell open. 'Feck sake. That's all we need.'

'I was up with Joyce Rafferty yesterday. Alice has been writing to Nancy since March.'

'What? You're joking!' he said in a high-pitched voice. 'How the hell did that come about? Is she staying? Nancy kept that quiet. Y'know, Mary'll kill Alice if she darkens our door. Does Rose know?'

'I'm not sure.'

'Is she staying with Joyce?'

'No. She's in Billy's old place.'

'That run-down auld shack?'

Flossie curled her lips. 'Yes. Sure only for Joyce she'd have nowhere.'

'Did Joyce keep in touch with her all these years?'

'Here's Rose coming. Hush.' Flossie put on a smile.

'How are you, Rose?' asked Flossie.

'I'm fine. You know.' She lowered her eyes to the ground.

Flossie turned back to Jim. 'Tell Mary I'll call this evening.'

'She'd love to see you. I'll tell her surely.' Jim gave a slight nod and arched his eyebrows to convey to Flossie that he would warn Mary of Alice's return.

§

Goretti had Molly round for Sunday dinner. Their idle chat about the upcoming tour to Knock distracted John and

Flossie from thoughts of Alice. Benny hadn't seen Rose or Nancy over the weekend, so he still didn't know Alice was back.

'Could I borrow the car next weekend, Dad?' Benny asked casually as he cut into his beef.

'What do you mean, borrow it? For what?'

'The Champions are playing in Granada and I want to take Nancy.'

'Well, I don't know about that. Spinning around the town is one thing. But gallivanting off to Kingscourt is an entirely different matter.'

'You said I could... soon.'

'I meant when you're older. Seventeen at least.'

'That's not 'til September.'

'I can't see Mary letting Nancy off over there, especially with the whole Maureen business and Ali...' John looked across his glasses at Flossie.

Benny looked up from his plate. He swallowed, raised his eyebrows to his mother. 'And what?'

'And also, Benny, she's only gone sixteen,' John said. 'That's what.'

Goretti's head bobbed. Her cheeks flushed from drinking sherry. 'Do you have a wee notion of her?'

Molly giggled. 'Aye, she's a nice wee lassie. You'd be lovely together.'

'That's ridiculous,' John snapped.

'Why is it ridiculous?' Benny scowled. 'Maybe she is my girlfriend. So what if she is?'

Flossie's fork dropped from her hand. She stared at her son. 'She's not your girlfriend.'

'How do you know if she is or not?' Benny sighed and slumped back in his chair.

'You said maybe she is.'

'She's not my girlfriend. Okay?'

Flossie's blood pulsed through her like it was lava. She sat up straight and focused on her breath, her hand pressed on her chest. She picked up her fork, pointed it at Benny. 'Maybe you should just stay away from her in future.' Her surprisingly raised voice and aggressive tone stunned everyone at the table.

'What's wrong with her?' Benny asked, palms turned to the heavens. 'I thought you liked her.'

'I do like her.'

'We're friends. Nothing else. And if you must know, it's Rose I like.'

'Benny don't be so stupid... at your age talking about girl-friends.'

Molly and Goretti sat wide-eyed, Molly's face tinged pink with embarrassment.

'Your mother's right,' John said.

Flossie and John held each other's gaze for a moment too long. Benny left the table—and his half-eaten dinner—and stormed out the door.

'That wasn't very nice of you, Flossie,' said Goretti. 'There was no need for all that.'

'He's better off not getting attached to any local girls. He'll hardly spend the rest of his life in this place.'

'But I thought this is where you wanted him to spend the rest of his life. In this place,' Goretti said. 'Make up your mind. Or better still, let the lad decide for himself.'

'Oh my God, Mammy, shut up. You didn't say things like

that about us when we were children. Catherine and Danny didn't exactly get to decide for themselves, did they?'

Molly coughed gently and shifted in her chair.

'That's not fair,' Goretti said. 'And don't tell me to shut up.'

Flossie regretted her words but made no apologies. The air was suffocating her; she needed to get out. 'Enjoy the rest of your dinner everyone.' She wiped her mouth with a napkin and stood up. 'I'm going to visit Mary.'

She went to her room and changed into a pair of trousers and a jumper. She had someone else to see first.

§

The sun radiated its mellow rays down on the green fields and ditches, seeking out the last frost of spring hiding in the shady nooks. The crisp, icy air hit the back of Flossie's throat with each breath she took. She pedalled hard up the Institute Road. Her heart pumped courage and rage through her veins. She was determined to stand up to Alice's intimidation. She owed that woman nothing. How dare she threaten to ruin John's reputation. She had no right to come back here. She had no rights to Rose and Nancy either.

The narrow road was quiet on any day of the week, and more so on Sundays. Flossie eased the pressure on the pedals as she got to the flat of the road coming close to Billy's. She wondered if people knew that Alice was back. It didn't take long for news to get around town. With Maureen running away as well, the gossip mongers would have themselves confused with their varied accounts of whys and wherefores. She pedalled hard again.

The chimney crumbled on the patchy roof of Billy Rafferty's old, derelict house. The walls still maintained their dull grey appearance. It looked miserable under the shade of the tall evergreen trees that surrounded it. Billy had left the place to Joyce, his only niece, but she showed little interest in it. She still talked of moving to London, but people said she was too attached to her mother and if she hadn't gone by now, she never would.

§

Flossie parked her bicycle against the ivy-smothered fence. The black metal gate creaked loudly as she pushed it open, startling the nestled crows into fleeing the trees. They cawed into the distance and silence resumed. She shivered in the shade of the trees. Damp pine needles covered the stone-clad path. She trod carefully to avoid the wet slippery algae. Yellow paint cracked and peeled off the old wooden door and window frames. Water trickled down the wall from the broken guttering, leaving behind a trail of green slime. The curtain twitched. Flossie's heart skipped a beat. Deep down she'd hoped the house would be empty.

She knocked on the door. As soon as it opened, a scrawny cat hissed and zoomed out past her.

Alice hadn't changed much. Her eyes... it was always Alice's eyes that got to Flossie. Olive green—perhaps attractive if they belonged to someone else, but in Alice they breathed darkness. They stabbed at Flossie, like two pins pressing into a voodoo doll. 'Can I come in?'

Alice opened the door wider and stepped aside. 'Straight through,' she said.

Flossie brushed past her into the gloomy hallway. Alice plodded behind. The smell of cigarettes almost masked the fusty smell in Billy's house. Wallpaper hung from the damp walls and patches of plaster blistered and bled white powder. Mould on the walls resembled miserable faces.

The kitchen was cluttered with boxes and useless junk, and apart from a couple of cups and a milk bottle on the table, no one would have guessed that anyone inhabited the place. A box of kindling and a bucket of coal sat on the floor beside the open range. Alice got on her knees and resumed the task of lighting the fire.

§

John sat through the rest of his Sunday dinner in a state of apprehension. Goretti and Molly removed themselves from the earlier embarrassment by engaging in a meaningful and poignant conversation about their late husbands. They barely noticed when John excused himself from the table.

Upstairs in his room, Benny played records—louder than was acceptable. John stood outside for a moment, a fatherly urge came over him; he wanted to talk to his son about Rose and Nancy. In his head, he tried to put the appropriate words together, but they wouldn't stay in the right place. Other words, unwanted words, stole their way in, so he walked away. He went to the end of the landing to his own room. He closed his door tight behind him. Today was a rainy day, he decided. He reached down behind the mahogany chest of drawers to where the frayed carpet met the skirting board. From there he took the key of his cash box, which he kept hidden in the jackdaws' nesting place: the chimney.

§

Mary smiled when Jim told her Flossie would visit later that evening. It was the first smile Nancy had seen on Mary's face since Friday. The atmosphere remained fragile. Still no news from Maureen and Dougie. Nothing from the Taylors either, except for the note from Dougie to say goodbye. When Jim went to their house to fight about their son taking his Maureen away—and her just a child—Mr Taylor made Jim angry by saying Maureen was a bad influence on their Dougie. He promised to find them and land her straight back where she belonged. Mrs Taylor, like Auntie Mary, cried for days.

Rose and Nancy cleaned up after dinner. They were back on speaking terms, but tension still hung over them. Nancy wanted to tell her what she found out, the secrets hidden away in the babby house, but she couldn't—not yet. She had to be certain, find out the truth about Benny.

'I'm going now, Auntie Mary. I won't be late,' said Nancy as she buttoned up her coat and pulled on her red knitted gloves. She left the house with her camogie stick. She had nearly two hours to spare before she was due to meet Jenny at four o'clock.

§

Still on her knees with her back to Flossie, Alice scrunched several sheets of newspaper into balls and stuffed them into the grate. 'What do ya want?' she asked.

'Why are you back?'

'What business is it of yours?'

'I know all about the blackmail, Alice, so you're not getting another penny from us.'

'Do ya?' asked Alice, snapping a piece of kindling in half.

'Yes, I do. And I know all about what happened at the lake. You killed Frank. You, along with that Stanley man.'

Alice paused. 'What are ya rambling about?' She piled the kindling sticks on top of the newspaper and cracked a match. The burning paper rustled in the hearth.

'John has proof. You're a murdering bitch.' Flossie took a couple of steps backwards as Alice stood and turned to face her.

'I didn't kill him. He drowned. So you'd better watch your mouth.'

'You hit him and left him lying in the water. That's why he drowned.'

Alice turned back to the fire. She put a few lumps of coal on top of the blazing sticks. 'I know you were with him that day. I saw ya snaking away on yer bike, stinking of your rich perfume. I smelt it off him often enough. Trying to make fool of me, the pair of ya.' She poked at the fire as the flames crackled up the chimney.

'I loved him, you didn't. You never loved him,' Flossie said, struggling to remain composed.

Alice closed the range door, got off her knees and lit a cigarette. She turned and blew smoke rings into Flossie's face. 'You're nothin' but a tramp. It was all your fault, the whole thing,' she said. 'And them photographs prove nothing. They could've been taken any day of the week. 'Tis only a picture of a man and wife paddling in the lake. So tell him he's wasting his time.'

'You shouldn't get away with it.'

'If people were to find out about his life of lies, they wouldn't believe a word he says. And if they knew that his wife had been carrying on with the dead man, sure he could get the blame for murder himself.'

'You can't prove that.'

'Maybe not, but it doesn't sound too good, does it?'

'Frank hated you. Even your so-called friend Joyce doesn't like you.'

'Oh, shut up. Feck off home now and tell Johnny Boy that I want what's owed to me.'

'I'm going to make you pay for this. I'm going to the guards. Today. Right now. People can say what they like about John and Julie. I don't care and John doesn't care.'

'Julie?' Alice smirked with narrowed eyes. 'Julie? What's she got to do with it?'

'Yes, Julie. I've known about her for years. John and I have an arrangement, if you must know, and what he does in his own time is none of my concern.'

'An arrangement?' Alice took a long drag on her cigarette and laughed the smoke into the air. 'Miss Fuckin' Perfect,' she said, looking down her nose.

'I'm leaving now.'

'Do ya think Julie is his bit on the side?' Alice flopped into a chair at the table and flicked her long ash into a cup. She smiled, keeping her menacing eyes on Flossie.

'Don't say it like that.'

'Don't say it like that,' Alice mocked. 'God, you're such a fool.' A look of satisfaction spread across her face. 'Johnny Boy hasn't told ya everything at all, has he?'

'What are you talking about?' Icy needles pricked at Flossie's scalp. Tears threatened, and she blinked them away.

'Do ya know who Julie is?'

'I'm not discussing my husband's business with you. Go back where you came from. Nobody wants you here.' Flossie felt the shakiness in her own voice. She clenched her fists, willing herself to stay in control. 'And stop blowing your damn smoke in my face!' she yelled.

'I hate people like you. Pretending ya don't care what your husband gets up to. As long as it's kept a secret, that's all that matters, isn't it? Brush it under your swanky carpet and nobody's any the wiser. Ha!' Alice reached for a near empty bottle of whiskey on the table. 'I could've ruined you years ago, y'know.'

'So why didn't you?'

'The money came in handy.' Alice poured the whiskey.

'You don't deserve to come back here. You don't deserve Rose and Nancy either.' Flossie's stomach churned. She had to get out of there. She felt sick looking at Alice, and sick at the stench of the place. She wished she hadn't come.

'Julie is Alfie's big sister.'

'Who's Alfie?'

'D'you wanna sit down, Mrs O'Malley?'

'I'm fine. Who's Alfie?'

Alice stuck out her chest. 'Johnny Boy's bit on the side.' She downed her drink, keeping her probing eyes on Flossie, who turned grey. 'A man.'

'You're... demented. Vicious!'

Alice put her hand on her heart and tilted her head to one side. 'It's not his marriage he's protecting, y'know. He doesn't give a damn about what you think. Him and Alfie Moore were caught red-handed in the Grand Hotel when they were young lads. Auld Freddie was horrified, imagine his face.' Alice faked a shocked expression. 'Ruthie never knew. Jaysus, she'd have dropped dead on the spot. Freddie made it clear to his son that he'd only inherit everything if he was married with a child.'

'You're lying. That's all lies,' Flossie said.

'I'm not fucking lying. He's a big mammy's boy who loves a man, and money is the only reason he married you. 'And while we're at it, Miss Fancy Pants Holier Than Thou, I know and your husband knows that Frank was Benny Boy's daddy.'

'You're a bitch, Alice.' Flossie lunged at Alice and walloped her across the face. Alice grabbed at Flossie's hair, pulling her head towards the floor.

'Two bitches.'

Alice let go and turned towards the voice in the doorway.

'Nancy!' said Flossie as she moved towards her.

'Get away from me.' Nancy held up her camogie stick and pointed it at Flossie. 'Get back over there.'

'What are you doing here?' Flossie asked.

'Why are you here?'

'I needed to talk to your mother.'

The camogie stick trembled in Nancy's hand as she pointed it at Alice. 'What did you say to her about Benny?'

'I said what's true. You heard rightly.'

She glared at her mother, her eyes hot pokers. 'You killed my father.'

'Don't be stupid,' said Alice, reaching into her cardigan pocket for her cigarettes.

'I heard,' Nancy said.

Nancy lowered the stick and looked at Flossie. 'Is that what you meant about Benny... in your diary?'

'My diary?' Flossie's heart swelled with pity for Nancy. She reached out to her. 'What diary are you talking about?'

'Get away from me,' she said. 'Is it true? About Benny.'

'Yes. But Nancy, please.' Flossie took another step closer.

'You're a liar, Mrs O'Malley.'

'It's true. I'm not lying.'

Nancy's shoulders fell and the colour drained from her face. She stood motionless for a moment. She opened her mouth to speak, but no words came. She pressed her knuckles to her trembling lips and turned her back on Flossie.

'I know how you must feel, Nancy,' said Flossie.

Nancy swung round, her eyes bulging. 'How the hell would you know how I feel? Do you even care how anyone feels? Benny is my friend and now... now he's my brother. I feel sick, punched all over. I feel like my friend has just been wiped out of my life.' Nancy stiffened as she wiped away tears. 'You've all been deceiving us. Rose wanted to be his girlfriend. Did you know that?'

Flossie hung her head in shame. 'I'm so sorry.'

'You're not even supposed to be here. I came to see her and now you're in the way.' Nancy lifted her camogie stick and struck Flossie across the side of her head. Flossie yelped as she fell to the cold cement floor. Alice yelled out as she dropped to her knees beside Flossie. 'Jesus, Nancy, what did ya do that for?'

'Why do you care?'

'I care that you're bringing me trouble I don't need, ya stupid fool.' Alice shook Flossie. 'Are ya alright?'

'You killed my father. You killed him.'

'It was an accident,' said Alice.

A trickle of blood ran down from behind Flossie's ear and dripped to the floor. She whimpered, her eyes closed.

'I can't believe any of you,' Nancy said.

Flossie opened her eyes.

Nancy raised the wooden stick as high as she could reach and whacked it down on her mother's head. Alice cried out as she slumped to the floor beside Flossie.

'Nancy, stop!' Flossie cried.

'You weren't meant to be here, Mrs O'Malley,' Nancy said.

Alice squirmed on the floor with her hands on her head.

Nancy looked from one woman to the other. She dropped her camogie stick to the floor. 'Sorry,' she said. 'Sorry.' She walked around the table, tapping it with her knuckles as she went along. 'I didn't mean to do that.'

Flossie pulled herself up and staggered towards the back door.

'Where are you going?' Nancy asked.

'Fresh air.' Flossie's wobbly legs carried her out into the overgrown garden. She opened her lungs and sucked in the cold air. She looked at the blood on her hands, on her coat, lots of it, thick and sticky. The throbbing in her head was like a bomb ready to explode. She had to get help. *But can't leave Nancy.*

She retraced her steps back to the kitchen door. She leaned against it, watching as Nancy dragged her stunned mother across the floor. She sat Alice up against the fridge, her legs stretched out in front of her. Nancy crouched beside her. A band of sunlight streamed through the window showering them with particles of dust.

'Ya didn't have to do that, y'know. Feisty like your mother, huh?' Alice said.

'I'm nothing like you,' Nancy replied calmly.

'In the press, Nance... over there.' Alice beckoned towards the sideboard. 'A wee drinkie.'

Nancy took a naggin bottle of vodka from the press.

'Ah good girl, Nance.'

'Stop calling me that. No one calls me that.'

'But you're my wee girl.'

Nancy opened the bottle and handed it to Alice.

'I need a fag.' Alice fumbled for them in her cardigan pocket. Nancy helped her. She put a cigarette between Alice's lips and removed her glove to light the match. Alice took a long pull, then exhaled grey streams of smoke out her nose. Nancy put her gloves back on and clapped her hands together. She opened the range door, poked the roaring fire, and threw in more coal. She banged the door shut and opened the damper.

'Help me up, Nance. There's no bother on me now.'

'No. Stay there. Keep drinking,' Nancy said. 'And if you call me that again, you'll be sorry.'

'Don't want any more, I've enough. Help me up.' Alice began to gather herself.

'No, you don't have enough. You never have enough.' Nancy shoved her back up against the fridge.

'For fuck sake.' Alice held her head in both hands.

'Drink it.' Nancy put the bottle to Alice's mouth and tipped it up.

Alice coughed and pushed her away. 'I can do it myself,' she said, grabbing the bottle.

'I hate you,' Nancy said. 'You're going to burn in hell.'

'I'm sorry, I really am. That's why I came home, for you and Rose. To make things right.'

'Drink it.'

Flossie continued to watch in silence, disconnected from their voices, rooted to the spot, like a spectator at a stage show. Fresh blood trickled down through the dark red stain on the breast of her grey coat. The sun had moved behind the trees and the kitchen reclaimed its dingy light.

Alice's heavy eyelids drooped. The bottle fell from her hand to her lap, splashing the vodka over her thighs. She put the cigarette to her mouth but dropped it before it got to her lips.

Nancy opened the range door and stared at the red-hot flaming coals. Her face and eyes burned. She looked towards Flossie. 'You can leave now, Mrs O'Malley.'

Nancy scattered the small bundle of newspapers across the floor and kicked the box of kindling upside down. She used the coal shovel to scoop the burning hot embers from the range. She watched in awe as the glowing coals burned right through the paper, expelling thick dark grey smoke. Flames emerged from the pile of old, yellowed newspapers. Nancy pushed the kindling closer to the blaze.

Alice groaned and gestured towards the fire. Nancy backed away as thick smoke filled the kitchen. She covered her mouth with her scarf. She kicked her camogie stick closer to the fire and took long strides towards the back door. She grabbed Flossie by the arm and led her out into the back yard.

'See what I've done for you. She'll be gone for good now. Every cold bone in her body will sizzle. You're free. We're all free.'

'I shouldn't have come.' Flossie shook her head. 'We can't leave her... we can't.'

'Yes, we can. Now, come on.'

§

As they turned the corner of the house, a black car pulled up at the gate.

'It's John,' cried Flossie. She released herself from Nancy's grip and floundered towards the car. John got out and opened the gate. 'What the hell happened to you?'

Flossie sobbed through bloodstained fingers. 'The kitchen's on fire,' she said.

Nancy neared the gate. 'We have to go now.'

'What's going on?' John looked from one to the other. He looked towards the house. 'I see it, I see the smoke.'

'Alice is in there. There was a fight and she's hurt,' Flossie said.

'Leave her,' said Nancy.

'We can't leave her, for Christ's sake,' John said. 'Flossie... get into the car.' He ran towards the house.

'We know everything, John. She told us. We know about the Moore man!' Nancy shouted.

John stalled, but only for a second. Then he continued running until he disappeared at the gable of the house.

Nancy grabbed Flossie's bicycle and took off up the road, further out of town. Flossie tried to replay her conversation with Alice in her head. *How much had Nancy heard? Did Alice lie about that man? It wasn't true. It was a lie. She had made it up to hurt them.*

She blinked as black spots flashed before her eyes. A

tightness spread across her chest, as if she'd been wrapped in a bandage. She couldn't get enough air into her lungs. She wound down the window. The air was smoky. She looked to the house. *Where was John? He should be back.* She got out of the car and stood at the gate. Smoke bellowed from the chimney, spraying ash and sparks into the sky. Pale grey wisps spewed from the crevices of the old walls, and black clouds puffed from the back end of the house. The darkened windows lit up one by one as the flames spread. Windows shattered as Billy's old place crackled and hissed.

The front door was flung open. John stumbled out, coughing and gasping. He swayed like a drunk as he rushed to the gate, muttering. 'Get in,' he shouted as he pulled Flossie through the gate.

'Where is she?'

'It's too late for her. Too hot, I couldn't get to her.' John opened the passenger door and nudged Flossie into the car.

Flossie pleaded with John as he started the engine. 'Please, John, we can't leave her,'

'We can't save her. She's as good as dead and I'm not risking my life for her,' he said, still panting and coughing. His face was black and his eyes red. He drove out the Institute Road and looped to the right, to head back into town via the Kells Road.

Flossie took a headscarf from the glove box and put it on her head, tying it under her chin. She took off her coat and folded it up—inside out—and tucked it under her seat.

'What the hell happened in there?' John asked.

'Nancy hit her. With her camogie stick. She caused the fire, John.'

'What happened to you?'

'Nancy did it. She was angry.'

'Why?'

'She knows everything. She read my diaries and the letters I wrote to Catherine.'

'What did you expect, Flossie? Even I read your diaries. Not that I needed to because I knew everything anyway.'

'How dare you?'

'Oh, Flossie, shut up.'

'Why did you come out here anyway?'

'To pay her the money, of course. I wanted her to go away. Don't pretend you didn't want the same thing.'

Flossie admitted to herself that yes, she did want her to go away. Forever. 'Is it true what she said in there? About you and a man?'

'Yes, it's bloody true. Whatever she said about me and Alfie and my father's will is all true.' John shoulders dropped; his jaw relaxed.

She didn't really know him at all, yet he knew her inside out. 'You used me.'

'We used each other.'

She couldn't deal with this right now. 'We can't go home like this,' Flossie said, looking down at her bloodstained hands. She felt the congealed blood sticking to the inside of her scarf.

'There's no one there,' John said as he pulled up at the house. 'Benny went off with the lads. Your mother walked Molly home, so she won't be back 'til evening.'

The street was quiet.

'Straight into the house, as quick as you can,' John said. Then the fire siren began to wail, stirring the town from its Sunday afternoon idleness.

CHAPTER SIXTY-NINE

The Legion of Mary women gathered together in their little room at the back of the community centre. Their prayer intentions were for the Connolly family.

'An awful tragedy,' Ruth said.

Mrs Brennan shook her head. 'Poor Joyce is in an awful way,' she lamented. 'She blames herself, you know, for not having the place in better shape. Sure Billy was an awful hoarder. I heard you wouldn't get through the rooms with all the rubbish he had.'

'It's the two girls I feel sorry for,' Molly said. 'Well and truly orphans now, so they are.'

The circle of women prayed for the soul of Alice Connolly and for the girls she'd left behind.

§

The hardest thing Flossie O'Malley ever had to do in her life was tell her son the truth about his father. She felt every ounce of the pain that she inflicted on him. All she could do was pray that one day he would understand and forgive her. Look her in the eye again. Meet her in the hallway with a smile rather than a look of contempt. She and John spared him the details about Alfie Moore, for the time being.

They depended on Nancy's discretion—just as she depended on theirs—fearing that the fine line that separated her stable mind and her irrational one might snap at any point. Flossie had to build up Nancy's trust again, work with Mary and Jim to help repair the damage.

Flossie called to see Mary and they went for a stroll through the woods. Just like Josey, Mary had suspected many years ago that Benny was Frank's son. 'Sure, he has his walk,' she said, after she scolded Flossie for not confessing years ago.

'Maybe if you had asked me, I might have admitted it.'

'I wanted to, but Josey told me to mind my own business. He didn't want us all falling out.'

'In all honesty, Mary, I don't think I could've admitted it. With Frank dead, I didn't think there was any point in saying anything.'

'Did you not worry that Benny and the girls might get involved... romantically?'

'I did, but I kept a close eye on them.'

'Nancy was always in your house. She and Benny got on fierce well together.'

Flossie pressed her knuckles into her burning cheeks. 'Nancy reminds me so much of Frank. I wanted her near me all the time. I feel so selfish, Mary.'

'I know you wanted to adopt her and Rose.'

Flossie stopped and faced Mary. 'How do you know that? I never told anyone.'

'Now, don't get mad with Jim, but he didn't destroy that

letter you wrote to me years ago... when you thought I was still in Manchester. He believed you were over-reacting, telling him to burn it. He just didn't feel right burning a letter addressed to me.'

'Why didn't you tell me?'

'I didn't want to embarrass you.' Mary grinned, and Flossie buried her face in her hands. Then they both laughed and walked on.

'You're an awful eejit, Flossie O'Malley.'

'I know. But I see now it was better things happened as they did. You and Jim have done a good job with them, Mary, but I do worry about Nancy.'

'Why? She's grand.'

'No, Mary, she's not grand.' Flossie paused, thinking before continuing. *If people knew how unstable Nancy was, they might lock her up. She couldn't let that happen. Not yet. She couldn't say anything just yet.* 'What I mean is, losing her father and her mother, then to lose her mother a second time —in such an awful way. It can't be easy to deal with that.'

'Rose is devastated too. And very angry that no one told her Alice was home,' Mary said.

They reached the river that flowed from the Castle Lake. Instinctively they both sat on the stone walls of the small bridge, one on each side looking across at each other.

'Do you think she'll be okay?' Flossie sighed heavily.

'Rose is a sensible girl. She'll be fine. How's John?'

'He just wants to be the best father to Benny as he can be.'

'His parents will find out eventually, you know. Those things don't stay secret forever.'

'They can't find out. If they knew they weren't Benny's

true grandparents, it would kill them. Please don't tell your Maureen. She'd tell Dougie for sure.'

Mary's posture dipped. 'Maureen wrote.'

'That's good news, isn't it?'

'It is.' Mary folded her arms.

'What's wrong? Is she okay?'

'She says she's very happy and has no intentions of coming back, but she doesn't want us to fall out.'

'It may not last, Mary. The novelty might wear off and she'll be back before the end of the year.'

'That's what Jim said.'

Flossie crossed over the bridge and sat on the wall beside Mary. She put her arms around her. They hugged each other tight, a silent promise that they would always be there for each other.

§

'Thank you,' Flossie said as Nancy handed her the bag of diaries.

'And I'm sorry for taking them.'

'Maybe deep down I always wanted them to be found.' Flossie sat on the grass and looked out to the lake. Nancy looked normal, Flossie thought, glancing at her. Not traumatised or... *she had to stop this. Nancy's not normal. Her behaviour's not normal.*

'How's your head?'

Flossie put her hand to her scarfed head. 'Wasn't as bad as it looked.'

'Sorry. I was very mad with you.' Nancy picked up a stone and skimmed it across the calm water.

'You were mad at your mother too.'

'So were you.'

'Yes, but I don't think I am anymore. A lot of what she said to me was true. She just didn't have a very nice way of expressing herself.'

'And I thought I did you a favour.'

Flossie frowned. 'What do you mean?' Flossie stood so that she was at the same level as Nancy.

Nancy skimmed another stone. 'Do you not remember? In your diary you wrote about her burning in hell. As if you wished for it to happen. So it's sort of your fault. But it's okay... I won't tell anyone.'

Flossie cringed. She had the urge to move away from Nancy, but her feet wouldn't move.

'Do you think Daddy's spirit roams the lake?'

'Who knows? Maybe.'

'I think it does.' Nancy faced Flossie. 'Are you going to stay with John forever even though you know about him?'

'When the time is right, we'll do what has to be done.'

'You won't leave here, will you?' Nancy picked up a stone, too big to skim across the water.

'Who knows? I might, sometime.'

Nancy glared at Flossie, took a step closer, hopped the stone from one hand to the other like it was a ball. 'You can't leave.'

Flossie looked around the deserted woods, her pulse quickened. 'If I do, you can come with me... if you want.'

'Promise?' Nancy fired the stone far across the water.

'I promise.' Flossie picked up the bag of diaries. 'You're a better thrower than me; must be from playing camogie.' She took the diaries out of the bag. 'Show me how far out into the lake you can throw these.'

Nancy grinned and, one by one, she threw the diaries with great force out into the middle of the Castle Lake.

Relief flooded Flossie when she heard voices approaching. She turned to the path. 'Oh, it's the McGuirks and Jenny's with them.' Flossie felt her voice tremble. 'We'll walk with them.'

She went to the path to meet the McGuirks; Nancy followed, close behind.

'Bet you never thought all your secrets would end up in the lake with Daddy's spirit,' she said in a loud whisper. Then she skipped towards the woody path to join Jenny.

§

Flossie stood by Frank Connolly's grave for the last time. The mound of fresh clay was a reminder that it was also Alice's grave. His wreath of artificial flowers, old and faded, was barely visible behind the build-up of dirt and condensation inside the cross shaped container. A new wreath of vibrant flowers encased in a hard plastic bowl had Alice's name on it. *Rest in peace. From Mary, Jim, Rose and Nancy.*

Flossie clasped her hands and closed her eyes. *Would saying a prayer be hypocritical?* She spoke silently to Alice rather than to God. *I hope you do find peace now. Everyone deserves peace in death, especially those who knew no peace on earth. What made you who you were? God? Your strange family? The people around you? Those who judged you... me included? Yes, I judged you because I was jealous of you. My jealousy turned to hate and for that I'm sorry.*

'Rest in peace, Alice Connolly,' Flossie said. She had to let go.

She turned her thoughts to Frank. *I hope that one day, the children will understand the love we had for each other, Frank. I hope you understand why we couldn't tell the truth about Nancy and the fire. They would've taken her away. I couldn't let that happen. I'll do the right thing for her now. I'll get her the proper help she needs. I'll write to Auntie Bridgey for advice. Yes, that's what I'll do.* She closed the back of her throat, tensing her tongue. *No more crying over you. This is the end now.*

Flossie walked away from the graveyard, her mind full of plans for the future. Plans for her, and for Nancy. She held her head high and her shoulders back, steadfast under the weight of secrets old and new.

ACKNOWLEDGMENTS

Writing this novel has been the most challenging thing I have ever done in my life. I knew from the beginning that it wouldn't be easy, but I didn't think it would take as long as it did. Even though I have enjoyed every torturous moment, there were times when I felt defeated and frustrated. I persevered and saw it through, but only because I had some amazing people behind me.

The biggest thank you must go to my husband, Stephen, for his support and encouragement from beginning to end. I really could not have finished this book without him. Thank you for your patience, Stephen.

Thank you to my children, who believed in me and asked a thousand times, 'How's the book going, Mam?'. They always believed that I would finish it—sometime!

Massive thanks to my youngest child, Lucy. She sat with me, encouraged me, listened as I talked about my characters, scrunched up her face when something sounded stupid, and never complained on the days when my writing came before other things.

I have the best bunch of friends anyone could ask for. Thank you to each one of you for all your encouragement. A special thanks to Roisin and Jackie, who have supported me since I put my first word on paper. Thank you for your genuine interest and encouragement. Thank you, Roza, for always shining the brightest light upon the West of Ireland. There were times when I really needed it!

Stories come from other stories. They prompt us and feed our imaginations. Thanks to my parents for all the stories of times gone by and for always encouraging me to read when I was a child.

Thank you to Uncle Philip and my mother-in-law, Betty, for sharing memories of your younger years. Every little detail helped me to visualise what life was like for my characters in the 1950's and 1960's.

Thanks to Tania and all the team at GetCovers for designing my book cover, not forgetting Des and Kathleen Connors for providing me with the front cover image. It was just what I had in mind. I love it!

A huge thanks to my editor, Alison Williams. Thank you to Aimee Dyamond, manuscript evaluator & developmental editor. Thanks to Alex Blackwell at White Seahorse, Publishing & Copywriting Services, who inspired and encouraged me to self-publish my novel. Thank you, Alex, for telling me not to rush it. I certainly didn't rush it!

Thank you to my author friend Jacinthe Dessureault for reading, tweaking, advising, encouraging, and most of all for helping to turn my Word document into an actual book. Jacinthe has saved me from a lot of stress in the tech department.

THANKS TO YOU, THE READER

I hope you enjoyed reading *Secrets in the Babby House* as much as I have enjoyed writing it. Reviews are important to authors, and I would be so grateful if you would consider leaving a review on Amazon, or even just a rating. Thank you so much!

ABOUT THE AUTHOR

Gloria McBreen was born and reared with her four brothers in Bailieborough, Co Cavan. Some of her fondest memories were formed during her childhood in the Drumbannon neighbourhood. She currently resides in Ballina, Co Mayo with her husband and youngest child. She is surrounded by inspiration, with the River Moy on her doorstep and a stunning view of Mount Nephin. She is just a short distance away from dipping her toes in the Atlantic Ocean.

Secrets in the Babby House is her first novel.

For more about Gloria,
visit her blog www.gloriawriteshere.wordpress.com
or follow her on Twitter @GloriaMcB
and Instagram @gloriawriteshere.

Printed in Great Britain
by Amazon

19637026R10277